Before & After

by

Jamison Thomas Meyer

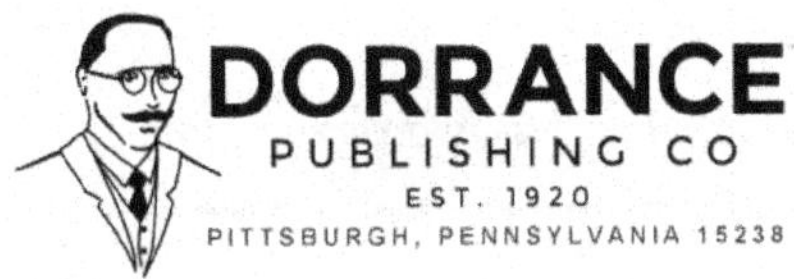

Dorrance Publishing Co
585 Alpha Drive
Pittsburgh, PA 15238
Visit our website at *www.dorrancebookstore.com*

ISBN: 978-1-6376-4354-9
eISBN: 978-1-6376-4666-3

After

Chapter 1

I open my eyes to the night sky. There are so many stars. It's an odd first thought, followed by the second of *where am I?* There shouldn't be this many stars. There are more stars than I've ever seen. I sit up and realize I'm lying on the ground. I don't remember how I got there, or rather here. I look around, and it appears I'm on a dock. It also appears I'm not alone.

There is a woman lying next to me. Her face is turned away from me, but I can already tell from looking at her that I know her somehow. The same way you can see someone from across a crowded restaurant and pick out the face of the one person you see there every night but don't yet know their name. I nudge her to wake her up, as well, but she doesn't stir at my touch. I turn her head towards mine and her open eyes stare straight into my soul.

It's now that I notice the wetness. I'm sitting in what I had at first thought was a puddle of rain, but now I discover is something stickier and more viscous. I hold my hand up to my face and see it for what it is. I'm sitting, and until just now was lying in a puddle of blood, and given the cold unmoving face next to me, I believe it's hers, whoever she is. Given that upon looking at her face, while I recognize it, I still cannot place a name.

I stand up quickly to back away from this morbid scene I've woken up to and something clatters to the ground. I look down and notice it's a knife. One which I'm sure is the cause of all this blood. I feel my blood rise as I start to panic. The words and confusion clattering around my brain faster than I keep track. What's happened? What did I do? Did I do this? Why can't I remember anything beyond a moment ago?

I look around to get a grasp of where I'm at, hoping for a clue somewhere that might help me remember something, anything, about what happened here. As I thought, I am on a wooden dock, a dock that juts out onto what looks like a lake. A lake I don't remember ever seeing in my life. There doesn't seem to be any buildings or structures to give me any point of reference. It's just a field with a single walking path leading away from the dock. The edge of the lake continues in both directions beyond my sight line, so it must be a rather large lake.

If it even is a lake? I have no way of knowing one way or the other. For all I know it could be the ocean. I don't know where I am or how I got here and, most importantly, I don't know who this woman is that is lying next to me. All I do know is that it appears like something that could never have happened. At least I hope it could never have happened because it sure as hell looks like *I* killed her.

Don't think that I tell myself. I didn't kill her. Why would I? I'm not a killer. At least I don't think I am. It's in that moment that I realize, I'm not even sure I remember who *I* am. No, I'm sure. I don't remember my name. *Oh, God... Who am I*?

I decide to take stock of my surroundings. Look at everything and see if there are any clues whatsoever. As much as I hate to, I must start with the dead woman lying at my feet. She is blonde, looks to be about twenty, maybe older, maybe younger. She's wearing a blue cocktail dress, it looks expensive, and it's stained with blood, her blood. She isn't wearing any shoes and her feet look dirty like she was walking through mud. She doesn't look to have any personal belongings with her; no purse, no phone, nothing.

Next, myself. I'm wearing a T-shirt and jeans. Nothing that tells me anything. They are, of course, stained with her blood, as well, but they show no resemblance to her attire. Wherever she was going tonight I wasn't going with her. I have shoes on; boots, to be exact. The knife at my feet looks to have been resting on my chest. That's where most of the blood on the front of my shirt is located, around a bloody outline of it. This is good, it was on my chest not in my hands, so it may not be mine, but I can't be sure.

The knife itself looks like a kitchen knife. A big one, about six inches in length. I pick it up to examine it and immediately curse myself. I just put fingerprints on it. Granted, for all I know, my fingerprints were all over it anyway. I glance around and a knee jerk reaction makes me want to throw it.

It's in that instant I realize what I need to do. Looking around one more time to make sure I see no other landmarks. When I'm positive of this, I chuck the knife as far into the water as I can. Even if the knife is ever found the water will have washed away all the fingerprints… I hope.

Now I get to the task of moving this woman, whoever she is. Looking down at her, it looks like she is simply sleeping on the dock. If it weren't for the fact that her eyes were open with that cold dead look or the puddle of blood that seeps out from under her onto the dock you wouldn't even know she was dead. I lean down and turn her over. Here I see the cause of the bleeding.

She has a gaping wound in the back of her neck. I don't know much about knife wounds but to my eyes that's what it looks like. Like someone, maybe myself, maybe not, stabbed her straight in the back of the neck with the knife I just chucked into the ocean.

I can't believe that I am already thinking of this as if I am covering up a murder but what else can I call it? It's what I'm doing isn't it? There must be some explanation that doesn't involve me having just killed this woman, and once I figure it out, I'll go to the authorities and explain everything. This is at least what I tell myself as I begin to pick her up.

It's with that thought that the idea of the dead body catches up to me and I become overcome with the urge to throw up. I make it to the edge of the dock just in time to avoid anything with my traces on it being left on the dock. After I wipe my mouth off, I wish I had puked on the dock. If I could have examined it, maybe seen what my last meal was, if it was recognizable. Who am I kidding, how would knowing what I ate help me to understand any of what had just happened? No, the only way was to get rid of the body and all the evidence and then see about finding some help.

I pick her back up and carry her to the end of the dock about twenty feet from shore. When I get there, I hesitate. This is the last thing. Once I do this, I will be helping the murderer of this poor woman, whether it was me or not. If I drop her into the water, I've made my decision. No going back.

"I'm sorry." I'm not sure why I said it out loud as I dropped her off the end of the dock and watched the mass sink to the bottom of the water and out of sight. It isn't as if there was anyone around to hear it.

Her arms, being more buoyant than her body, float towards the surface as she sinks. It almost appears as if she is reaching out for me to save her. But it's too late. She sinks into the abyss and disappears.

I turn to walk off the dock and it dawns on me. My clothes. After having picked her up, dropping her, and picking her up again, I have completely covered myself in her blood. Not to mention the puddle of blood from beneath us that seeped out while I was unconscious.

I have no choice but to strip down to the nude and throw my clothes in the water, as well. I note that it takes this act for me to discover that I wear boxers. *How much do I not know about myself?* I think, and I realize that the easier question to answer would be how much *do* I know, and the answer is sadly, nothing. I consider keeping the boxers, but I decide I don't want to risk it. I stop before throwing the wad of clothes into the water and think for a moment. If I'm going to do this, might as well do it all the way.

I walk along the edge of the water for five minutes, not running into anymore landmarks along the way, in order to wade out and drop the clothes off in a different location than the body. No sense in making it easier for people to find the evidence. I feel like I should burn the clothes but since I have no lighter, I had checked my pockets and there was nothing but lint in them, I have no choice but to set them out to the depths like everything else.

I'm treading water by the time I release the clothes to sink to the bottom. Afterwards, I slip myself beneath the surface in order to try and wash off any of her blood that is on my skin. When I do this, I discover that there is a stinging pain on the back of my head. I feel with my hand and discover that at least some of the blood is my own.

I can't see it, but I can feel a rather gnarly wound on the back of my head. I'm not sure how I got it or even what would have inflicted such a wound but perhaps that is the cause of my amnesia. I consider this as I break the surface of the water and doggy paddle in place. It is only now after having gotten rid of the last of the evidence that I begin to realize that this was the end of my plan.

Where can I go? What can I do? I'm naked in a lake that I don't want anything to do with. A lake that holds the dead body of a woman I do not know and the evidence that points to my guilt. I'm completely nude, without a thing to my name; a name, by the way, that I don't even recall. I haven't got a shred of a plan but I'm going to have to come up with one. I swim to the shore, hoping I come up with one before it's too late.

I wander along the shore, shivering in the cold. I'm not sure what season it is but it's definitely not warm out. My nakedness and the fact that I'm dripping wet do not help either. I look up and see the slightest sliver of a moon among the stars. When I look back down, I notice that I've found my way back to the dock. I decide I need to get away from the lake. Both because

I can feel the breeze blowing off it against my exposed skin and to try and separate myself from the crime scene.

I turn down the foot path that leads away into the field. I mentally try to think of anything, but I cannot bring anything to my mind before waking up on the dock. It's almost as if I was born in that moment. Born in that poor woman's death. There is a part of me that fears that no one will ever find her body. That her story will remain a mystery known only to a man who doesn't know his own. But then a deeper part of me is saddened by her death for the simple fact that she might have known who I was. She might have been able to help.

Looking ahead, I see a shape appear in the darkness. As I get closer, I see it take form as a small shack. The path ends right next to it in what appears to be a small gravel parking lot. Perhaps it is used for storage of boating material, oars, fishing nets, fishing poles. I reach forward to try the door and it is unlocked. The moonlight doesn't reach inside but I feel against the wall and find a light switch.

The shack is exactly as I expected and then some. What appears to have started out as a fishing storage location has now morphed into the beast of a mess that is before me. There is a kayak, an old truck tire, a stone bird bath, a pre-lit Christmas tree, as well as a million other knickknacks and doodads. All of them are covered in dust and cobwebs. Whoever's stuff this is, they obviously haven't used any of it in quite a while. I let the door close behind me as I step inside. That's all the further I go as there isn't room to go in beyond three feet due to the junk piled up waist high.

I begin to scan the piles to see if there might be any clothes. My nakedness, while a minor inconvenience now, will become a much larger issue should I run into anyone. A man with no memory and no clothes is guaranteed to be on the first bus to the loony bin, if not the police station. I wonder if that's where I should be anyway. It might be safer for me, if this amnesia is a recurring event; or it might be safer for others, at least it would have been for the woman on the dock.

"Don't think like that." I tell myself I don't know for sure what happened. There must be an explanation of some sort. Anything could have happened out there. I can't jump to conclusions. I have to stay calm and take time to figure out what I'm going to do. To begin with I need to leave this shed. It doesn't appear to contain any clothes, so I turn around towards the door and am met face to face with a young girl.

"What the fuck?"

"Look, I can explain!" My mind immediately starts running a mile a minute. "Please, listen; don't call the cops or anything." The girl looks to be about thirteen. I quickly cover myself up with my hands after I see her eyes flick downwards.

"Where are your clothes, and what are you doing in our shed?" Her hair has streaks of color in it that suggest a rebellious personality, but her pajama bottoms contradict that with their baby blue color and yellow duck prints.

"My umm…My clothes are… umm…" I panic, "stolen."

"Someone stole…. your clothes?"

"Look, I was…" I grasp at straws. A decorative sign catches my eye hanging on the wall to her left. It says: "I don't skinny dip, I chunky dunk." It will have to do. "I was skinny dipping."

"Really?" She looks like she might be buying it. A little at least. She is on the verge of laughing at me but that's better than doubting me.

"Okay, sorry, I was skinny dipping with a… a friend." I didn't want to say girl, mainly because I didn't want there to be a chance later that this conversation would tie me to the dead woman that was now sitting at the bottom of the lake. "And they um… must have run off with my clothes."

"Sounds like a great friend." I see her begin to relax slightly. She doesn't seem as tense; her face looks a little less threatening and her voice sounds a lot less interrogational. "Well, lucky for you, my older brother is about your size. I think he might be able to lend you some clothes. Come on." She turns off the light as she leaves the cabin. "What's your name, by the way?" she asks as I exit the shack.

"Kevin." The name comes to me in a heartbeat. I don't know if it's mine, I don't feel anything when I say it, but it was the first name that popped into my head. I didn't even need to think before answering. Perhaps my subconscious remembers things that I don't.

"I'm Alex. Nice to meet you, Kevin."

I finally relax as the hot water rushes over me. I have been tense ever since Alex led me back to her house. Her father was asleep she said, and she hadn't wanted to bother him when she saw someone breaking into the shed. This seemed odd to me at first, but I snooped just a few moments ago when she left me alone in the bathroom and from the amount of prescription bottles in the medicine cabinet, I have a feeling that Dad isn't a very healthy man.

Alex had led me up to this old house with peeling paint that is in desperate need of being redone. There was a wraparound porch with a screen that needs repairing. I counted three trucks in the driveway, it was hard to tell given that they were all in pieces, one with no wheels one with the engine taken out.

Inside, the house looked in dire need of cleaning. She led me through the kitchen to get to the stairs and I saw plates with moldy food stacked up everywhere. I won't swear to it, but I might have seen a mouse scurry across the yellow tiled floor that I'm pretty sure used to be white, I might add. Alex's brother is working, she told me as we walked up the stairs. He does that a lot she said. We went into his bedroom. She gave me some of his clothes out of his dresser and suggested I take a quick shower to avoid getting sick from being out in the cold.

I glanced around his room and saw a calendar hanging open to the month of August. At least I know what month it is. I'm glad she didn't ask me any more questions before leaving me to take a shower in the bathroom. I'm not sure I could answer anymore just yet. I'm not sure I could make up any answers, I guess I should say.

Now, I sit down in the shower and let the hot water burn the top of my head. The stinging intensifies but somehow its cathartic. Like as it cleans out the wound on the back of my head, it's also cleaning my mind. I barely even notice as the tears start to run down my cheeks. My mind reels as the reality of my situation begins to settle in and the adrenaline wears off.

I killed someone. Even though I keep telling myself to think of other possibilities and consider all the other answers, the simple answer must be considered. I must deal with the idea that I might have, very possibly could have, done this thing. I could have taken a life. A life that I don't even remember. I try to rationalize that I must have had a good reason but what good reason could there possibly be. She wasn't armed. I wasn't in danger.

I smack myself both figuratively and literally. I can't sit here in a stranger's shower weeping over what I might or might not have done. I have to act. I have to move forward. And yet the tears won't stop. I keep seeing her face behind my eyelids. The cold dead stare. The strikingly blue eyes that would have been riveting if it weren't for the shattered light behind them. She was young. She hadn't looked older than twenty-five. A whole life ahead of her. A whole life she'll never know now.

And what about myself? A whole life behind me that I can't remember. I continue to fight with myself for a single detail, a name or a face, anything that might give me even the slightest hint to who I am. Who I was before waking up on that dock? Nothing. Just blackness. A knock at the bathroom door takes me out of my head. I hear Alex calling from the other side. I can't make out what she's saying and I'm not sure I care.

Regardless, I stand up and turn off the water. I step out onto the blue tiles and grab a towel off the rack. It's then that my reflection catches my eye. For the briefest of moments, I thought there was someone else in the bathroom. I don't even recognize my reflection. A stranger looks back at me, standing there holding a towel to cover my naked body. I must force myself to remove the towel, fighting with my own brain to remember that it isn't another person in the mirror and my modesty is unnecessary.

I take a moment to look at myself. Looking at the crevasses and marks that cover my body. I'm not sure what I'm looking for, but I feel that one should know one's own body. I'm thin but not unhealthy. I have some muscle, though it doesn't look like I work out. I have a tattoo across my right shoulder. It's an eye. I look at it and it stares back at me through the looking glass, and I am mesmerized by it. Why did I get an eye tattooed on my shoulder? Was it a spur of the moment decision? Does it mean something? I feel almost like that eye knows something, something it's not telling.

I return to the rest of my body. My hair hangs wet from my head. It falls just below my ears, but doesn't look like it's intentional, more that I just haven't gotten a haircut in a rather long time. I have a five o'clock shadow but it's nowhere near a full-on beard yet. I see that the wound on the back of my head isn't bleeding anymore, thankfully. Looking into my eyes, I feel the connection I've been looking for. It's not that I recognize them. They look no different to me than any other eyes, no more revealing than the one on my shoulder, but they do feel different. Perhaps it's the simple fact that my brain realizes they are mine, but I sense a oneness looking into my own eyes. Like the blackness of my pupils might be hiding the answers to all my questions.

I realize I've walked up to the mirror and am almost nose to nose with my own reflection. The towel on the floor, forgotten. My modesty lost in the slow connection that is growing between me and the man in the mirror. If nothing else, I am beginning to gain a sense of self. Even if that self began on that dock.

I pick up the towel and dry myself off before dressing. I take one last glance in the mirror before heading out to face Alex. Heading out to face a world I don't know. A world in which I might be a criminal. A world where I am most definitely lost.

Chapter 2

"I made you some hot cocoa." I find Alex in the kitchen. She has cleared some dirty dishes off the small wooden table where she has placed two mugs of steaming chocolate. Her mug has a broken handle while mine says something about not being a morning person.

"Thanks, you didn't have to." I take a sip as I sit down, all while trying to avoid her eyes. She has very adult eyes for a twelve-year-old. I'd say she has an old soul if I didn't want to avoid sounding like a cliché.

"So, what happened to your girlfriend?" She takes a long sip of chocolate and raises her left eyebrow at me.

"My… my girlfriend?" My mind begins to real as I think back to the girl on the dock. Did Alex see us walking to the dock earlier? Maybe did she hear us? She might have even been spying on us she could know everything!

"I assume that's who you were skinny dipping with, wasn't it?" Realization dawns on me as I inwardly sigh with relief. She saw nothing.

"Oh, no, it wasn't my girlfriend… It was just a … just a friend." I try to look innocently into my chocolate. I don't know if I'm successful, but she lays off of the questioning and we sit in silence for a few moments.

"Well, there's a blanket on the couch if you want to stay." I glance around the room and realize when I see no clock that I don't know what time it is beyond it being the middle of the night. "It's three in the morning, so I imagine it'd be best if you just stay," she says with an odd clairvoyance.

"Won't your parents mind?" It's her turn to stare into her cocoa before she replies.

"My dad won't notice." I respect her secrets as much as she respected mine by refraining from interrogating her further. We sit and sip from our cocoa, neither of us looking at the other. Basically strangers, and yet we have reached a silent understanding. Ask me no questions, and I will ask none of you.

Suddenly, I see lights outside the windows. She notices, as well, and I see an immediate change in her demeanor. She jumps to her feet and I see her tense up and panic.

"You've got to hide." She grabs my mug of half-finished cocoa and pours it out in the sink before grabbing my arm and pulling me out of my chair. She leads me over towards what looks like a pantry.

"What do you mean hide?" She shuts the door on me leaving me in darkness.

"Just don't make a sound," she whispers through the door. I see the light at the bottom of the door turn off and hear her head out of the kitchen when, suddenly, the screen door leading to the porch bangs open and the light claps on again.

"What the fuck are you still doing up?" This voice is gruff, old, and slightly slurred.

"I… I couldn't sleep." I can't see but I can imagine Alex standing in the doorway to the hall, ready for a quick escape.

"Little girlies like you should get their beauty sleep."

"Yeah, right… I'll go do that." The desperation in her voice is tangible. Dangling in the air like mist.

"Did I say you could leave just yet? Come over here!" Silence. Painful pregnant silence. "That's right. Sit next to me. Uncle Benny ain't gonna be here long. Just getting a little somethin' from the cookie jar. Then I'll be on my way." My brain jumps into hyperdrive as I put two and two together and make four.

I consider the consequences of doing as she said and sitting in the dark, not acting, not stopping what I can feel is about to happen. I hear the chair scrape across the tile floor with a screech and I wince as if it were nails on a chalkboard.

I can't take it anymore, this silent hiding and letting this happen. I slowly turn the handle of the door and open a crack. I intend to burst into the kitchen until I see he's nowhere near Alex. He apparently meant a literal cookie jar. He is standing next to the counter, opening a cookie jar while she sits at the table staring at her cup of cocoa. I can only see her back, but I can see her shaking in silent tears.

The man standing at the counter looks exactly as you would expect him to. With an aptly named wife-beater and jeans that look like they've been through a woodchipper, the red trucker hat acting as the cherry on top of this redneck cake. He pulls his hand out of the cookie jar and instead of baked goods in his hand, I see a wad of cash. Even if it's all small bills, there's quite a stash hidden in that cookie jar.

I decide that the situation does not require my insertion and all it would do is cause yet another person to know of my trespassing. A certain person who does not appear to be as understanding as Alex. I slowly pull the door closed with as little noise as possible.

"You know I love you, baby." I hear him walk back towards Alex. I can see her cringing in the chair in my mind. "You're so beautiful. You're looking to be a pretty young lady you are. Just like your momma was." I hear a whimper. It's an odd deep whimper that I wouldn't expect out of a little girl.

"That's enough of that. I'll be back later this week. Till then, tell yer pop I said hi." I hear the screen door bang, but I remain in the pantry. I want to give Alex the room she needs to compose herself. As much as I want to comfort her or offer my help, I remind myself that not only am I a stranger, but a stranger with problems of his own.

After a few minutes of silence, the light turns off in the kitchen. She doesn't come to the door or open it; she simply speaks to the kitchen as if I am a ghost somewhere in the room.

"Wait to make sure he doesn't come back. My brother's room is at the top of the stairs on the right. You can stay there if you'd like. It would be more comfortable, I guess…" And with that, I hear her footsteps leave the room without a word of farewell. I wonder what made her change her mind about my sleeping situation. Is she concerned her uncle will return and find me on the couch? Or is she thanking me for not forcing myself into the situation in the kitchen? Is she giving me a more comfortable sleeping arrangement in return for my silence?

Regardless of the reason, I have no other options at this point. I leave the pantry and find the kitchen dark. I feel like I can't turn on the light, like this isn't my home, like I'm not supposed to be here, so I feel my way through to the living room and find the stairs. Earlier when I went up to take my shower, I didn't notice the pictures lining the stairs. Now in the bright moonlight coming through the windows I see the story of a family. It starts exactly as you would expect. A wedding photo, then pictures of two babies growing up. His first game of tee-ball, her first bicycle, the two of them sitting on Santa's lap at the mall. There are a few pictures of the family all together. The four of them happy and smiling. What happened? Where is their mother? I mentally note that she is not the woman from the dock. I didn't honestly believe it would be, but I wanted to check regardless.

Then the pictures stop. Given Alex's current age, I'd say they stopped over five years ago. There is a picture of what might be her first day of school, and then one of her brother going to homecoming, and then the lifelong picture collage ends. It's like the family ceased to exist. Was that when their father got sick? Is that when the mother left? I want to ask Alex, but I know it isn't my place. I can't be poking around in other people's lives. Besides, my curiosity is probably only fueled by my own lack of knowledge about my past. My mind is trying to fill the gaps in my own past with the past of this family. This family in which I do not belong.

I can't sleep. I toss and turn in the bed that isn't mine and try to be comfortable. I look at the alarm clock on the desk and see that it is now six in the morning and I have perhaps dozed for half an hour at most. I did a little light snooping and have discovered Alex's brother's name is Daniel. Daniel J. Evans. I have found out quite a bit about Daniel. It's weird to think that from a light perusal I now know more about Daniel than I do about myself.

It looks as if he is still in school, college. And that gives me the biggest clue about my situation so far. He goes to Fareport Community College. His class schedule was left on his desk. It mentions the address of the school. Fareport, Ohio. I may not have discovered anything about myself, but I have discovered at least where I am. I am in Ohio.

It's interesting in that I know where that is. But I have no recollection of whether that is where I'm supposed to be? Did I live in Fareport? If I didn't, what brought me here? Did the woman on the dock bring me here for some reason? I looked to see if Daniel had a yearbook from his high school. Given my inspection of myself in the mirror I don't believe I am that much older than him. I could have gone to school with him. After I failed to find it in the first ten minutes, I realized it was a fruitless mission. I don't know my exact age or name, so I'd have had to look through every single photo of every single grade. Add to that, the fact that I don't know myself well enough to recognize a picture of myself from years ago means it wouldn't have done anything except waste my time.

I discovered he had continued to play baseball through high school. His team even went to state once. It looks like he was the pitcher. He reads a lot; his desk and floor are littered with books. Some of them are textbooks and between the large number of creative writing textbooks and the abundance of English classes on his course schedule I assume he must be an English major.

Part of me felt like I was breaking his privacy to pick apart his life like this. Another part of me felt that this was simply practice for myself, this is how I'm going to have to discover my own past, finding clues and making assumptions. But the largest part of me felt that it was oddly appropriate for me to be snooping. When you keep private things, your intention is for nobody to see them. Who fits the qualification of nobody better than a man with no name, no memory, and no possessions?

So, now I lay in Daniel's bed, trying to decide what next to do. I know I should sleep but my mind keeps spinning towards what next. Where can I go? What can I do? Do I stay here and try to start over, or do I go out into the world and try to figure out my past? I need to find someone who knows who I am. There must be someone out there who knows me. Perhaps I live here in Fareport, perhaps not. All I know for sure is staying here at this house isn't going to do me any good. My past isn't going to come knocking at the door. I need to go and find it.

I get up and head for the door. I pause as I'm about to leave and look back at the room of a stranger. Although is he really a stranger when I know him better than I know myself? I notice a backpack on the floor and grab it. It's filled with books, these I have no use for, so I take them out and leave them on the desk. In their place I put two changes of clothes in the bag. I swing it over my shoulder and head down the stairs.

I try to be as silent as possible as I head through the kitchen and open the screen door. It is just as I am about to step outside when I hesitate. I realize what I'm about to do is wrong, but the rational part of my brain tells me that this is what needs to be done. This is what's necessary.

I turn back and go to the cookie jar on the counter.

There is at least $2,000 in twenties, if not more. I take half of it and then realize that if I'm going to do it, I might as well finish it. I stuff the entire wad of cash into one of the pockets on the backpack and replace the lid on the cookie jar. I am halfway back to the screen door when I hear a creak behind me. I turn and see, through the shadows, Alex enter the room. She doesn't turn on the light, and all I see is her silhouette.

"Kevin? Did you need something?" I realize that in her fatigue and in the darkness, she does not notice the backpack. I notice I'm standing next to the sink. There is a half-empty glass of something, and I make a split-second decision.

"Nope. Just came down for a glass of water. You go back to bed." She shrugs a goodnight and turns back to the stairs and leaves. I don't breathe until I hear her door close at the top of the stairs. What I have just done hits me like a ton of bricks. Is this the kind of person I am? The scene at the dock is becoming more and more believable. If I'm willing to steal all this money and lie to the face of the only person who I can even claim to know, why wouldn't I be willing to murder someone?

As I walk down the driveway towards the road, I see the sun start to peek over the horizon. As I reach the end of the gravel drive and come up to the seemingly endless road, I make a decision. Looking both ways, wondering which direction to take, I decide that whatever way I go I will not be the man I was on that dock. I will not be the man who just left a kitchen with a backpack of stolen money. I will be a new man, with a clean slate and with no past. I leave Kevin behind as I head out west, walking down the road, the rising sun on my back.

Chapter 3

I am stumbling by the time a car passes me. I have walked for what feels like days, though the sun tells me it has only been an hour or so. Once I left the safety of Alex's driveway the fatigue began to settle in. The stress of the night before and the lack of sleep makes me feel like I haven't slept in days. I began to get a headache a while ago but now it has progressed, and I feel as if someone has put a scalding piece of coal behind my eyes.

The truck that approaches is driving slowly. I don't know if they see me, but I've been watching them since they slipped over the horizon. I have been debating with myself whether to stop them. Do I risk it being Uncle Benny? What if it's Alex's brother and all I manage to accomplish is to return to the house that I robbed? But it could be a completely different person. It could be someone who knows me. The decision gets made for me when the truck slows to a halt without so much as a signal from me.

"You look like you could use a ride." The old woman behind the dash is squat with short, cropped hair. Her face looks artistically put together, through hours spent in front of the mirror. Sadly, it doesn't cover up her sixty years of stress and toil. She is dressed rather smartly given the state of her truck, with a white dress shirt, black bow tie, and black suspenders. "Well, you gonna stand there staring all day, or are you gonna hop in?"

I come around to the other side of the truck and open the passenger door. The inside looks like it hasn't been cleaned in ages. I can count at least ten paper bags from someplace called Beer 'n Burgers, and that's just the ones I can count. The smell doesn't hit me until I get in. It's a strange smell that I don't necessarily recognize but is comforting, even though it is laced with the smell of fast food.

"You got a name?" We start driving back in the direction in which I had come, and I realize that I must have picked the wrong direction when leaving the driveway. Not that there is a right or a wrong direction when you have no idea where you are headed. I consider her question for a few moments before answering.

"Sam." I don't have the immediate response to Sam the way I felt about Kevin. I have to search for it. I force myself not to use Kevin almost as if using that name will bring back the man that stole money from a little girl, the man from the dock.

"Nice to meet ya, Sam. My name's Christine; you can call me Chrissy. Sorry if I'm taking ya the wrong way. I assume you were tryin' to get to town?" It takes me a moment to realize she's asked me a question. The way she said it, it was as if she were telling me what I thought rather than asking.

"Yeah." I hope she doesn't press to find out why I don't know where town is.

"Well, lucky for you I came along; 203 is a bitch of a road to walk. You had about another ten miles the way you were going before you ran into anythin' worth runnin' into." She begins to fiddle with the radio. It looks old, it must have been the original radio that came with the truck. All it has is a power button and two knobs, one for volume and one for tuning, one of which has broken off revealing the metal rod beneath.

"Thank you." I look forward and lean my head against the window and listen to the static of the radio. She finally settles the radio on a blue grass station playing some song about wanting a long lost lover. She is silent for a few moments almost waiting to see if I will give up information willingly or if it will require work on her part.

"So, where you runnin' to?" I had been on the point of dozing off when her scratchy voice, a chain smoker by the sounds of it, or at least used to be, yanks me back to the cab of the truck.

"Nowhere in particular." I feel that in this there's no reason to lie. I wouldn't even know what to say other than the truth anyway. I really have no idea where I'm going. I don't even have options.

"Ah. So, what are you runnin' 'way from?" She smiles a little as she looks over at me. Her eyes twinkling with a joke. She digs in her pocket and pulls out a half empty box of Pall Malls. She offers me one and I accept. I have no idea if I'm a smoker or not, but a cigarette sounds really good right now.

"I'm not running away from anything," I say, trying to sound nonchalant about it, hoping she doesn't see the cigarette tremble in my mouth as I light it with the lighter, she has offered me. It's a simple red Bic lighter but it says on the side: "Buy your own fucking lighter."

The cigarette feels good, but I can feel the tinge of heat in my throat, and it almost makes me cough. I don't think this is my first cigarette, but I also don't think that I smoke regularly. Although all of this is just guessing on my part, of course.

"Suit yourself, but trust me, everyone's running. Whether it's towards something or from something that's their business, but there ain't a fuckin' person on this damned planet that ain't runnin', and that's a fact." She slips the lighter back into her pants pocket and takes a long drag from her own cigarette.

"What about you, then?" I ask, immediately regretting it. Neither of us say anything, we don't even look at each other. The song on the radio ends and the static takes over as a commercial for a used car lot begins. We pass a sign that says "Welcome to Fareport! The happiest place to call home!"

"Where do you want me to drop you off?" It's a moment before I realize she's talking to me and expects an answer. I stop myself from admitting to the fact that I have no idea. I don't want her to know how lost I truly am, but what choice do I have.

"You don't have to drop me off anywhere. I can walk from your work. I assume that's where you're headed?" We stop at a red light. I don't see any other traffic lights nearby. Fareport must not be a very large town.

"You don't think I wear this get-up by choice, do you?" As we turn right, I see the neon sign come into view. The second "e" in "Beer" is out, and the picture of the old-time beer cask is flashing almost as if it's sending out a Morse code signal. She pulls into the parking lot and parks in the first spot. I get out and allow myself to have a good look around.

I still only see the one stop light. There's a post office across the street next to an all-night laundromat. I see a few people walking the street. A man is walking his dog and waves to an elderly gentleman waiting to cross the street with his walker. A young woman has stopped in the middle of the sidewalk to search through her purse while she holds her phone between her shoulder and her ear. A boy skateboards around her effortlessly and heads down the street. I search each of their faces hoping for something, anything, to trigger in my memory. Hoping that I know one of them, hoping that one of them might know me.

"Why don't you come in an' have an omelet? You look like you could use some food." Chrissy has stopped at the door into the diner, her hand on the push bar. I think on it for a moment, and when my stomach begins to grumble, I follow her inside.

It's like I've stepped back in time. Everything is black and white tile. The booths have red cushions and the pictures on the walls are of fifties style cars being driven by James Dean wannabes. A man a little older than me is wiping down one of the tables with a rag. He is dressed just like Chrissy except with a black apron overtop.

"How was your night, Jimmy?" Christine asks as she walks behind the bar into the kitchen. I see an extremely overweight cook far in the back working over a stove. Christine doesn't notice Jimmy quickly pull his headphones out of his ears and shove them in his pocket, but I do. He frantically returns to wiping down the table. "Dougles, make my new friend here one of your famous omelets." Dougles comes away from the stove and comes up to the counter. He is a very overweight, very dirty, very hairy man with a very disgruntled look on his face.

I take a seat on one of the bar stools and he begins to leer at me. After a few moments of this, I scoot myself off of it and walk over to a booth.

"Just put cheese in it, Doug," Jimmy calls from across the room. "Ignore him. He likes to fuck with customers. Can I get you anything to drink?" I try to think about what I even like to drink. Loads of sodas and drinks come to my head but I have no opinions about any of them.

"I'll just take a Coke." Jimmy nods and walks back behind the counter to the drink fountain. I grab a menu and begin to look at it because I have nothing better to do. It's beginning to dawn on me that I have no plan. My first step was to get away from the dock. I know that I need to try and figure out who I am, but I'm so clueless, I don't even know where to begin.

"Did you want anything other than the omelet?" Jimmy has appeared with a glass of Coke for me. He sets it down in front of me and pulls out a small pad of paper and pen.

"No, I'm okay, thank you." An idea hits me. "Hey, do you have a spare pad and pen I could borrow?" He chuckles and reaches into the pocket of his apron.

"Asking a server if he's got paper and pen is like asking if a cop's got donuts. Here ya go. I'll go make sure Doug isn't spitting in your omelet." He walks away, and I take the pen and pad he has placed on the table. I look at the blank page and try to think of what to write.

I need to figure out what to do, so I might as well start by making a to do list. I write "To Do List" at the top of the page. Here is where I falter. I consider putting down something about finding out about what happened at the dock, but I hesitate to even put that on paper. Just in case this were to fall into the wrong hands should I lose it or something.

Find out what happened last night. I put that down, figuring as long as I never put a date on it no one but me will know what it means. I put a small box next to it in the faint hopes that one day I'll be able to put a little checkmark in it.

Find out who I am. I put below that then immediately scratch it out. I remind myself that I have to put obtainable goals on here and instead write, *Find out my name.* A small box goes next to that, as well. Slightly bigger than the first, as if it were more important.

Pretty soon I'm able to come up with more short-term goals. After a few minutes of writing, I pause to look at what I've got so far:

Find someone who knows me
Find out where I'm from
Find a way to make money
Find a place to stay

"Find a place to stay?" I quickly shove the pen and paper into my backpack as Jimmy sets a plate full of egg in front of me. I hope he didn't read any more of the to do list, especially the part about trying to find out about my name. He does give my backpack an odd look for a moment but then snaps out of it and returns to looking at me.

"If you need a place to stay, I'd check next door. Ronnie's got a room to rent." I pick up the knife and fork he has laid down next to the plate and try not to make eye contact. Hoping against hope he doesn't inquire into the rest of the list, meanwhile silently cursing myself for being so stupid as to write any of that down.

"Who's Ronnie?" I ask after I take a bite of the omelet. It really is good, Dougles makes a pretty mean egg.

"He's this vet next door." Suddenly, Jimmy is sitting in the booth across from me. "He rents out his guest room all the time. He does it because he's lonely ever since his wife died, which I get but the dude goes through more roommates than a kid goes through shoes. He never has good luck with renters. They always turn out to be crazy."

"How do you know I'm not crazy?" I don't even realize I've said it out loud until he responds.

"You seem alright. How's the omelet?" I see him glance behind me, no doubt checking to see if Chrissy notices him sitting with me and not working.

"It's really good. My compliments to the chef." Jimmy smirks as I say this. He bites his lower lip and looks about to say something when, suddenly, the most ungodly sound comes from behind me. I turn around to see what it is, and I see Chrissy coming out of a small door next to the kitchen marked Restroom.

"What the hell happened in there, Jimmy?" Chrissy looks as if she is about to throw up and runs into the back room. Jimmy groans and gets up from the table.

"You should definitely look into Ronnie's room if you're looking for a place to go. Anyway, I gotta go take care of the bathroom, but I'll see you around." He heads off to the back, presumably to grab a mop or cleaning supplies.

I turn back to my omelet and begin to eat more as I consider his proposition.

Staying next door might not be a bad idea. I want to stay nearby, see if I can find out any clues to my identity, or that of the girl at the dock's. And staying there won't be like staying at a hotel I may be able to avoid needing an ID. I quickly scarf down the rest of my omelet and drink some of the Coke before getting up to leave. I fish around in the bag for the wad of cash and pull out a ten-dollar bill from it, leaving it on the table I go to head out.

Part of me feels bad for leaving without saying anything. But another part of me says it's for the best. Until I know my own situation and what I'm going to do, it's probably best not to make friends. Or anything else, for that matter.

There's a faded quilt across the double bed. I set my backpack down on top of it and look around at my room. Ronnie offered it to me for a couple hundred a month. I figure I have enough in the money I stole to last me a few months before I start to worry. The room has an ugly yellow wallpaper with a design of birds flying in repeating sets of seven. If you think about it, it almost looks like they are circling you, waiting for their prey to keel over and die before they strike.

Ronnie is an interesting fellow. He has a prosthetic leg that he kept reminding me he lost in "the Gulf." I had interrupted him eating cereal and watching a daytime soap in order to discuss the room for rent. The conversation was interrupted every few moments with him commenting towards the screen. "That's more like it, Rufus! Show her you love her, goddammit! Sorry anyway, yeah, the first month's rent up front if you could, would be fine."

I stuck with the name Sam this time. I figured being in such proximity to the diner it would be best if people didn't call me different names. He asked for a last name and I gave him Smith. I figured it was common enough.

He didn't seem too interested in finding out too much about me. I wouldn't swear to it, but I saw a half empty six pack on the counter, and I was pretty sure it had been full when Ronnie woke up. He asked me what brought me to town, and I lied through my teeth. I told him I was just passing through on my way west. I kept it vague in the hopes that he would leave it at that. Luckily for me he did. I made a mental note to come up with a more believable story later.

Any qualms he might have had about me disappeared when I offered him cash on the spot.

There is a small vanity next to the chest of drawers. I catch a glimpse of myself in the mirror. I can see that I need sleep. I decide to take the rest of the day and sleep. I collapse onto the bed without even bothering to undress or to get beneath the sheets. My consciousness sinks faster than my eyelids.

Flashes of color sprout up behind my eyes like wildflowers. Soon the colors morph into faces. Faces I don't recognize. I don't recognize them because they are wearing masks, fancy Venetian masks like they were at Mardi Gras. Everyone is in fancy costumes too and spinning, spinning, spinning in circles. As each of them passes me they reach out a hand almost to offer me a dance, but they fall short and stroke my arm, my shoulder, my face.

Then there she is. A man with a long-nosed mask moves just so and I see her across the way. She's wearing the same dress; she is the only one without a mask. She looks exactly like she did on the dock. Complete with the neck wound which I see when she turns and begins to run away from me. I chase after her, pushing my way through the crowd.

Cackling laughter erupts around me as the caresses around me turn into grabs as hands hold me back from getting to her. They rip at my clothes and scratch at my skin, but I ignore it. I have to get to her. She knows who I am. I have to ask her who I am. I have to get to her.

She looks back one last time before they overpower me and pull me to the floor. Except when I hit the ground, I fall through it as if it were water. I look up at the ballroom from beneath the floor. A floor of rippling glass. I fell through it, but they can't cross, and as I swim back up to try to break the surface, I realize that I no longer can.

I also can no longer breath. I open my mouth, and nothing comes in or out. I clutch at my throat and try not to panic. This is a dream I tell myself I can't drown in a dream. I can't die in a dream. I can't die before I find out who I am.

"Sam!" My eyes open to the bedroom. It's dark except the bedside lamp. Ronnie is sitting on the edge of the bed his walking stick in one hand, his other hand on my shoulder. I'm sitting up and I'm sweating all over. "You were screaming somethin' fierce."

"I'm… I'm sorry. I didn't…" I swallow. "I didn't mean to wake you."

"That's alright. I was awake anyway. Just on my way out, actually." He stands up awkwardly leaning on his cane and heads for the door. If you didn't know any better, you would just think he had a limp. I only knew his leg was a prosthetic because when I showed up that morning, he had it in his lap.

"Why are you going out so late?" I look over and see the small alarm clock on the bedside table reads eleven-thirty. I must have slept for almost fourteen hours.

"Why I always do. I keep Jimmy company on his night shifts. Care to join me for a coffee?" He doesn't stop at the door to wait for my answer he just keeps limping on down the hallway leaving me with the question hanging in the air like a streamer after the party has ended.

"Sure. Just let me change my clothes," I call to him. I grab my bag and instinctively check the money. I haven't gotten a chance to count it yet, but it looks like it's all still there. I have no reason to not trust Ronnie, but then again, I don't have much choice other than to not trust people right now.

A few minutes later, I emerge into the hallway dressed in the same pair of jeans but a new t shirt. Ronnie is nowhere to be seen. I look in the kitchen but it's empty. I step out onto the front stoop and look through the windows next door and see him sitting in the corner booth. Jimmy is setting a cup of coffee in front of him.

I didn't notice the bell ring when I opened the door earlier, but I notice it now. Jimmy looks over when he hears it but Ronnie either doesn't notice or doesn't care.

"Hey. I wondered if you'd be back." Jimmy goes to grab me a menu.

"He'll be back quite a bit. Sam here is my new roomie." Ronnie holds his hand out offering the seat across from him. I take it and grab for the menu Jimmy offers me.

"So, you took my advice. Sam, is it? I'm Jimmy. We didn't get a chance to introduce ourselves earlier." He hands me the menu, and I notice he keeps a grip on it for a moment longer than needed.

"Yeah. Thanks for the help." I smile at him and then look at the menu.

"Well, just holler if you guys need anything. I'll be back in a bit. Ronnie, you know where the coffee is." He nods at Ronnie and heads towards the back.

"That I do." Ronnie takes a sip of his coffee and then looks straight at me, almost like he was trying to see into my soul. "So, what were you dreaming about?" He grabs a packet of sugar from the counter and opens it without taking his eyes off of me.

"I don't remember." I avoid his eye contact, but I still feel his eyes boring into me.

"People don't remember dreams all the time. Not nearly as often, though, do they wake up screaming from them. Those dreams are much more… memorable." He takes a hint, however, and quits the staring contest, choosing instead to look at his coffee as he pours in another sugar.

"Why are you getting coffee at eleven-thirty at night?" He laughs and a little bit of spittle bubbles on his lip. He digs in his pocket and pulls out an old hanky to wipe it up.

"Why did you sleep away the entire day?" I can't decide if Ronnie wants to be my friend and is just jerking me around or if I've done something to piss him off. "Look, everyone's entitled to their own business. I just want to get to know the kind of guy I'm livin' with, is all. Forgive me for bein' curious." He looks at me and smirks.

"I didn't get much sleep last night." I can't blame the guy for questioning, but at the same time I need to get him to stop before he realizes that I don't know the answers any more than he does.

"Too busy staying up with Angela?" A bell rings in the depths of my soul.

“Did you decide you wanted something?” Jimmy has appeared out of nowhere at the worst moment.

“Wait, yes, but what do you mean ‘Angela’?” Ronnie gives me an odd look before setting down his coffee.

“That’s who you were screaming for earlier. You kept screaming, ‘Angela! Come back!’ I assume she must be the reason you were up all night previously. Nothing like girl troubles to keep a young man like yourself up late at night.” I can’t believe what I’m hearing. It’s exactly what I wanted, what I was hoping for. A clue. It isn’t much but it’s a name.

“Another omelet?”

He looks at me questioningly, but I don’t make eye contact or even register that he is standing there. I am too busy dealing with the new information.

So, her name was Angela. That tells me I knew her or at least knew her name. It wasn’t a random killing. Although what had I thought? That I had killed some random girl in a party dress and dumped her in the lake? Of course, I knew her. Now I am one step closer to figuring out how.

“I said, did you want another omelet?” I finally look up at Jimmy, from his look and Ronnie’s I figure I must have zoned out.

“Sorry, yeah, that’s fine.” Jimmy, obviously frustrated, turns and heads to the back. Ronnie chuckles again this time catching the spittle before it hits his lip with his hankie. His chuckle turns into a coughing fit.

Chapter 4

I sit in front of the computer at the library. I had quickly woken up today to the buzzing of the alarm next to me. Ronnie had confirmed for me that the library would be open and told me how to get there. Part of me cursed the fact that I didn't think of this yesterday, but Ronnie tells me that the library wouldn't have been open anyway given that yesterday was apparently a Sunday.

I had some minor difficulties getting access to the computer, however.

"I'm sorry, but without a library card, I can't let you use our computer systems." The blonde woman behind the desk looked late forties with a twelve-year-old's taste. She had a bubblegum pink head band and matching glasses. Her shirt had hello kitty on it as did the cellphone case of the newest iPhone that vibrated at that moment. She checked the text from "Lilly." I glanced at the preview and it said, "Call me right away." the smiley face at the end implied some juicy gossip for the wannabe-young-again club.

"Well, can I get a library card?" She frustratingly messaged Lilly back and didn't look at me as she responded to my query.

"Sure, no problem. I just need a form of ID." She put the phone down faceup. No sooner did it hit the counter and it vibrated again. "But this can't wait! Trust me!" I glanced at her and saw her frown as she put the phone in her purse to avoid temptation.

"How about we forget the ID, you give me a library card, and I won't tell your boss if you go out back and leave the post unmanned while you call Lilly?" Desperate times call for desperate housewives to be taken advantage of.

I now sit here staring at the results of my most recent Google search. I had started with "Angela" and, of course, came up with a million useless links. I narrowed it by adding "missing person" and got nothing from it either. I narrowed it further by adding in "Ohio" and didn't get any hits. None that were useful anyway. Not unless she was a fifty-five-year-old woman or went missing ten years before she had looked to be born.

"Hey, look who it is!" The voice came from in front of me. Across the room at another desk with a similar computer sitting in front of him, a young man about nineteen has turned and is looking at me. Not only is he looking at me, but he is looking with recognition. He knows me.

"I'm sorry?" He gets up and walks towards me. My mind tries to handle this. I definitely do not remember him. I don't even feel the dim recognition I felt from seeing Angela at the dock. I try to think how we could know each other. It would be possible we would have gone to school together, but he would have been four years behind me or so. He might be around the same age as Angela, though. I might know him through her.

"Remember me from the bus?" He pulls up a chair and sits across from me, his face staring at me right next to the computer full of my dead-end search. Bus? What bus? "The bus from Boston?" he clarifies based off of my confused expression.

"I'm sorry, but… I don't remember." I tread lightly. I don't want him to know that I have no recollection of anything. His first suggestion is going to be go to the authorities, but that obviously won't work given I might have killed someone. At the same time, I need to get information from him, he is the only person I have met who met me before.

"I thought you'd be gone by now." He pulls out a pencil and begins to balance it on its point on the table. I scratch an itch on the back of my neck as I try to decide how to continue.

"Why would you think that?" I try to gauge his reaction. He doesn't seem to be concerned with much beyond the pencil. I'm not sure my lack of memory has sent up any red flags for him. Thank goodness.

"Well, you said that you wouldn't be staying longer than the week. It's Monday now." He finally gets the pencil to balance by shoving it into a small gap in the wood and getting the point stuck there. "Anyway, I'll let you get back to what you were doing." I saw my hope of answers start to dwindle in front of me and I began grasping at straws.

"Do you remember why I was coming here?" He turned back with a confused look on his face, halfway between his desk and mine, halfway between giving me the answers to my past and disappearing forever.

"You said you were coming home. Why, do you not remember?" His face morphed slowly from confused to concerned.

"What if I said I didn't?" My mind went through the possible outcomes of this conversation and ultimately decided that if I really wanted to get any information, I'd need to give a little bit. You can never learn what fire is without getting burned. "Look, I woke up yesterday with no memory of the past few days. I was in an accident and hit my head." Not exactly a lie. Not exactly the truth.

"Oh, my God. I'm sorry. Have you gone to the hospital or something? They might be able to help." Not the solution I expected but would probably still result in police involvement.

"Yeah, they said that if I could talk to people I met, it might help me regain my memory." I could feel Kevin crawling back into my skin as the lies easily slipped off my lips.

"Well, we didn't talk much. We sat next to each other the whole way from Boston, but you weren't very talkative." He took his seat again this time, though he seemed much more attentive. He felt he was doing me a favor, and he was, he just didn't realize who he was helping.

"Boston?" Was that where I was actually from? If so, why was I coming to Ohio, and why did I say I was coming home?

"You got on from another bus, so I don't know where you were originally coming from. I was just coming back from a concert in Boston. You just said you were heading home and then you pulled out a notebook and sketched the rest of the ride."

"I sketched?" So, I'm an artist? I hadn't felt the urge or the need to draw in the last two days, but then again, I didn't see any reason why it didn't make sense for me to be artistic and not know it. If I don't know my own name, then there's no reason I'd know my hobbies.

"Yeah, you kept sketching this picture of this woman. I think she was blonde. I don't know, you weren't showing it to me or anything I just looked over your shoulder most of the trip." His concerned face was trying to be comforting but all I felt was frustrated. If what he said was true and I saw no reason to doubt him, that meant I wasn't from this town, at least not currently. That meant it was going to be even more difficult to find people who knew me.

"I didn't happen to mention my name, did I?" His eyes widened, my full condition finally hitting him for the first time.

"Dude, you don't even know your own name? That sucks, man. I'm sorry I don't remember. I mean you might have mentioned it, but I don't remember it." Of course not. I smile and try to look grateful. He turns around and returns to his computer leaving me with my thoughts.

I try to tell myself that this is good, that it is a clue, even if it is not the clue I wanted. I now don't need to worry about being recognized by anyone from my past since I didn't live here before. But that means I am severely limited on my possible leads. Luckily for me the most pertinent information I need is that of the last couple of days leading up to the events on the dock.

"What day were we on the bus?" I ask the guy from the bus. He quickly pulls out his headphones and I have to repeat my query.

"It was just last Sunday night. Like late Sunday night. We got off the bus at probably half past midnight. Sorry I can't be more help." He shrugs and returns to his computer. I add this new information to my slowly growing knowledge of my life before the dock. If I was only here on Sunday night and I woke up on the dock late Saturday night I was here for an entire week before he dock. What did I do for a week?

What was I doing here? Did it involve Angela? Had I met her before, or did I meet her here? These questions and countless more circled around and around in my brain, going around and around in circles like dogs on a racetrack. rushing at breakneck speed to try and catch the mechanical rabbit that was my past. Running faster and faster but still getting me nowhere.

After twenty minutes of more fruitless Google searches trying to find Angela, I noticed that the desk in front of me was empty. The computer had returned to its log in screen. The only person in this town that knew me was gone. I didn't even know his name.

"You gonna tell me why you've got a wad of cash hidden under my mattress?" Ronnie asks as I enter the kitchen. His leg is unattached and sitting on the counter. He has a bottle of polish and is polishing the wooden facade. It was an old-fashioned wooden leg, nothing like the fancy metal ones they used for the Paralympics and such. This was nothing more than a wooden stump with a hinge at the knee.

"You went through my stuff?" I immediately panic. Does he know what happened? Why is he searching my room if he doesn't have some reason to suspect me of being devious?

"I was just taking the sheets off of your bed to wash. Relax I don't care how much money you got. I just wanna know why someone's got almost $1,000 in small bills. Makes me think someone's into something not quite legal." I actually have closer to two thousand. I counted it last night before I went to bed. It was exactly $1,874. I make a mental note to count it again later to make sure that Ronnie didn't have sticky fingers.

"So, tell me straight, are you a drug dealer? Cause I ain't gonna have any of that bullhockey in my house." He points at me with the polish rag in his left hand and the way his head tilted I see one of his eyes through his bifocals and the other not, giving him two different sized eyes. I don't know which part of it I find funny, the fact that even if I was a drug dealer I wouldn't know, his eyes, or the fact that he called it all 'bullhockey.' Regardless of what it is, I laugh in his face.

"I promise I'm not a drug dealer." He sighs with relief and returns to polishing his leg.

"Thank goodness for that. I didn't think you was. I got a good eye for people. I can tell when someone's bad. Hell, you can't even lie to my face most times. I got a keen sense o' when someone's pullin' my leg." At this he looks at me and winks. "Pull up a stool and sit a while."

The small kitchen looks like it hasn't been redecorated since the seventies. It still has a retro looking fridge, lots of wood trimming, and ugly yellow wallpaper. The counter and bar are all polished wood and the T.V. that sits upon it still has knobs to change the channel, as well as a screen that looks smaller than most tablets.

"I'm 'bout to watch the wheel if you care to make yerself some tea 'n watch. Just one rule. No givin' the answers out loud. I like to figure 'em out myself." I get up and got a coffee mug out of the shelf he points to.

"Would you like some?" I notice that he doesn't have anything to drink in front of him, but he shakes his head.

"Drinkin' tea this late would keep me up all night." He leans over and turns the television on. A commercial for a weight loss program comes in and out of focus as he plays with the rabbit ears above the screen. I glance at the clock on the wall, it has a different hummingbird at each hour. The hour hand is only pointing to the little bird where the three should be.

"But you have no problem drinking coffee at eleven-thirty at night." I grab a tea bag out of the box sitting on the counter. I notice he has an insta-hot faucet in the sink. It's the only part of the kitchen that doesn't feel like it's older than I am.

"Coffee's different." He leaves it at that as his eyes become glued to the colorful opening of the *Wheel of Fortune*. Pat Sajak smiles, arm in arm with the dashing Vanna White, as they introduce the show and then the guests.

I sit awkwardly steeping my tea as they introduce the three college students who were competing. It dawns on me that I can't remember if I have been to college. Even if I have, would it still count now that I remembered none of my classes. Although, I am capable of remembering how to make tea without anyone explaining it, and I had no trouble with the computer at the library so my functional memories must still be in place. So, perhaps it would depend on my degree.

I think again about what the guy from the bus said. I had been sketching, so perhaps my degree had been in art? I laugh at my ineptitude and luckily it lines up right with a joke from Pat, so Ronnie doesn't ask me what is so funny. Suddenly, an idea hits me.

"Do you have any paper and pencil?" Ronnie at first looks confused.

"Sure, over there in the drawer is a bunch o' pens and pencils. I think there's a pad in there too but if not, I've got a pad or two in my bedroom." I open the drawer and grab a pencil but there is no pad in sight. He goes to get up.

"You don't have to put your leg on; I'll go and get it." He chuckles at me as he hops out of the room, using the walls to support himself he finds his way without the use of his prosthetic.

"If I can make my way out of a prisoner of war camp, I can make it to my bedroom without a leg." I hear him call from the hallway. He misses the solution to the first puzzle while he's gone: "Time and Time Again." Hope he doesn't hold it against me.

"I never liked my left leg anyway, my right one was always better. Here you go. What do you need that for?" He sits back down, and his eyes are, once again, glued to the screen. I feel he is still paying attention, so I feel the need to respond even if I don't have the words to express what I'm trying.

"I'm just gonna try drawing something." I hold the pencil in my hand and the pad I place on the counter. I close my eyes and put the tip of granite to the fibers of the paper. I suddenly can feel the connection between paper and stylus, between white and black, between blank and art. I keep my eyes closed and I let my mind wander. I try to think about not thinking. I let go of the cage around my mind and let it explore the inner depths of my mind.

I'm only slightly aware of my hand moving but I try to keep from concentrating on anything specific. I simply let my hand do what it already knows it needs to do and move about the page like an ice skater dancing across a rink, leaving lines in the ice but unlike the skater, my lines are black. And it's not me that is the art, but rather it is what I leave behind.

After a moment, I open my eyes and look at what I have done.

Nothing. Unless I was a Jackson Pollock impersonator, this is not how I drew my sketches. I see an eye randomly in the middle of the page but it's pupil is off on another part of the image. An image that is dominated by many squiggly curves that seem to serve no real purpose. The image has neither definite shape nor any recognizable characteristics. It's the drawing of a four-year-old.

"Don't quit your day job." Ronnie chuckles to himself. I look up but he isn't looking at the paper, he's looking at the screen. "Oh, it's the answer to the riddle, I promise. I wasn't making a comment on your… art there." He smirks as I leave the pad and pencil and leave the room. I notice half an hour later that I also left my tea. I hope Ronnie didn't think I left because of his comment. I simply left because I didn't want to look at my failure. My inability to do what I apparently was able to do two days ago with ease.

I wake up in the middle of the night, drenched in sweat. I had a similar dream… or at least I think I did. The details are already leaving me, disappearing like the steam on a bathroom mirror. I practically reach my hands out to try and hold onto the tiny pictures. I have this urgent feeling that if I could just remember what I was dreaming about it just might answer my questions.

It's 4:15 A.M., and I don't feel like rolling over and going back to sleep is going to work, so I get up and throw on a pair of pants. I listen at Ronnie's door before I head into the kitchen. I can hear him snoring. In the kitchen I get myself a glass of water and stare out the window into the dark street. Fareport isn't a night town. The street outside is vacant, though I can see the light spilling onto the pavement from the diner next door.

I suddenly have a constricting feeling. I feel trapped and my blood pressure begins rising to a boiling point. I quickly but silently slip shoes on and get out of the house before the claustrophobia completely takes over and stops me from breathing.

I hesitate standing on the road and I realize the mistake I made. When I left the house by the dock, I thought I had two options. To go left or right. But I forgot that roads don't work like that. There isn't one single road. In either direction you hit loops, and turns, and intersections, crosswalks, lights, stop signs, countless things block your path and make you change your direction. I've set myself on a course, and I don't even know my destination.

I hear laughter behind me. I quickly turn and see the hint of the edge of a ghost turn the corner around the edge of the street at the end of the block. I walk towards it to find the source of the laughter. But just when I round the corner it disappears behind another even further down the street and to the left. I follow the phantom laughter through the village of Fareport. It consistently is at the end of my gaze, just beyond my ability to see, always one step ahead no matter how fast I went. I try to trick it and circle around it but all that results in is more laughter. I now can tell that it is not just laughter. It is her laughter. I recognize it. It's Angela. I don't know how I know, but I know.

I'm partially aware of the insanity of following a dead woman's laughter through a town you don't know in the dead of the night, but I have no other choice. My legs don't listen to me; they only follow the alluring sound of her laughter. That is until the laughter disappears. Leaving me alone on a street in the middle of the town. A street I've never seen before, yet I recognize. I know before I reach the end of the street that it is a cul-de-sac. That the house to the left has a double garage. That the brick is brown and pale. I know without the garage doors being open that inside is a mess on one side and perfectly pristine on the other side.

I know this house. I don't think I've ever been in it, but I've been here before. More importantly, I feel like I know who lives here.

I can see her face now. She's in the kitchen. She's gotten herself a glass of water. She is blonde like Angela. She doesn't have the same natural beauty, but she is pretty nonetheless, although she is much older than myself or Angela. She must be in her forties, but she looks good for it. She is in a silk robe with an Asian design. It was cinched tight at the waste at one point but the journey downstairs to water has since loosened it and it almost gapes open. So much so that I can almost see her nudity beneath it. She stands up and walks towards me, not towards me but towards the sink that is below the window. She rinses out the glass in the sink and glances outside.

Our eyes meet. I see in that moment, recognition. Not recognition like at the library. A deeper recognition. We know each other. We know each other in an intimate way. In a way that you only know those who are closest to you. I remember the feel of her hand in mine. The smell of her perfume. I also remember tears on her cheek.

She snaps the curtains closed on the kitchen window and the light in the kitchen goes out. I wait for what feels like hours, but she never shows herself. I know she saw me, but she evidently didn't want to. Whatever relationship we might have had before I lost my memory, it did not end well. Something must have happened. Is she the reason I came here from Boston? I feel a closeness to her, but I don't feel a love, or rather I don't feel a lust. There is something deeper, rooted more in my chest than in my groin.

I wander and find my way back home in the dark. Without the laughter to guide me I circle back on myself a lot and get lost a couple of times. It takes me a while but eventually I make it back. I notice that Jimmy is alone in the diner. He is sweeping and I catch his eye. His reaction is the opposite of the woman in the window. He beckons me in.

"Where are you coming back from that has you out so late?" he asks over the tinkle of the door as I walk to a booth. He leans the broom against a table and walks over and sits across from me in the booth.

"I was just out for a walk." I try to avoid his eyes, but he is simultaneously attempting to keep my contact. I also find that there is a part of me that doesn't want to look away.

"What were you thinking about?" He leans gracefully back in the booth. I almost laugh as I realize what he is doing.

"I wasn't thinking about anything. I was just walking." I counter and sit forward my elbows resting on the table.

"No one just walks at five in the morning. Something must have been bothering you. Keeping you awake at night." He leans forward, as well. Our faces a seemingly endless distance apart, we couldn't be closer, but we couldn't be farther apart.

"What do you think about at five in the morning?" I am acutely aware of every nerve on my face. I feel the corners of my eyes tighten the slightest degree, almost as if they are preparing to close. I feel the edges of my lips rise less than a quarter of a millimeter, as my cheeks warm just the smallest of degrees. I feel my pupils dilate as I try to take in every aspect of this moment.

"Did I hear a new customer?" Dougles' grumbling from the kitchen pulls us quickly out of the moment. Jimmy goes from sitting to standing with the broom in his hand faster than what seems possible. Leaving me alone in the booth and disappointed. I'm not sure what just happened or didn't happen, but I do know it was ruined by Dougles' entrance.

"It's just Sam." I hear all the layers of the sentence. The surface layer, the layer that's intended for the grumpy cook, and the layer that's intended for my ears only.

"Whip me up one of your omelets like the other day Dougles. I liked it." Dougles heads back to the kitchen. Jimmy returns to sweeping the floor, as if we are going to pretend the last few minutes didn't exist. "So, is it always this busy?"

"On Mondays, yes. Fridays and Saturday nights can be kind of crazy." He looks at me trying to gauge whether he should return to his seat. He decides against it and instead continues to sweep.

"Fareport doesn't seem like the kind of town to have a crazy night life. Most of the houses around here look like Stepford houses. Light's out at ten o'clock." I feel the twinge of thirst but don't want to ask for a drink, afraid it will break the line of connection we have. A line that was already struck once by the knife of the cook's presence.

"It's only a forty-minute drive to the outskirts of Cleveland. It's not a bad drive if people are looking for a night out. And it's just long enough of a ride home for them to get hungry and this is the only place open past eleven." He puts the broom down and my hopes rise like a balloon in my chest. "I need to go to the back and clean up a bit before Chrissy gets here in an hour. Do you need anything to drink while I'm back there?" And with a pop my hope is burst like a balloon.

"No, that's okay. I'm actually gonna head to bed." I get up and head towards the door.

"But what about your omelet?" I almost don't respond but I don't want to leave it like that. I pause at the door. My hand on the glass.

"You can have it. I wasn't really hungry. I was just trying to get rid of him." With that I leave him and walk the short distance back to Ronnie's house. It will take the entire time until I wake up to process tonight's events.

Chapter 5

"Are you sure you don't want anything else sir?" I look up from the book I'm not really reading to find the waiter standing over me. A disapproving glare on his face. It's understandable. I've been sitting here in his section for over three hours and all I've gotten to eat or drink is a single Coke. I'd get more but I can't afford to waste any of my money if I can avoid it. At least until I find a job.

"I'm okay. Thank you." He walks away grumbling under his breath. I return to not reading my book and look over the edge of it at the beauty salon on the other side of the street. I have been waiting for the last three hours for her to leave. This morning I woke up with the energy of the first real lead on my identity. Regardless of the woman's reaction to seeing me last night, there was no denying that she knew who I was. So, my first step in getting to know who I was included getting to know her.

I considered just walking up to her door and knocking but I wanted to gain some information first. I needed to know who this woman was and how I might have known her. So, instead, I went to her house and I watched where she went. Lucky for me she was a walker and did not drive her car. I wasn't sure what I would have done if she had done that. I only had to wait about twenty minutes after I hid behind her neighbor's rose bushes before she came out and began to walk down her street.

I had followed her throughout town and saw her stop by the bank, the post office, and get lunch with a woman. I sat in this same cafe and watched her from outside while she sat inside with her red headed friend and talked their way through a light lunch. I didn't recognize her friend and I tried to catch her eye to see if she recognized me, but I was wary of the blonde woman catching my eye. I had gotten a very clear message from her last night. She did not want to see me and knowing that I was basically stalking her would not help matters.

Both ladies had looked rather wealthy. They were wearing designer brand clothing and had those obnoxious purses that match their outfit but don't look like they are efficient at keeping belongings. Neither of them ate much of what they ordered but they each got two courses and at least three drinks apiece. Given that my Coke by itself was $3, I figured this was a rather expensive lunch.

Soon she had left the cafe and I had almost gotten up to follow her when she walked straight across the street and went into the beauty salon. That was two hours ago, and I hadn't seen her leave. I had brought a book along just in case I got stuck sitting and waiting. It was some old novel off of Ronnie's shelf in the living room, called *The Awakening*. I had tried to read it, but I was too afraid of getting engrossed in the book and missing her leave. Instead, I watched the street that separated us.

We were in a different part of Fareport than Beer 'n' Burgers. There was a clothing boutique on the corner and a couple of upper-class looking cafes. The edge of the lake came closer to town here. So close, in fact, that I could see it down the street to my right from where I sat. There was a dock that was populated by a bunch of sailboats across the road, I had to stop myself from picturing Angela's body floating beneath the bulks of those boats.

I return my attention to the salon just in time to see her walk out of it. She smiles and waves to the lady inside. She must have had something done to her hair but what exactly, I can't tell. I try to hide my face with the book while also keeping an eye on her as she walks down the street. I don't want to get up and follow her till she's far enough away to not notice me.

I notice that she's heading in the same direction from which we came. I hope she's heading home and decide to let her go for now. I have a surge of an idea that takes me across the street to her beauty salon. I step inside and see that I'm the only man in the salon. I glance quickly at the sign on the wall behind the counter and notice they don't have men's hair cut prices listed. I quickly improvise.

"Can I help you?" The young brunette with glasses and a headband sitting behind the counter has one pencil in her hand and two more through the bun in her hair. She is wearing a very low-cut top with a matching skirt. I approach the counter trying to ignore the looks I'm getting from the other women in the room. One blonde is looking at me like a rat just walked through her living room. It's obvious that no one walks into this salon in jeans and a t-shirt, let alone a young man.

"Yes, I'm here to make an appointment for my mother." I glance at the clock and do some quick math in my head, counting back the time to when the woman had walked in.

"When were you hoping to get her in?" The brunette is smiling, now that it appears I might bring in a paying customer.

"Do you have any openings later today?" She looks down at her book, and I do, as well, gleaning the information I was hoping to get. My job was done, now it was simply a job of getting out.

"No, but we can do tomorrow around four-thirty?"

"That sound's great. Angela…" I hesitated on a last name. "Angela Cartwright." She smiled and wrote the name down and I walked out of the salon proud. I may not have learned anything about myself, but I did learn that I knew an upper-class woman by the name of Helen King.

I walk down the street towards Ronnie's, I guess I can say my, house, when I see Jimmy walking out of the diner. He sees me and waves. I wave back. He looks like he is about to call out to me but then thinks better of it. Instead, he goes over to his beat-up truck and gets in. I have been so distracted with tracking down Helen today that I haven't given last night much thought. I wonder why he is just now leaving the diner as his shift would have ended much earlier this morning. Then I chastise myself. It's none of my business. I have enough on my plate to worry about without keeping track of Jimmy's work schedule. Perhaps it's just guilt from walking out like I had the night before.

Stepping into the kitchen I see Ronnie sitting at the counter eating a bowl of cheerios.

"How are you?" I ask as I sit next to him. He has the T.V. turned on like I had never left. Right now, it is just a commercial for a dentist's office.

"Lousy, as usual." He smiles at me and takes another bite of Cheerios.

"Welcome back to 2 News at Two. For those just joining us, we are keeping you updated on the story that is unfolding out on Hudson's Beach. Melissa Ethridge is on the scene." My throat goes dry as I see the screen go to a shot of a dock. At first, I panic, but it does not look like the dock that I awoke on the other night.

"Thank you, James." The newswoman stands in front of the lake, while behind her there are police officers searching the dock and the surrounding areas. There is crime scene tape up blocking off the access to the dock. "Just last night a major breakthrough was made in the missing person's case of Emily Bradshaw." I sit down, my head begins to thump, and my vision begins to go fuzzy. "Last Friday night, Emily Bradshaw was kidnapped from her home on South Plymouth St. in Fareport. Her house showed signs of a struggle, and the victim's blood was found at the scene."

They plastered Emily's photo across the screen. I felt the bile begin to rise up in my throat. My stomach did a summersault and I felt sweat crop up all over.

"After talking to Emily's neighbor, they began searching for the blue Toyota that was seen parked in her driveway that day. Last night the Toyota was found abandoned here on Hudson's Beach. After an initial search of the area, the search party found what appears to be the body of the missing girl at the bottom of the lake."

"God, isn't that terrible." Ronnie shakes his head, but I don't trust myself to speak, besides my tongue feels like it weighs a thousand pounds.

"We have just received confirmation from Detective Callahan, the lead on this case, that the family has confirmed the identity of the body as Emily Bradshaw." They once more plastered her picture across the screen.

I can't take it any longer. I bolt out of the kitchen and run into my room and slam the door behind me. I lean against the door and collapse to the floor. I shut my eyes, but I can't get her face out of my mind. It is etched into the back of my eyelids. The picture of the dead girl. The picture of the girl they found at the bottom of the lake. The picture of a girl I don't know. The picture of a girl I don't recognize. I don't recognize it because it isn't the girl I woke up next to Saturday morning.

What if I killed them both?

I hear Ronnie stumbling down the hall before I feel him knocking on the door behind me.

"You alright in there?" I search for an answer, but I can't seem to string two words together. I lick my lips and wonder if he'll go away if I don't answer. He doesn't knock again but I don't hear him walking away either. After a few moments, I stand up and turn to face the door. I reach to open it but hesitate at the last minute.

I know in the back of my mind that I should tell someone. Say something. Go to the authorities, do something to turn myself in. I have an obligation to Angela, to Emily apparently, as well to their parents. I am breaking the law simply by not going to the police. I'm making a criminal out of Ronnie by letting him inadvertently house a murderer.

Instead, of opening the door I turn away from it and throw myself on the bed in frustration.

"I'm okay. Just need a little time to myself." The voice coming out of my mouth doesn't sound like my own. Although who am I to say so? I don't know who I am. I don't know anything. I don't even know my own name let alone the sound of my own voice. I have evidence to the fact that I killed not one but two women the other night. For all I know there's more. For the last few days, I've been trying to figure out my life by following a trail of bread crumbs, when all along that trail could have been of dead bodies.

I hear Ronnie walk away from the door. I get up and quickly leave the room and then the house. Ronnie looks at me as I leave but I give him no excuse.

I don't know where I'm going but I need to clear my head. I need to get my thoughts in order and decide what I'm going to do. Do I turn myself in, or do I continue to hope that there is some other explanation, any explanation that doesn't include the fact that I may have killed someone?

Before I realize it, I'm running. I'm bolting around corners, I almost collide with a woman who's walking her corgis, but I dodge past her without giving her a second glance. I continue to run till I feel the sweat dripping down my back from the exertion. I need to get out. Out of this town, out of this life, out of my skin. So, that's where I run. I head out of town.

I am on the same street I came in on. I am running back towards Alex's house. Back towards the dock. Back towards the scene of the crime. That's what criminals always do isn't it? Return to the scene of the crime. So, I run.

I collapse of exhaustion in the middle of the road. I lay there for a few moments considering if it would be best to just let someone run me over. Let it all go away with a quick thump. A scarlet spray of blood on the road that will get washed away with the next thunderstorm. Will that be enough to wash away my guilt, to wash away my past? Will my past continue to matter if I have no future?

The sun moves behind some clouds and I feel the coolness of the shade.

It gives me the chance I need to clear my head. I relax and sit up. I crawl over to the side of the road. There is an electrical fence that separates the ditch from the corn field beyond. I lean against a wooden post and rest my legs. It is five minutes before a car passes, and I try not to think of what would have happened if I hadn't moved to the side.

As much as I want to, I can't fight against my need to survive. I feel so guilty that I know I should die for what I have done but I don't want to die. I also cannot turn myself in. Not until I know for sure. Not until I've proven it to myself beyond a doubt. I have to know if I did it. If I killed them.

Chapter 6

I'm back at the masquerade, but this time, no one is dancing. No one is moving. Everyone is frozen in time. Angela isn't there. I weave my way through the crowd looking for her among the stationary mannequins. I notice that while they don't move, their eyes do. Their eyes are all following me. I can feel them burning into my skin from all angles. I navigate myself to the wall and follow it until I find a large set of double doors.

I open them and step out into a forest. There are trees as far as I can see. They reach up farther than I can tell and create a dark green roof making it impossible to see the sky. I turn around and the doors I came through are replaced with a standing mirror. A mirror that doesn't show my reflection but instead shows hers. Not Angela's, but Emily's. She is covered in blood, her shirt is buttoned wrong, and her jeans are ripped. She stands there in the reflection of the wood and stares at me.

"Look at what you did." She glares at me and I slowly back away from the mirror. I turn to run and find myself face to face with Jimmy.

"What did you do?" He seems angry with me. He pushes me so hard I crash into the mirror behind me. I land on the ground amongst the broken pieces of mirror and feel the shards cut into my palms. I vaguely wonder whether the seven years of bad luck still occurs with dream mirrors but am distracted by the blood that begins to stain Jimmy's work uniform from the inside out. He is bleeding but he doesn't seem to realize it. He just stands there looking down at me like I was caught with my hand in the cookie jar. I move back from him driving more shards into my hands.

"I don't know what I did." This is when he leans forward and grabs my face and pulls it close to his. Intensely close. I can see my reflection in his pupils. He forces his lips onto mine, but blood pours out of his mouth and I feel it running down my chin. He pulls away and he has been replaced with Angela. When she speaks, Jimmy's voice comes out.

"You know what you did. And you're going to do it again. It's what you do. It's who you are, Kevin." She smiles, and her teeth are rotted. They are all old and cracked and half of them are missing. She throws her head back with laughter and it fills the forest as everything begins to spin around me. I feel like someone pulled the plug on the drain of the world and everything is swirling around and around and down and down until everything gets sucked down through a hole.

"Sam?" I open my eyes and see that it's dark out. I must have passed out along the side of the road. the only thing that has woken me up is Jimmy's truck is stopped in front of me. He has his head out the window and is squinting to get a good look at me in the dark. "Is that you? What are you doing on the side of the road?"

I stand up and stretch my back, I feel the soreness from leaning against the post for what was probably a couple of hours. He opens the door and jumps out.

"I'm okay. Look I just, I went for a walk and got tired is all." He looks at me as if I told him I was the pope.

"Get in the truck, I'll give you a ride home."

"You don't have to do that. I'm okay." I shrug his hand off of my shoulder and try to get my bearings. I can't remember which direction is towards town.

"I'm headed into work. Get in." He hops into the truck and looks expectantly at me. I give in and walk around the cab and get in the passenger side. Where Chrissy's truck looked like a landfill, Jimmy's looks like it came off of the lot today. The carpets are spotless, and the windows are clean of fingerprints. The only thing it is missing is the new car smell.

"Never heard of a clean truck." I don't mention the fact that I only have memory of two trucks to go off of.

"I like to keep things neat and tidy." He revs the engine, and we get on our way. "So, are you going to tell me why you were passed out along the side of the road?" He looks at me out of the corner of his eyes.

"I told you I was out for a walk and I got tired, so I decided to take a nap." I can tell he isn't buying it, but I hope he will let it go and not question me further. I can see from the look on his face, though, that his questions are just beginning. "Look, if I told you it was none of your business, would that stop the Spanish Inquisition?"

"Okay, maybe it isn't my business, but I do think I deserve some sort of an explanation. I did care enough to pick you up. But if you aren't willing to give it to me, then that's fine." He flips a switch, and the radio begins to play some pop song.

"Look I appreciate the ride, but I don't owe you any sort of explanation. You don't know me and no offense but that's probably for the best." He bites his bottom lip, and I can feel the unsaid things emanating from him like heat. "Ok, about last night…"

"What about it. Nothing happened." He adjusts his grip on the steering wheel and checks his rearview mirror in an attempt to avoid my gaze.

"Okay. Nothing happened. But like I said, that was probably for the best. So, if you don't mind, I'm going to just go home, and I'll try to avoid falling asleep on the side of the road in the future." I leaned over and turned up the radio, letting the music drown out the blaring silence between us.

After I left him at the diner, I went into Ronnie's and I took a shower. I needed to wash off the person who had been almost hurtful in Jimmy's truck. I mentally tried to argue that it was for the best, but I still hated myself for it. Ronnie was silent watching Jeopardy and didn't ask where I had been. I momentarily wondered how long he would put up with me disappearing and acting strange. Part of me said I should give him some excuse, but I felt like lying outright was somehow worse than silence. After my shower, I went outside. I knew where I was going before I left but I tried not to think about it.

Now I find myself standing in front of her house again. I can see Helen sitting at the kitchen table in the same robe. This time, though, she is not alone. Her husband is sitting with her. He is wearing a white T-shirt and striped pajama bottoms. They are each nursing a mug of tea. They don't seem to be talking but I can see from across the street the tension that fills the kitchen.

He leans over and kisses her on the cheek. She turns ever so slightly at his touch and when she does, she sees me. In one infinitesimal second, we understand each other. She understands why I'm there and I understand that she doesn't want him to know. She nods her head ever so slightly and turns back to her husband to say goodnight.

He leaves the kitchen and heads upstairs. I stand in the street until I see the light upstairs turn off five minutes later. She doesn't do anything, but she looks back out the window at me. Her jaw is set, and she grips her mug of tea as if it were a life raft. I walk across the street and up their driveway, my eyes never leaving hers until I turn towards their front door and the window falls out of sight.

When I get to the door, I open the screen door to knock. I don't want to ring the doorbell. We have made a silent agreement to not tell her husband. I don't understand why she would agree to talk to me, but I understand that I am at a disadvantage, she knows who I am, while I have no idea. I need to play by her rules until I find out more.

She opens the door before I can knock. She stands there in the doorway, not opening the door enough to invite me in but enough to show she's willing to talk to me.

"You can't keep doing this." I hear a slight accent, it's almost European but not quite. I am ever aware of her nakedness beneath the silk robe. The robe that's slightly loose at the neck, revealing the tops of her breasts.

"I need to speak to you." She closes her eyes and leans against the door. That isn't what she wanted to hear.

"I don't want you to come here again. I can't risk him seeing you." She keeps her eyes closed almost hoping that if she can't see me that I will just go away. I, however, am not moving. "I don't know what you want me to tell you. I said all I had to say the other night. I understand your situation, but you have to understand mine." I highly doubt she understands as much as she thinks she does. "Philip can never know you exist. It wouldn't be good for him, or our marriage."

My mind works to try and put together the pieces, trying to make sense of the puzzle that is our history. But it's like trying to put together a puzzle without the picture or half the pieces. All you get is a pile of wooden pieces. I need to keep her talking I need to get her to give me more information.

"Why can't I meet him?" She tucks a lock of golden hair behind her ear. From her glare at me she has told me why and she is assuming that I'm refusing to listen. I let her assume because it is better than the alternative.

"He would be devastated. It has taken me years to get him back I'm not going to lose him again. Not to you or to her." Her? who is she referring to? The puzzle has a new piece, a new character. "Now I've said everything I'm willing to say please leave." She goes to close the door, but I stop it an inch from the frame.

"Do you know where I can find her?" I don't know who she is, I'm not even sure what I'm asking but I need something. I can't walk away from this encounter with nothing but a pronoun. I need a name, an address, something that can lead me to the next bread crumb. She gives me a confused look. I realize too late that I should know where she is, whoever she is. I'm afraid I've said to much, perhaps revealed too much. I turn to walk away. When I step down onto the path through the front garden, I hear her whisper.

"Over on Westchester Street. You'll find her at the back." I barely hear her, even in the silence of the night the words in my head almost drown out her quiet voice. I turn back to thank her, but the door is closed. I hear the click of the dead bolt. I can't be sure, but I still feel her presence on the other side of the door. Both of us waiting to see who will be the first to leave. Neither one willing to go first, like lovers, who refuse to hang up the phone even when the conversation is dead. We have a connection, something that has brought us together. Something that we can't deny no matter how much we try.

On the way home I look at every street sign looking for Westchester Street. I never see it. Part of me is afraid that she has given me a fake street. Something to get me off her porch. But I know in my gut that what she's said was true. As much as she doesn't want to, she needs to help me. I can see it in her eyes. She may not know my whole story, but she knows more than I do and she's the only one that's helping me.

When I come to the kitchen in the morning, I find Ronnie eating a bowl of cereal and reading the Fareport Daily. A black and white picture of Emily Bradshaw dominates the front page, but Ronnie is reading the comics.

"Good mornin'," he says without looking away from the paper in his left hand. His right precariously poised before his mouth with a spoonful of frosted flakes. I go over to the cabinet and pull out a bowl for myself and pour the cereal. I haven't offered to pitch in for groceries yet, but Ronnie hasn't asked me to either.

"Do you know where Westchester Street is?" This causes Ronnie to put the paper down and give me an odd look. I realize I don't even have an excuse for the address. I don't have a lie to tell him about where I'm going or where I got the address from.

"Course I do." He raises an eyebrow.

"A friend of mine lives on Westchester Street," I lie, hoping that will be enough for him to tell me where to go. Instead, he chuckles to himself.

"Is this friend of yers a lady friend?" I'm not sure how it's relevant but I nod my head yes, and he falls into another batch of giggles. "Well, I hate to tell ya, but you've been fed a line o' bullhockey. The only people on Westchester Street ain't living there. That's where Fareport Cemetery's at." He chuckles once more and returns to his paper. Leaving me with the bowl of dry cereal and the realization that this new character, this mysterious "her" that Helen mentioned, must be dead. How many dead women are there in my past?

I don't know why I go to the cemetery. Without a name I have no way of knowing who at this cemetery is the woman that Helen referenced in our conversation. Any of the people buried beneath the hundred slabs of stone could be the next stop on my bread crumb trail.

I wander among the tombstones, some of them fresh and new with easily read names while others are old and rotted to the point that they lose all indication of engraving and become formless rocks that, other than their strict, placement, imply that they came to be here naturally. I read thirty names or so, but I skip over most of them. The dates range all the way back to the 1950s, but there are some as recent as last month. Flowers are in abundance, as well as little pebbles on top of the gravestones. One grave for a Roger Klint has an immense amount of floral decoration, I see from his marker that he passed merely a week and a half ago. I wonder how long it's been since the funeral, how long till the remains of it will disappear like all the rest, leaving Roger to fall into obscurity like the rest of his eternal neighbors.

I stoop to examine the epitaph on a particular stone: "Evan, whom God loved so much. He needed him more than we did. August 3, 2011 - July 27, 2012." A teddy bear rests his head against the stone. When I rise, I see that I'm not the only one in the cemetery this morning. Chrissy catches my eye from a few rows over. I almost don't recognize her out of uniform. She is wearing jeans and an overly large turtle neck, even though it's not cold.

I worry that she will come over and ask who I'm visiting, but she doesn't. She walks over and acknowledges me with a hello. But then we continue to walk along the path in silence. Neither of us say anything or question the other. We reach the end of the aisle and turn down another without asking the other. We move as one without thinking. It's fifteen minutes before she speaks up.

"I come here a lot. My father is buried across the way." I feel like I need to say something in return, but I clam up and bite my tongue. She assumes my silence is emotional and doesn't inquire. Instead, she continues, "Cancer. It's been fifteen years, but I still come at least once a month. Just to say hello. I like to wander sometimes, though."

She stops and looks at a particularly old stone. The name is illegible, but the year is still visible: 1964. She stoops and puts her hand on it.

"I feel sorry for some of them; those whose family have moved or joined them. No one comes to visit them anymore. It's inevitable to happen. So, I try to wander and visit them all. I may not know them but at least someone sees them. Someone remembers."

She takes a deep breath and I see her eyes bead with tears. She closes them to try and hold them back, but one escapes and rolls down her cheek. She stands up quickly and we continue our walk and resume our silence.

The next time we stop it's my turn to pause. I've been glancing at the names and most of them simply enter and exit my consciousness like people getting on and off a subway. There for a moment but then gone into the crowd and never to be recognized or noticed again. Until one stands out among the others:

Angela Cartwright

April 19, 1974 - January 18, 1992

I try to rationalize it in my brain. Angela isn't uncommon. And I might have seen or heard of this woman before I lost my memory. So, it's understandable that when I go to make up a name, I pull one from my subconscious. They say that you can't make up faces. That if you see a strangers face in your dreams or if you imagine a face, it is actually a face in a crowd that you've seen before. Perhaps names are the same. Perhaps we can never come up with completely original names. If that's the case, then I shouldn't panic. But a part of me says that this is a clue. This may not be the woman I was sent to find here but I can't ignore the fact that when I had to make up a name for the hairdresser yesterday, the name I came up with was none other than Angela Cartwright.

But if she died in 1992 and I just arrived in town last week, then how could I know her? Chrissy doesn't ask me why I've stopped. She is polite and silent. I mentally try to memorize the dates and act normal as we continue on our way, but this time, when we find ourselves at the edge of the cemetery, instead of continuing I turn towards the gate.

"I've got to go." She smiles and turns towards the next aisle. Just before she gets there, she turns back to me and looks at me. She doesn't say anything at first, but I wait for her to speak. She looks again like she might cry but she bites her bottom lip and stop the tears, all of them this time.

"Thank you… for walking with me." With that she returns to her walk among the dead.

Chapter 7

Jimmy is sitting on my doorstep when I get home. I see him sitting there from a block and a half away. I consider calling out to him until I see a cop car pull over in front of the house. I quickly hide behind a hedge that separates a little house and the street. I peek around the edge and watch as a man in police uniform gets out of the car. He walks up to Jimmy and they exchange words. I'm too far to hear what is said but the policeman hands Jimmy a card after a few minutes and then gets back in his car.

Why are the police talking to Jimmy? Do they know where I'm living? Are they already looking for me or is it just a coincidence? I see a woman walk into the kitchen of the house next to me and I realize I have to leave my hiding spot if I don't want a nosy neighbor wondering what I'm doing on her property.

I try to act casual as I walk up the street. I have to stop myself from looking over my shoulder, both for the nosy neighbor and for the police car that I'm sure is tailing me. When Jimmy spots me, he quickly stands up.

"Hey. I was waiting for you." It strikes me that this is the first time I've seen Jimmy out of his uniform. Unlike Chrissy earlier he isn't unrecognizable. His blue button-down shirt and jeans don't make him seem out of place.

"Oh, yeah, what for?" I decide not to mention the police. Part of me wonders if I could get information about what they are investigating but I also fear looking too interested. Besides, they didn't talk for long, it's entirely possible that the policeman didn't give him enough information for me to benefit anyway.

"I was wondering if you wanted to get lunch or something?" He looks me in the eye, and I hear the word he's afraid to say. It's just now that it's beginning to dawn on me exactly what's been going on with me and Jimmy the last couple of days. And it appears to be mutual. I'm not sure I want it to continue yet. But I'm also not sure I don't.

"Sure. Where did you have in mind?" I see the muscles in his neck release tension as we begin to walk back the way I came. We fall into stride with each other easily.

"There's this little place on Main Street. It's Mexican if that's okay? They make the best chimichangas."

"Sound's good to me." We walk for a bit in silence. I can't speak for him, but I know I am beginning to freak out about this situation. I don't want to distract myself but at the same time I'm beginning to relax in ways that I haven't since I woke up on the dock.

"So, tell me about yourself." He chuckles at the cliche but I'm too busy racking my brain to notice how silly it sounded. I'm trying to come up with an answer to a question that I've been asking myself for three days.

"What do you want to know?"

"What brings you to Fareport? It isn't exactly a popular spot to move to this time of year." I try to decide whether to be honest at all and tell him where I might have come from or to make up a story from scratch just in case I have to disappear.

"What do you mean this time of year?" Evasion is always a good tactic.

"Well, it's lakeside, so spring and early summer we get a lot of people coming up to spend time on the lake and go boating, but now that it's almost fall it's gonna get colder. This place kinda dies down in the fall and winter." I realize he's looking at me to answer his question.

"I just needed to start over." I figure it's true enough to not be a lie, but it's vague enough to not cause questions.

"Well, it's a good place for that." God, I hope so. I decide to take control of the conversation.

"What about you? You grow up here?" I figure his past is safe territory, definitely more safe than my own non-existent past.

"Yeah. I was born and raised here. My dad raised us just outside of town on my family's farm."

"Oh, a farmboy?" I laugh for what feels like the first time. The sense of relaxation is growing stronger.

"Well, I say farm, but it hasn't been a working farm in a decade or so. Ever since my dad retired." I see him swallow with the word retire. I realize I may not be the only one who has subjects they would prefer to avoid.

"Well, it must be nice to stay in one place your whole life."

"Did you move a lot growing up?" We turn a corner and almost barrel into a woman jogging. She separates us for a second, a second which I use to come up with an answer.

"Yeah, I never really felt like I had a home." I try to come up with a believable reason for my constant movement. "I was in foster care, so I got moved from home to home a lot."

"Oh, wow. That's gotta suck. I'm sorry." I feel my grip on the conversation slipping. I'm saved by the fact that we finally arrive at the restaurant.

La Fiesta is a typical Mexican food joint with lots of vibrant colors and advertisements for tequila and Dos Equis beer plastered among murals of mariachi bands and Latinx women. Jimmy holds the door open for me and ends up getting stuck holding it for a family of seven who are on their way out. When we get past the front door, a woman asks us how many, although I can barely hear her over the music from a live mariachi band in the back and the chatter of the lunch crowd. I hold up two fingers and she leads us to a corner on the opposite side of the restaurant from the band.

"I had no idea it would be this busy." Jimmy confesses. I'm actually glad it's crowded if for no other reason than because it makes it feel less intimate. I'm feeling torn between wanting this to be what it is and feeling like I'm standing on a precipice and one wrong answered question could push me over the edge.

A waitress comes and takes our drink order. It's a few minutes before we start talking again instead of awkwardly looking at the menus, Jimmy, trying to decide which of his favorites to get, I'm sure. Meanwhile, I'm trying to decide if I even like Mexican food to begin with.

That's when I see her.

She's sitting at the bar on one of the multicolored stools. She's in a white strapless dress, no purse to be seen and a margarita in her hand, halfway to her pink lips. She smiles at the bartender who smiles back as she throws the last of the drink back and scoots away from the bar. She calls to someone else behind the bar in the kitchen and waves. And as if there's no reason for her not to, she turns and looks straight at me, removing any doubt in my mind. I almost swear she winks at me.

Angela.

She turns and walks out of the restaurant. I mumble something to Jimmy but I'm not sure what I say. I'm not even sure I'm awake right now. I pinch myself as I try to follow her out, but it doesn't awake me from this daylight slumber that I must be in. She can't be here. She can't be at a bar. She can't be alive. I killed her.

I push through the front door into the bright sunlight, and it blinds me momentarily. When my eyes adjust, I look in every direction possible, but I see nothing. Not a slip of her white dress, nor a single strand of her blonde hair. She vanished as easily as she appeared. I walk to the edge of the building and look into the back alley. Unless she jumped into the dumpster, she's gone. I go back into the restaurant hoping that maybe she hadn't left, and I had just assumed from the direction of her walk. I notice the restroom is right next to the front door. I quickly check and make sure no one is looking, and I enter the door marked *Niñas.*

I check every empty stall before I'm able to force myself to believe that she's gone. I run some water on the tap and splash my face with water. Looking at myself in the mirror I wonder if I'm going mad. I'm seeing dead people in Mexican grills. I try to tell myself that it was just a woman who looked similar, but I know in my heart that it was her.

"What are you doing in here?" I remember too late that this is the women's room and I excuse myself as I walk past the confused woman heading to the bathroom. I stand in front of the bathroom door trying to decide whether to return to my date.

It's funny that's the first time I've even thought the word. I've known that in my subconscious that's what it was, but I never said it, even to myself. Not that there's any denying it. It is a date.

"Where'd you go?" Jimmy looks utterly confused when I come back to the table. Apparently, my mumbled exit was not sufficient in any form. I try to smile it away and tell him I had to go to the bathroom. The waitress picks the perfect moment to come to our table and we order our food. I order the chimichanga's at Jimmy's suggestion, but I don't pay attention to his order. My mind is still searching through the restaurant. I watch the bar; I watch everyone in the place for a glimpse of her golden hair.

"I asked if you had any siblings?" I notice too late that the waitress has left, and Jimmy is talking to me. I shake my head no and try to concentrate on him. "I've just got the sister. But trust me, she's enough." I try to laugh along with him because I know it's expected but I just can't bring a laugh to the surface right now while my insides are in the process of a panic attack. I take a long drink of the water in front of me. I don't remember it being put in front of me. I don't even remember ordering it.

My head starts to pound, and my palms start to sweat. a buzzing in my ear grows to a swell and drowns out Jimmy's words but I can read his lips. He's asking if I'm okay, and I try to tell him no but all I can do is shake my head which makes the pounding worse. It also starts the blurry vision. I try to take another drink of water and knock over the glass. I hear the glass shatter but it's like it happened at the bottom of a deep well, and the sound reverberated and overlapped itself to the point that it became a cacophony of sound that is no longer similar to the sound of breaking glass.

I close my eyes to try and get rid of the blurred vision and it helps, but then I feel my consciousness slip away as I pass out.

Chapter 8

My eyes open and it takes me a few moments to realize where I'm at. I panic at first, worried that it happened again, but the simple fact that I recollect that it happened once means it didn't. I still have my memory, or at least as much as I had before I passed out. Although as the room around me comes into focus and I realize I'm in my bed at Ronnie's, I begin to wonder how I got here. Did Jimmy bring me back here?

I look out the window and the crescent moon shines enough light into the room that I see I'm not in the clothes I was in at the Mexican restaurant. In fact, I'm not wearing anything. I lay on top of the covers, my manhood exposed to the darkness and the cold. I lean back my head and try to remember how I got here but I can recall nothing after the restaurant. But I do remember Angela. She was there. I saw her.

But maybe she wasn't. Maybe even I wasn't. What if it was all a dream? It would make sense. It explains the surrealistic find of Angela Cartwright at the cemetery, as well as the ghost of my past sitting at the bar in the Mexican grill. What if the entire day had been a dream and I'm just now waking up from it. I breathe a sigh of relief. It makes the most sense. I didn't black out, I didn't see a dead girl, and I didn't follow the only lead I had to a dead end in a graveyard.

It doesn't explain how I came to be naked in my bed, though. I sit up and that is the first time I realize the pressure on my chest. Somehow, when I looked down at my nude form, I failed to note the arm that fell across my chest.

Jimmy lays next to me, asleep.

It wasn't a dream. It really happened. But even worse than that, something happened in between the Mexican grill and here. Something I can't remember. Jimmy isn't the type to take advantage of me when I pass out which means I didn't pass out at the restaurant. Instead, something else must have happened. Something else took over while I tapped out of reality and dissolved into nothing.

I close my eyes and try to rack my brain for anything that I can remember from the past few hours. I look again around the room and it is only now that my eyes are adjusting that I notice our clothes thrown around the room. His and mine mixed up like tangled weeds. He stirs next to me, but it is only to pull himself closer to me and fall back into his slumber.

I can't fall back asleep like this. With him lying next to me and the memory of what happened gone. I glance at the clock next to the bed and see that it's half past midnight. I'm missing almost twelve hours of the day. In the grand scheme of things, I shouldn't be so panicked over those twelve hours in comparison to the twenty odd years I'm missing from before the dock, but these seem more important. If it happened once, it could happen again.

I succeed in pushing his arm off of me and rolling out of the bed. If I stay in here with him a moment longer, I might have another panic attack. I need to clear my head. I need to get out of here and figure out my next move. He stirs as I put on pants and a shirt, but he doesn't wake up. I freeze and realize that while I don't remember getting here it isn't as if I don't want to be here.

A part of me wanted this. Obviously, a large enough part of me to take over and get me here. But it's more than that. The part of me that was pushed aside wanted this too. I shake my head trying to stop the thoughts before they overpower me. I need to think clearly, and I can't do that with him here. I need to get out of the house. I need to go somewhere and think through this.

On my way out I faintly see Ronnie sleeping in the living room on a recliner. His leg is unattached and, on the floor, his one hand clutching the remote, the other on a bottle of Jack Daniels that sits on the side table. The T.V. is blaring some late night advertisement for a bathroom stain remover. I pause and almost turn off the T.V. but I'm afraid the sudden silence will wake him up. Instead, I leave him to his troubles and his solutions as I go out in search of my own remedy.

I'm beginning to get a good feel of how to get around Fareport by walking late at night like this. I realize, though, that tonight I'm going to a new location. I'm not going to Helen's house as before. I'm going to check and make sure that yesterday was not a dream. Jimmy's naked body in my bed isn't enough proof. I need to see it without a doubt, in front of my eyes, written in stone.

The cemetery is lit enough by the streetlights that I'm able to find the gate and stumble my way to her row. I only trip over one rock, a rock that I secretly pray is not a tombstone. I mutter an apology to the deceased just in case. I don't remember how far along the row it is, but I remember what the stone looked like. It was flat against the ground, almost sinking into the ground as if it were trying to hide itself from view. As if it didn't feel it was worthy of visitors unlike the angel to its left that begged for it on its knees.

I find it but in the side light I can't read the words on it. The moon is behind a cloud now and all I have to go off of is the street lamp that is a hundred yards away. I try to feel the stone like braille, but my hands aren't sensitive enough to recognize letters among the engraving. I curse myself for not thinking to bring a flashlight or something.

I haven't come this far to go home without my proof, so I sit down and wait for the moon to expose itself from behind the clouds. Meanwhile, I take stock of what has happened. I run through the last few days in my head, from Helen's refusal to talk to me, to the sighting of Angela at the restaurant. I try to make sense of the possibility of another girl dead at my hands, while also trying to grapple with my most recent loss of memory.

Perhaps it's a mental condition. Perhaps I can plead insanity. If my mind took over without my control as it did yesterday, then I can't be blamed for Angela's death or anyone else's. It wasn't me it was someone else in my body. I realize I sound like a schizophrenic and my mind jumps to the next conclusion of me in a straightjacket in a padded room and Angela sitting across from me, dead, but alive enough to ask me why I did it. Alive enough to never let me get a moments sleep as the years trudged by.

No.

That isn't what is going to happen. That isn't the only outcome. There has to be another explanation. This blackout isn't the same thing that happened before. For one I still remember everything before it, and secondly, I didn't kill anyone this time.

I don't think I did.

Even if I take into account what I assume happened with Jimmy, that still leaves plenty of time blank. What did I do? Was Jimmy there the whole time or did he leave me alone? Is that what made this time different? Was it because I wasn't on my own? If Jimmy hadn't been there, would I have gone and found another victim? No, I tell myself. If that were the case Jimmy would have become my victim. He wasn't my savior.

But how can I be sure?

The solution is staring me in the face but I'm afraid of the fallout. I have to ask Jimmy. When he wakes up, I have to tell him that I don't remember what happened and explain to him that I don't know what I did yesterday and hope he knows.

Fueled with the knowledge that I know what to do, I try to will the moon out from behind the clouds, so I can get what I came for and return to Ronnie's house. When it does, I'm not shocked. There it is as it was before, as I knew it would be, and as it will be until the weather wears the stone down to illegibility.

I leave the cemetery with no new information but with a new plan. I'm not going to be alone in this. I'm going to tell Jimmy about yesterday. I'm going to ask for his help in figuring out my missing hours. Who knows, maybe if I find out what happened yesterday, I can begin getting closer to figuring out the missing years.

I re-enter Ronnie's house and at first it seems nothing is different. Ronnie is still asleep, and the T.V. is still on. But I notice that the dishwasher soap ad doesn't account for all the sound I'm hearing. There is a rustling in my room. Jimmy apparently woke up while I was gone.

I come in to find the room torn apart. He is no longer nude, but he hasn't thought to put a shirt on, and I see faint scratches on his back. I don't have long to consider whether I put them there because instead, I am more concerned with his opening every drawer of my dresser and pulling what few things that are in it, out.

"What are you doing? Why are you riffling through my stuff?" He turns to look at me and I realized that I have not only missed twelve hours from yesterday, but I have now missed something here. Something happened or was made apparent to him in the half hour that I was at the cemetery.

"*Your* stuff? What do you mean *your* stuff?" At first, my mind doesn't quite understand what he means. I worry that I might not be the only one on the brink of the deep end, but then the puzzle pieces begin to fit together in my mind.

I see flashes in my mind as I put it all together. An image of him at the restaurant saying he had a younger sister, him at the diner giving my shirt a funny look the first day we met, him finding me on his way into work on the same road heading out of town, a name that I barely registered from that first night spent in a stranger's house. David J. Evans.

"Jimmy isn't your first name, is it?" He looks at me incredulously and slams the drawer in front of him closed.

"How dare you! You steal from me and then you have the gall to throw it in my face like this!" He approaches me like he's going to hit me, but then he thinks better of it and goes over to grab my backpack. His backpack, I correct myself. "Helpful note! Next time you steal from someone. Don't leave them alone in your room with *their* backpack. The one that's got *their* name written on the inside!"

"Look, Jimmy, I can explain. Just let me explain." I panic as I realize my plan has been derailed. The one person who could help me understand everything that has happened to me. The one person who knows what I did yesterday is about to storm out and not return. Drastic measures are necessary.

"I don't care how you got into my house and got my stuff. All I care about is that I never see you again and you better fucking never come around me again." He grabs his button up shirt off the floor and throws it on. I don't remember if it's the same one he wore yesterday, but it doesn't matter as they are all his in reality. He picks up the backpack and begins throwing everything into it.

"Please, Jimmy, listen to me. Let's talk for a second." He ignores me at first until I grab his arm and turn him to face me.

"I'm not going to talk to you! Did you think I wouldn't find out? Do you get off on this? Tricking people into sleeping with you while you steal from them? Is it some fucked up fetish or what? Was it all a con?" He storms past me and just as he gets to the door, I throw out the one weapon left in my arsenal. The truth.

"I don't remember yesterday!" This makes him pause with his hand on the doorknob. "I… I blacked out and I don't remember anything." He turns, and this time pissed isn't the only emotion on his face. It's still there but it's joined by confusion. "It isn't the first time it's happened either." I mentally try to decide how much to tell him but once I start, I can't seem to stop.

I confess to stealing from him and not knowing that he was the same person when I met him at the diner. I tell him about Helen and stalking her and going to her house and the cemetery. I confess to meeting his sister and waking up on the dock and having no recollection from before. The only thing I leave out is Angela. I may be desperate, but I'm not suicidal. With his current opinion of me, telling him I may have killed someone would be a one-way ticket to the police. By the end of it, he hasn't moved but I have sat on the bed.

"So, you don't remember anything from yesterday?" This is the first thing he's said since I started. I can see he is searching for the words to say what he truly thinks. I'm sure one of them is crazy, I just hope another is believable.

"I don't remember anything from yesterday and everything from before this week is a complete blank. You have to understand I never meant to hurt you. I just didn't know what else to do."

"Wait. Did you have anything to do with that girl?" I see fear begin to get thrown into the mix of emotions on his face.

"No! I mean I don't think so. I don't know." His eyes do a dance across the room almost as if he's looking to make sure I don't have a weapon hiding somewhere in the room. Waiting for him to let his defenses down.

"Why didn't you go to the police? I'm sure they could have helped you."

"And they would have jumped to the same conclusion you did. A man from out of town confesses to waking up at the scene of a crime with no recollection of who he is or how he got there? I'd be behind bars before noon. I didn't have a choice but to try and figure this out on my own. I was coming back here to tell you everything. I need someone. I need you. I need your help. I need to figure out what's happened." He begins to relax but he still doesn't leave the door.

"How could I help? I didn't know you until you walked into the diner on Saturday."

"Because you know what happened yesterday. Or at least more of it than I do. Please. Don't leave. Stay and help me understand what happened. Maybe if I can figure out what happened yesterday, I can start to understand what happened before I woke up on your dock." He considers me for a moment. I can see the struggle going on in his eyes. Can he trust me? Should he?

"What is the last thing you remember from yesterday?"

You came back from the bathroom and you were acting strangely. I honestly thought you had been sick in the bathroom. You were holding your head like it might explode beneath your fingertips. I suggested we go but you shook your head, and then suddenly, just as quickly as it started, it was over, and you were back to normal. Or at least you looked normal.

You began to talk a lot… smoother. Your voice sounded a little different. It was deeper somehow without actually being different. I figured I was imagining things, but then when they brought our food, you wolfed it down like it was your last meal. You didn't think before you spoke like you usually do. I asked you questions about your family and your life. You told me that you were an orphan.

You said that you didn't have a job but that you had a trust fund of some sort. You said the important thing was that you didn't worry for money. You finished your food before I was even halfway through with mine, but then, suddenly, you said that you had an idea. You grabbed my hand and practically dragged me out of the restaurant. When I said we ought to pay, you laughed instead of responding.

You smiled with this devilish smile that was intoxicating but scary at the same time. You pulled me around the building we were in an alley. There was a dumpster that you pulled me behind. You pushed yourself against me and something just came over me. I went with it. I went with you. We stopped when a Mexican man in a chef's apron came out and yelled at us in Spanish. We hastily buttoned up my shirt and ran out of the alley straight into the street. We almost got hit by a car!

You didn't seem fazed by any of this. You laughed and continued running across the road, all the while dragging me with you. I didn't know what had come over you, but it was almost contagious. I felt like laughing along with you. I tried it out as we ran but it didn't come as easily to me as it came to you.

I asked you where we were going, but then you suddenly stopped. You turned to me and said you had no idea. Then something caught your eye. It was a car, a red convertible, actually. You dropped my hand and jumped into it without opening the door. I panicked wondering what you were doing. You said it was a friend of yours. Don't worry you said. I didn't even notice you had ripped the plastic away from beneath the steering wheel. I hopped in, as well, just as you put two wires together and the car started up.

Looking back, I don't know what came over me. It was like I would be willing to do anything with you. I knew in the back of my mind what had just happened. We had stolen a car. But I didn't care. You had said not to worry, so I didn't worry. I just went with it.

We sped out of the parking spot and merged with traffic, a lot of car honks blared at us and I saw a woman in the rearview mirror running after us with shopping bags in her hands. I'm sure she was screaming at us to come back with her car, but you didn't even notice. You weren't looking at the road, you were looking at me. I looked at you, but your eyes looked different than they did before. They were deeper. The color wasn't different, but it felt like it was wrong.

When I finally looked away from them and towards the road, I saw that we had sped out of town. We were barreling down the road, the speedometer slowly but surely getting closer and closer to the triple digits. I hastily put my seat belt on, but you told me I didn't need to worry. Once again, you said it. Don't worry. Then you leaned over and kissed me again. I knew you shouldn't keep our lips locked this long while we were flying at a hundred miles per hour, but your lips were so intoxicating I couldn't tell you to stop. I didn't want to.

Then you took it away. You took away the drug that was your lips and turned down a dirt road. I had no idea where we were. We had left Fareport behind, but I could see Lake Erie in the distance to our right. I vaguely could figure out what direction we were heading but it didn't matter to me. You screeched the car to a stop in front of a house. It was an old farm house, it looked like it was built in the 1800s and it looked like it hadn't been lived in for many years. It had huge columns in the front. Four huge white columns that wouldn't have looked out of place on a governmental building. Except for the fact that these were worn and stained from the weather. One of them had a piece of it chipped away and there was a bird's nest in the crevasse.

You left me in the car and ran towards the house. You stopped halfway and called me to follow. I got out of the car and followed you inside. The furniture was all there but it was covered over with sheets like the chairs and tables were pretending to be ghosts for a Halloween party. Everything was covered in a layer of dust. Dust that hung in the air like a fog giving everything a sepia tone to it. I felt almost like we had actually walked into a nineteenth century picture.

We wandered through the abandoned house without a word. You smiled the entire time as if you were about to burst out into that laughter again at any moment. That infectious confection of laughter that got us here. Occasionally you uncovered a piece of furniture, ripping off the sheet with a flourish, sending dust flying through the air. You practically danced through the house. Dancing to music that only you could hear.

Most of the furniture looked as old as the house but some of it was more modern. The kitchen had a microwave. It wasn't a new one for sure, but it was definitely no older than twenty years. The fridge looked like it was from the seventies, I almost opened it, but you drug me into the dining room instead. The chairs were all covered but you must have already removed the sheet covering the table. You grabbed hold of my shirt and pulled me against you. You gave me a quick taste of my drug before pulling away with a smile on your face.

You then pulled me close and whispered in my ear. You told me to hide. I didn't know what you meant but you pushed me away and put your hands over your face and began to count. It wasn't until you got to fifteen that I realized you intended to play hide and seek. Looking back, I realize now why your laughter had been so strange and so infectious. It was the laughter of a child. It was innocent and carefree laughter.

I went along with your game and ran upstairs to hide. I found my way to the bathroom, but I didn't see any place to hide other than in the bath tub and it looked full of mold. Instead, I returned to the upstairs hallway and tried the next door. This one was locked. I pushed and shoved but the door wouldn't budge. So, I moved on to the door at the end of the hallway.

This was the door to the master bedroom. There was a four-poster bed complete with curtains. I quickly pulled the curtains aside and jumped onto the mattress. There were no sheets on the mattress, so I saw all the stains and holes from age. I would have gotten off at that point and found a less dirty hiding spot, but then I heard you call out.

"Ready or not, here I come!" You followed it with another bout of laughter, and I heard you barrel around downstairs looking for me. I felt your mania creep into me as we played hide and seek. You found me after five minutes of searching and immediately told me I was it. It took me longer to find you because as much as your attitude was seeping into my veins, I didn't have the energy you had. You were like a dog who's master had just come home to play, or a bullet flying out of a gun.

The final time we played you were the one hiding. I searched for you for what felt like an hour but I'm sure it wasn't longer than twenty minutes. I looked through every room in the house and never found you. It wasn't until I noticed the string hanging down from the ceiling at the top of the stairs that I realized the house had an attic. I pulled the string, and a ladder came down with a rainfall of dust.

When I got to the attic, I found you sitting on the floor. Saying you were sitting crisscross applesauce seems fitting given we had spent the last hour playing hide and seek in an abandoned house. You were sitting in front of an open trunk. Without seeing your face, I could tell that something was wrong. Your childlike wonder was gone. Replaced with whatever you were looking at in the trunk.

I said I found you, but you ignored me. I crawled over to you, the ceiling in the attic was so low I couldn't stand up straight. You had both your hands in the trunk, which was full of old toys it looked like. They were all children's toys; I could see building blocks and a marionette clown among the remains of a wooden train that was missing a few, colored wheels. You were holding onto a little toy pop handgun in one hand and a small multicolored abacus in the other.

I asked you if everything was okay, but you didn't respond. You simply stared at the toy chest as if I hadn't said anything. It was as if you were alone in the attic. I wasn't there at all. I was a ghost hovering over your shoulder trying to bring you back to reality. I finally reached in and grabbed the abacus out of your hand, and it was like I had flipped a switch. You whirled on me and shoved the popgun in my face. You pulled the trigger and the pop resounded in the silent attic.

The mania I had caught from you earlier completely wore off in the moment as you spoke for the first time since coming into the attic.

"You're dead." I looked into your eyes and the childlike wonder was gone. It was replaced by coldness. A coldness so deep it penetrated my bones. I felt like I was all alone at the bottom of a well, darkness surrounding me. But then you pulled me out of it as you smiled again. The light at the end of the tunnel grew brighter with your face as it burst into laughter. You screamed that you got me. I laughed a little, but I was beginning to grow concerned. The reality began to press back in again as I realized that we had stolen a car, driven to an abandoned house in the middle of nowhere and spent the afternoon playing hide and seek. The sun out the small round window in the attic was hovering just above the horizon.

"We should go back, Sam," I said, and you said okay. You suddenly were somewhere between the child from earlier and the seriousness of the box. We climbed down the ladder and pushed it back into the ceiling. Before we went downstairs you pushed me against the wall and kissed me.

"Just because," you said when I asked what that had been for.

We got outside just in time to see the sun break the horizon and begin it's descent beneath the edge of the earth. Slowly sending us into darkness.

We got back in the convertible and you started it up. I told you that we should probably return it to your friend. Even though I knew the lady was not your friend. You said, of course, and began to drive back to town.

I hadn't paid any attention to how we got here but you apparently had, or else you knew the way from some time before because you didn't hesitate on finding your way back to town. We drove the speed limit this time, so it took us longer to get back to town. Although we either were driving much faster than I thought on our way out of town or else I was more out of it than I thought because it took us almost an hour to get back to town. I know it was because I turned on the radio and we made it through an "entire forty-five minutes of music on K99.1 FM."

We left the convertible back where we found it. I wanted to do more but with no name for the woman who owned it we couldn't have found her or anything. I pulled out my wallet and left a twenty in the glovebox hoping that would keep her from trying to find out who stole her car. I guess we will find out.

Anyway, we walked back here, and I said, I had had fun, but you grabbed my face and kissed me again. You told me to stay over. It wasn't an inquest, it wasn't even a request, it was a demand.

I can't believe what I'm hearing. He keeps saying "you," like he's referring to me, but I can't imagine myself doing the things he's saying. I not only have no recollection of the events that transpired it's almost as if someone else who looked a lot like me took over me and just took him for a spin. I glance around the room at the mess of clothes on the floor. most of them are from him taking clothes out of my dresser but I know that there was some there when I woke up.

"Did we…?" I don't know how to put into words what I'm asking, but it isn't necessary.

"No. We started to, but you… you didn't quite make it that far." He averts his eyes as if this one thing is the only part of the story that I might be embarrassed about.

I suddenly realized the absurdity of the situation. We were simultaneously discussing my lack of memory, my strange behavior yesterday at the abandoned house, and also having the awkward conversation that comes the morning after. I look at the clock and it is, in fact, the morning after as the clock now reads two o'clock.

“Thank you… for staying and telling me everything.” He has come to sit next to me on the bed. We are incredibly close but also so far away again. I realize that of the two people it appears are living inside of me only one of them really knows what to do in this situation. The one that I am aware of is completely clueless.

“Look. I should probably go.” He gets up to leave. I decide to take a leaf out of my doppelgangers book, and I grab his hand stopping him from getting to the door.

“Please stay.” This time it is a request, but I hope he responds the same.

“I don’t know that it’s such a good idea. You obviously need to figure out stuff. I mean—” I can see in his eyes there’s a part of him that wants me to ask again, so I do.

“Please don’t leave me alone. I don’t want to be alone.” He struggles with what to do. I can imagine the debate going on between his head which tells him I’m crazy and his heart that wants him to trust me and stay.

After a few moments, I decide to make the decision for him. I stand up and put my hand on the side of his face. He doesn’t relax into my hand, but he doesn’t push it away either. I pull him in to my lips and with that it’s decided.

He’s going to stay.

Chapter 9

It's exactly as he described it. We walk through the French entryway doors into the abandoned home. I woke up this morning to him gone and I panicked that I had imagined everything or that there had been another blackout. But he had left me a note on the door saying he had to go to class and that he would be back.

I used the free morning to go to a thrift store down the street, I found its existence from asking Ronnie during the commercials. I figured now that Jimmy knew I'd stolen his clothes it was time for me to get some of my own. I mentally chastised myself for not coming clean about stealing the money, but the survival instinct part of my brain told me I didn't have a choice. I'd pay him back someday.

Jimmy was back by the time I returned with my bags full of t shirts and jeans. He told me I didn't have to go to the trouble, but I said I'd have had to get some of my own clothes eventually anyway.

When I told him that I wanted to come out here, he said he wasn't sure if he remembered the way. It took us about two hours of driving to find the place but eventually we got here.

And now we walk through the house that yesterday I recognized and knew. Not me, but rather Kevin. I've thought about it and it's the easiest way for me to separate blackout me and well, me. I'm not sure if it qualifies for multiple personalities but it makes the most sense to me.

I wander through the rooms trying to look for something that is familiar. Some reason for how I knew about this place. Some clue as to how I even knew it existed. Nothing sparks even the faintest glimmer of memory. I even go so far as to sit in the chairs and to force myself to smell the dusty air. They say that smell is the sense most attached to memory, but it does nothing to help me remember. Instead, all I do is dirty my new clothes and fill my lungs with dust to the point that I have to step outside to hack up a lung.

"Maybe we should try the attic," Jimmy suggests. I see no reason not to but when I start to climb the ladder up, I begin to get a feeling. It's not quite fear, but it's more than simple trepidation. I feel goosebumps raise on my arms and my throat constricts slightly but more than that it's something in my gut. A feeling not dissimilar to deja vu.

It intensifies as I get into the attic and crawl across the dusty floor to the toy chest that was left open from yesterday. I swear I could have told you the toys that were in it before I looked inside, even the ones that Jimmy didn't mention like the wooden race car or the black and white dominoes, but I don't realize this until after I already look, so there isn't any way to be sure.

"Do you remember anything?" I shake my head and close the box, even if I did feel something it isn't anything solid, or anything useful. I am ready to give up on the whole idea and leave when, suddenly, Jimmy stops me. "Look at that."

"What?"

"There's something engraved on the top of the box." I look and sure enough the thick layer of dust is obscuring something on the lid of the wooden chest. "When I came up here yesterday, you already had it open, so I never got a chance to see it." He brushes the dust away with his hand, but this time, I'm sure. I know what it says before my eyes see it. In fact, I might have even slipped and said the word before it was, in fact, visible.

"Kevin."

"Do you recognize the name? Do you remember something?"

"I think it's my name."

"But you said—"

"I have no memory, remember?" I almost laugh at the irony of my statement, but Jimmy's shocked look stops me.

"You said you forgot everything, but I didn't think you meant *everything!* I mean, your own name?" The workings of his thoughts run madly behind his piercing blue eyes as he tries to calculate exactly how little I know about myself.

"It was the first name that came to my mind when your sister asked me my name. I gave it up because…" I realize that the reason for my new name was because of the money. The money that I stole and haven't told Jimmy about.

"Because you wanted a fresh start. I know. It's just hard for me to wrap my head around. But I mean, if you think that's your name, then that's something to start with!" I hated to dash his cute smile.

"A first name isn't anything to go from, especially when I'm not even sure that it's my name at all. And on top of that Kevin isn't an uncommon name. What are we going to do search for all the Kevins from Boston? If that's even where I'm actually from," I say as I sit back on my heels.

"No. We don't look for Kevin in Boston. We look for Kevin here." He begins crawling over towards the ladder.

"But I just arrived in town last Friday. At least according to Helen and *that's* the only real lead I've got. She's the only person who recognizes me."

"And yet you knew exactly where this house was? Or at least your alter ego or whatever you call him did. No. You didn't just arrive last Friday. That might have been when you got here this time, but you've been here before. You were in this house before, and luckily I know how we can get a last name to search with that Kevin." And with that, he climbed down leaving me no choice but to follow him down the ladder. When I get to the bottom, he pushes up the ladder.

"And, for the record, I like Sam a hell of a lot better than Kevin."

Kevin must have been taking the scenic route in the car because on our way back Jimmy is able to find a much faster route and thirty minutes later, I find myself back at the library, but this time, I don't have to convince this volunteer to let me in. She barely even gives me a glance, too busy checking out Jimmy's ass as we walk towards the filing cabinets in the back corner, beyond the children's section.

"The dopey eyed volunteer is checking you out."

"I know. She went to school with me. Two years behind me and obsessed. Almost had to get a restraining order. She had this weird affinity for my hair." It is her hair that she seems attached to now, although the attachment is sadly on her tongue given that a lock of her hair hasn't left her mouth for the last fifteen minutes.

"What's in these filing cabinets anyway?" He opens one up and it is full of papers, some looking organized and new, but most of them are yellowed and look like they were organized by a toddler or a monkey, or both.

"When I was in high school, I did a report on the properties in Fareport that had been owned by the same families for the longest times. You'd be amazed at how long some of the people in this town have lived in the same place. There are homes in here that have been with the same family for over a century." He starts leafing through, doesn't find what he's looking for and closes the drawer to open another.

"That old house I'm sure is owned by someone. These hold all the property listings in the surrounding counties, and they are *supposed* to be organized by district. But somewhere in here is a public domain copy of the deed telling us who owns that plot of land and more importantly who lived there."

"But I'm not a century old Jimmy. I mean isn't this stuff on the internet?" I wish she would stop staring.

"It is but you can't look it up from the address. You can look up someone's address from their name, but you can't go the other way around. But you can if they aren't alive anymore. A big house like that, chances are it's a family house. Whoever owned it fifty years ago, their last name will be a good place to start at trying to remember yours. Now what was the house number again?"

"5781" I double check on the small piece of paper in my pocket. Jimmy had me write it down before we left. "5781 Plymouth Road."

"Great. I found it." He pulls out an official looking form. He hands it to me and lets me read it. I silently thank him. It's a bill of sale from 1935. "Well, what does it say? Do you recognize the name? I mean at least as much as you did Kevin?" He looks at me expectantly, but I'm caught up in reading the name under the title of buyer.

Evan Cartwright.

Well, that explains why Angela Cartwright came to my mind when I was trying to make up a fake name for my mother. Cartwright is my name. Which would make me and Angela Cartwright related. I do the math quickly in my head, or as much math as I can do, given I don't know my own age beyond an estimation.

"I think Angela Cartwright was my mother." Just as I say this, Jimmy's phone begins blaring some poppy tune.

"Hold on. This is Alex. I've gotta take this. But while I'm out, go look her up on the computer and find out what you can. I'll be right back." He kisses me on the cheek and then answers his phone as he heads towards the front of the library, briskly whisking by the stunned librarian. I smirk at her as I make my way over to the computers.

I open up Google and this time, instead of searching for a simple name, I have a last name and some dates to go off of, as well.

Angela Cartwright doesn't pull anything up, but when I couple it with Fareport and the date of her death it does pull up an obituary. I click the link and it shows the small body of text. There was no photo that ran with it, but it is a nice paragraph about her family. It, however, does not mention her having any children. It doesn't even mention a husband. Instead, it says that she is survived by only her parents Robert and Elizabeth Cartwright, and her brother Samuel.

"Well, did you find anything?" I've done a few more Google searches in the meantime waiting for Jimmy to return. I show him the first obituary in response to his question. "Wow. So, you had a sister? That's depressing. It's strange, it doesn't mention what she died from." I hadn't even noticed.

"More than that though, Elizabeth, my actual mother is dead, as well." She had a larger obituary telling all about her church activities and her volunteerism in the town. She just died a few years later in 1994. It, however, doesn't mention me. It only says she's survived by her husband Robert. It does have a nice bit about her joining her daughter in heaven, however.

"Wonder why it didn't mention you?"

"I don't know but my father is still alive." I pull up the results of my last Google search. This one is a white pages name and number.

"Is he still local?"

"I don't know. It has an address listed but it says he still lives out on Plymouth Road. We saw today that he obviously doesn't. I imagine the phone number is the landline there so that isn't going to do us any good either." I notice that he hasn't sat down. He also hasn't said what the phone call was about.

"Well, at least he's alive. So, there's something we can go off of. Look, my sister is having some issues with my uncle, so I have to go."

"I'll come with you."

"No. You should stay here and looking up stuff about your family." His words say no, but I can tell his voice is saying he wants me to come.

"Look. We spent all morning searching for my family and none of them are even here. Your sister is, and she needs you. I kind of met your uncle, so I know he can be a handful." I realize too late that I hadn't mentioned the run in with Uncle Benny when I gave him my recollection of events.

"You know my Uncle Ben?"

"Know is an awfully strong word. Here, let's just go and I'll explain on the way." I couldn't help myself from grabbing his hand as we walked out. He didn't reject it, but the best part was the look on the girl behind the counter's face.

When we pull into the driveway, it is like I am dreaming. Seeing the house again, the first house of my memory, it feels like I'm going back in time. The only thing that keeps me in reality is the bright sunlight that wasn't present last time, that, and the man standing out front in nothing but his underwear.

It isn't Uncle Benny, given his sagging skin and long flowing, but sparse white hair I'd give him a strong eighty or maybe a weak sixty. He is currently standing in the front yard with his boxers on, decorated with little red hearts on a pink background. Alex and Uncle Ben are on the front porch and they seem to be arguing about something as me and Jimmy pull up.

"Try not to judge me based on my family." Jimmy smiles over at me.

"Do you want me to just stay in the truck?" I can tell he doesn't want me here and is regretting letting me come.

"That might be best for now. Let me sort this out and then we'll go from there." He parks the truck and leaves the window cracked for my benefit. Along with the late summer breeze that it lets in, I also am now able to hear what is happening on the porch.

"I didn't touch it!" Alex is in green shorts and a tank top that both look a size too small, and like they haven't been washed since she wore them last. He hair is pulled back into a messy pony tail.

"If you didn't touch it, then who the fuck did? And don't say yer pops did cause we all know he doesn't have enough sense to know what to do with it anyway!" Uncle Ben is wearing tattered jeans and a work shirt that's covered in oil stains. I may be imagining it, but I swear I can smell the mix of cigarettes and alcohol wafting off of him from the truck.

"What are you doing here Uncle Ben?" Jimmy either hasn't noticed the man standing in the front yard or he feels the argument on the porch is a more pressing matter. I feel awkward watching this family drama but at the same time it's like a train wreck, the fascination doesn't allow you to look away.

"You're not supposed to be here!" Jimmy looks like he wants to pull his uncle off of the porch by brute force. I figure he could take him. Especially in Ben's current state of inebriation. Jimmy stops instead beside his sister and stands there, looking like a guard dog at the end of his chain.

“I only came to get my fucking money and the cunt’s gone and stolen it!” Ben points at Alex with the half empty bottle of Yuengling that I hadn’t noticed before. I keep an eye on that bottle. It probably would take a situation from bad to worse if he started swinging that thing around at people.

“Look, you probably spent it all on booze. What would Alex want with your money?” Jimmy moves to stand in between his sister and his uncle, which is no easy feat since Alex, regardless of her small stature, seems to want to face her uncle alone. The two of them have a silent pushing match to see who stands in front of the other, luckily for her sake, Jimmy wins.

“I didn’t touch your goddamn money!” Suddenly, three things happen almost simultaneously. Alex steps forward around Jimmy and makes to go after her uncle. Ben sees this and swings the bottle at her, it misses, however, as Jimmy shoves her out of the way and takes the bottle to his own arm. I hear the glass shatter but I’m not close enough to see if any of the shards broke his skin. In the next second it doesn’t matter because it broke the chain on Jimmy’s collar, and he throws himself at his uncle like a linebacker going in for a tackle.

Uncle Ben had been standing at just the wrong spot and when Jimmy tackles him they both go through the railing that borders the edge of the porch. It was an old railing, so it didn’t take a lot of force to break through what fifty years of weather had worn down. When they crash into the ground, it sounded like it hurt both of them pretty good.

The two of them become a mess of arms and legs and wood as they both tried to get power over the other. I throw open the door of the truck without thinking about the consequences of involving myself. All I care about is helping Jimmy. There is plenty of cursing and shouting in pain, especially when Uncle Ben sinks his teeth into Jimmy’s left arm. I grab Jimmy by his shoulders and drag him away. Jimmy is so out of it that it takes him a moment to realize that it is over, and he is being pulled out of it.

“Break it up before you guys kill each other.” I yell as Jimmy stands. I try to help him up, but he brushes away my hands, not even looking at me.

“Who the hell are you?” Uncle Benny says still trying to get up from the ground. This is quite a feat given his level of intoxication. I feel all the courage drain out of me in that instant. Hearing the question I’ve been asking myself put into words is like a knife in my heart. I go cold immediately and struggle to respond.

"It doesn't matter who I am." I don't even believe the words coming out of my own mouth. I try to cover up my insecurity by turning things back to Uncle Ben. "Why don't you just get out of here and sober up."

"I don't take orders from you." Benny finally gets to his feet and then proceeds to almost trip over the pieces of wooden railing at his feet. He looks like he was a trapeze artist with his arms out trying to keep his balance.

"Benny? What are you doing here?" Everyone looks around to see who had spoken up. It's Jimmy who remembers first that his father is there and notices that he has turned away from the road and is facing the four of us. He still doesn't seem to notice or care that he is standing in the front yard wearing nothing but his boxers.

"Dad, let's go inside." Jimmy walks away from me and reaches a hand out to his father. He doesn't take any notice; instead, he only looks at Uncle Ben.

"I haven't seen you in years! It's so good to see you." He takes a step towards Ben and it's like they are magnets with the same pole. Ben shifts backward, so the distance between them doesn't change. "How are the girls?" It's like his words are a light switch and Uncle Ben's anger immediately melts into despair. His eyes immediately turn red as if he is allergic to the words coming out of his older brother's mouth.

"Fuck you." Ben turns and storms away towards his truck.

"Ben, you know he doesn't understand!" Jimmy calls as Ben gets into the truck, turning on the diesel engine to drown out his words. I can see that Ben is full on crying as the truck pulls out of the driveway.

"Why did he leave? He just got here." Jimmy's father seems genuinely confused but at the same time does not seem that upset by the situation. Jimmy takes his arm and begins to lead him into the house.

"Alex, go inside and put a pot of tea on. I'm gonna take dad to bed." It is now that Jimmy noticed Alex staring at me. Of course, she would be. I hadn't even noticed myself. When I meet her eyes, the questions behind them seem to throw themselves like arrows at me. She knows me only as the naked guy she found in their back yard.

"What are you doing with my brother?" She directs the question at myself, which Jimmy notices and doesn't care for, if his face is anything to go by. I don't know how to respond. We didn't discuss what we were going to tell Alex. I don't know who's decision it is. Mine, since it's my story to tell or his because it's his sister. After a few moments, however, Jimmy answers.

"I'll explain; let's just go inside." When she doesn't move, he adds, "Please." Finally, she turns and heads inside, but she stops on the other side of the screen door and stares at me for a moment before heading into the kitchen.

"It's great to meet your family." Neither of us laugh.

Ten minutes later, I find myself right where I was a few days ago. Alone in a room that isn't mine full of things belonging to someone I don't know. Now at least I have met him but how well do I really know him? Jimmy is downstairs explaining to his sister who I am or at least what we know of who I am. Whether he will mention our sexless night spent together or even the details of my awakening I don't know.

I've left that decision up to him.

For myself, I am looking at the pictures that sit on his desk. Pictures of Jimmy as a young boy, playing on a play set. Eating ice cream with his father. A woman who looks like she could be his mother holding his hand. A myriad of different characters that have passed through his life whether family or friends, but definitely memorable enough to earn a place on his desk. To earn a place in his life.

Do I have this? People that are important to me? People whom I am important to? If so, where are they? Why aren't they searching for me? I tell myself that they must be searching. They just haven't found me yet. Perhaps I told them where I was going and they have no reason to be worried, or maybe I intentionally didn't, and they don't know where to look. But a small voice in the back of my mind wonders if I'm wrong.

You are all alone it says in the back of my mind.

Why wouldn't I feel alone? I try to recall images of faces. The attempt, that for any normal person, is simple; however, escapes my ability. I can't even bring to mind nameless faces. My mind is like a never-ending void that I know is supposed to contain something, but instead, is nothing but darkness. Darkness that is consuming and complete.

I pick up one of the pens littered across his desk and realize that I can't even for sure say that I can write my own name. Not through lack of ability to write but rather by the simple fact that I don't know what it is. Is it Kevin? The evidence seems to point to that but at the same time I don't know for sure. I struggle with the idea that I can't remember my own birthday. I would have to measure myself to figure out my height. All the things that a normal person can answer without thinking are a complete mystery to me. It's like I'm stuck in someone else's body or like I'm not even a someone.

Like I'm a nobody.

The last couple of days have been full of my attempts to figure out who I am but I feel like the little success I've had is dwarfed by comparison with the immense amount of knowledge that is missing. And what worries me the most is the little facts that I have discovered are just that-facts. They don't feel familiar to me at all. Is the rest of my life going to be like living in a stranger? Even if I find my family, my past, will I recognize it as my own? Will there ever be a moment of ascension? A moment in which it all clicks into place and my memory returns? Or will the facts of my life before the dock be forever like facts in a textbook? Stone cold facts with no emotion or feeling attached to them.

I lay down on Jimmy's bed and stare at the ceiling going through the facts that I know. Angela, whom I assume was my sister. Helen King who knows me, but how, I have no idea. The house that I believe had to belong to my parents. One of which is still alive. Is he looking for me? Was I looking for him? Was that why I came here from Boston? Was I searching for him? Did I find him?

And all of these questions about myself seemingly have nothing to do with the question that festers in the depths of my gut. The question that I'm afraid to answer. The question that doesn't seem to have any clues other than the constant reappearance of a girl who also happens to be the earliest memory I have. A girl who I misconstrued was Angela. A girl who is now dead.

Did I kill her?

I want to say with confidence that I didn't. I'd like to say that I couldn't. Doesn't everyone hope to be able to say that they couldn't take another human life? But can I say that when I don't know the situation leading up to us being on that dock? Can I say it not knowing who she was, or what she was to me? And even if I knew those answers, how can I say that I'm not a cold-blooded killer? I don't know if the person I am today is the person I was a week ago. For all I know I lived a different life and perhaps she isn't my only one. There is Emily Bradshaw to consider, as well. Was she another of my victims?

Kevin seems to be a man of many talents. He is able to highjack a car without even thinking about it. He knows of the farmhouse and knew that it would be empty and available for a game of hide and seek. Perhaps he killed her. But how much separation is there really between us? Me and Kevin. In reality we are the same, but he does things without my knowledge or my consent. But is it just that he doesn't ask me? If he did, would I really have stopped him? What did I do, besides stealing the car, that I wouldn't have done if I simply had the courage? I wanted to sleep with Jimmy. I wanted to find my past. Kevin just knew where to look.

Perhaps Kevin isn't so bad.

But if Kevin isn't so bad, then why would he have killed the girl on the dock? If he didn't, then who did? One of us had to have killed her but that's splitting hairs. When you come right down to it, this separation between him and I is nonexistent. He is me. I am him. We are one. And it would appear that we are a killer.

But where do I go from here? Do I turn myself in? Do I run away? How can I stay here and figure out my past when I'm going to be constantly afraid that someone will find out I killed someone? How can I leave? What would Jimmy say if he knew? What would he do? It's impossible to say we aren't close after the last few days, but is it close enough that knowing my possible guilt wouldn't push him away? He is the only secure thing that I have right now. He is my anchor in this sea of confusion. If I lose him, I'll drown for sure.

He can't know. I can't tell him. I have to figure out this part of my story alone. He can help with the things leading up to the night I awoke. But I have to come up with the events of that evening. I have to find out if I killed her. If I didn't, I need to know who did. And if I did, then I have to cover it up. I can't have just started to figure out my life to lose it behind bars. Whether a jury would agree or not, the person I am now is not who I was five days ago. I can't be held accountable for actions I didn't intend to commit.

Unless it happens again. In which case I don't know what I'll do.

"I'm ordering pizza." I didn't even notice that Jimmy had poked his head into the room. For a moment, I laugh internally at the fact that even if he had bothered to ask me whether I liked pizza, I wouldn't have been able to answer him either way.

"Okay." He opens the door a bit further but doesn't enter. He is trying to give me privacy I feel but at the same time it's his room. He struggles with what to do; I can tell. This is just as confusing for him, I'm sure. This person he has only met a few days ago, but that has suddenly become so much more than an acquaintance. But how can you consider yourself close to someone who can't even tell you their favorite pizza toppings?

"How did she take it?" He chews it over for a second before answering.

"Better than you might expect. We've had an… unusual life. She's had to grow up pretty fast." With that he finally decides and goes to close the door. "I'll let you know when it's here." He closes the door on me, shutting me off in his room, all alone.

I find that I actually like pizza. Alex isn't surprised; she says everyone likes pizza. I'm not a fan of the mushrooms but I suffer through. I already feel awkward enough joining them for dinner. The awkwardness isn't helped by Jimmy's father.

He is able to feed himself for the most part, but he keeps forgetting what he's doing, and Jimmy has to remind him to sit back down and finish his dinner. He's like an extremely old toddler, constantly distracted. He struggles with the glass of water, but Jimmy puts a hand on his arm to steady him.

"I'd pitch in for the pizza but…" I begin without knowing where I'm going. I feel awkward. We haven't said a word since he came to get me to tell me the pizza was here. I feel like having been shoved into his family life has shown to us both exactly how strange this situation is. When it was just the two of us, we could pretend it was okay. Pretend it was normal. Now there is nothing but weirdness.

"You don't have any money, do you?" The thought has just occurred to him. How funny that money is so important normally but it's a last thought when our life gets turned on its head.

"I have some." My stomach pangs with guilt from having stolen from him but I insist to myself that I had no choice and it's done now. I'll pay him back somehow.

"Well, I'm gonna see about getting you a job at the diner."

"You don't need to—"

"It'll be best for you. They won't have to actually put you on the books. Chrissy can just let you work for tips. That's what she does for one of the servers who's undocumented." What would I do without Jimmy? I literally owe him my life and more.

"I don't look Mexican."

"Neither is Tania. She's Cuban." He glares at me across the table. "I'll figure out something to tell her. Don't worry it won't be the truth." He hasn't looked me in the eye through this entire conversation. This back and forth has lasted all of a few minutes in time, but in my mind the silences between our lines have dragged on forever.

"Thank you."

He doesn't say anything back.

We finish the meal in silence, except for the one time that his father spills the water all over himself and Jimmy has to use a napkin to clean him up. He tells his father it's alright even as his father begins to cry. I can tell from Jimmy and Alex's reactions that this isn't the first time. This probably isn't even the hundred and first time.

As we are putting away the dishes, I glance at the clock and notice the time. It's almost eight o'clock.

"I think I should probably go." I put down the towel. I had been drying while Jimmy washed. Alex had been in charge of putting the plates away.

"You can stay." I give him a questioning look as he dries his hands. He doesn't meet my gaze. I look at his sister and she smiles politely at me. I can tell she doesn't care for me. I still don't know what all he told her, but she doesn't trust me. Perhaps she figured out about me taking the money. Perhaps she is just being protective of her older brother.

"It's time for bed, Alex."

"No, it's not." She isn't fighting him. She is sincerely confused.

"Just go to bed." I realize that as much as they are brother and sister, they are also in some ways parent and child.

"I wanted to watch T.V.!" She begins to pout. It's clear to me that it's not real-she simply knows what buttons to push to get her brother to see her way.

"Why don't we watch some T.V.?" I'm not sure if I'm overstepping but I feel like I might be able to alleviate the situation. "I could use some mindless television right about now." I smile at him trying to make light of the situation. I get the closest thing to a smile and he finally looks me in the eyes.

In that moment, I realize that he is tired. He is confused and he doesn't know what to do about me. It really clicks into place the fact that he is the one holding this family together. Everything falls to him and I have complicated things beyond their usual chaos. He doesn't know what to do from here anymore than I do.

We go to the living room and all three sit on the one couch as Alex takes control of the remote. I take note of the fact that Jimmy has sat in the middle. I don't know if it is his need to separate me and Alex or if he wanted to be seated next to me.

Alex settles on an old black and white film.

"I don't understand your love of these old movies," Jimmy insists and reaches for the remote. Alex shoves it into the side of the couch and away from his grasp. Just like that they have become brother and sister again.

"Just because they are black and white doesn't mean they are bad!"

"It also doesn't mean that they are good. Come on, let's watch something else." They continue to struggle over the remote while my eyes are pulled to the T.V. A man sits on a couch and is talking to a woman writing notes at a table and an old man who stands behind his couch. It's clear that they are therapists and he a patient.

"But I haven't seen this one before!"

"You don't know that; you don't even know which one it is."

"It's *Spellbound*." It comes out of my mouth before I can even realize it's me saying it. I didn't intentionally say it. It came out the same way expletives come out when you stub your toe. We all freeze.

"You know this movie?" They have forgotten about the remote.

"I do. I don't know anything other than the name, but I know this movie. It's *Spellbound*. That's Gregory Peck and that's Ingrid Bergman sitting behind the desk." The names of the actors comes out of me before I can even consider if it's true or not, but at the same time, the minute I hear it I know it's true. I feel confident that if you had asked me a minute ago who Gregory Peck was, I wouldn't have even been able to tell you if he existed, let alone recognize him in a line up. But I recognize this. I recognize this film. I've seen it before.

We watch in silence as the film changes into a dream sequence that is just as strange as the dreams I've been having. We are all aptly Spellbound by the film for the rest of the runtime. We don't even look away when it cuts to commercials. Not until the credits roll do any of us take our eyes off of the television.

I did notice, however, that a few minutes after the dream scene, Jimmy took my hand and never let go.

Later, I lay in his bed.

There was no discussion about sleeping arrangements. At least not in words. We had watched another film, this one also starred Gregory Peck. They were running some sort of special, but I did not recognize it. When Jimmy suggested we go to bed after the second film was over, we shared a look. I saw I didn't need to suggest a couch for myself. He didn't want me, too.

Alex didn't question it. I don't know if she was used to her brother having men over to stay the night, or if she didn't even realize what it might mean.

We lay separated but looking at each other. The bed wasn't the biggest so there wasn't much room, but we kept a few inches of no man's land between us. We were both in a t-shirt and boxers. Ironically enough, of course, both his.

"So?"

"So." Neither of us knew what I had asked yet we both seemed somewhat content with his answer.

"What all did you tell her?"

"I told her you were a friend of mine who was in trouble."

"Not exactly a lie." I silently think that friend didn't quite cover it, but it also was almost too strong a term.

"I told her you lost your memory. She didn't ask too many questions beyond that." I nod a little, not sure if that was it or if there was more.

"I honestly don't know much more." He says this with questions in his eyes.

"Sadly, I'm in the same boat." I try to force a chuckle, but it comes out all wrong and leads to an awkward silence.

"Can I be totally honest?"

"Please do." I prepare myself. I immediately start to sweat; my arm hairs stand on end. This is where he tells me that he wants me to go away and disappear. This is where he says he never wants to see me again. Where he tells me it's too much for him and I have to handle it on my own.

"I don't care." I don't even have time to register his words before his lips slam against mine with such force it takes my breath away. He opens his mouth and gives me his.

The three inches between us disappears, and we are suddenly forcefully and madly together. Entangled, mixed up and fused together without even a hair's breadth between us. I can't get enough, and he craves my touch. My eyes close and I see him with my fingers, with my tongue, with my skin. The awkwardness is gone. It's been ignored, it's been pushed out the window in favor of carnal knowledge. I may not know my name, but I know what I want. Him. All of him. Nothing but him.

Without any memories there is a part of me that worries I will not know what to do but my hands do the work without my brain having to do a thing. My self sits back and simply enjoys the feeling of his hands on my waist, his tongue in my ear, his breath on my neck, our sweat blending together making our hands slippery. We simultaneously decide the minuscule distance created by his clothes we share is too much and soon it is just us. Connected, unseparated from head to toe.

Suddenly, we have so much more area to discover, so many new sensations to test. I don't know what all happened the other night with Kevin and him, but for me this is all new territory-he is new territory-and I am ready to explore it. At the same time, he finds soft spots on my body I didn't know I had, places that send shivers down my spine and make me bite my tongue to keep myself quiet. It's a rush that accelerates beyond lips and hands. It moves so quickly I lose track of it until suddenly it comes to a screeching halt just before we cross that final threshold. That singular act from which there is no going back.

We have both simultaneously stopped. I look him in the eyes. We don't say a word aloud for a moment, both of us catching our breath. He has a look in his eye. A look that tells me this has gone beyond where he had anticipated. It's not exactly fear-it's less than that-but it's in the same vein. Trepidation.

"I'm sorry." He pulls away from me, the three inches suddenly back in play. He turns away from me for the first time since we got in the bed. I reach out a hand to his back and he breathes into it.

"Don't be sorry. We don't have to." He rolls over to face me. I can see from his eyes that he doesn't quite believe me. But it's the truth. I am unsure if I have done this before, become one with another person like that, but if he doesn't want to, I do know that there are plenty of other *things* we can do. I may not know my past, but I do know that.

"It's not that I don't-. It's just…that…I've never done… *that.*" I silence him with a finger on his lips.

"Do you want to stop?" He considers for a long moment.

"No. But…"

"It's okay. We don't have to do that. Now, where were we?" And with those four words the three inches disappear for good.

Chapter 10

"You really need to be quieter when you sneak out." I turn at the sudden voice.

I've been sitting on the edge of the dock with my feet hanging towards the calm water for what has felt like eons. Staring into the surface of the water, daring her to float to the top, hoping she would, if only so that I could try to ask her dead corpse the questions I have been asking myself for the past few days. She wouldn't answer, of course. I had to find the answers on my own.

I had woken up and slipped out from between the sheets. Jimmy had clutched at my arm as I did, unconsciously trying to keep me close, keep me there. It was a lot harder emotionally than physically to break from his grip. But I needed to be alone. I had had another dream that was just as confusing and pointless as the ones before.

I was in a bar, like Gregory Peck had been in his dream, but instead of playing cards, I was playing chess, and my opponent was the dead girl from the dock. Then Jimmy had appeared behind her and shoved a knife in the back of her neck, right where I had. She had collapsed onto the board but did not bleed; instead, lake water had started to pour from her wound until the bar began to flood and we all drowned.

"Can't sleep?" Alex sits down next to me.

"You shouldn't be out here."

"Says who?" She gave me a challenging look and I realized that Jimmy was absolutely right when he said she had to grow up fast. She may only be twelve, but she acted like someone much older.

"So, you couldn't sleep either?"

"Are you lying to my brother?" The accusation came out of left field and startled me, not only because of it's strange source but also because of the strange acuteness in which she had pinpointed the heart of the guilt that had brought me out here.

After I had woken from my dream and lay with Jimmy in the crook of my arm, I felt this sinking in my stomach. Jimmy, this man whom I had come to care for had just inadvertently slept with a murderer and he didn't know. What was worse was that it was me and I hadn't told him. I felt like I had taken advantage of him.

"Why do you ask?"

"He didn't bother to ask about you being naked that night." Not only was she adult she was smart. That was the one thing she knew that Jimmy didn't. I had told him I had awoken on the dock, but I couldn't tell him I had gotten rid of my clothes without telling him they were covered in blood.

"Don't worry, I didn't tell him either. I figured I could use the information."

"Use it for what?"

"If I find out that your trying to hurt my brother in any way. I'll tell him and your whole facade will fall. He won't trust you again. Something happened out here, and I don't know what, but what's more important is Jimmy doesn't know, and you haven't told him." I had unexpectedly found myself next to a regular Nancy Drew.

"What if I told you I don't know either?"

"If that were the case you wouldn't have lied to your boyfriend." A small part of me flinched when she said the word, not out of disagreement but out of embarrassment. "Don't worry, I don't care." And apparently don't miss much.

"I really don't know."

"But you know more than you've told. There's got to be a reason and my gut tells me it isn't good. So, I'd figure it out if I were you. Because if you don't, I'm going to tell Jimmy that you're keeping secrets." This whole time she hasn't moved from sitting next to me. She hasn't shifted her body position. She hasn't even looked at me. This girl is strong.

"I'm trying to." And with that, she stands to leave. Her threat has been spoken and her job as a protective sister is done. Just as she walks away from me, I turn.

"Does Jimmy know about Uncle Ben?" There is a long silence before she answers.

"No."

"I'm not the only one with secrets. "Her face dares me to continue the threat. "You should tell him. There's no reason—"

"You don't understand. Don't tell him. He can't know. He'd do something…. something stupid." I hear her walk back but then stop. "You should see a therapist."

I chuckle thinking it's a joke.

"Like in the movie. Maybe they can help you remember."

I have to admit, it's not a bad idea.

"You can't go to a therapist." We are sitting at the kitchen counter. Alex and I are eating cereal, while Jimmy gets his things together to head to class.

"Why not? It might help me remember something."

"How are you going to pay for it? Therapy isn't cheap. And as far as I know there isn't one in town. You'd have to go to Cleveland."

"It can't be that expensive and I'm sure I can figure out a way to get there."

"Look it doesn't matter because some quack job isn't going to be able to make you remember. All they are going to do is dope you up and screw with your head. Look, I've got to go to class. Just stay here and forget about the therapist." He starts to walk out the door.

"Fine."

"Look I don't mean to be angry with you, I just don't think it's a good idea. I'll be home after class." He winked and was gone. Leaving us alone with our corn flakes.

"Don't worry about him, he'll come around to the idea. He just doesn't trust doctors of any kind." Alex takes her bowl to the sink.

"Why not?"

"He blames doctors for Dad's condition. It's a long story and I don't know much, I was too young. I'd ask him later when he's cooled down."

"What do you do all day? Shouldn't you be in school?"

"No, silly, it's August." I realize this is the first time that I've even worried about what the date is. "School hasn't started yet."

"So, what do you do, then?"

"I read a lot, and I watch T.V. I've taught myself solitaire. I keep an eye on Dad." She puts the bowl away now that it's clean.

"Don't you have friends?"

"That's a mean thing to say." Her face tells me she is kidding but nonetheless I apologize.

"I just meant why don't you go see any friends or have anyone over?"

"First of all, no one is allowed to come over, especially when Jimmy isn't home. We can't risk anyone finding out about Dad." I give her a quizzical look. "That's more for the talk you'll have to have with Jimmy, but basically no one knows that Dad is this bad. Jimmy insists that if they did, they would take me away. I think he's exaggerating, but he's the boss. Secondly, I'm twelve, how am I supposed to get anywhere? We live in the middle of nowhere." And with that, she turned and waltzed her way out of the kitchen.

I sit in the kitchen for a few minutes before I decide that I have to find something to occupy my time. I go upstairs and look on Jimmy's bookshelf for something to read. You can tell a lot about a person by what they read. Jimmy's shelves are full of mystery books mostly. He has a few schoolbooks and a couple of books that I recognize. This baffles me as much as the movie did the night before. How can I recognize the Harry Potter books but I can't remember my own name?

While I recognize a few, I can't say for sure if I've read any of them. I decide to pick one at random and begin reading for no reason other than to kill time. I settle into his bed and open up *The Girl with The Dragon Tattoo* by Stieg Larsson. At first, I find it hard to concentrate with memories of what had happened in the bed last night, and then this morning flooding my brain, but eventually Miss Salander pulls me in.

There's a knock at the door. Not at Jimmy's door but at the front door. I glance at the alarm clock on Jimmy's desk. I've been reading for about an hour or so. I sit for a moment, pondering what to do when, suddenly, I hear the doorbell ring. This person isn't going away.

I calmly walk downstairs and try to practice in my head what I'm going to say to whoever it is at the door. I'm not a hundred percent sure what it will be, but I feel like I should have something prepared. Nothing could have prepared me for this, however.

"Hello, I'm Detective Callahan. I was wondering if I could ask you a few questions." It's not the cop that I saw talking to Jimmy. This one is in plain clothes rather than a uniform. He's mid-fifties, unshaven, and has dark circles under his eyes. His tie isn't very tight, and I notice a small stain on the collar of his shirt. He probably has been wearing the same clothes for at least two days.

"What about?" I stand there in the doorway not opening the screen door. I want to slam it in his face and run upstairs and hide but my gut tells me that would be a mistake. I have to answer his questions, but I can't tell him anything. I have to insist I don't know anything.

The irony of the thought almost brings a smile to my face. Almost.

"Can I come in?" I have to think fast. I don't want him in here anymore than I want to talk to him, but it would be rude and suspicious if I didn't comply. I have to come up with something quickly.

"I don't think you should…. See I…. I don't… This isn't my house." I settle on the truth. May not be all of it, but it's the part that serves my purpose. I just hope it doesn't bring up a red flag in his brain.

"Well, can I talk to someone who does live here?" I realize too late that that was the wrong thing to say. He's suspicious, I see his eyes dart to the windows, and I can tell he doesn't trust me.

"Well, the only one here is a little girl." The answer comes to me in a heartbeat. "I'm her babysitter, sort of." He looks dubiously at me. "Her brother has to go to classes during the day and her father… He can't watch her, so I come over and watch her."

"How old is she?"

"Twelve."

"A twelve-year-old girl." I don't know anything about kids. I don't know how old they have to be to be left alone. I realize now that obviously they don't regularly have a "babysitter," so she must be old enough. Old enough to make my cover story look stupid.

"Yeah, she—" He holds up a hand. This isn't going well.

"Can I speak to her? This… twelve-year-old?" He gives me a warning look. I can tell he doesn't like me, which is the exact opposite of what I wanted out of this conversation. I'm about to mumble something when, suddenly, Alex appears between me and the door. She has squeezed herself between me and the door jamb to get a look out the door.

"Hello, officer." She is all smiles. I'm embarrassed that she seems to be much more adept at this than I am. Of course, she has no idea why I would be scared of the police anyway.

She doesn't know I have to lie.

My heart almost explodes out of my chest.

"Well, how are you, little lady?" He stoops down almost to one knee to be eye level with her. Suddenly, I feel like a third wheel on this wagon that's speeding towards a cliff and I'm the only one who knows to put on the brakes.

"Look, I don't—"

"It's alright, young man, I think the little lady can answer some questions. Hey, little girl, are your parents around?" I can't see her face because she is directly below me, but I can tell from the shake in her voice that I'm not the only one with secrets and questions I don't want answered. I reflect to the conversation we had about Jimmy being afraid someone was going to come take her away. Little does she know he'd be much more likely to take me away.

"No. My daddy is… out and my brother is at class." He shoots me a look. I try to wear a face that says I told you so but not in an offensive manner, more simply: "I said you could trust me."

"Do you know when they might be home?"

"Jimmy is gonna be home in like an hour. I don't know when Daddy will be here." She has reached her arm behind her and is holding onto my pant leg.

"Do you mind if I come in and ask you guys a few questions?" I am having an internal war with myself over whether to let him into the house. On the one hand, if I do, he might find their father and then start to not trust us quite as much. But if we don't let him in he won't trust us anyway. I need to just answer his questions and send him on his way.

"As long as it doesn't take too long," I say, taking control of the wagon before it careens off the road. I open the screen door and he takes an awkward step back to avoid getting hit in the face as he stands up.

"In a hurry?"

"We were actually going to go out soon." He looks around to the driveway that only has the old beat up truck in it. I never noticed before that it was missing a wheel.

"Weren't planning on going too far I hope?"

Shit.

"We were going to go for a walk." It's the only thing I can come up with and I can feel my blood pressure rising as he takes his first steps into the house. He is looking around with a peering eye. He doesn't trust me, and he doesn't like me and he's trying to catch me in something I can't get out of. I'm madly playing chess with him and I don't have nearly enough pieces.

“Do you go for walks often?” The question catches me off guard. It isn’t where I expected him to go.

“Sometimes.”

“Ever walk down by the lake? I noticed that the property goes all the way to the shoreline.” I can’t say no. It wouldn’t make any sense.

“Sometimes.” I can hear the lies in my voice. I’m sure he notices them, too, but he can’t catch them. They are like flies in the room, he can see them, and they catch his attention, but he can’t quite kill one. But at the rate they are multiplying it’s only a matter of time.

“Did you take a walk last Friday night?” The night Emily Bradshaw disappeared. I do some quick date checking in my mind. I woke up on the dock five nights ago. It was Sunday night. Two days after she disappeared.

“I don’t think so.”

“No pesky policeman to avoid that day?” He smiled at his joke that wasn’t really a joke.

“Friday night is movie night.”

“What about Sunday night?” Is that when the other girl disappeared? Have they already realized there was two of them? Have they found her already? It wouldn’t have taken them long once they realized I left the first one in the lake. I correct myself. I *allegedly* left her there. Other than the similarities between the two I have no proof that I killed Emily. I don’t have any evidence against it either.

“Nope.” I don’t have an excuse for our staying in that night, but I don’t feel the need to give one.

“Sure don’t seem to go for many walks, do you?”

“Was that all you wanted to ask?” He walks into the living room without asking and begins to have a look around.

“Where do you live? I’m sorry, I didn’t catch your name.”

“It’s Sam.” Alex gives me a strange look when Officer Callahan turns his back. I realize she knows me as Kevin. Somehow, I had lucked out in her and Jimmy not mentioning to each other my name. Between that and the lie she caught me in about my clothes I realize I now have two people who don’t trust me.

“Well, Sam, where do you live?” I realize that this is a question that I can’t make up an answer to. The only two places I know of that I could tell him is Ronnie’s or here. If I tell him Ronnie’s, then he’ll go and check with Ronnie. Then he’ll know I just arrived here conveniently into town on

Sunday morning, just after those girls went missing. Not to mention it would make him question how I got here without a car.

"I'm living here."

"I thought you said you didn't live here."

"It's just temporary until I get back on my feet." He gives me a questioning look. His trust in me if possible has dwindled even further.

"When did you get here?"

"About a month ago." Long enough that the murders won't seem connected but not so long that it would be strange that I haven't moved out yet.

"And where did you come from?" He has now pulled out a notepad and is scribbling on it with a Number 2 pencil. I fight the urge to snatch the pencil from him and break it in two.

"Boston." The city is the first one I can come up with, and I'm not sure where I'm going to continue with this line of questioning, but I simply take it one question at a time. If he asks me a question I can't answer… Well, I'll jump off that bridge when I come to it.

"That's quite a ways."

"I needed to start over." Alex is trying to keep her face controlled. I can tell she is just as confused and mistrusting as Callahan is.

"What brings you here?"

"I wanted to be by the lake."

"I mean, what brings you here to this house? You just stopped by and asked for a room?"

"Her older brother and I have a mutual friend. She put us in contact, and I asked Jimmy if I could crash here for a while." He takes a note on his pad.

"I might want to talk to this friend of yours." This has gone on long enough. I consider the consequences but, ultimately, I have to act. I have to take this bull by the horns.

"Look. I'm not sure how any of this is your business. I haven't done anything wrong, and I don't appreciate being questioned about my entire life story. Ask the questions you came to the door to ask and then please leave." I'm not the only one shocked by my guts. Alex and Callahan both look at me like I've just cursed at the Pope.

"And what questions do you think those are?" A thought crosses my mind. I need to be the opposite of myself in this moment because Kevin is very suspicious and leads to problems.

"You are asking about the missing girls." He blinks. I've taken him aback. He didn't anticipate me bringing it up. That will show him. Why would I bring it up if I was involved? Take him off the scent.

"Girls?" In that moment, I notice that his face has changed. He's no longer curious. He's calculating. I've misspoke. He may have known about the second girl, or he may not have but definitely jo schmo off the street wouldn't know. They haven't announced that there was a second missing girl.

I've screwed myself.

"I think it's time you left." I walk out to the entry way. He follows me but doesn't show any intention to leave the house.

"Do you know something you're not telling me?" He's beginning to get angry now.

"I know you need to leave." I can be angry, too. He hesitantly steps outside and turns on the porch before I close the door.

"I'll be back again when this Jimmy is home. I have some questions for him."

"You'd better be back with a warrant." I go to close the door, but he puts out a hand and stops it a few inches from the jam.

"Look kid. You should listen to me when I say that you need to be friends with me."

"And why is that?" I'm struggling with keeping up the courage to continue this conversation. I'm beginning to lose those guts I magically grew.

"I'm not going to rest until I figure out what happened and whether you know something or not. A drifter from out of town who doesn't like answering questions isn't exactly in a good spot in the middle of a murder investigation." He let's go of the door. I try to come up with something to say but I can't, so I simply close it and lock the deadbolt.

"What was that?" I turn around. I have gotten rid of one detective, but I forgot I still have Nancy Drew to deal with.

"It was nothing."

"I watch the news. I'm not an idiot. There was only one missing girl."

"Leave me alone." I push past her and start up the stairs towards Jimmy's room.

"Did you have something to do with her? Who's these other girls? How many of them are there?" She hasn't started up the stairs she's just standing at the bottom screaming at me. I barrel my way back down the stairs. I don't know what comes over me, but the fear of the windows being open or the wall not being thick enough to muffle her words gets my blood flowing.

"Look, Alex. There are things you don't know about. If I could tell you I would, but I can't, okay? Just stop yelling about it when there is a policeman on your front door step!" We have a stare down for a moment.

"Did you kill them?" She doesn't beat around the bush, does she?

"No." A fly buzzes in between us.

Chapter 11

"You told him what?" We sit at opposite ends of the kitchen counter with Alex between us. The bag of burgers Jimmy has brought from Beer 'n' Burgers lays forgotten on the table.

"I didn't know what else to say; I had to get him out of here." I am treading on eggshells as I explain to him what happened with Callahan. On the one hand I need to tell him what I had said so that if Callahan comes back, which he undoubtedly will, we will have matching stories. But on the other hand, I can't tell Jimmy why I was so wary of the police. Every time I get dangerously close Alex gives me this smug look. She may not know what I am hiding but she knows it's something. It is her silent threat. She could say something at any minute and this house of cards I am building will come crashing down.

"Why was he here to begin with?"

"He was here about the missing girl." I catch myself before I pluralized girl. Alex noticed and glares at me.

"Why would they be stopping by here of all places?" I haven't thought of that before he says it. They had no reason to stop here, they had no idea there had been a body on the dock in the back yard. They had no idea that the possible killer had spent the night here.

"I guess they were stopping by any house with access to the lake. That's where they found the body, wasn't it?" I hope that that was the reason. If not, the police know a lot more than I was counting on.

"Well, next time, don't lie to the police. I still don't get why you did it to begin with."

"Because I couldn't tell him I had just woken up here on Sunday night. It doesn't sound very plausible or very innocent."

"Why would they have something to suspect of you?" This is a genuine question.

"Yes, why would they suspect you, *Kevin*?" This is the first time Alex had spoken.

"Someone who just happened to wake up next to the lake with no memory of who he is or where he's from just days before a dead body was discovered there? It doesn't look good. I'd be in lock up before you got home from class."

"Did you have something to do with her disappearance?"

"I don't know. I don't remember anything before Sunday night. I told you that."

"So, for all we know, you *could* have." The pit in my stomach sinks deeper as the look of suspicion grows on his face.

"I wish I could tell you more, but I honestly don't know anything else." Alex's eyes see right through me. Her glare clearly says she doesn't believe the shit I was spewing.

"Look I think it would be best if you went back to Ronnie's tonight. I'll drive you home after we eat." With that he pulls one of the bags over to him and pulls out a burger. The conversation was over. But I won't leave it like this. I can't.

"I don't think I did it." Jimmy looks at me for a moment before returning to his burger. I am going to have to let him think things over.

We eat in near silence. It is like the previous night didn't happened, and we are back to square one. I can't blame him for not trusting me. I'm not even sure I trust myself at this point.

I sit in his truck as we drive down the road towards town.

"I talked to Catherine, the store manager, today. She said you can come in and work tomorrow. She isn't sure she's going to keep you but she's willing to give you a shot." He doesn't look at me while he says this.

"I'm sorry for all of this." He doesn't respond. "Please talk to me. I'm not doing all this on purpose; you know that, don't you?"

"Look, it's just a lot to process. I hadn't even been thinking about the missing girl until today. I don't think you did it either but… I don't know." I know he's thinking of the other day when I blacked out. When I became a different person. A person that was capable of anything. Perhaps even murder.

We don't say a word until we get to the house.

"If you don't want to see me, I understand."

"Oh, no, I have to see you. You live with me now, remember?"

"That's not fair. What was I supposed to say?" He turns and faces me in his seat.

"You could have told the truth. Or do you know how to do that? Ever since I met you, you keep changing your story. You lie about your name. You lie to me about your past. Then when I think you've told me everything you turn around and lie to the cops for some strange reason. How do I know there isn't something you haven't told me? How do I know you've really even lost your memory? All I have to go on is your word, and as of right now that isn't the most dependable source."

He's right. How could he trust me? How could I expect him to trust me? But then again, if he didn't trust me, who would?

"I—"

"Don't bother. I won't believe any more of your lies anyway. Just go."

I open my mouth to say something, but I change my mind. Instead, I open the door and get out. I stand there on the side of the street watching him drive off. I don't know what to do. I turn and let myself into Ronnie's house.

"Hey, sonny! You didn't come home last night. Where'd you go?" Ronnie's sitting in front of the T.V. Some sitcom from the nineties is playing.

"I stayed at a friend's." Even that felt like a lie. Could I really call Jimmy a friend? A friend is supposed to trust you.

"Oh, well, I was thinking of going over and getting a burger. You care to join me?"

"I'm not hungry." I go into my room, and even though it's only the early afternoon, I collapse into the bed. I feel so lost I don't know what to do. I don't know where to go. I don't know who to talk to.

I wake up on the dock.

My blood starts to pound so hard I can feel my neck muscles tighten. It's pitch dark, middle of the night, starlight reflects off the water. But as I look at it, I realize it isn't water. It's darker than water. I crawl to the edge of the dock and reach over, dipping my hand into the liquid. It's thicker than water. I scoop out some of it in my hand and realize it's blood.

A hand explodes out of the lake of blood and grabs my arm. It's her hand. It's already begun to decay and rot. I can see her bone through the holes in her flesh where the fish have started to eat away at her. She is dragging me down into the pool of death with her. I can't get a grip on the dock at first and fall until I'm almost in the blood. I am able to get a hold of the last board on the edge of the dock and keep myself from being pulled deeper. A second hand comes out to help her. This one is Emily Bradshaw's. My fingers can't hold onto the dock much longer. I already feel the strain.

They keep pulling and pulling me. I scream as I feel my fingers break and lose hold of the board. When I hit the surface of the blood, I don't sink into it as I thought I would. It's solid.

I wake up on the floor of the bedroom.

It was just a nightmare.

I take a moment to catch my breath. I had fallen off the bed, not the dock. I sit up on the floor and lean my head against the side of the bed. What am I going to do?

I can't continue like this. I can't just keep thinking about one step at a time. I have to figure out what happened. I have to solve this mystery. Eventually it's going to catch up with me. I tried talking to Helen King, the only person who I know for sure knew me last week. I wasn't successful before but now I have no other options.

I have to try again.

With a clear objective in mind, I get back in bed and this time I sleep straight till morning without a single dream.

"I thought I told you to leave us alone." Helen and I stand exactly where we did the other day. Her with the door open just a crack and me on the porch. This time, however, I refuse to leave so easily.

"I'm not going away."

"My husband isn't even home."

"I don't need to talk to your husband. I want to talk to you." I can tell this isn't what she expected.

"Do I need to call the cops?" She threatens but she has opened the door an inch or two more. I've begun to crack her guard.

"No. Look, give me fifteen minutes. That's all. I just need some information, and you're the only person I know of who might be able to help." She thinks for a minute. I can see her weighing the pros and cons of what I was saying.

"You can have ten." She opens the door, but instead of letting me in, she steps out onto the porch. She gestures to a bench to the right of the door that I hadn't noticed before. We sit at opposite ends. I can see she is on the edge of the bench trying to keep as much distance between us as possible. Am I paranoid or is she physically scared of me?

"I have some questions but in order for them to make any sense I have to tell you something first. I've lost my memory."

I had thought this over on the walk over here. I realized that the only way I could make anyone trust me is if I start telling the truth. I may not be able to tell all of it, but if I told enough, perhaps I could gain her trust. Besides, it was the only way I could ask the questions that were really important.

"You…what?"

"I lost my memory. I was… in an accident." not even two minutes into the conversation and I was breaking my rule, but I allowed myself this one. It would take up too much time and wouldn't have the desired effect if I told her what had really happened. "You're the only person I remember from before the accident. I need you to tell me anything you know about me."

"I don't know." She seemed wary.

"You don't have to tell me anything that I didn't already know the first time I came here to talk to you. Just tell me what I told you? You've got to help me figure out who I am."

"No, that's what I'm saying. I don't know who you are. You never told me your name."

"Tell me anything you do know. Any little detail could help."

"Well, you didn't come here for one thing. You came to my husband's work first.

"Philip told me about it when he got home that day. It was last Monday. He was quite upset about it. You had gone to his office. He wasn't at the office-he was in court. His partner was, however, and when you said you wanted to talk to Philip, he had let you wait. When Philip got there, you started asking him about Angela." I already had so many questions but decided that this was an instance when I should hold my tongue and let her tell it to me her way.

"You have to understand. Philip doesn't talk about Angela." I make a mental note when she says the name. "He told me about her when we were first dating, years ago. They had apparently been high school sweethearts. They had even discussed getting married. But then something happened, and they broke up. He never told me all the details and I never really asked because… Well, because he became a different person when he talked about Angela.

"He was in a deep depression when I met him. I was able to pull him out of it. It took me three years before I was able to convince him that there really was any point in spending the rest of his life with me, and another two years to convince him that marrying me wasn't going to be a betrayal against her.

"Angela has always been the third member of our relationship. I'm constantly being compared even when he claims I'm not. But I love him. He may love her, but I know he loves me too, just a little less. But I've come to terms with that. I've learned that having a part of him is better than not having any of him, so I let her have a little bit." I feel a surge of sympathy for the woman sitting next to me. I almost reach out and touch her hand but I'm afraid of her shying away.

"The only thing that I know about her is she's dead. She died shortly before we met. That's why he was so depressed. So, I, at least, never had to worry about her coming back and taking him away from me. But then you came along. You came along insisting that you were looking for her. Claiming that you knew her. I don't know if you really did or not. You're much too young to have really known her. She must have died when you were a child.

"But just bringing her up sent Philip off the deep end. He came home and it took me hours to get him to even talk about it. He had stopped by the bar on the way home and was obviously drunk when he walked in the door. All he kept saying was "It was like I was seeing her again."

"He never told me what exactly you told him but the next day when you showed up at the house, I told you that you couldn't see him. You told me that you were going to give him a little time but that you would be back.

"I thought that's why you came back the other night. To talk to him again. But I'm sorry, you just can't. You can't talk to him about her again. I'm afraid I've already lost him again as it is."

"But it's been over twenty years." She was crying now.

"When I say he loved her, I'm not talking about a simple love. I mean that the two of them were soulmates. I'm aware of that. If she were alive today, he would leave me in a heartbeat and go to her. I always have been and always will be a second wife. He and Angela may have not gotten married, but something happened between them that he'll never get over. I can't have you dredging all that up again." I put a hand on her shoulder to comfort her. I expect her to pull away, but she stays, accepting my attempt.

"Did I ever mention my name, where I came from? How I claimed to know Angela? Anything?"

"Not to me. You might have to my husband but as I told you he was drunk when he came home, and he was rambling. The only coherent thing I got out of him was that it was like seeing her again. I had to talk to his partner to get any more of the story and even he didn't hear most of what you said. The two of you talked in Philip's office."

"Could I talk to your husband's partner?" She thinks on this for a moment before responding.

"As long as you don't speak to Philip."

"I won't." I tell her this, even though I feel eventually I will have to, whether it breaks up her marriage or not. I need to know why I would have been searching for my sister's ex-boyfriend.

"His name is Duncan, Evan Duncan. Don't go to his office. He lives in the neighborhood. I can get you his phone number." She gets up and heads into the house. There is still not an invitation for me to follow. I sit on the bench and wait for her to come back. When she does, she has a slip of paper with her.

"You should go. Your ten minutes are up." She hands me the slip of paper and I step down from the porch.

"Thank you for telling me what you knew."

"I hope you find out what you're looking for. I really do."

"One more question." She has headed back into the house but stops. "You say I went to the office on Monday. Then I came by the house on Tuesday?"

"Yes. That's right."

"But then you never saw me until this week." She thinks about it, then nods.

So, I *was* in town on Friday when Emily went missing.

In town and with no alibi, at least not one I can remember.

"So, you have no experience?" Catharine is an overweight woman who is probably in her forties, but she looks late fifties. She has long stringy brown hair that doesn't look like it has seen any conditioner, if it has even seen shampoo. She is wearing a dress shirt that has a large mustard stain on the chest and khakis that are frayed at the bottoms.

We sit across from each other in one of the booths in Burger 'n' Beers. Jimmy hadn't told me when to come by, so I just stopped on my way home from Helen's. I don't really care to be here, but I need the money.

"No, I don't." I had gathered from what she told me that Jimmy hadn't told her of my past, or lack thereof. Rather it appears he has only told her I need a job and can't give her my information. I can't tell if the nasty look on her face was a reflection of her opinion of me or if it was just her face.

"Well, I can let you serve for tips but if you don't make any money that's not my problem."

"That isn't a problem." I briefly consider asking Jimmy for some pointers but then rethink the idea. I'm not sure he is going to want to help me right at this moment. I make a mental note that I need to figure out how to get him to trust me again. I need an ally.

"Well, I'm gonna pass you off to Holly. She's gonna show you the POS system and how to put orders into the computer. I don't have any room on the schedule this week, but I can get you in sometime next week."

Holly turned out to be another overweight, middle-aged woman, but she was much cheerier than Catharine. She was almost too cheery in my opinion. But she explained everything to me and got me out on the floor, following her in just a few hours. She even gave me a cut of her tips.

Now I sit in my room counting out the few tips I made. Twenty dollars. It isn't much but it's a start. I put it in a desk drawer and pull out a pad of paper and write down exactly how much I stole from Jimmy and start a tally on how much I've made. It may take me a while but paying him back will get me one step closer to gaining back his trust.

Of course, it would if he knew I had stolen from him, which he doesn't. Shit. Yet another reason for him to hate me. I realize my number of secrets has grown to the point that I can't even keep track of who knows them and who doesn't.

"I'd like to buy a vowel." I am sitting on the couch in the living room. Ronnie is sitting in the recliner drinking a beer. We have been watching what I hope are reruns of Wheel of fortune. I hope because if not the ladies in it are a few decades behind on their choice of hairstyle.

It continues to baffle me how my knowledge of pop culture seems almost unaffected by my amnesia. Earlier today when I was first working on the floor with Holly, she asked me if I liked the song that was playing in the dining room because, I hadn't noticed, but I was singing along. I had known every single word without even being able to tell you the artist.

"There are four E's."

"Are you hungry?" I ask Ronnie. I'm not really hungry but I'm hoping to run into Jimmy when we go next door.

"Why waste your money?" He screamed at the television. His words kind of slurred together. I wasn't sure how long he had been drinking, he had already started when I got home earlier. There is a part of me that is somewhat worried about Ronnie, but he doesn't seem to be hurting himself. He just doesn't seem happy.

I haven't seen him talk about anyone else in his life. I have never asked him if he had any family. I've never felt like it was my place. I mean what were we? Landlord and tenant? Friends? He didn't seem like he particularly wanted to talk but at the same time all I ever saw him do was drink and watch *Wheel of Fortune*.

"I think I'm going to go over to the diner to get some food. Do you want anything?"

"I'd like to solve the puzzle." Dorothy on the T.V. was about to take the lead.

"Nah, I'm good. Thank you, David." I pause for a minute. I run through my few memories that I actually have trying to see if I gave Ronnie yet another name. I don't remember doing so nor can I come up with a reason for why I would.

"It's Sam." Ronnie looks at me and blinks a few times. He looks sincerely confused for a moment before he finally swallows back what almost looks like tears.

"Of course. Sorry. One too many of these things will mess with your brain." He gestures with the half empty bottle of beer. "I'd stay away from the stuff if I were you." He turns back to the T.V. in time to catch the solution. *Rebecca*, by Daphne Du Maurier.

"You sure you don't want to join me?"

"What the hell is that? It's not even English?" He yells at the screen before chucking his half empty bottle of beer at the T.V. He luckily misses and it crashes against the wall, but it makes me jump.

"Ronnie? Is everything okay?"

"What? Oh, yeah, I'm fine. These dimwits just don't know how to make good television." I stand there tensely in the doorway to the living room not sure what to do in this situation.

"Well, I'm going to go now I'll be right next door if you need anything." I feel like I ought to stay but I'm not sure what I can do.

"Grab me another beer on your way out, will ya.?" I pretend like I didn't hear and leave him to his television. On my way out I glance at the time: 9:45. I am going to try and be home in an hour or so to make sure he's okay.

When I get over to the diner, Jimmy isn't there.

"He'll be here in about ten minutes or so. He doesn't start till ten. Can I get you something while you wait?" Danielle said as she gave me a menu.

"Just a Coke." I'm her only table, so when she brings back my drink, she sits across from me.

"So, are you the new guy?" I give her a quizzical look before I realize she means new guy at the diner. I nod and am about to say something when she cuts me off.

"I knew it! I always said that Jimmy was a little… you know… but no one would believe me, and then he comes along and says he needs to get a job for his friend. And Holly, she's my mom, she told me that you definitely were. She has a perfect gay-dar. So, how long have you guys been together? When did you meet? Where? Tell me everything?" She said all of this in the span of about three seconds. Her mouth moved so fast I wasn't sure I would be able to make it stop. But I held up a hand and she finally stopped but she still looked like a horse ready to start a race.

"We aren't together."

"Come on you can tell me. I've got tons of gay friends. They tell me everything. Like my one friend, Gary…" She keeps going on about Gary and his myriad of what she refers to as 'sexcapades.' I stop really paying attention and let her ramble. I figure it's safer than trying to say anything. I'm afraid if I say too much it might just fuel the fire and I'm also kind of afraid that she might bite my head off if I try to interrupt her again.

“Anyway, so he says to me, ‘Dany, all my friends call me Dany. You can, too, if you want.’ I’ll answer to Danielle, too, but I don’t really like it my mom calls me that and I feel like a kid every time I hear it. But he says ‘Dany, you won’t believe what he said to me.’ And you know what he said? He said—” I am saved from hearing what Gary’s ex said by the ringing of the front door.

Danielle, or rather Dany, leaves me alone to my thoughts for a few glorious minutes while she seats the old couple who has come in and gets them their coffee.

She has me thinking, however. Are we together? Jimmy and I? We have slept together twice and at least one of those times it had definitely not been platonic. We have been on a date technically even if I had not been present for most of it. I know I have feelings for him, and I feel like I could say he has feelings for me, but how can you even attempt to say you’re in a relationship with someone who you just met five days ago? And then there is the added complication of my lack of a past. If things were different, I wouldn’t have a problem saying that we were involved, but as it stands now, I’m not even sure I can call us friends, let alone- I’m saved from even thinking that word by Dany resuming her seat across from me and continuing her monologue about Gary and his exploits as if she had never left. I let her ramble and sip my Coke watching the clock on the back wall tick closer to when Jimmy might come in and save me. That is if he even wants to save me from her. He may see I’m trapped and leave me there. He’d have every right to.

Almost like he could hear my thoughts, Jimmy comes walking through the door. He immediately sees me, but he tries to act normal as he walks towards the back, not saying a word to me.

“So, I tell him that he needs to ditch this guy—” I have completely lost track of what Dany is talking about, but it doesn’t matter to me at this point.

“Look I need to talk to Jimmy. Thanks for the Coke, though.” I leave her looking a little flabbergasted as I walk to the back. Jimmy is at the computer clocking in.

“I can’t talk right now. I’m about to work.”

“You have one table and Dany is still here.” He walks further into the back and pretends to check the schedule, but I can tell he is simply trying to avoid me. “Will you please talk to me?”

“I don’t want to talk to you right now. I have work to do.” He proceeds to go into the walk-in freezer. I follow him in and close the door behind me cornering him inside. He is rummaging through boxes.

"I want to talk to you." He turns to face me holding a big box of ice cream. Our breath hangs in the air between us along with all the unspoken secrets.

"Please get out of my way. I need to go stock the ice cream."

"The ice cream can wait." I have to try and keep my teeth from chattering, I can't show any weakness. I have him alone and cornered-I'm not going to let him go without talking to me.

"What do you want to talk about?"

"I went to Helen King's house today."

"Alright, and…?"

"I think I was coming here looking for my family." He looks at me expectantly waiting for me to continue. "She said I was asking about where I could find my sister Angela. I think I was looking for my family."

"So what? Can we go out where it's warm now?" He reaches for the door, but I cut him off.

"Why would I have done anything to that girl? I wouldn't have had any reason to. I was just looking for my family."

"That's all what you wanted to say?"

"What do you mean that's all? This is a big deal!" He drops the box to the floor.

"So, what? It doesn't tell us anything! So, you were in town looking for your family. I never thought you came to town with the intent of killing that girl but that doesn't mean it didn't happen. We have no idea who she was, or whether she was connected to your family or anything at all. You don't know any more than you did yesterday. You just want me to think you do, so I'll sleep with you again."

"That's what you think this is about? Sex?" My blood would be boiling except for the fact that my skin is ice cold. "I don't want to sleep with you, I want you to trust me! I want you to believe me when I say I didn't have anything to do with that girl's disappearance!" I'm glad for the cold because it keeps my eyes from watering.

"How can you say that? How can you say you had nothing to do with it when you have absolutely no idea what you were doing or if you even knew the girl! You don't even know your own name for sure! How can you say you're innocent when you don't know?"

We stand in silence staring at each other in the freezing cold. I don't know how to answer him, so I remind myself of the commitment I made to myself earlier about telling the truth.

"I don't know for sure."

"Then how am I supposed to believe you? How am I supposed to trust you?"

"Because…" I swallow back my fear. "Because I care about you. And I don't know what happened before I woke up on that dock but whatever happened, whoever did those things, that wasn't me. The me that you know, the me that's falling for you, the me that is here and now didn't exist before Sunday."

"Did you say—?"

"Let me finish." I don't know where this is all coming from, but it's as if a dam has broken and everything that I haven't allowed myself to even think is coming pouring out of my mouth. "I can't explain what happened before Sunday, but I'm trying my best to figure it out and I can't do it on my own. I'm going to go crazy if I don't have someone else to help me. So, if that's all you want, that's fine. I'll be okay with that. We don't have to be… we don't have to… sleep together, but don't ignore me. I have nothing right now. I have no family, no friends, no past, nothing. All I have to anchor me is you, and if I lose that, too, I don't know what I'll do. So, please, just don't leave me."

Silence.

I try to catch my breath, but the cold makes it hard to take in a breath. My fingers have gone completely numb as they hold onto the door handle, but I refuse to give in and open the door until I have his trust. He begins to bite his lower lip but stops.

"I can't say I trust or believe you. I still don't know how I feel about it—" I'm about to start in again but he doesn't let me. "But, but I'm willing to try. I don't think you did it. At least I don't think the you that… is here… as you put it… I don't think *you* did it. But it is a lot to take in and it's going to take some time. Is that okay?" I try to look in his eyes and see if he is telling the truth or if he is just telling me what I want to hear. I realize that this trust is going to have to be mutual.

"I can live with that."

"Now can we get out of here? Because it's really cold." We both laugh a little as I go to open the door. Unexpectedly, he puts a hand on the door as I do. We are suddenly very close. I remember the first time we were this close. It was only a few nights ago but already it feels like I've lived an entire life since then. So much has happened. "By the way… I think I might be falling, too."

I think he's going to kiss me, but he doesn't. He opens the door and heads out into the kitchen leaving me alone in the freezer. Suddenly, the warmth coming from in my chest is keeping the freezing temperatures at bay.

I stay with him for an hour or so. We don't talk much, but I'm there as he takes care of the factory workers on their breaks. I watch him serve the truck drivers who just got off the high way. I chuckle at the jokes he tells to the drunk girls who never made it to the clubs in Cleveland. I bask in the wonderful feeling of him being there. Of those last words he said in the freezer.

I don't know if I've ever felt this way before, but I can't imagine that I have. If I had, I don't see how I could have forgotten about it. Every second is crystal clear and I'm fighting a constant battle to keep it fresh and perfect in my mind, but I needn't try because for now, he's not going anywhere.

Finally, I decide I had better get some sleep.

"What are your plans for tomorrow?"

"It's Sunday, so I have no classes."

"Well, don't bother going home if you don't have to, just come next door."

"I don't want to wake you."

"I want you to." I ignore the giggles coming from the drunk girls as I kiss him on his cheek and walk out the door.

Ronnie is still in front of the T.V. but he has passed out. I turn it off and pick up the empty bottles off the floor. I take a towel from the kitchen and attempt to soak up what's left of the stain on the floor, but it's mostly dried by now. Luckily, his carpet is dark shag, and the stain may not show up. I consider waking him up and taking him to his bedroom, but I figure he's sitting up and less likely to get sick on himself that way, so I leave him be and go to my own bed.

I'm not awoken by any dreams, but I am awoken by Jimmy's arm slipping around me in the morning.

Chapter 12

"Sam. You need to wake up." I roll over and feel him missing. Peeling my eyelids back slowly, I see him standing next to the bed. I reach out for him.

"No, you need to come back to bed."

"Wake up! You need to come see this now." He leaves the room leaving me to drag myself out of bed. I glance at the clock, it's noon. I slept for almost twelve hours straight.

I groggily put on some pants and a t-shirt and stumble out to the kitchen. Jimmy is sitting at the counter watching the television. Ronnie is sipping a cup of tea and glaring at me.

"I'd appreciate it next time if you tell me we are going to have visitors," he grumbles to me.

"Sorry you were kind of… busy last night, I didn't want to bother you," he mumbles under his breath.

"Shh… Look, Sam." He points at the television, and it's like a nightmare come to life.

It's the dock.

It's breaking news coverage and they are standing on the dock. There are policemen and police tape everywhere and a couple of other news stations in the background. I don't need to read the ticker across the bottom or hear what's being said to know what's going on, but I lean over and turn up the volume anyway.

"Early this morning, based off of an anonymous tip, when they searched below the dock, they found the body of Sara Jefferson." A picture came up next to the reporter. It was like a cruel version of deja vu. I was in the same room as the other day watching the same reporter. Except this time the picture that came up was familiar.

It was the girl I dumped in the lake.

"It is unconfirmed at this point, but it is suspected that this case might be connected to that of Emily Bradshaw." A picture of Emily is pulled up next to Sara. "Both girls were roughly the same age, both were found with wounds to the back of their neck and dumped in the lake. Sara, however, was never reported missing. It appears she lived alone and was self-employed. As always if you have any information—" Melissa was cut short when Jimmy turned off the T.V.

"Come with me." He grabs me by the arm, and I don't even have time to say anything to Ronnie before he drags me outside.

"Where are we going? I need to watch the rest of that!" I don't know what he's doing but I am struggling to try and get back to the television. I need to know what the police know. Or at least what they are willing to tell the public they know. At this point, any information is better than what I've got, which is practically nothing.

"You can watch it when they show it again at five. Get in the truck." He practically throws me in the truck and goes around and gets in the driver's seat. He puts it in gear and drives in silence for a while until we are out of town, then he pulls over and looks at me for a moment before speaking.

"How did you know there was a second victim?" I feel the sweat form on the back of my neck, and I yearn for twenty minutes ago when we were in bed together cuddling and content.

"What do you mean?" I evade.

"Alex told me that you said 'girls' to the detective the other day. You knew there was a second victim. I promised you I would try to understand and try to help, but I've got to know the facts. I have to know everything. I can't do this with half the deck. How did you know there was a second victim?"

I evaluate his face. I have painted myself into a corner, and there are no escapes. I have to tell him. I try to cherish the memory that I have of us together this morning. I try to remember the feeling of his arm on my stomach because after I speak, there won't be any more cuddling. There may not even be any speaking. There may not be anything. He could turn me in. But I have no choice. Trust is mutual. I have to trust him.

"Because I dumped her in the lake."

We sit in silence. Me waiting for his reaction, and him contemplating what I said.

"Go on." It looks like those are two of the hardest words he has ever said in his life, but I appreciate that he said them. It tells me he isn't going to just turn me in. He is going to listen to my side of the story.

"When I woke up on the dock, she was there, dead, next to me." He waits for me to continue. "I don't know anything before that. But when I woke up, she was dead next to me. I was covered in her blood, and so I dumped her in the lake and my clothes with her." He looks confused at this. "Alex apparently didn't tell you I was naked when she found me. Well, I was. That's why I took your clothes."

"Why didn't you get help? Why did you dump her in the lake?" The worst question he could of asked was, of course, the first one to leave his lips.

"Because I thought I might have killed her." He looks away from me and stares out the front of the windshield. "Not me, exactly, but the me before I woke up. The me before I lost my memory. I didn't want to get punished for something that I have no memory of doing!"

"But what about her? Did you even think of her? Someone killed her and you could have ruined any chance of finding out who did it whether it was you or not!" He looked at me in a way he'd never looked at me before. Like a monster. Like someone to be despised.

"I didn't think about her because at the time I was trying to figure out who and where I was! You have no idea how terrifying this is for me. I honestly don't know if I killed her. And if I did, then that means there's a very good likelihood that I killed the other girl, too! I don't know what to tell you. No, I didn't think. I didn't think about her because I was too busy trying to think about me and trying to figure out who that was." He stares at me trying to process this and trying to decide if it's sufficient.

"If you didn't kill her.... why wouldn't you be dead?"

There it was. the question that essentially proved my guilt. Logically there was no answer that satisfied it. Either I was the killer, or the killer would have killed us both. There is no reason I would have been left alive.

"Perhaps he didn't know I was still alive." Even as I say it, I realize how little sense it makes. He would have dumped us both in the lake like He did with Emily. I can see the same thought is crossing Jimmy's mind.

He looks at me out of the corner of his eye and I become sick to my stomach. He is looking at me like I might pose a danger. Like he might be scared of me.

"Don't look at me like that."

"Like what?" He looks back at the road, but I can feel his muscles tense.

"Like I'm a murderer." I reach for his hand, but he pulls it away.

"How am I supposed to look at you?"

"Like you did this morning." I feel tears building up behind my eyes.

"I can't do that now." I search for something to say. Anything to say that might make him forgive me. To make him not hate me. But I come up dry. I've made my mistakes, and now I'm paying for them.

"If you killed her...." I almost vomit as he says these words. Just uttering them out loud gives them credibility. "If you did... then how did you lose your memory?"

It was a thought that I hadn't considered. Every time I considered the idea that I was the perpetrator in this crime I forgot that I was also a victim. Something had to have happened to me to make me lose my memory.

"You're right.... It couldn't have been me."

"I didn't say that. I just said.... How did you lose your memory?" I hated myself before my words even left my mouth because they were a cop out that I had become much too used to using.

"I don't know." I want to scream at the top of my lungs. My head hurts from the sheer multitude of things I do not know.

"Well, we need to figure it out." He starts the truck and I stare at him.

"We?" He doesn't answer me he just drives. I don't know how to take this. He seems to be at the end of his rope with me, but then there is always more. Just when I think he is about to run, he sticks around.

There are a half dozen cop cars in his back yard when we pull up to the house. There is also a couple of news vans and a bunch of people, most of them newscasters and policemen but a few civilians have also parked their cars by the side of the road and are watching the drama unfold.

Neither of us had thought about the fact that the body was found right behind Jimmy's house. Sure, the dock was about a half mile from his house, but it was next to his property and therefore his house was the logical next stop.

I recognize Detective Callahan standing on the front porch talking with Alex and another officer, this one in uniform. Jimmy pulls into the grass, past the newscasters, and jumps out of the truck like a bullet out of a gun. He is on the porch before I can even get out of my seatbelt. I slowly follow him, knowing that my flimsy story is going to be put under the microscope. I realize this might be the end of everything. I hear the reporters yelling questions at me as I head for the porch, but I ignore them.

"Alex, get inside." Alex turns to go but the uniformed cop puts a hand on her shoulder.

"We were just asking her a few questions is all." This came from Callahan. He eyes Jimmy, then sees me.

"Get off my property. You have no right to be here."

"You happen to know what was found by your dock back there?" The cocky uniform is chewing some gum. Between that and his bushy mustache he looks rather stupid.

"It isn't my dock. I'd like to see your warrant." Jimmy takes Alex by the arm and pulls her away from the two cops.

"Woah, son, just relax. We're just asking some questions now. No need to get all anxious." Callahan waves the uniform away. "Why don't we go inside and get away from all these cameras." I turn and notice that all the news reporters are facing away from us, but the cameras are pointed right at us. I count at least three different channels that we are being broadcast to.

"Why don't you show me your warrant or get off my property."

"Is this your property, boy? Because I'm pretty sure it's that gentleman over there's." Callahan points a thumb over his shoulder. As Jimmy looks, I see the color drain out of his face. I turn and look and see his father standing and talking to a uniformed police officer. He's wearing his tightey whiteys and two different colored socks.

"Why the hell would you let him be out here like that? There's cameras everywhere!" He pushes past Callahan and runs to his father, a trail of newscasters following after him.

"Don't matter kid, he's been out here for a good thirty minutes talking to us!" Callahan yells after him. I have to suppress the urge to punch the cop in the face. "I'm glad you showed up. Got some questions for ya." My eyes are so glued to Jimmy attempting to shield his father and pull him toward the house that I don't even notice Callahan is talking to me.

"I'm not answering any of your questions." I push my way past Callahan and am not light about it. I head towards Jimmy and begin to pull at his father with him. His father doesn't seem to fully understand what's going on and is rather excited to be on T.V.

"I'd like to say hi to my son Jimmy and my daughter Alexis; oh, hi Jimmy! I didn't see you there. Did you know we are on T.V.? I don't know what for, though. I can't understand anything these pretty ladies are saying." The officer who was questioning Jimmy's father is cracking up laughing.

"Come inside, Dad." Jimmy is shoving his father away from the cameras and I'm shooting a dirty look at the uniformed cop.

"What are you doing Jimmy? You're embarrassing me! And on T.V.!" We drag him kicking and screaming to the front door and push him inside. Callahan follows inside and neither of us have the ability to stop him because we are so concerned with getting the elderly man calmed down and away from the spotlight.

"Now that your pop is inside, will you answer some of my questions?" Callahan closes the door behind him shutting off some of the noise coming from the reporters as they update the world on the situation.

"I told you I'm not answering any of your questions until I see a warrant. Now get the hell out of my house!"

"Now, don't get your panties all in a twist. As I was telling you, this isn't *your* house. It's his. And he's been very cooperative and told us we were more than welcome to have a look around." Alex and the Uniformed Gum Chewer have followed us inside without me noticing. Gum Chewer smiles at me as if he is asking for a punch in the face.

"He's obviously not mentally competent to understand his own rights to the Fifth Amendment." Jimmy suddenly begins to not sound very much like Jimmy. He sounds more official. More sure of himself. More… in charge.

"Oh, I think he's plenty capable. We explained the whole thing to him, and he said he'd be happy to help. Now if you insist that he's mentally incompetent, then that's fine, we will have the state psychiatrist out here to check and get the whole thing cleared up. I hate to tell you this but if we do, and he is the legal guardian of this cute little one over here, we're going to have to find her a suitable home." He pats Alex on the shoulder. "One that isn't full of crazies." He looks at me as he says this.

"I'm more than competent as a guardian."

"Are you her godparent? Seems to me a good father like yours would have taken care of his beautiful little angel in case such an eventuality would come about. But that's fine, we can have the lawyers and doctor's all figure it out. Meanwhile, we will just put her in a home where we are sure she's well cared for until the courts decide." His pat on the shoulder has become a grip and he begins to lead her to the front door.

"Wait! You can't just take her!"

"You just told me that her legal guardian is mentally unstable. You can't expect me to leave her here now, do you? I wouldn't be a very good detective if I did that."

"She is perfectly safe here." I'm beginning to feel lost in the conversation about guardians and mental capability.

"Now, you can't have it both ways, boy. Either her guardian, your father, is cuckoo for cocoa puffs and therefore unable to allow us on the property, or he's fit as a fiddle and perfectly capable of taking care of this little angel. Now which is it?" His hand doesn't leave Alex's shoulder as Jimmy tries to figure out what to do.

"You can look around all you want. There's nothing to find," I say, and Jimmy stares at me.

"Good. Jefferson, go get the boys. We're gonna sweep the place. Thanks for the invitation." He heads out the front door and Jimmy grabs my arm and pulls me into the kitchen.

"What the hell do you think you're doing?"

"What difference does it make? He was going to look around anyway. Standing here arguing about it only makes us look guilty."

"We already look guilty, your dead girl you left for them in the lake did that quite well," he says through his teeth.

"There's nothing in the house. They won't find anything. I cleaned up at the lake before I came here. What are they going to find?"

"Are you sure? You didn't have a single hair or drop of blood on you? Under your nails, in your hair, anything?" He's panicking as he stares into my eyes, willing me to remember.

"I'm pretty sure. I cleaned myself off really well in the lake water."

"That probably didn't do a good enough clean. You can't get rid of that stuff with just water. And besides, you probably tracked lake water into the house."

"So, you live by the lake, you go swimming." He closes his eyes and shakes his head.

"Lake water with traces of her blood." As he says this, I hear the front door open. We look and there are men in uniforms walking in with boxes and equipment. Callahan follows them in.

"We are going to have to ask you to leave the house while we search," he says, leaning against the doorframe. "Oh, I'm sorry, did I interrupt? What were you two whispering about?"

"We aren't answering any of your questions." Jimmy walks past him and I follow suit. I try to shoot him a dirty look, but I'm not sure it does anything to the detective's triumphant smile.

Jimmy runs upstairs and grabs a robe for his father before leading us all out into the barrage of reporters and cops. We all stay silent except for his father, who continues to prattle on about being on T.V. for the first time in his life.

We watch from outside for the next two hours as they search the house looking for anything that might tie us to the dead body. The news crews eventually leave as they realize there isn't going to be any major finds anytime soon, leaving us alone on the lawn as the sun passes its apex. When they were finally done, Callahan came out onto the front lawn to us.

"Well, we will have to wait for the results on some of the tests, but I think you guys came out of this one clean."

"As we said we would. Now please get off my property." Jimmy pushes past Callahan and heads towards the house. I go to follow him, but Callahan grabs my shoulder as I try to pass him.

"Not so quick fella. You know what else we didn't find?" I can't bring myself to respond. "A suitcase, or bag, or extra clothes, or any sign that there was a fourth person living in this house."

"So what?" Jimmy has returned to my rescue.

"Well, this guy here, told me yesterday he was staying with you. But I couldn't find any of his things. I find that… peculiar."

"Please get off of our property. We told you we won't be answering any more of your questions." I turn with Jimmy and walk back to the house. This time Detective Callahan doesn't have anything to keep us talking.

Jimmy takes his father upstairs and then we congregate in the kitchen.

"New rule. No one says a word to the police." He stands at the head of the table while me and Alex sit on either side. It's extremely clear who is in charge here.

"But we can't just ignore them forever. Eventually we have to answer their questions."

"No, we don't. Not until we are subpoenaed, and they can't do that without strong evidence, which they don't have. Just refuse to answer. If they refuse to listen, ask for a lawyer. They can't ignore that."

"But do we, I mean, do you have a lawyer?"

"Duh silly Jimmy is our lawyer." This is the first that Alex has spoken in quite a while. She has been silent and withdrawn ever since Jimmy and Callahan had the argument about Jimmy's father. I haven't been too worried about her because I was more concerned with Callahan, but now, I notice that her eyes are puffy like she's been crying.

"I'm not your lawyer. I'm not even a law student. I'm just in pre-law." I realize now that I didn't even know what Jimmy was studying in school. I make a mental note that perhaps we should spend some time actually getting to know one another. Of course, it'll be a one-sided conversation. "But it doesn't matter if we don't have one, if we ask for one, they will be forced to provide us with one. It'll be a crappy public defender, but it will at least stop their questioning."

"I'm sorry I let them search the house. How could I anyway? It's not my house."

"Technically, according to them, you're a resident. All they need is a resident's permission to enter and search a dwelling. Since they didn't find anything I'm glad they got your permission. It's something maybe we can use in court in the future."

"You don't think that's going to happen, do you?" I've never really thought about the possibility that any of this confusion could lead to that. I never thought anything beyond the possibility of being caught by the police. I just pictured getting handcuffed and thrown in prison, but, of course, there would be the court case to follow before they decide my fate.

"Let's hope not, but we have to plan for that eventuality. Now rule number two. You two aren't allowed to leave the house without me. I don't want you getting ambushed and saying something you're not supposed to."

"Where would I go?" Alex doesn't look up from her lap when she says this.

"What about the diner?"

"You're quitting. We will figure out the money situation. I've got some money stashed away." I hope he doesn't mean the cookie jar. If he does, then that secret will have to come out as well. I still have quite a bit of the money left, so maybe it wouldn't be so bad if I told him now.

“Why don’t I just leave. They suspect me. I can tell every time Callahan looks at me. I’ll just go and then you guys can return to your normal lives.” I stand up at this.

“Sit down. We are in this. Whether we wanted it or not, we would now be considered accessories after the fact for housing you and helping you to avoid the police. We are in this together. But if we follow the rules and don’t do anything stupid, we might come out of this without having to worry about anything like that.”

“Then what are we going to do? Just stay in this house locked up like hermits forever? Eventually they will figure out what happened. Why run away from the inevitable?”

“Because we are going to figure it out first. That’s the next step. We have to figure out if you really killed her. We have to figure out who did if you didn’t.” I almost laugh at how easy he makes that sound.

“How are we supposed to do that? We don’t have any of the knowledge or capabilities that the police do. We don’t have access to her body for clues, we don’t have a chance at figuring it out before they do.”

“There is one thing we have that they don’t. We have you, and your memories.”

“But Jimmy, I don’t remember anything.” I feel silly reminding him of this.

“Not yet, but we have to get you to remember. As much as I hate to say it, I think we need to go through with Alex’s suggestion and get you to see a therapist. Maybe if we can make you remember, we can figure all of this out.” I don’t know if he’s correct in thinking that we can figure out what happened before the police catch on, but I’m willing to give it a shot if it means I might get my memory back.

“Well, then, let’s find me a therapist.”

Chapter 13

"Ronnie, are you home?" I look around the apartment, but Ronnie is nowhere to be found. We have come back to get my stuff out of the apartment. Jimmy thinks it would be best if I stay at the farm for the time being. It's best to stick together and, also, we don't want Ronnie finding out too much and saying something to the police.

"He doesn't seem to be home," I say as I head to my room to grab the few things I left there, mostly clothes, but there is also the money stashed under the mattress. I've decided that I can return the money tonight while everyone is asleep and while some of it is missing, Jimmy may not notice. He obviously doesn't check it often or else he would have known by now that it was missing.

"Well, maybe that's best. It saves us having to explain why your suddenly moving out. Just get your stuff and lets go home." I throw my clothes in a duffel we brought and shove the money in one of the side pockets.

"What are we going to do if he goes to the police to look for me?"

"I don't know."

"Maybe I should leave a note." I grab a pen and pad on the kitchen counter and do just that: *Had to leave unexpectedly, thanks for the room. See ya around.*

"That's fine. Come on, before he comes back."

Please don't creak. I think to myself as I tiptoe down the stairs. Jimmy is asleep upstairs, and I don't want him or anyone else to wake up and find me sneaking into the kitchen and putting the money back. I walk into the kitchen but don't turn on the lights. It's eerily similar to my first night here when I took the money.

I hear something. I turn but it's only an animal outside. I look out the window to be sure and that's when I see him. I only get a quick glance but I'm sure it's someone. He's walking in the back yard. My mind jumps to Jimmy, but he was asleep in bed when I left. We didn't do anything but sleep tonight but he was definitely in bed with me. He couldn't have gotten past me without me noticing. It's not his father, they were too slim for that. I think of Uncle Ben, but he had too sure of a walk, I highly doubt Uncle Ben would be out this late in the dark unless he was drunk. Besides, we would have heard his truck pull up.

But then who else could it be?

Suddenly, the kitchen light turns on. I whip my head around and see Jimmy standing in the doorway rubbing his eyes. Thankfully, I haven't pulled the money out of my pocket but when I turn back to the window, the figure is gone.

"What are you doing up?" Jimmy asks but I'm already heading to the door to go out into the yard. I don't bother to say anything to Jimmy, I know what I saw and if I tell him, it will just waste time. Who knows who was out there? But whoever it is, we need to know. Perhaps it's Callahan, perhaps it's… I realize it could be whoever attacked me and Sara.

Jimmy chases me out of the house asking what I'm doing. I break into a run when I hit the grass and realize the trajectory the figure had been walking. He had been walking away from the road across the back yard, I had noticed that. But it wasn't until I was outside heading towards where I had seen him that the map in my mind was completed. He was walking towards the lake, more specifically towards the dock.

I shush Jimmy and try to make as little noise as possible but also move fast enough to catch up to the intruder. I don't see him anywhere, but he can't have gone far.

We make it to the dock but it's empty. The only sound I hear is the ripples of the water and the chirping of a cricket. I turn around and look in all directions, but I don't see anything.

"What is going on?" Jimmy whispers.

"I thought I saw someone. No, I know I saw someone. He ran off this way."

"Are you sure you're not just having another one of those dreams? There isn't anyone out here. Come back to bed." He takes my hand and tries to lead me back to the house, but I don't move. I know he was out here. I wasn't hallucinating.

I can't be.

Suddenly, I don't even know for sure if I saw it myself. How can I be sure when I can't trust myself when I don't know myself? Since I awoke, I haven't had the most reliable senses. I've had strange dreams, sleep walked, blacked out and even had personality shifts. Is hallucinating really out of the realm of possibilities. I did see Sarah Jefferson in the restaurant before Kevin showed up. Suddenly, I'm afraid he may show up at any minute.

"Jimmy… you believe me, don't you?" I look him in the eye to see if he is telling the truth.

"Sam, I'm sure you saw something."

"No. Not about that. About…. everything. You believe me, right? You believe that I don't remember? That I don't know who killed her?" He looks at me for a few moments before responding.

"I believe you. And I don't think you did it. But I want to prove it. So, tomorrow, I'm going to find you a therapist. We have to go and get some professional help to get your memories back. But right now, you have to come back to bed." I pull my hand away from him.

"Jimmy. I have to tell you something." I put my hand in my pocket and summon up my courage. If he's stayed through everything else this shouldn't be a big deal. "I stole your stash of money in the cookie jar." I pull out the wad of cash.

"What are you talking about? Stash in the cookie jar? Sam where did you get this money?" He takes it from me and quickly thumbs through it.

"Sam, this is almost $2,000! Where did you get this?" This isn't the reaction I was expecting or had even considered.

"I got it out of your cookie jar in the kitchen. If it isn't yours, then whose is it?"

"I don't know. Alex couldn't get her hands on this kind of money."

Suddenly, I remember Uncle Ben yelling at Alex the other day when we came to the house the first time. Well, the first time together. He had been screaming something about her taking his money. I had assumed he was drunk and making things up, but this must have been what he was talking about.

"Do you think it might be Uncle Ben's?" Jimmy laughed at this.

"He couldn't stock up this much money. There's no way. He would have spent it all on booze. Come on let's talk inside. I'm getting cold." I give the dock one last look before following him up to the house. The water almost taunts me with its stillness.

"Are you sure you are alright?" Jimmy has turned on the light and is pulling out mugs from the cabinet. He doesn't ask if I like tea, not that I could properly answer, he just makes me a cup.

"I'm fine. I swear I wasn't hallucinating. I know what I saw. Someone was out there."

"I believe you. I'm just worried. You never seem to sleep through the night and even when you do you say you have those nightmares. Have you had anymore blackouts?" I sit at the counter and glance at the clock for the first time since I woke up. It's three in the morning. He isn't lying when he says I don't sleep through the night. He would know since he's been there.

"No. Not that I know of. Maybe the therapist will be able to help explain that. I'm sure it has to do with my lost memory, but I don't know how." He sets the cup of hot tea in front of me, and I see his face darken at the mention of the therapist. "What do you have against therapists?"

"It's not therapists. It's just doctors in general." He doesn't meet my eye when he says this.

"Is it because of your mother?" He doesn't answer. "What happened to her?" He sits so long in silence that I begin to think he isn't going to answer.

"It wasn't her. It was what happened after." I decide that I'm just going to sit back and let him tell it as he is ready, I'm not going to push him or ask questions. Whatever he wants to tell me I'll be okay with.

"She died in a car accident. It wasn't anyone's fault. She hit a patch of black ice and went off the road and into a tree. They say she didn't suffer. They say it was quick… But how can they really know?" I see his eyes are starting to tear up. "I was fourteen and I was at home with Dad and Alex. She was only a baby, so she doesn't remember most of all this." I think this is going to be the end of it but I'm wrong.

"My father. He changed. He wasn't the same. It wasn't just her death. Something happened between him and Uncle Ben. I don't know what exactly, but I have my suspicions. Anyway, that's when Uncle Ben became a drunk. Or at least when he started drinking. We used to be really close. He was like a third… Like a third parent. He was always over here spending time with me and Alex. But then he became… well, you've met him. You understand." I do. To a point that I'm not sure Jimmy is aware, but I'm not going to say anything about that at the moment.

"My father, though, just became depressed. He sold off most of the farm. It used to be four times this size. He claimed it was because he was thinking of retiring but I knew it was because of Mom. He became a hermit. He wouldn't leave the house most days. I began doing most of the grocery shopping as soon as I got a license. Then I was getting a job to help pay for some of it. Dad sold off more of the farm and stopped working the other part. It wasn't until later that I found out he was taking pills. He had prescriptions for them but there were just so many… uppers, downers, stabilizers. He had an orange little box with all the days, and it was packed full.

"Well, it didn't matter how many pills he took, he just got worse. Every year that he went without her he just deteriorated. Alex didn't really notice because she was too young. She doesn't remember what he used to be like. She only knows him… the way he is now." He's quiet for a long time. I'm tempted to ask for the missing link, the tipping point between the depressed pill popper he described and the invalid that was snoring upstairs, but I don't need to. He reads the question written in my eyes.

"Then, April 4th, three years ago. I remember because it was her birthday. It was always a rough time for him but that was a particularly rough year. You know it was such a small thing but looking back on it I think it was because of Alex's hair. That was the year she decided to start growing it out. She had always kept it short to be like us guys. Without mom she felt like she was one of us. But that year she started wearing it long and well, the resemblance was uncanny.

"I found him unconscious on the bathroom floor when I came home from work that morning. He had emptied his entire little orange box. It was only a Tuesday so there was at least twenty pills. I don't know how long he had laid there but I picked him up and carried him to the truck. He hadn't been eating much so he wasn't too heavy. I drove him to the hospital, and they pumped his stomach. He didn't wake up right away. They thought that he had completely scrambled his brain beyond the ability to wake up." He isn't trying to hide the tears at this point. They are falling like rain, diluting his tea.

"Then about a week later, he just woke up without any prompting, or any reason. The doctors said it was a miracle. But he came out of it…. lost. He never really came back all the way. He is a child. He can't care for himself. He doesn't remember things beyond five minutes. It took me forever to get him able to recognize Alex. He still thinks sometimes that she's a baby. He forgets that time has passed.

"You want to know the funny thing though? He never asks about Mom. He's never mentioned her. Not once since he… since he lost himself. It's like he was successful only part-way. He was able to kill the part of himself that missed her. I don't even know if he would recognize a picture of her, I've never asked. I've never wanted to.

"They gave him yet more pills that were supposed to eventually help his brain get back to normal. I let him take them for a little while, but they didn't seem to help too much. Finally, I stopped giving them to him. Honestly, I would have stopped regardless. I'm not sure I want him to get any better.

"He may not realize it but he's happy now. He doesn't think about her. He may not live a very full life but… at least he'll smile now. Alex used to tell this joke. It was some silly joke about two guys walk into a bar and the third one ducks or something. It wasn't that funny, but he thought it was the most hilarious thing he'd ever heard. He laughed so hard every time he heard it, and because his memory is shot every time, she said it, it was like the first time." He finally took a moment to wipe his face. I put a hand out on the table between us. Not forcing it, just offering. He accepted before he continued.

"Anyway, that's why I hate doctors. All they do is make things worse." We sit in silence for a few minutes before he stands up to head upstairs.

"Would you rather your father be like he is now, or depressed like he was before he started taking pills?" I finally ask as he heads out of the kitchen and I take the half drank mugs to the sink. He turns and considers the question.

"Do you know what I'd really prefer? More than anything else?" He chews the words up before he spits them out. "I wish I had come home and gone to bed that night. I wish I'd never gone into the bathroom until it was too late." With that he goes upstairs not waiting for a response.

I rinse out the mugs and put them away. I remember just before I head upstairs myself and return to the counter. I open the cookie jar and place the wad of cash inside. I turn off the lights and go upstairs, and crawl into bed. On every other occasion, I've been the vulnerable one. I've been the one who needed to be held. Tonight, I hold him. Tonight, he is the one who can't sleep. For him it isn't lack of memories that terrorizes him, it's too many.

Chapter 14

I lean my head against the window of the truck watching the countryside fly by the side of the road. The heat is on, but it has a musty smell to it, and I consider that I'd almost prefer to be cold. Jimmy came home from work two nights ago to find me on his computer. He had given me his password and I was unable to sleep.

I had found her.

Dr. Green.

She had a practice over in Cleveland. She specialized in abuse victims and repressed memories. I admitted to Jimmy it wasn't the exact same, but it was close enough to be a good start. I called the next day and she didn't seem too expensive per hour. The best part, however, was that she wasn't a psychiatrist, she was a psychologist. She couldn't prescribe any medicine. When I mentioned that, Jimmy's attitude towards the whole plan changed. Suddenly, he was all for it.

After I called and scheduled an appointment with her, Jimmy had requested the time off work and we decided we would stay the night in Cleveland.

"It's too far to drive there and back in the same day; besides, we could use a daycation." He didn't say it, but I think he also thought it might be good to get away from Detective Callahan. He had stopped by the house every day since they discovered Sara's body. First, he knocked, but then he just got out of his car and stared. I began to consider he might have been the shadow I saw, but he never came anywhere close to sundown, let alone in the middle of the night.

I hadn't seen the figure again, and I had been looking for it. I didn't sleep when Jimmy wasn't there, so I sat by his window and tried to read, but mostly I watched and waited. Waited for the figure to appear, to give me some sort of clue about his identity. But nothing. Perhaps I really did hallucinate him. I tried not to consider the possibility. If I admitted that there hadn't been a figure, then suddenly, anything I saw came into question.

I had tried to call the number for Mr. King's associate, Mr. Duncan, but his wife answered. She said that she would let him know I called, and she would have him call me. I didn't want to pester him, so I decided I'd wait to try again until we got back from Cleveland. I wasn't even sure what I was going to ask him anyway. From what Helen had said it didn't seem like he would know much. I apparently only really talked to Philip. And Helen had made it very clear she didn't want me talking to him.

Perhaps I won't even need to talk to him; I think to myself as we pass yet another barn. For all I know this time tomorrow I'll know everything. Perhaps Dr. Green will be able to unlock my brain and release the memories that seem to evade my grasp. I certainly hope so because if not, I'm not sure what my next move is going to be.

I look over at Jimmy, and smile. This past week has been great. Ever since we talked in the kitchen Sunday, we haven't had a single misstep. He goes to work and comes home to sleep with me. We wake up and he goes to class while I spend the day with Alex. She has taught me how to play a few board games, she's exceptionally good at Scrabble. I keep blaming my amnesia for my poor vocabulary, but I don't think she buys it. I keep saying it because otherwise I'd admit that I got creamed by a girl half my age.

Then Jimmy comes home from class and we have dinner. One night Jimmy cooked this chicken pasta dish. But every other night we've either ordered pizza or Jimmy has brought something home. I have yet to find something I don't like. We watch a movie or play cards and then he heads off to work and Alex goes to bed.

If it weren't for this time when I'm alone, I'd almost forget what all I've forgotten. I feel like a part of something, like I know who I am when I'm with them. But then when I'm alone it all comes rushing back. I suddenly don't know how to be with myself because I don't know how to just be me. What do I do? I finished *The Girl with The Dragon Tattoo,* I want to read the second one, but Jimmy doesn't own it and I don't want to ask him for it.

So, I tend to sit and stare out the window. Watching for the figure, trying to remember something. Failing to move forward.

Now I'm moving forward for sure. I tell myself that even if Dr. Green doesn't unlock all of the answers for me, then it will be a step in the correct direction for sure. If a psychologist can't help, then who could?

With this thought to calm my nerves I turn and look at Alex, asleep in the back seat of the truck. She doesn't have much room, but luckily, she doesn't need much. I forget how little she is sometimes. This little girl who has had to deal with so much but is so quick to smile and keep going. She has gumption. I trust in ten years she'll be quite the heartbreaker, perhaps even sooner than that whether Jimmy wants her to be or not. I whisper a secret prayer that she doesn't grow up too soon.

Jimmy changes the radio station as we drive out of range and into static. I've gotten to know him better over the last few days. We stay up after he comes home and talk. Even though I don't have much to contribute, we spend a lot of time talking. I've learned about his favorite color, movie, and song: green, *Back to the Future*, "Don't Stop Believing." He told me stories about his childhood, talked about his classes. He confessed he didn't really want to stay in Fairport. He wants to move to the city, maybe Cleveland, maybe larger, but he can't as long as he is taking care of Alex and his father.

He told me he wants his father to go into a home once Alex graduates. Until then, he thinks it's important to keep him at home and happy for the time being. I tried to tell him he doesn't have to take care of his father, that he could go to a home now, but Jimmy shut down as soon as I tried. I decided that for now, it was Jimmy's decision and I had to respect that.

Just like Jimmy had to respect my decision to see Dr. Green alone. I had been thinking about it since we decided to go, but I didn't bring it up to Jimmy until this morning. We had decided that the best way to get me into the office was to masquerade me as Jimmy because I'd have to fill out insurance forms and medical history forms in order to get in the door. I could explain to her the situation once I was in the session. Jimmy wanted to be there with me to help explain and to reassure her that I hadn't simply stolen Jimmy's information and that he was helping me.

I told him this morning, however, that I'd prefer to go in alone. Not that I didn't want him there but because I wanted to be able to talk freely. I have been one hundred percent honest with Jimmy about the facts, but I haven't confessed just how much I honestly am afraid that I might have killed those girls. I'm sure he's thinking it, too, but thinking it and hearing it said out loud are two different things. I don't really care what Dr. Green thinks of me, but Jimmy on the other hand I do. I don't want him coming out of this, if things go poorly, thinking that I'm a murderer.

Finally, I was able to convince Jimmy that he needed to stay with Alex, if he came in with me, then she would have to be alone at the hotel or in the waiting room. He wasn't happy but he agreed. we decided it would look suspicious if the two of them were going to wait in the lobby and besides, if he wasn't coming in with me there wasn't a reason for us to both go. So, we planned to go to the hotel first, check in, and then we would walk the few blocks to the building where Dr. Green's office was. From there Jimmy and Alex would visit some of the sights in the city and I would meet up with them after my appointment. I was scheduled, or rather Jimmy was scheduled, for three-thirty. We had booked an entire hour, so we figured there would be time for dinner and a little sightseeing for all three of us afterwards before we headed back to the hotel.

That was if Dr. Green didn't decide I was unfit to be a part of society and locked me up in a nuthouse. I'm not sure if they still do that but it is a fear that had popped into my head last night and was yet another reason for Jimmy not to join me. I'm not sure I want him there if that's what it comes to. But I hope it doesn't.

"Go ahead and have a seat, Daniel."

Dr. Green's office is very red. I don't know what I expected it to look like, but I guess I thought it was going to be… well, green. But instead, it has a dark brownish red colored wall that would look like mud if it weren't so multifaceted. She has a brown leather couch with red accent pillows that I assume is for me. It isn't a chaise couch like I expect a therapist to have; instead, it is a regular, three-seater couch. Her desk is large and imposing but she sits in an auburn swivel chair close to the couch. She was reading a book when I was let in by her secretary. I can't see the title, but it is rather large. She stands up and puts it on a shelf full of similarly large books. They don't seem to be in any sort of order, but rather are haphazardly put away, some of them stacked rather than shelved. I would have figured a doctor would be more organized but I kind of like this. It makes me feel like she isn't uppity or too self-important. Perhaps she will have enough compassion to not ship me off to the nuthouse.

I sit on the edge of the couch, afraid to get comfortable. She grabs a notepad and pen off of her desk and returns to the swivel chair. She isn't what I expected either. She has blonde hair that is straight and just barely brushes her shoulders. Her thick brimmed glasses match the color of the walls, but her blouse is bright hot pink. It's sleeveless and I see she has a tattoo on her left shoulder. I can't see it very clearly, but it looks like a Chinese symbol of some sort. Her black pencil skirt has quite a high side slit that shows off her pale legs. She would be about a half a foot shorter than me if it weren't for the stiletto heels she is wearing.

She sits and stares at me as I sit on the couch. I didn't notice the grandfather clock in the corner behind me until our silence made it's ticking overwhelmingly powerful.

"What brings you in today?" She finally says as she takes a note on her pad. How can she already be taking a note? I haven't said a word. Maybe she's commenting on my lack of introduction. Or I tell myself, she could just be writing down my name. I try to calm my nerves, but I feel the sweat break out on the back of my neck.

"Well, it's kind of…." I start, but then a cat grabs my tongue. I have tried to think of how I would explain this all the way here, right up until the point where Jimmy and Alex dropped me off out front. Jimmy assured me he would come in if I wanted him to, but I insisted, even though there was a part of me that was scared to death to come in here alone.

Now she's waiting for me to continue. This isn't going well. Or at least it isn't going like I planned. Suddenly, I remember one of the things Jimmy told me I had to ask her. He told me he was pretty sure of the answer, but he wanted me to be sure before I told her too much. I don't think he intended it to be how I started talking but I was at a loss for where to begin at the moment, so it was better than nothing.

"Everything I tell you is privileged, right?"

"Of course, Daniel." She makes another note but doesn't look at the page while she's doing it.

"What if hypothetically I confessed to a crime. Would you be forced to tell the police?"

"Do you have a crime to confess about?" That wasn't the answer I was hoping for. I don't know how to respond. If I say yes and she says she has to report it, then I've painted myself into a corner.

"Maybe." I figure it's close to the truth anyway.

"Well, unless someone is in imminent danger, yourself or others, then I am not compelled or even able to say anything to the police. You could claim you shot the president, and unless you were planning to do it again, I couldn't tell a soul." I breathe a sigh of relief. Jimmy had said that was what he figured but he didn't know for sure. He was only a law student, not a full-fledged Lawyer.

"Well, okay, then. That's good."

"So, you do have a crime to confess to?" She hasn't moved or changed her demeanor since we started. I expected her to panic or freak out once I started hinting that I'd committed a crime, but she remains calm and collected.

"Sort of. Or at least I don't think so. But maybe." I realize that I'm not making any sense and close my eyes and try to get a grip on what I'm saying.

"Just start at the beginning, Daniel."

"Well, for one, you can stop calling me Daniel." I don't know why but every time she says Daniel my stomach clenches with guilt. Perhaps because I'm using Jimmy, or because it reminds me of the fact that I don't even know what my real name is.

"Do you have a different name you'd like to be called?" She makes another note.

"I don't know." I shake my head hard to try and organize my thoughts. If I continue like this, I'm going to definitely go to the nuthouse. "I have no idea who I really am."

"Okay. What makes you think you're not Daniel James Evans?"

"I know I'm not him because he's taking his sister sightseeing right now. He dropped me off." She is unfazed by this. She takes another note and looks at me again.

"If he's out there, who is in here talking to me?" I realize she thinks I'm delusional. I need to be more clear I need to actually just tell her what's going on.

"I have amnesia. I lied on the form about my name and everything because I have no idea who I really am. I was afraid that if I said that on a form you wouldn't see me. So, I had Jimmy, or rather Daniel, let me pretend to be him, so I could get in the room. I put down his information not mine because I haven't got any information of my own. Like I said, I have no idea who I am." It finally clicks for her. I can see it in her eyes. She makes a note and waits. I assume it is an invitation for me to continue. "I wanted to come in here and talk to you to see if you could help me remember who I am."

"Well, I don't know if I can do that or not. Why don't you tell me when all this started? What's the first thing you remember?" She seems to be taking this all in stride. She didn't even bat an eye the entire time. I figure she either still thinks I'm delusional and making this all up or she is the most understanding person ever.

Of course, that will be put to the test when I tell her what I do remember.

"So, no matter what I tell you, as long as no one is in imminent danger, you can't tell anyone?" Just making sure before I drop the bomb.

"That's correct." I take a deep breath and close my eyes. I'm not sure I want to see her facial expression when she hears my next statement.

"I woke up next to a dead woman." I wait for her to gasp or make some sort of noise but when nothing happens, I crack my eyes a steal a look at her. She is exactly the same. She hasn't moved or even adjusted her seating.

"I woke up covered in her blood." I feel like I'm almost testing her at this point. Trying to get a rise out of her. Trying to get her to be shocked. Trying to make sure I'm speaking the same language because I'm positive there's no way she hasn't called the cops yet.

"Did you know this woman?" she asks when I don't continue.

"I don't know for sure. I don't remember anything before waking up next to her on the dock."

"Did you have any head injuries when you woke up?"

"Yes, I didn't notice it at first, but I did when I went in the water to… " I stop not because I don't want to tell her but I'm almost ashamed to say the words out loud.

"Went in the water to do what?"

"To dispose of the body." I look at her out of the corner of my eye. She finally moves but it's only to pick up her crossed leg and switch it with the other. She returns to almost the exact same position only in reverse.

"Do you think you killed her?" I wince as she cuts right to the heart of it. I was hoping it would take longer to get to that part of the questioning.

"I don't know."

"Was anyone else around when you woke up?" I am shocked that she so quickly moved past what I thought was the pivotal and most important question. I didn't have an answer, so she just moved on like it was no big deal.

"I mean Alex and Jimmy… well, Jimmy was at work, but it was practically in their back yard."

"And did Jimmy and Alex… I'm assuming that's Jimmy's little sister?" I nod. "Did either of them know you?"

"No. They had no idea who I was. They also had never seen Sarah before."

"So, you knew the name of the dead woman?" I realize I jumped. It's really hard to explain this situation in chronological order without confusing myself or her.

"Not at the time. I know now because the police have found her body and are searching for her killer." I nervously look behind me at the clock, but it's only been ten minutes.

"Don't worry about the time. I'll let you know when we are getting close. Now I take it since you were so worried about me going to the authorities that you yourself have not talked to the police?"

"I have talked to them, but I haven't told them anything. I've… well, I've lied through my teeth." She makes another note. I start to panic. What if she's been doing the same thing? What if she's lying to me and is taking notes to go and tell the police the minute I leave the room?

"And why have you done that?"

"Because I'm afraid of incriminating myself."

"So, you think you killed her?"

"I don't know for sure. I mean there is that possibility isn't there? I can't know for sure, and I don't want to go to jail for a crime that I'm not even sure if I committed." She makes another note.

"Do you feel like you killed her?" I pause for a second, confused that she would ask the same question twice.

"I just said—" She puts a hand up to stop me.

"You misunderstand. I'm not asking for facts. It's clear that there is no definitive answer to whether or not you killed her yet. The police will have to figure that out. But what I'm asking is do you *feel* like you killed her?" I take a moment to digest this. This isn't going the way I want it to, but I don't quite know where it is going, and I feel like she does. I decide to trust her.

"Do I *feel* like I killed her? I mean I feel guilty. I feel bad that I've been keeping this a secret, but I also don't think I'd have the ability to. I mean I don't feel like I'm a murderer, but I don't know how a murderer feels. Maybe a killer feels guilty after they kill someone. Maybe they don't. I don't know. I don't even know what kind of movies I liked before I woke up, let alone what state of mind I was in." She makes another notation this one seems longer than the others. Or at least she doesn't look up quite as quick.

"Let's come back to that question. Have you remembered anything since you woke up?" I try to think and the only thing I can remember is when I recognized the name of Angela.

"I think I remembered my sister's name." Another short note.

"Which is?"

"Angela Cartwright."

"And have you tried to contact her?"

"She died twenty years ago." She makes a note.

"So, you remember that you have a dead sister?" I sink my head into my hands. I feel like I'm trying to swim upriver, explaining things that I'm not sure I fully understand without the benefit of time or Jimmy. I was able to explain things to him so much easier. I don't know if it was because I did it in small bursts rather than all at once or if it was because I simply felt more comfortable with him.

"It's not like that. I remembered her name. Then I, well… I happened to remember this other woman's face. Her name is Helen King. I followed Helen and talked to her. I didn't know how I knew her at the time but that's not really important."

"Why isn't it important?"

"I mean it is, but… I'm trying to explain it in a way that makes sense."

"Do you find it hard to explain things a lot of the time?"

"Not particularly." She ignores my frustrated tone and waits for me to continue. "Anyway, she told me where I could find 'her' I didn't know she was referring to Angela at the time. I just knew it was someone I had talked to her about anyway." I can see as she writes another note that I'm digging my hole deeper. I'm not doing a very good job at making things clear. "Anyway, I found her tombstone at the address Helen told me."

"So, her address was a graveyard?"

"Yes."

"And what makes you think this Angela Cartwright was the woman you were talking to Helen about?"

"Because I recognized the name. I knew the name before I saw it, but I didn't know that I knew it if that makes any sense. It wasn't until I saw it that it fell into place." She nods and writes something down.

"And what made you realize this was your sister?"

"Well, that was because I found our house… Sort of." This was another part that might land me in the looney bin.

"Go on."

"Well, when I was out with Jimmy, I sort of had an episode." She sits and waits for me to explain. I chew over my words before I let them out of the gates. "Well, I sort of hallucinated, I think. I thought I saw Angela, but it was actually Sarah." Before she even opens her mouth, I realize how confusing I made that sound.

"So, you saw the girl from the dock."

"Yes. I didn't know her name was Sarah at the time, and I didn't know Angela was dead yet. I'm getting this all out of order and I'm not doing a good job of explaining it."

"Just take a breath." I hadn't even realized that I was panicking. I took her advice and tried to take a long breath to lower my heartbeat. I was getting so frustrated with myself and my inability to tell this story that I was freaking out.

"So, I saw her. It was a hallucination, but I blacked out. I didn't lose consciousness I just… my brain shut off and according to Jimmy, I became a different kind of person. I mean I acted differently and… Well, I hijacked a car."

She takes a note, and my blood starts burning again. I can feel the sweat dripping down my forehead. I wipe it away before I continue.

"Anyway, I hijacked this car and took Jimmy to this house." I decide to not tell her about the game of hide and seek. For one I'm not sure it would be helpful at this particular moment, and I also feel like I'm inching closer and closer to a nervous breakdown. I don't know what is coming over me but I'm finding it really hard to concentrate.

"Would you like a glass of water?" Dr. Green is finally showing some sign of emotion. She has gotten out of her seat and her face is no longer the calm stone that it has been. Instead, it's concerned.

"Yes. Please," I force myself to say. I'm not able to say much else because my throat suddenly closes up on me. I try to force myself to calm down but all I'm able to do is think how crazy this makes me look and that just sends me further and further into my anxiety.

She hands me a glass of water. I'm not sure where it came from. I can't seem to focus my eyesight at the moment. Things are getting fuzzy. I feel her gently push me back, so I'm lying down on the couch. I hear her say something to her secretary out the door. I close my eyes and lay back trying to calm myself.

Then, suddenly, it all disappears.

My blood calms down to a reasonable pace. My eyes pop open and I have the ability to focus. My mind stops reeling and my stomach is no longer doing somersaults. I test it for a second, then try to sit up. When I do, Dr. Green is sitting back in her swivel chair. She looks up from her notes that she is taking. I don't know exactly what it is that tips me off to it, but I can feel that time has passed.

"What just happened?"

"I think you had another… episode as you called it. Are you feeling better now?" I sit up fully and look behind me. It's almost the end of my hour. I must have passed out for a good chunk of time. I curse myself for having wasted the time that I spent Jimmy's money for.

"I am. Did I pass out or was I talking?" She looks at me confusingly.

"Were you aware at all during the episode?"

"I was aware up until the glass of water and then I woke up just now. Why what did I do?"

"How did it feel before you passed out?" I don't understand why she wouldn't just tell me what I did.

"I felt panicked like I wasn't in control of anything. What did I do? What did he do?" Instead of answering, she gives me an interested look. I can tell there is a vast difference between her current demeanor and that which she had before my episode. She is intrigued.

"Who is he?"

"Kevin!" I'm so frustrated that I realize she doesn't know that that's who I refer to him as. This Mr. Hyde that came out.

"So, you're aware of your other Identity?"

"What do you mean 'other identity'?" I'm so confused. I feel my head pounding and, at first, I am afraid I'm going to have another episode, but it doesn't get worse. I'm just frustrated.

"Well, I can't say for sure, but it would appear that you are suffering from some kind of a mental break." I still am trying to figure out what I could have done while I was passed out. I worry about what I told her but at the same time what could I have said that would be any worse than what I already told her. Unless Kevin told her that I definitely did kill Sarah.

"What did I say?"

"Well, who do you think it was? You or Kevin?" She's dodging the question.

"Look it doesn't matter. Just what happened?" She looks at her watch on her wrist.

"Look. It's about time. I want to see you again. we have only just scratched the surface of what needs to be discussed. Can you come again tomorrow? I have a slot open in the morning." She gets up and goes to her desk, but I follow her. I don't intend to scare her, but my sudden advance seems to startle her. This makes me even more concerned about what must have happened while I was out. What could I have done to make her fear me?

"What did he say?" She considers me for a moment before responding. I can see in her eyes that she is weighing the pros and cons of telling me.

"You told me not to believe a single word you said. You were very insistent on that. You told me that you were a stark raving lunatic and that you needed to be put in an insane asylum. You insisted that you'd never heard of any of these people you had discussed and that you were making it all up."

I don't know how to respond at first. It isn't the words she says so much as the intention behind them. When I last became Kevin… or rather last had an episode, I didn't do anything I didn't want to do in reality. I wanted to get together with Jimmy, and I wanted to find out about my past. Kevin wasn't so much a different person from me he just was willing to do things I was scared to do like make out with Jimmy or steal a car.

But if that's the case, then I must deep down honestly feel like I'm crazy and that I need to be put in an insane asylum. But I know I don't feel like Jimmy and everything is made up. I know that for a fact. I can prove that to Dr. Green if need be. But I don't think that's what she thinks. At least she isn't sending me off to the nuthouse right away. She's asking me to come back which means she is letting me go. I venture one last question.

"What do you think is wrong with me?" She considers this for a minute.

"I don't want to tell you just yet. I will if you insist because ethically, I can't deny you your own information if you ask me directly. But I'm telling you that in my professional opinion that I think it would be detrimental to your mental health if I told you right now when you are leaving. I would much rather tell you tomorrow when we have time to discuss it at length and talk about your options." She looks at me for a second to see if I respond. When I don't, she continues, "If you think you can, I'd urge you to hold onto that question and to come back tomorrow morning at ten and ask me then. Are you okay with that?"

I try to process what she said. I understand her reasoning and I somewhat agree with her. I just had a panic attack of some sort or as she said, a mental break, if she told me now it could spark another attack and I don't want that to happen right now.

"All right. As long as you promise to tell me tomorrow."

"I will. Just go and get some rest. I'll explain what I think is going on tomorrow." She leads me out into the outer office. Jimmy and Alex are sitting there waiting in two of the comfy chairs in front of the secretaries desk.

"You must be Jimmy." I didn't anticipate her meeting, Jimmy. I feel weird because I don't think I adequately described my relationship. If you could even call it that.

"Yes. So?" Jimmy obviously had a million questions but was unsure of what to ask at the same time.

"I've asked Sam to come back again." I give her a weird look. I don't remember referring to myself as Sam or giving her that name at all. Did I give her that name while I was out of it?

"We need to head home."

"I understand but I really think it would be beneficial. Do you think you could come tomorrow at ten? I promise I won't keep him more than an hour. Then you all can head home if you want." What did that mean? If we wanted? Did she think we wouldn't want to? That I wouldn't or that they wouldn't?

"Alright. We will come back tomorrow at ten."

Chapter 15

I'm not able to concentrate on any of the sights we are seeing as we wander the streets of Cleveland. Jimmy tries to ask me about what happened in my session, but I avoid the questions and tell him I'll tell him about it later. I claim I don't want to talk about it right then, but honestly, I don't want to talk about it at all.

Every time we turn a corner, I'm afraid I'm going to have another episode. I had thought that my attack in the Mexican restaurant had been a one-time event and that it was just a fluke but now that it's happened again, I don't know what is causing it. Dr. Green seemed to have an idea, but I won't know what that is until tomorrow.

Until then, I try to act interested in the Rock and Roll Hall of Fame or in the Museum of Art. Eventually, though, Jimmy realizes I don't feel like sightseeing anymore so when we are eating dinner at some Italian restaurant we found, he suggests we go back to the hotel afterward.

"No, it's such a waste. We came here to have a little vacation." I don't even buy my own argument.

"It's okay. We will go back to the hotel and get some rest. You've had a long day. We can watch something on T.V. before bed."

We go back to the hotel and do just that. There are two double beds in the room, so Alex lays by herself to watch T.V. and me and Jimmy lay in the other bed. We watch a few rounds of *Jeopardy* before Alex dozes off to sleep.

"So, it's later. Tell me what happened," Jimmy says as he presses the mute button on the T.V.

I knew he was going to ask, and I know I have to answer him now that he has, I just wish I had been able to make it past tomorrow, so I could tell him whatever Dr. Green says tomorrow. I don't think that I can convince him to wait the way she made me. I have to tell him something.

"I had another episode." He gives me an odd look. "I blacked out and began to act oddly. I'm not totally sure what I did but she said I told her to put me in an insane asylum while I was out. Then she told me that she wanted me to come back tomorrow. She seems to have an idea of what's going on, but she wouldn't tell me until tomorrow. Or at least she didn't think it would be smart to tell me. She wants time to explain it accurately."

"Okay. But did she say she could help you remember anything?"

"No." I had been so caught up in my panic attack and following episode that I didn't even think to ask that as my session was ending.

"Well, I guess if you know what's causing these episodes, it's something." He un-muted the T.V. just in time for the final *Jeopardy*.

After a few more episodes, I started to doze and was only slightly aware of Jimmy turning off the T.V. and the lights.

I open my eyes and I'm in a circus fun house. There are mirrors everywhere I turn. I reach my hands out to try and feel my way because everywhere I turn, I see my reflection. I bump into my reflection as I try to make my way through.

Suddenly, one of my reflections stops moving. I continue walking, but he just stops and stares. He's followed suit by another reflection. Pretty soon all of the reflections have stopped. I try to find my way through but I'm walking in circles, surrounded by these doppelgängers that look just like me but don't reflect my actions.

Then they start laughing at me. They are pointing at me and laughing, not in unison but rather like a gaggle of friends making fun of someone, except I'm the one being made fun of. I can hear their laughter as it grows louder and louder as I try to push my way through the maze. It becomes deafening as I hit a dead end. I use my hands and follow the wall around and see that I'm closed in with six walls that reflect each other and create an endless number of Sams. But none of them are my reflection, they all are maniacally laughing at me.

Frantic to get out and angry at being made fun of I take a swing and punch one of the mirrors. a giant crack spreads from where my fist hits and spiderwebs out. When I do this, the doppelgängers stop laughing and get angry. One of them, the one in the mirror I punched, reaches out beyond the edge of the mirror, and grabs a hold of my shirt. He pulls me towards him, but I hit the glass and taste blood in my mouth.

Another one grabs my hair on the back of my head and slams my head into a mirror as another one kicks me in the chest. I scream in pain and find myself sitting up in bed in the hotel room. Jimmy stirs next to me but doesn't wake up.

I must not have screamed in real life.

I'm covered in sweat and my blood is burning in my veins. I swing my legs off the bed and try to stand up. My blood rushes to my head and I get fuzzy, so I sit back down again. Finally, after a few minutes of sitting up I feel able to stand. I pull on some pants and feel my way out into the hallway. As I pass, I look at the clock on the bedside table. It's twelve-thirty.

In the hallway I realize I didn't put on my own pants, or rather the pants I had been wearing today. I had accidentally slipped on Jimmy's pants. I can feel his wallet in my pocket. This is good since he had the room key, and I just closed the door and otherwise would have locked myself out.

I did not, however, think to put on shoes. I consider it for a moment, then decide that if I'm going to wander the hallways I should probably put on shoes. I get out the key card and slip back into the room. I put on my own shoes before letting myself back out into the hallway.

It's not until I get downstairs to the main lobby of the hotel that I even think about where I'm going. I'm not really heading anywhere in particular I just need to clear my head. I walk past the front desk without hesitating and step out onto the street. It is a lot different than my late-night walks in Fareport because I'm not alone. There are plenty of cars on the street and even a few people walking along the sidewalk, granted a few of them look homeless, but at least I'm not the only one lost at night.

I take a left and begin walking. I do take careful note of the name of the street and where I'm headed as I walk. Cleveland is a lot bigger than Fareport and I need to be able to find my way back before Jimmy wakes up in the morning.

Rather than being distracting, the lights and sounds of the city are calming. Once I stop paying attention to the individual noises and let it ride over me like waves it becomes a continuous hum. I ride the hum of the cars and subway system and let the lights of the various twenty-four-hour convenience stores and bars lead me down my path to nowhere. The night is chilly, however, and it isn't long before I am looking for a place to get in from the cold.

I find a bar called the Mad Hatter that has lights on, although doesn't look very well-lit inside. I open the door and find it extremely warm inside; in fact, it's almost hot. The inside is crowded with people and there is a low beat playing in the background. I don't see anyone particularly paying attention to the music though, most are standing around drinking and talking, but mostly drinking. I feel somewhat out of place as I'm the only guy in a tee shirt and jeans, but no one else seems to notice or care. In fact, I feel practically invisible in this room full of strangers.

I navigate my way to the bar, pushing my way through the throngs of people trying not to bump into anyone. I find a barstool empty, and I sit and wait for the bartender to make his way over to me. He doesn't seem to be in much of a rush, but then again, neither am I. My mind tries to process what happened today but at the same time I don't really want to think about it. I want to forget all about it. I laugh at the irony.

"Something funny?" I didn't even realize I had laughed out loud until she said it. I turn to face the woman in the skin tight dress sitting next to me. When I say it was skin tight, that doesn't quite do it justice. The bold purple dress came down to her upper thigh covering just enough to make it decent for public. I find my gaze pulled to her voluptuous chest that is practically begging to be let out of its restraints.

"Just had an ironic thought." She's drinking a pink drink out of a martini glass, and while she has half a glass left, she tips it back and swallows it all. Her asymmetrical blonde hair falling back to reveal dangling earrings that matched her dress.

"Buy me a drink," she says, placing the glass on the bar. This gets the bartender's attention, and she waves him over. I don't know how to respond, so she does it for me and says something to the bartender and before I know it there are two drinks sitting in front of me. One is another martini glass for her and then there is a darker drink in front of me.

"I trust you can handle your whiskey?" She smiles at me from behind the rim of her martini. I nod, even though I have no idea. I take a swig and the burn makes me almost wear it. I try to keep a strong face, though, and swallow. I don't know if I'm much of a drinker, so I don't know whether I can handle my liquor, but I can sure tell I'm not a fan of whiskey.

"Not a fan?" She smiles at me like a Cheshire cat.

"Not particularly," I say as I take another swig. I refuse to look like a wuss. Besides, alcohol is supposed to help you forget, isn't it? And isn't that why I came in here?

The bartender makes me give him a credit card before he will give me another drink. I pull out Jimmy's wallet and find one. I'll pay him back I tell myself. Part of me says I shouldn't be doing this but a larger part of me says that I deserve some stress relief. I've had a lot of stress. And I'm about to have a lot of relief. This time it's a clear liquid he pours for me instead of the whiskey. This goes down easier but is still not the best. I hear her say something to the bartender at this point, but the noise of the room seems to have risen in volume.

The lights are also getting brighter, but dimmer at the same time. I can't seem to focus again like I did earlier today. It's similar but also different. I have caused myself to have another attack I think but it's not that. My blood isn't pounding, it's not rushing, it's *dancing*. I don't feel panicked I feel free. The third drink he places in front of me is in a different kind of glass and is a lot prettier. It has multiple colors to it and at least one of them matches her dress, but her dress isn't the same purple it was five minutes ago.

It's green. I don't know how that could be, although everything is starting to look different. The crowd around me has gotten thicker but at the same time when she grabs my hand and pulls me further into the bar, I find it's easier to navigate than it was getting in. We go away from the front door and towards the back. The bar is a lot deeper than I thought it was. When we get to the back, I notice that the dull beat was dull because it wasn't coming from here, it was coming from upstairs.

Up the stairs and towards the music we go. Everything is dark but at the same time I'm able to see everything in bursts. Colors and sound blend together as we become a part of the crowd rather than fight our way through it. The heat of the room is intense, but I barely notice the sweat that is already dripping down my neck and face.

Me and the green or purple dressed woman are extremely close but at the same time free to move on our own without bumping into each other. we pulsate with the crowd as a single giant organism made up of individuals that are at once in unison and also completely unique. I see glimpses of the people around us, but it comes in flashes as the lights change position and color so that every time I blink, it feels like the entire crowd has shifted.

My head feels light, and my vision is beginning to blur at the edges but as the music pounds through my chest I lose the ability to care. I don't even notice as her hands begin to grab a hold of me. We move and sway finding our own rhythm among the others until we are dancing together as one.

Then just as soon as she is there she is gone and replaced by someone else. I don't know how, but suddenly, the woman I'm with is shorter, brunette and wearing a skirt instead of a dress.

The shock of her transformation pulls me out of the dream I was in and I begin to frantically look around for her. I think I see her across the crowd but when I push my way to her, I see it's not her, just a different blonde drinking from a martini glass.

I am near the stairs, so I go down to see if she went down to get more drinks. When I get there, I see that the crowd has grown even larger. Suddenly, I'm suffocating and can't breathe. I stumble my way over to the bartender and see that it's a different bartender but when I ask for my card, he doesn't hesitate. I'm coherent enough when he hands it to me to check and make sure it's Jimmy's. It is. I sign the little paper he hands me with it and try to ignore the very large number next to it. Either those drinks were much more expensive than I thought, or I bought a lot more than the four I could recall. Or was it three? I'm not sure now. I notice on the Budweiser clock behind the bar that my sense of time is extremely off.

It's past three o'clock already.

I force my way back out onto the street and immediately run to the alley to lose the contents of my stomach on the concrete. I feel better when I do, but things are still spinning. In fact, now that I'm outside and it's actually brighter because of the street lamps, it seems to be spinning faster, or at least in a different direction than what I had become somewhat used to.

I lean against the brick wall of the bar and close my eyes for a minute to try and calm my stomach and brain. I try to piece together what had happened in the Mad Hatter. It aptly felt like I just got back from Wonderland. Except I wasn't out of the rabbit hole yet. I still had to find my way back to the hotel.

But I couldn't go back like this. I had to walk it off. I had to sober up. I have no idea if Jimmy has noticed my absence yet but if he has it, he won't appreciate me coming back wasted. I can't think of a better word to describe how I feel at this moment. Like a complete waste. This attempt at trying to forget my life and problems was not how I planned it to go.

I stumble out of the alley and almost run into a homeless man begging for change that I hadn't noticed. I don't respond to his questions as I try to get my bearings for where I'm at. I turn right and head back towards the hotel. I desperately hope that my brain is working enough to get me back there because if not I'm drunk and lost without a clue of where I'm going or who I am. Once again, a complete waste.

The breeze whips past me reminding me that I didn't bother to bring a jacket with me. At least the cold will help sober me up. A taxi pulls over and offers me a ride, but I wave him away. Not that a warm car wouldn't be welcome, but I don't want to spend any more money than I already have if I can avoid it. Besides, I need to sober up before I get back to Jimmy.

I stumble along the street trying to follow my spotty memory back. I am pretty sure I took a left here earlier so now I should turn right because I'm going backwards…right? Or did I turn right the first time? I distinctly remember the all-night pharmacy across the street, but which way was I walking down the street?

After twenty minutes or twenty hours of wandering, my sense of time has gone out with my sense of balance, I finally cave and flag down a taxi. I tell him to take me to the Days Inn. Thankfully, the Islamic gentleman in the front seat takes pity on me and lets me know it's only a block down the street and around the corner if I'd rather walk than pay the $5 it would cost to get me there.

I thank him and have him recount the directions again just to be sure I'm clear before I head off towards the hotel.

The five-minute walk takes me ten minutes because I pause and lean against a wall for a bit. When I get to the front door of the hotel, I think to myself that I am going to have to come up with an explanation for Jimmy because at this point, he's going to know what I went out and did. Even if I were one hundred percent sober walking in, which I'm not, he would be able to smell it on me and on top of that I'm sure I will have a serious hangover when I wake up in the morning for my appointment. My appointment that according to the lobby clock is in a mere six hours.

I find my way up the stairs and let myself into the hotel room and see the bedside light is on. I'm found out, but not by who I planned on. Alex sits up in her bed with the T.V. on mute. I pause for a moment as she looks at me. She holds a finger up to her mouth, then points to the bathroom. I go in and she follows me in.

"He hasn't noticed you're gone. I'd shower before I go back in there. I smelled you the minute you got off the elevator," she says in an almost silent whisper. I mouth a quiet thank you to her as she opens up the door to leave me to my shower, but she pauses and closes it again.

"I don't know what kind of game you're playing, but my brother really likes you. He's never acted the way he does when he's with you. He's… he's happy. Don't hurt him please." She doesn't wait for a reply she simply leaves me alone in the sterile bathroom.

Chapter 16

I wake up to the alarm before the first beep is even over. I quiet it with my hand and immediately try to return to the same position. Jimmy had woken up when I showered but he was too groggy to care why I showered in the middle of the night. Instead, he just welcomed me back into bed with open arms and held me the rest of the night.

Suddenly, I don't want to get out of bed. Part of it is my hangover that I can already feel in my head and stomach, but more of it is simple dread. Dread for what Dr. Green is going to tell me. Yesterday I wanted to know so badly but now I'm frightened. What if it is something that I can't fix? Something that spells the nuthouse? What if this second appointment was all a ruse to give her time to get the paperwork in order for me to get picked up from her office today? I close my eyes and try to will time to stop and leave me here in Jimmy's arms for eternity.

Eternity doesn't stop, however; it keeps inching forward with each breath whether we take it or not. Soon it is time to check out and then I find myself standing in front of Dr. Green's office again. This time, however, I am not expected to go in alone. Jimmy is coming in with me to be there for me. For whatever it is she has to say.

"So, we have a guest with us today?" Dr. Green asks as we both come into the room. We left Alex in the capable hands of Dr. Green's secretary. Everything is exactly the same as yesterday except that she is sporting an aptly green dress today instead of the hot pink blouse. This one has sleeves that cover her tattoo, but it shows a little more cleavage.

"If that's alright?" Jimmy asks as we take a seat on the couch. There is ample room for both of us, but I feel uncomfortable regardless. That dread and hangover are both still very present.

"Whatever Sam would like is fine by me." She takes a seat and holds her notepad and pen ready. I wonder if it's a new sheet or if she is continuing the same notes from yesterday.

"I'd like him to be here." I grab Jimmy's hand lightly. I notice she makes a note of this but for once I don't care.

"Well, then, that's fine. The more the merrier as they say." She smiles at us, but I am not sure any of us feel particularly merry. I know I don't.

"So, you said you would tell me today. What's wrong with me?" You could hear the thought of a pin dropping.

"Well, for starters, I don't like the phrase 'What's wrong with you?'. It implies that what you're going through and how your brain chooses to deal with it is well... wrong and it isn't. It's different and you can change it but it's not like you have a disease. It's not something that can be cured with a pill." At this, I feel Jimmy squeeze my hand.

"Now pills may help you get there and that's okay, but I am not able to prescribe them to you. I also don't want you to take my word as gospel either. Psychology is not an exact science. What I'm giving you is my opinion. You are more than welcome to get a second opinion. I would almost insist on it because what I am going to suggest is very abnormal.

"But before I say it, I have a question for you. Why haven't you turned yourself into the police?" The dread suddenly boils, and I feel like I might vomit. Has she called the police? I thought she couldn't. Jimmy grips my hands in reassurance.

"Why would he?" Jimmy stands up for me like my knight in shining armor.

"I'd like to know what Sam thinks." Dr. Green doesn't look at Jimmy when she says this, but I can see she doesn't particularly enjoy having someone to stand between her and I.

"Because I don't want them to arrest me."

"So, you assume that you must have killed Sara?" She says this matter-of-factly with barely the hint of a question mark.

"No." I'm beginning to feel a splash of confusion mixed in my dread cocktail.

"Don't you think that if you didn't the police would be able to prove that? If you turned yourself in and it proved you didn't kill her you wouldn't be arrested."

"But they might not be able to prove it."

"Aren't the chances of them proving that improved by your turning yourself in?" I feel like a witness in a trial. Or worse yet like the suspect.

"Well, yes… but." I'm not sure what she wants me to say, or what I should say.

"But then, what if they can't prove it because it isn't true. What if you did kill her? If let's say you were to figure it out yourself without the police? If you knew you had killed her. Would you turn yourself in then?" I suddenly feel extremely small.

"I don't know…"

"Wouldn't you feel morally obligated to turn yourself in?" My stomach is tied up in so many knots a sailor couldn't untie it.

"What are you trying to get at?" There's my knight in shining armor again slaying my dragons.

"Sorry if that was combative," she concedes, the cross examination disappears and is replaced by the kind face from yesterday. "What I'm trying to say is I think you feel that even if you killed her, and that's still a big if, then *you* still didn't kill her. Does that make sense?" It doesn't. I try to think it through, but the confusion must show on my face.

"You told me how you had separated your normal self from the person who was acting when you were having your black out episodes. Kevin, you called him, correct?"

"That's right."

"Well, whether it was Kevin or whoever you were before you lost your memory, it wasn't Sam who killed her. Because you can't remember it."

"I still don't follow."

"Have you ever heard of Dissociative Identity Disorder?" Neither of us respond. "No? Well, I'm not surprised. It's an extremely rare subsection of schizophrenia. You probably know it by its more common but incorrect name, now don't be frightened when I say it but I'm sure you have heard of Multiple Personality Disorder."

I can't say for sure where I've heard of it, but I know I did. One of those many things that I somehow just know, even though I don't know my own age. However, what I do know of it does scare me whether she warned me or not.

"Now most of what people know about DID is what they've seen in films. Like everything else, it's been very much dramatized by Hollywood. In fact, it's not even able to be an actual diagnosis because it isn't prevalent enough to be studied. They aren't even sure it exists. The basic idea, however, is that whether due to physical trauma, emotional trauma, or drug usage you could cause your brain to act as if there are two or more people in a single body. One moment you could believe yourself to be one person. But then, in a moment, you could be someone completely different." She stops to let all that information sink in.

I try to comprehend it. What she is saying makes a lot of sense with what I've been feeling. I even thought that first night that the person who woke up on the dock was different than who must have laid there unconscious. I have thought of that night as my first night, not just since my amnesia but first night of my life, like I was born that night.

"So, what do you think caused it?" Jimmy always the practical one.

"I think it was possibly caused by the amnesia. The stress of not having a self, added with the emotional trauma of the murder would mean that your brain might create multiple selves in order to compensate."

"But that would mean that I wasn't afflicted by it … before." I don't want to say out loud what I was thinking: *When I killed her.*

"Not necessarily. I mean, yes, in that scenario, you are correct. But as we don't know what happened prior to your waking up, there is no guarantee that you didn't have this same disorder before. We would have to find someone who knew you before you lost your memory."

I think of Helen, but she didn't really know me. She met me once. Then I think of her husband who obviously knew my sister, but that doesn't mean he knew me. She died when I was very young, I don't even know if I really knew her.

Does anyone know who I was?

Sara might have. But there wasn't any chance of talking to her any time soon.

"What does this all mean?" I say not necessarily looking for an answer. It is less a question and more a cry for help.

"Well, as I said, it's not been studied at length, so there isn't a known way to treat it. Firstly, I'd like for you to meet with me regularly. Your case seems to be mild and doesn't seem to affect your ability to function. Yesterday's episode did not last very long and there was only a short part of it while you were switching personalities in which you were incapacitated. So, I don't think we need to think about confinement."

"By confinement you mean the nuthouse?" Jimmy's hand is clenching mine with such force I can feel my knuckles cracking, but somehow, it's more comforting than painful.

"I mean more along the lines of hospitalization, but as I said, I don't feel in this case it's necessary. Your episodes seem to be caused by stress, so as much as you can learn to deal with your stress the better off you will be. I would like to start working with you on some stress controlling techniques, some meditation exercises so when you start to feel an episode coming on and you start to feel stressed like yesterday, then you can try to control it."

"Wait, hold on; I still don't understand. Did this cause his amnesia?"

"I don't know for sure. It is common for those who have claimed to have DID to report amnesia of what happens when their alternate identities present themselves; however, I've never heard of complete self-amnesia being a side effect. It is possible but it is also just as possible that the amnesia was caused by something else completely, perhaps the head injury, and is, in fact, the root cause of the DID itself. Right now, it's a chicken and egg situation. Either could have caused the other, we need to get more information first to understand fully.

"For that reason, I would like you to go see a neurologist."

"We don't have that kind of money." I say this and grip Jimmy's hand back when I see he is about to protest. "We can't afford to pay for regular sessions with you let alone a neurologist."

"Look, you need help. You need to figure out what is going on before these episodes become stronger or more prevalent. As I said, your case seems quite mild, but it could progress if not handled correctly. I might be able to work something out if you needed me to and, given the rarity of your situation, I'm sure a neurologist could be willing to do the same." I see true concern in her eyes.

"Let me help you. You can't tackle this on your own."

I nod my head in agreement and spend the next forty-five minutes going over breathing techniques and meditation exercises to calm myself during times of stress. Jimmy doesn't say much but he's there for me whenever I need a hand.

As the clock whittles down our time to nothing, we stand to leave.

"I realize it's quite a drive for you, so I don't think that weekly meetings will be beneficial or effective. But here is my number and my email. I want you to keep in contact with me and let me know how things are progressing. I will get you in contact with a neurologist and if you need to come see me again don't hesitate."

I thank her and I go to follow Jimmy out to the outer office.

"Sam. Wait a moment." She deftly moves up beside me and closes the door, so it is just the two of us.

"What was that about?" Jimmy asks when we all get back in the truck. I mumble something about her asking me about who's money I had used to pay for her session.

"I think she wanted to make sure I didn't use your money without telling you," I say without looking at him.

I stare out the window as we pull out onto the highway. Heading back to Fareport. Heading back from our getaway.

Chapter 17

We pull into the driveway and we see that Callahan is standing on our porch waiting for us. Christine is standing on the other side of the screen door and we can hear them arguing the minute we get out of the car.

"You can't just stand there forever! They told me not to let anyone in while they were gone. That includes you." We had asked Christine to watch Jimmy's father for the night while we went over to Cleveland. Jimmy had thought that Callahan would stop by.

"They are here now, so I'll be getting off the porch real shortly now." He turns to us with a smile on his face.

"What are you so smug about?" Alex pipes up.

"Why don't you ask your friend Sam? Or is it Kevin?" I stop in my tracks one foot on the porch, one foot on the ground.

"What are you talking about?" Jimmy speaks for me.

"Well, it's kind of funny. You see you've been telling everyone your names, Sam. At least that's what the word is down at the diner." Chrissy looks at me funny, almost asking me to explain what Callahan is talking about.

"That's because it's my name." I desperately think through my head and try to figure out how he would have gotten Kevin's name. I didn't use it any time after that first night.

"Then how come I found this ID with your picture on it and the name Kevin Price?" He holds up a clear evidence baggy with a driver's license inside. I step closer and sure enough it's my face.

A waterfall hits me in the chest. I don't know what to think or how to feel. Everything is happening so fast. I start to feel dizzy. How should I react? With joy at finally knowing something about who I am? Confusion at the different last name? Or fear at the implications of it being in the hand of Detective Callahan?

"Found this in a purse we got out of the lake. Would you like to tell me what it would be doing there?"

"I have no idea." I grab the baggy out of his hand. He at least allows me to take it and have a closer look.

"I think you and I need to have a serious talk." I don't even fully process his words as I stare at the license eating the words upon it like a starving man who finally finds himself in front of a smorgasbord.

"Don't say anything, Sam." Jimmy puts his hand reassuringly on my shoulder. I lean against the banister of the porch.

Birth date: January 7, 1992. Height: six feet, two inches. Weight: 175 pounds. Address: 3612 Rudy Road, Greensboro, NC. I have an address. I have a home. I don't know anything other than the address, but I know that I live there. My heart feels like it's going to beat right out of my chest.

"I'm twenty-six." I turn to Jimmy. I don't understand his expression, but I don't care. I know how old I am. I know how tall I am. I know where I'm from. I even know my middle name. Andrew. Kevin Andrew Price. "Kevin Andrew Price." I feel the words cross my lips and it's like a smell that you can't quite place but you know you love. It makes you feel all warm inside. "Kevin Andrew Price." I say it again, this time turning and facing Detective Callahan. His face shows his confusion.

A voice in the back of my mind reminds me that he doesn't know I lost my memory. I know I shouldn't let him know that, but I can't stop myself from saying it again.

"Kevin Andrew Price."

I have a name.

"Okay. Enough. You care to explain this?" The detective snatches it out of my hands. I have to fight the knee jerk reaction of wanting to hit him. I reach out to grab it back, but he holds it out of my reach. I feel a little like a bullied kid on a playground.

"Give it back. It's mine, isn't it?" A smile crosses his confused face.

"You can have it back if you explain how it ended up in a dead girls purse." A glint crosses his eye. Chrissy gasps.

"Chrissy, take Alex inside." Jimmy points to the door without taking his eyes off of Callahan. Alex is about to retort, but then Chrissy takes her by the shoulder and leads her inside.

“Give it back.” I try to hold it back, but I feel my rage seep through my words.

“Tell me how it ended up in Sara Jefferson’s purse.” He holds the bag up like a piece of candy. A treat for me if I just do his trick.

“Don’t say a word, Sam.” Jimmy emphasizes the name to Callahan as if to declare sides. “Not without a lawyer present.”

“Okay. If you wanna do it that way, we can go downtown and get you a lawyer.” He steps down off the porch as if to head to his car.

“Are you arresting him?”

“I could. His license was found in a dead girls purse and, as of yet, I haven’t heard an alibi or an explanation.”

“I told you he was here with us. Me and my sister.”

“You see that’s the funny thing. I checked that out. And he may have been here, but you weren’t.” I see the realization cross Jimmy’s face before Callahan speaks. “I asked your coworker before you got here. Yeah, she tried avoiding my questions, but I did get her to answer one question. You were working the night that Sara died. And that means that the only people here to vouch for mister Price’s whereabouts that night are a twelve-year-old girl and a very senile old man.” Callahan smiled like he had just won the lottery.

“Sam. Don’t say anything.” I look from him to Callahan and back again. This all is becoming very tense.

“So, here’s the situation boys. One of you is coming down to the station with me.”

“One of us?”

“Well, either Kevin is coming down to willingly answer any of my questions. Or I’m going to take you in for obstruction of justice.” He turns his glare from me to Jimmy. “You see it isn’t a good idea to lie to a police officer. Especially one who’s leading a murder investigation.”

This is too much for me at this moment. I take a hold of the banister.

“Come on, Sam. He’s bluffing.”

“Really? You think I’m bluffing? That’s funny. Because these cuffs say otherwise.” He holds them up and takes a few steps towards Jimmy. Then he pauses and turns to me. “So, what’s it gonna be Kevin? You gonna come down and answer my questions? Or am I gonna arrest your boyfriend?”

“Don’t do it, Sam. Let’s go inside.”

“Be careful. I might have to add resisting arrest to your rap sheet.”

"Alright. I'll answer your questions." I'm not fully aware of saying the words until I hear them for myself. Jimmy glares at me. Callahan's smile widens so much I'm afraid his face might split in two.

"You don't mind if I record this, do you?"

We sit in a room at the police station. I feel like I'm on an episode of Law and Order. It's the typical austere square room with a single table and two chairs. It doesn't have a two-way mirror, but it does have a window with blinds on the other side. Callahan places a recording device in the center of the table.

"Shouldn't I have a lawyer present?"

"It's not necessary, but if you'd like I can put you in lock up until someone from the public defender's office shows up. It is kinda late, so they may not be here till the morning." He sits back waiting for my response. When I don't give one, he continues, "That's what I thought. Look. You're not under arrest. I just have a few questions."

I try to wrestle with myself. I don't know why I let myself get into this situation. I thought Jimmy would be here with me but when he tried to come, Callahan told him that only a lawyer could be present while he was questioning me.

"Where were you the night of August 21?" The image of the dock flashes in front of my eyes followed by Sara's smiling face. I try to control my breathing, but I begin to panic. I don't know what I'm doing.

"I was at Jimmy's house."

Short answers. Just answer the question. Don't extrapolate. I don't know if that's what I'm supposed to do but it sounds right.

"Okay, and who was there with you? Who can vouch for you being there?"

"Alex and Jimmy's father."

"Right. For the record, Alex is Jimmy's twelve-year-old sister. Is that correct?"

"That's correct."

"And Jimmy's father, Harold Evans, has serious mental issues, isn't that correct."

"I don't—"

"He tried to kill himself with depression pills a few years back, isn't that right?"

"I don't think—"

"He needs pretty constant care, doesn't he?"

"I can't say—"

"Look, Kevin. I'm not trying to be mean. I just want to make sure we have the facts straight. For the record, of course." I glare at him in response. "So, let's just say he isn't in tip top shape mentally. How about that?

"What did you guys do that night?"

I try to think if he has asked that question. I don't remember. I make a mental note to say something to Alex to confirm this later.

"We watched T.V."

"What did you watch?"

"I don't remember."

"I see."

"Is that all you wanted?"

"Oh, no. We are just getting started. Do you know this girl?" He pulls a picture of Emily Bradshaw out of nowhere and places it in front of me.

"No." Finally, a question I can answer without lying.

"Let the record show I have just shown Mr. Price a picture of Emily Bradshaw. Now how about her?" Emily is replaced by Sara Jefferson as if he were doing a magic trick.

Sara's smiling face is the same picture they used on television but this one isn't cropped. It's her graduation photo. She's in a black robe, so it's from college. She looks so happy. This was probably one of the happiest days of this young girls life. And if it is being used by the police as a reference it was probably also one of her last. She'd never smile again. And I could be the cause of that.

"No." I say it as flatly as possible, but I can't look at the picture. I look to the side instead. Callahan notices this and leaves the picture on the table. I know he is doing it on purpose. Taunting me.

"Let the record show that I have just shown Mister Price a picture of Sara Jefferson." He pauses and lets the name hang in the air. "Have you seen this purse before?"

Now he brings out a photo of a purse. It's a small purple purse. It has a floral pattern on it. There's a ruler next to it showing that it's a small clutch. Hand sized and the perfect size for some money and credit cards.

"No." I feel a little like a broken record.

"Is this your Driver's License?" He places the evidence baggie in front of me with my license in it. Seeing it next to Sara's face creates a void in my stomach. She had a home, too. She had a birthday. She had a middle name.

An idea strikes me.

"No."

If Callahan had been standing, he would have taken a step back.

"I'm sorry. Let me repeat the question. Is this your driver's license?"

I look him in the eye.

"No."

"Do remember you are under oath."

"I remember." It's one of the few things I do.

"And you are saying that you are not Kevin Andrew Price?"

"That wasn't your question."

"Well, I'm asking that now." It's clear that I've flustered him, but the game is still on. I haven't won yet. "Are you Kevin Andrew Price?"

"No."

"Do I need to remind you that you stated your name at the beginning of this recording?"

"No, you don't; my short-term memory is fully intact."

"And what did you say your name was?"

"Kevin Price."

"So, is it your name or not?"

"Kevin Price is my name. Andrew isn't."

I'm not sure if this plan is going to work but I figure it's worth a shot.

"Do you have your driver's license on you at the moment?"

"No, I do not."

"Where is it?" I can see he is seething underneath his hard exterior.

"I lost it."

"If Andrew isn't your middle name, then what is?"

"It's Samuel."

"Do you expect me to believe that there are two Kevin Price's and they both happen to look exactly alike?"

"I don't expect you to believe anything. I'm just merely stating the truth as I know it to be. MY name is Kevin Samuel Price and that is not my driver's license. Now are we done here?"

"No." He sits back in his chair thinking.

I feel like we are playing a game of chess. I'm not sure how to play it but I think I just surged ahead.

“Where are you from Kevin?”

“I came here from Boston.” Not exactly a lie.

“And what did you do in Boston?”

“A little bit of this a that.” His eyes narrow at me.

“What was your last place of employment?”

“I was a server.” Also, not a lie.

“Where did you live in Boston?”

“I don’t remember the address.”

“How convenient.”

“What does this have to do with anything?”

“I’m asking the questions. When did you come to Fareport?”

“A few weeks ago.”

“Why did you come here?”

“I needed to start over.”

“Why did you come to Fareport?”

“Because that was the last stop on the bus.”

“Do you have any family in Boston?”

“No.”

“Anyone we can call to get confirmation about what you say?”

“No.”

“No one. Not a single soul in Boston knows you, knew you were headed here?”

“No.”

“If I took your picture and went to Boston and showed it around, would anyone recognize you?”

“I can’t answer to someone else’s memory.” He lays off of his firing of questions and takes a moment. He smiles at me. Not in a happy way but in the way you smile at an opponent when, despite yourself, your enjoying the game. He’s enjoying the struggle. He wants it to be over because he wants to win but at the same time, he considers me a worthy opponent.

“Let’s take a different angle. What is your relationship with Daniel Evans?” It takes me a moment to register that he is talking about Jimmy.

“We’re friends.”

“Is your relationship physical?” I can see from his face that he’s asking these questions to push my buttons.

“Is that any of your business?”

“I’m a detective in a police investigation. I need to know why you’re staying at his house. Answer the question.”

"Yes. Our relationship is physical."

"Would you say it's romantic?" I can feel the jeering going on in his voice.

"I don't have to answer that. That doesn't have anything to do with this."

"I need to know if you would be willing to lie for Jimmy."

"I'm not lying and even if I was, why would I be lying for Jimmy?"

"I don't know why you would. Why don't you tell me?" He's sitting forward on the edge of his seat, watching me squirm.

"Am I under arrest?"

"No."

"So, I'm free to go." I stand up.

"Sure. Go right ahead." I walk over and open the door. He reaches out and turns off the recorder. "Too bad you don't have your driver's license." The question seems so strange that I turn.

"Why?"

"Because when Mr. Evans comes to pick you up, I'm going to book him for obstructing justice and lying to a police officer. So, someone is going to have to drive his truck back out to the farm. But since you don't have your license… well." I close the door; just like he knew I was going to.

"How long are you going to hold that over my head?"

"Until you answer my questions. All of them."

"How many more do you have?"

"Just one more." He reaches out and turns on the recorder again.

"Did you dump Sara Jefferson in the lake?" I'm still standing at the door, so he isn't facing me. I'm not sure if it was just chance that he decided to ask that question and not ask if I killed her. To an observer the two questions mean the same thing but, in reality, they have very different meanings. Up until now, I can claim amnesia for all of the answers I lied about. I'm not sure if it would work or not but I could claim I answered them to the best of my knowledge. But this question here would be an outright lie. I know I did it. It happened after I woke up. After that night. After whatever happened before. After I lost my memory. After everything started to fall apart.

"No." I open the door and walk out of the interview room.

"I need to figure out what happened." I'm sitting back in Jimmy's kitchen. Chrissy is in the other room with Alex and her father. Jimmy sits across from me. I just finished telling him every detail of the interview. I left out the bit about our relationship. I know Callahan was just trying to push my buttons.

"I agree with you. What do you want to do next?"

"I need to find out why I was here. I know I told Helen I wouldn't, but I need to talk to Philip."

"What do you think he's going to tell you?"

"I don't know but when I came to town before I lost my memory, I tried to talk to him. I don't know why. I need to figure it out. It had something to do with Angela, who I thought was my sister. But I don't know. Now that I know my last name, I know that I wasn't a Cartwright. At least not legally."

"You could have been adopted."

"Maybe. I don't know. But I'm going to bed." I am just now realizing that because of my outing the night before I am running on very little sleep other than what I got on the car ride home. Which didn't amount to much.

"I think I'm gonna stay up for a bit."

I'm asleep when I hit the pillow.

My mind is a torrent of images with no fluid connection.

I see Jimmy standing in the middle of a field wrapped in a giant red sheet. the wind blows the sheet in front of his face.

Suddenly, I'm on the dock and Sara is standing on the still water as if it were solid. She walks towards me not causing a ripple. Just as she gets to me the dock crumbles and I fall through.

I'm standing in Jimmy's kitchen, but the entire room is on fire. But instead of hearing the roar of the flames, I hear Callahan's last question over and over and over.

"Did you dump Sara Jefferson in the lake?" The flames scream at me.

I'm standing in a hall of mirrors, but every mirror shows a different image of me. They are all the same but in different positions and with different facial expressions. Suddenly, they each shatter one by one.

I'm lying on the ground in a deep hole. Jimmy appears at the edge of the hole, holding a shovel. So does Detective Callahan and Sara. They all have shovels. Jimmy is the first to throw dirt in. They all three ignore my screams of protest as they bury me alive.

"Sam! Sam!" I am pulled out by Jimmy's arms holding onto me.

I'm back in bed.

"You were screaming." Jimmy's eyes look very worried. I don't know what time it is or how long he's been there.

“It was… just a nightmare.” I think of telling him what it was, but I think better of it. I’m not sure I could explain it. Besides, the memory of the images is slipping through my fingers like fog.

“Well, it’s over now.”

I roll over and enfold myself into him, trying to touch as much of my body with his. As comforting as his words are I fear that this nightmare is far from over.

Chapter 18

The next morning, Jimmy drives me into town. We leave Alex at home to keep watch on Harold. When we pull up to the law offices of Duncan & King, suddenly, a sense of wariness overcomes me. Jimmy opens his door, but I can't bring myself to do it. Instead, I sit there staring at the small building in front of me with the letterhead over the windows.

"Sam?" he asks and looks at me concerned.

"What if we find out I did it?" I don't take my eyes off of the brick building.

"Then we will deal with it." He takes my hand and I turn and look at him.

We get out of the truck and walk up to the front door. I open it into a small waiting room. There is an obese woman sitting behind a desk working on her computer. She is wearing a green blouse and obnoxiously blue jewelry to match her large, rimmed glasses that sit on the tip of her nose. She looks over them at us as we walk in. A momentary recognition crosses her face as she sees me.

"Mr. King is in a meeting with a client," she says without even asking. She must have let me in to see him the last time. "Have a seat. I'll let him know your here." She stands and turns to one of the two doors that lead to offices. I notice a condescending look she gives Jimmy just before she closes the door behind her.

We have a seat in some of the uncomfortable chairs by the front window. Everything in the office is beige or brown. there isn't any decoration on the walls except for a single award on the wall. I can't read it from so far away, but it has a small picture of the secretary inset in it. Perhaps an employee of the month sympathy gift. Her desk has a nameplate that read Ms. Blumenthall.

"He says he doesn't want to see you." Ms. Blumenthall reenters. This time I catch a glimpse of the room behind her. I don't see Philip King, but I see that there is no one else sitting in front of his desk.

"Please. Just ask him if we can have five minutes. It's very important." Jimmy says this and puts a hand on my knee to keep me from standing up to leave.

"I'm sorry, but he was very upset last time you came to see him, and he has said he does not wish to see you. Now, please leave." With this she places her overlarge self back in her chair and returns to the computer.

"Come on, we will come up with something else to try."

I'm not sure exactly what comes over me, but I don't accept it. Suddenly, I'm done with taking things that happen to me. In the past week I have been a passive onlooker, letting things happen to me but not taking charge. That stops now.

"You can't go in there!" I ignore her protests as I push my way into Mr. King's office.

"Excuse me, but I need to speak with you, and I am not leaving this office until I do, so quit pretending you have someone back here and let me talk to you! I just want you to help me understand—" I have more to say, but I am thrown off balance by who I see when I walk into the office.

Mr. King is a middle-aged man with glasses and a short haircut. He is wearing a suit with a tie that had Tweety Bird and Sylvester the cat on it. He looks different than what I had expected. I can't tell you what it was I thought he looked like, but I guess it would be more unique. The man sitting on the other side of the desk looks so bland, so beige like his office, that if he were in a crowd, you wouldn't be able to even see him.

It isn't him who stopped me in my tracks, however. It is the person on the other side of the desk. From my seat out in the waiting room it looked like there was no one in there with Mr. King but I see now that was because he is over to the side of the desk filling out paperwork.

"What are you doing here, Sam?" Ronnie looked at me quizzically.

"Get out of here!" Philip King stood up. His beige face was turning purple.

"I'm sorry, but I really need to talk to you. I'm not going to leave until I do." My tone is much less defiant now that I know Ronnie is in the room, but I am still insistent.

"Pamela! Call the police!"

"Now there's no reason to do that, Philip. Sam's a good cookie. I'm sure he didn't mean any harm. What's the matter, Sam?" Ronnie, of course, has no idea why Philip is kicking me out.

"Yes. I need to have an officer come to the offices of Duncan and King. I have a violent person who needs to be removed." Pamela is holding the corded phone and glaring at me through her thick glasses.

"Violent? Why, Sam isn't violent. He stayed with me for a few days this week. He's a good guy. Just talk to him." He leans over and signs the top document. "See, now I'm all done. And fifteen minutes early. So, you've got plenty of time to talk to him." Ronnie doesn't wait for a response. Instead, he just stands up, as steadily as a man with a wooden leg can and walks out of the room and closes the door. This leaves me and Mr. King alone in his office. I hear him talking to Pamela outside. He is trying to get her to call off the dogs, but she isn't listening.

"Well, have a seat I guess." Mr. King is obviously perturbed by the turn of events. He picks up the phone and presses a button. "Call off the police, Pamela." He hangs up without waiting for a response.

We sit in silence for a few moments. He is clearly waiting for me to start, and I am not sure where to start. Jimmy was supposed to be in here with me when I did this but, suddenly, I am afraid that if I try to get him in here too all of Ronnie's help will be lost and I'll be back where I started, stuck in the waiting room with the cops on their way.

"I didn't come here to talk about her." I say this, even though it isn't completely true. I do want to find out what he knows about my sister and my family, but it isn't the most pressing thing on my mind right now. It also would probably antagonize him further and lead to me out on my ass.

"Then what do you want?"

"I want to know what happened last time I came to see you." I get a confused look as a response. "I had… an accident." I feel horrible expecting people to be honest and tell me the truth while feeding them only lies. "I hit my head and I woke up with no memory of who I was or where I was. I don't have any idea what I was doing here." He doesn't look like he believes me.

"Well, perhaps that is for the best. You were just digging up the past that didn't need to be dug up." He uses putting Ronnie's forms away as an excuse to avoid eye contact.

“Did I give you my name?” I already know what Callahan believes my name to be, but I keep grasping at straws in the hopes that there is still some way to explain all of this with me not being Kevin Price, the man who’s driver’s license was in a dead girl’s purse.

“You said your name was Kevin. You came here looking for your parents. Your search led you to me. I’m not sure what else you want me to tell you.”

“Did I mention anything else about who I was? How did I find you?”

“I don’t know how you found me. I hadn’t talked about Angela in years. Your PI friend must have been extremely thorough to find my name.”

“My PI friend?” This is completely knew. I haven’t heard a word about a PI. I feel like a dog with a bone.

“You mentioned last time that your private investigator gave you my name.” He finally looks like he might believe that I don’t have my memory.

“I didn’t happen to mention my private investigator’s name, did…?” He pauses for a minute. Perhaps now that he actually believes me, he is actually trying to help.

“No, I don’t think you did. But I do remember you referring to a ‘her’ so that might help to narrow it down. I’m sorry.” His anger as almost completely left him now.

“Well, at least that’s something. Did we talk much about my sister?”

“Look.” He cuts me off before I am even able to finish my question. “I’m sorry, but I don’t want to talk about her. You have to understand that that was a lifetime ago. I’ve worked very hard to not think about … the Cartwrights for twenty-five years. I’m not about to start now.” I’m not sure why it didn’t click before just now, perhaps it’s because I didn’t really know my age until last night, but twenty-five years seems an odd length of time.

“Has it been twenty-five years?” He looks confused by the question. He thinks for a moment.

“Well, yeah, it must be somewhere around there. The last time I saw Angela was in 1992, just before-.” For a moment, I lose him to memories. He even gives me the oddest look, but then he shakes his head and brings himself back to the present. “But anyway, as I said, it was a long time ago.”

I’m not sure if there is or not but it feels like it is too close to be a coincidence.

“That would have been when my mother was pregnant with me.” At this the beige overtakes Philip once again.

"Look. I don't have anything else I can tell you. Now I have some work to do so if you'd please see yourself out." He stands up and gestures to the door. I realize that I'm not going to get anything else out of him, but I feel good that I have gotten something even if it was just a blip on a timeline and a mystery PI.

"Thank you for your help," I say as he closes the door without a reply. Ronnie is still in the waiting room. Him and Jimmy are talking much to Pamela's chagrin. She turns her glare to me until I greet Jimmy and we head out.

"So, did you take care of what you needed?" Ronnie asks in the parking lot.

"Not exactly. But I got something."

"Look, I don't know what you got going on and I'm not sure I want to." My mind flashes back to when Ronnie thought I was mixed up in drugs because of the wad of cash I had hidden under my bed. "But you seem like a good kid. Be careful you don't get mixed up in something you shouldn't be."

"I'm not I promise."

"All I'm saying is someone who has the kind of cash you do and disappears without a word only to show up at a defense attorney's office? Sure sounds like trouble to me." He turns and walks to his car. "Stop by the apartment sometime and I'll give you back your deposit. No sense in you paying for the whole month when you weren't even there a week."

"Wait. Ronnie." He stops and turns. "What were you doing at a defense attorney's office?" He smiles a devilish smile.

"You can't expect people to tell you things when you don't tell them yourself. You fellas have a good day. And don't forget to stop by and get your money." He gets in his beat up Buick and starts it up.

"So, what did you find out?" Jimmy asks as we get back into the truck.

"Not much, but I need to find a PI. I apparently hired one to help me find my family. That's who led me to Mr. King." I don't mention the odd year coincidence I noticed. It seems too trivial, and I'm not sure what it even means.

"Well, then, let's find the PI. Do you have any idea how to find him?" He pulls out onto the road headed for home.

"It's actually a *she*. Other than that, I have no idea how to find her."

"Well, if you came here looking for your parents and you hired a PI it would make sense if you hired one from here rather than from wherever you came from. So, we could look up Private Investigators in the area and see how many of them are women. Then it's just a matter of calling them."

"What would I do without you?" He turns to me as I say this and smiles.

He makes a few turns, and we end up at the library. We go inside and are greeted by the same prissy girl as last time. This time she doesn't say anything as we head to the computers.

"Why don't you try to find a phone number for my dad while I look up PIs. See if you can find any information about Robert Cartwright," I say as I sit at a computer.

"Well, someone's taking charge."

"Sorry, I just—" He smiles at me from his computer.

"I'm just messing with you. Honestly, it's cute." He winks as he pulls up Google on his computer.

I do the same and type in Private Investigators Fareport Ohio. I come up with a long list but most of them are companies rather than individuals. How am I going to figure out which ones have female investigators let alone which one I was working with?

I change my search to 'female private investigators' and hit enter. I'm about to go back and add in a location when the first article that pops up catches my eye. It's from the Cleveland Herald.

It's about the murders.

"Female murder victim identified as Sara Jefferson." I don't even notice that I read it out loud. I quiet myself but Jimmy doesn't notice, or he chooses not to react. I continue reading the article trying to see why it would have popped up for my search. I catch it on the third line of the article.

"I've found her." I curse to myself.

"Already? Don't you need to call her and ask first? There has to be more than one female PI."

"Oh, I'm sure there are plenty of female private investigators but only one popped up dead on a dock." I highlight the line and turn my monitor to him, so he can read it: "The second victim's name was just released. Sara Jefferson was a private investigator in Lake County."

"I can't call her to confirm but I don't see a need to. This explains how I knew her and what we were doing together."

"But it doesn't explain what you were doing on the dock." He looks at my face and sees I'm upset at the new dead end. "Look on the bright side. You knew her. That means something. We can talk to her coworkers or something and find out what she knew. Maybe someone can point us in the right direction." He turns back to his computer and quickly types something into the search bar.

"Are you having any luck finding Robert Cartwright?" I try to turn and look at his screen, but the article image just finally loaded on my screen and it's a picture of Sara and it pulls my eyes back. I close the window.

"Not a phone number. But I found out who he was. He was a police officer. In fact, he was a police chief. He retired in 1993. But it's weird, he wasn't that old when he retired. He was only forty-three when he retired."

I pull up my window again and type something into the search bar to confirm my thoughts.

"That was soon after my mother died. that's probably why."

"Well, I still haven't found a phone number or address but at least we know what he did for a living. That's gotta help us somehow. Besides, I haven't been digging for very long."

"I feel like all we come across are dead ends. I wish I could just flip a switch and remember what I knew a week and a half ago." I put my head down on the table in frustration. I feel his hand on my back, trying to comfort me.

"If you found it once you can find it again. Besides, you don't know, maybe you hadn't found your father even with the help of the PI. If you had I don't see why you guys would have been meeting on the dock." He raises a valid point.

"I wish I hadn't lost my memory to begin with. All of this would be so much simpler…"

"I for one am torn on that account." I sit up and give him a look of confusion. "Well, yes, I hate that you have no memory and wish you could remember everything but at the same time…" He chews his words for a moment before continuing, "If you hadn't lost your memory, you might not have ended up naked in my shed. And I might not have met you." He looks over at me and smiles. A sweet smile that tells me everything is going to be okay. If for no other reason than because we are going to figure this all out together.

He glances back at his screen and I see his eyes light up.

"Here's something! Not only was your father a police officer, but he also served over seas. He was a Gulf War vet. He technically didn't serve with the army. But he was recognized for being a part of a private security contractor over there around 1990. Doesn't look like he was over there for very long. I'm not sure if it can help us find him but it's something."

"I think it might help us find him. I happen to know someone else who was a Gulf War vet."

"Really who?"

"You just met him. Ronnie."

When we arrived at Ronnie's apartment, he wasn't home, so we went next door to grab a bite to eat while we waited.

"What will you boys have to eat?" Chrissy asks as she sets us down at a booth. Ironically enough it's the same booth where we almost kissed that night so long ago.

"I'm just gonna have a burger." Jimmy nods the same and Chrissy gets us our drinks.

"Either of you wanna throw on an apron and clock in today? We had a no call no show."

"Oh, really? Who?"

"Dany. I wouldn't be surprised except Holly called her and couldn't get a hold of her. Normally When her mom calls, she caves and comes in. Anyway, interested?"

"Nah, thanks, though." She shrugs and walks away.

"You should stay," I say to him. "You need the money. You haven't got class or anything today, do you?"

"No, but I was going to keep helping you—"

"I can manage on my own. You would be helping me by making sure that somebody has money. I'd stay and help them out, but you'd make more tips than I would."

"This is true." The one shift I had worked last week, the girls had not been quiet about the fact that Jimmy made a lot more money than anyone else at the restaurant.

"Look, I'll be fine. You stay and work for a while. I'll talk to Ronnie, see if I can get in contact with my dad, and I'll come back when I'm done. Then we can go home and have dinner with Alex."

"What are you gonna do if you have to drive somewhere to see your father?"

The thought hadn't occurred to me. Do I know how to drive? I assume I did before my memory loss, but I wasn't sure. And even if I did, that doesn't mean I could drive Jimmy's truck. I am almost positive I didn't know how to drive a stick shift.

"Well, If I do, then I'll just come back and wait, but I can at least talk to Ronnie and who knows, he has a car maybe he'd drive me? Look, the point is we need to not let this get in the way of things. I appreciate your helping me out with everything, but you have to think of your family, too." He sighs.

"Alright. But you are gonna take my phone. Call me on the store phone if you need anything."

"I'm just gonna be next door…" He glares at me like a protective parent. "Alright." He slides the phone across the table to me just as Chrissy returns with our food.

"Hey, Ronnie hasn't been in today, has he? I was trying to find him." Krissy seems taken aback by my sudden question.

"You mean Ronald?" She says this like she suddenly has a bad taste in her mouth.

"Umm… the one next door?" I'd never heard anyone say Ronald, but I guess Ronnie was short for something.

"No. He wasn't in today. At least not that I saw." With that she walks away and doesn't even ask if we need anything else. It's not until we go to pay that Jimmy is able to talk to her and tell her he would stay to work.

"Here let me help you with those groceries." I've been waiting on Ronnie's front step for about twenty minutes after I finished lunch with Jimmy. Ronnie pulled up with a car load of plastic bags from Kroger.

"I keep bumping into you today, don't I?" he says as he hands me a bag with a six pack in it. I notice that there are a few bags that have them. "I told you to stop by, but I didn't think it would be today." He chuckles as he searches for his keys.

"Well, I really wasn't stopping for that—" He turns and points at me.

"There will be no arguing on this. You're taking that money back." He shows his bottom teeth and I put my hands up in surrender.

"I will I promise. But I also had a question for you." He opens the door and hobbles into the kitchen.

"Well, ask away, but first let me get this damned thing off it is itching like mad today." He sits at the kitchen counter and removes his prosthetic leg. I avert my eyes as I start putting away his groceries.

"Do you keep in contact with anyone from your military days?" He looks at me oddly, at first, I assume it is because I was putting something away incorrectly, but he shakes his head.

"Why would I wanna spend time with them? It's not exactly a time I want to remember."

"I see. I just thought maybe if I was looking for someone you might be able to get me in contact with them."

"Who ya lookin' for?"

"Robert Cartwright? I don't know if you would even know him, I just know he did a tour in Vietnam."

"Cartwright? As in the old Police chief Cartwright?"

"Yeah. So, you do know him." A lead!

"Sure, I know him. He was in my platoon. He was my subordinate.... why are you looking for him?" He gives me a sidelong glance.

"Well..." I wonder how much to tell Ronnie. "I guess..." I decide it can't hurt to tell him some of the truth. "Well, the real reason I came to town was I'm looking for my family. I was adopted I guess—"

"You guess?"

"I mean, I guess I was adopted from here. Obviously, I know for sure I was adopted." I don't really want to go into my memory loss. Not only because I don't feel like having to tell Ronnie the entire story of the dock, but also, I don't really want too many people to know. God forbid word would get back to the police.

"What would Cartwright have to do with that?"

"Well, I think he might be—"

"Wait a second, did you know that girl who died?" My heart drops to my feet and I almost drop the eggs I'm holding.

"What?" I try to maintain a stone face and not show any expression. I'd try for a confused face but I'm afraid I'd screw it up and no expression is better than a shocked face.

"About a month ago, that girl from the T.V. came here asking about Cartwright. But she wasn't looking for him for family reasons. She had already interviewed him."

"She had interviewed him?"

"Yeah, she wanted to talk to me about what he was like as a soldier. Said she was writing some sort of article for the paper about him being a police chief and Vet." What was Sara doing talking to Ronnie about my dad? If she had already found him, then why was she looking into his past?

"What did you tell her?"

"I told her the same thing I'm tellin' you. He was my subordinate and that's all I'm saying. We weren't together for very long over there anyway. He wasn't even part of the Army, one of those private security company men. Not really sure what he was doing there anyway. But look we don't keep in contact anymore. I don't want to and I'm sure he wouldn't either." I could tell from his tone of voice that I wasn't going to get any further on the subject with him.

"Well, okay, then. Sorry I asked."

"Well, if you give up that quickly you ain't never gonna find your family. Don't you wanna know if I know how to get a hold of him?"

"You just said—"

"I said I don't wanna contact him. Doesn't mean I don't know how."

"So, you know his phone number or something?" Finally, I had found a thread that wasn't a dead end.

"Better than that I know where he lives."

"You didn't have to drive me," I say for what is probably the tenth time as we pull into the driveway. We are in an apartment complex on the other end of town. It consists of three buildings. Two of them are the actual apartments while a third looks like the front office.

"Enough of that. You weren't gonna be able to walk all the way here. Now I don't know exactly which one he lives in. I just know that girlfriend of yours mentioned he was living here."

"Why did she mention that?"

"Cause I asked. I hadn't heard anything about what he was up to. I may not be interested in talking to him, but I like to keep tabs on old colleagues." He parks in front of the office.

"Nosey, are you?"

"Knowledge is power."

"She isn't my girlfriend, by the way."

"Oh, I know you don't swing for that sort of thing. I'm not an idiot. I saw you with that Jimmy today."

"What? I—"

"Look. No worries. Anyway, I'm gonna sit out here in the car if you don't mind. Like I said, no interest in contact. Besides, I'm going to take off my leg. But if you go in and ask, they may tell you what apartment he lives in."

"Why would they tell me? And I'm not gonna just leave you in here all alone."

"I'm just gonna take my nap here instead of at home in front of the T.V. Don't worry about it. But as for talkin' to the office lady, you gotta learn how to lie." I don't mention that I have gotten pretty good at lying in the last week. "Come up with some story. Something believable. Something that they'd buy. You're a smart fella you can come up with something. Now get. I wanna take my nap."

I get out of the car, even though I have absolutely no idea what I'm going to say. I hope that inspiration will strike me as I walk towards the door to the office. But when I walk in, I realize I won't have to say anything. I glance around the room and notice a door that leads down a hallway to what looks like a weight room and maybe some other amenities. Then another few doors that lead to offices. But directly to the right of the front door is a wall of mailboxes. On each box is a name and a corresponding apartment number.

I do a quick sweep to see if anyone is watching. There is only one woman I can see in one of the offices and she is typing away at her computer. I go over to the wall of mailboxes and look through them all trying to find the one marked Cartwright.

Apartment 104A.

I glance again to make sure she wasn't looking, and I quickly walk out of the office. Hopefully not arousing any suspicion about why I just walked in and out for no particular reason. Ronnie is fast asleep in the car out front. I mentally tell myself that I'm gonna tell him I didn't need to lie at all. Just snoop a little bit.

I walk up to one building first but it's apparently the 200 Building, so I walk over to the other one and find 104A on the first floor.

I hesitate at the door with my fist an inch from knocking.

My father is theoretically on the other side of this door. Someone who, if he doesn't know me, at least knows of me. Some sort of connection to my past. I could get answers to a lot of my questions today. Was I adopted? Why was I put up for adoption? Maybe we had been in contact before I lost my memory. Surely if I could track him down alone, then Sara and I would have found him. She had told Ronnie that she had interviewed him. She wouldn't have seen him and not introduced us.

If he is my father at all. I might have hit another dead end. The only evidence I have is a hint of a memory of the name Cartwright and the fact that I knew where his old house was. It was mentioned in one article about Robert having a son, but then in his wife's obituary he wasn't mentioned. Maybe his son died. Maybe I'm barking up the wrong tree.

And even if he does know the answer to some questions, he won't be able to answer the most important questions that are wreaking havoc on my brain. He wouldn't be able to tell me why I lost my memory or what happened that night on the dock. He couldn't tell me who killed Sara or Emily.

But in order to find the answers to those questions I have to start somewhere. He may not be able to give me the answers I want but he has to be able to tell me something. I have no other routes to go at the moment and standing here in front of a door wasn't going to solve anything. I have to knock.

I rapped my knuckles against the door.

At first, I thought no one was home because nothing happened. I was about to walk away when the door creaked open.

A man stood on the other side of the door. He was wearing a plaid shirt and jeans and slippers. He was balding but what little hair was left used to be black, though, it now looked mostly gray. He wore glasses with bifocals in them. Other than his hair and a few wrinkles on his face he didn't look old enough to have been in a war with Ronnie. He looked much too young. He held himself upright like he was called to attention. There wasn't even a hint of a hunch.

He stared at me for a moment before he spoke.

"Can I help you?" This answered one of my questions. He must not have met me. If he did, he would have recognized me. Instead, he was giving me a rather blank stare. I don't see how Sara could have met him and not have introduced us. Unless he had turned into a dead end for her, as well. Perhaps she had talked to him and found out I wasn't his son and hadn't bothered to introduce us.

I realize I haven't responded to his question.

"Sorry. Look. I have a weird question for you. Would you mind if I came in?"

“You can ask it right here.” He made no move to open the door.

“I haven’t introduced myself. I’m Sam.” I falter at a last name. I don’t know that I want to give him the last name from my license. Price goes with Kevin and, no matter, what Callahan thinks I am not Kevin. At least not anymore.

“Well, nice to meet you Sam. I’m Robert. Now what’s your question.” He was very matter of fact about it. There wasn’t any inclination in his voice to opening the door any further.

“I don’t really know how to ask this…” I could feel I was trying his patience. I had to get to the point. “I think I might be your son.” There was no reaction on his face. It seemed the same as if I had told him the sky was blue. “Is there any chance I might be right?” Finally, he stepped backwards.

“I think you ought to come inside.”

I step into the apartment. There is a large couch and a coffee table littered with cigarette butts. The rug underneath is dark brown and covered in darker stains. The room has a musty feel to it, and it smells like he hasn’t opened a window in years. There is a small kitchenette with yellow tiles and a matching yellow fridge. He gestures to the couch and heads to the kitchen.

“Would you like something to drink?”

“No, thank you.” I sit down on the couch. It’s rough and itchy.

“What makes you think I might be your father.” He asks as he pulls a kitchen chair in from the other room. I note in my head again the difference in age, or at least appearance of age between Ronnie and Robert. Where Ronnie can’t carry more than two bags of groceries at a time, Robert picks up the kitchen chair one handed without even thinking about it.

“Well, I…” The question of evidence again appears in front of my mind. It makes logical sense if you look at the picture as a whole, but I can’t tell him all of that. I can’t tell him how I’ve lost my memory and knew his last name. I can’t tell him that I came here to this town specifically looking for him because I have no idea how my search led me to him or this town. I can’t even tell him about Sara because I’m not sure exactly how she got his name. “I know I was adopted, and I know you had a son that was about my age. But then when your wife died, you no longer had that son.” He looks at me without saying anything.

I figure that was enough information without arousing questions but also enough to give me an excuse for having tracked him down.

"Well, I did have a son. This is true." He says this slowly like he is picking his words delicately. "And true I lost him, but I didn't put him up for adoption." My heart sinks. Another dead end.

"I'm sorry to have wasted your time. I'm sorry—" I stand up.

"Where are you going?" He says without inflection. I pause. "Sit down. I wasn't finished." I do so. "I didn't put him up for adoption, but my wife did."

Maybe this wasn't a dead end after all.

"So, I could be—"

"I don't know for sure. I was never allowed to have information about what happened to my son. The orphanage wouldn't let me. Something about me not having been there when she dropped him off." He doesn't say any of this with regret or any sort of emotion. Instead, it is a matter of fact, like everything else. He sounds like he's talking about the weather instead of his lost child.

"What orphanage was it?"

"St. Elizabeth's Home for Children. It's about thirty miles east of town. It was one of my wife's final acts to take my boy there before she died. I didn't know where she had taken him until years later. By the time I did, they said he had already been adopted, and they were not allowed to say where just because I had changed my mind."

My heart starts to beat quickly. He might actually be my father. I could finally be on the right track. I suddenly don't know what to say. My head had been full of questions but now I can't formulate a single one.

"So…"

"So, I would imagine if you went there, they could tell you. But until then, I hope you understand if I don't want to get my hopes up. Sorry but I mourned the loss of my son for many, many years. Until I know for sure I'm not gonna lose him again I'm not ready to open myself up to that." With that he stands up.

"Now I don't mean to be rude but unless you have something else to say…" for the first time he seemed a little lost for words. I could see mist in his eyes. I stand up and walk to the door.

"I do have one more question."

"Yes?" He asked as he held the door open for me.

"This may seem weird. But have you happened to speak to a woman named Sara Jefferson?"

"No. I've never heard of this woman." He doesn't seem confused by the question. He was, in fact, quick to answer it and then quick to close the door in my face.

I stand for a moment, digesting the conversation I just had.

I don't know what I expected. It isn't like he would have recognized me. Unless I had met him in the week or so before I lost my memory, he wouldn't know who I was, even if he was my father. I guess I expected him to be more helpful or at least more understanding.

I understand his negative attitude. This is a man who intentionally has separated himself from others. He doesn't list his address. He retired early. He lives alone and judging from the amount of cigarettes and cleanliness of his apartment, doesn't have anyone over very often. Then here I come with nothing but a hunch, claiming to be his long-lost son who he had assumed he would never get to see again.

But something feels wrong. Why did he not at least look for me? I find it hard to believe that in twenty years he couldn't get any information about me. It is as if he didn't really want to find me. It seems like he wants to be alone and unhappy.

I will just have to figure out the truth without him. I will go to the orphanage and see if they can tell me anything. I'm not sure if they will be able to for sure but they can at least tell me if a Kevin Price was ever adopted from there.

I take a deep breath and head back to the car.

"Well, that wasn't exactly a dead end but—" I look over and Ronnie is still fast asleep. "Ronnie?" I nudge him a little on the shoulder.

He doesn't stir.

Chapter 19

"What's going on?"

"Are you family?"

"No."

"Then I'm sorry, but you are going to have to wait in the waiting room."

"Wait can you at least tell me what is going on?"

"You're going to have to wait. I'm sorry."

"Why won't anyone tell me if he is at least going to be okay?"

I sit down again on one of the ugly, uncomfortable couches in the waiting room of the hospital. It's not a very large hospital. I had driven here after the ambulance took Ronnie. I had wanted to ride in the ambulance with him in order to avoid driving, but the EMT wouldn't let me because, once again, I wasn't a family member. I tried to explain to him that we lived together and that he didn't have anyone.

At least I don't think he does. The doctor asked if I knew of anyone I should call, and I couldn't think of anyone. I don't know that I ever got any information about Ronnie's family. I know he had a wife that died but I don't know if they had any kids or even when she died. I never even heard that from him, Jimmy told me that.

Jimmy.

I looked at the clock. It was eight o clock. I had been at the hospital for a good few hours waiting for someone to talk to me about Ronnie's condition. None of them would tell me a thing. I had gotten here quite a while after he had arrived. I had gotten lost on my way here, even though the EMT gave me directions. He seemed confused that I needed directions until I explained I had only just moved to town.

The doctor tried to ask about Ronnie's medical history, or what I knew of it for a while but when he realized I didn't know anything about his health other than that he drank way too much and was missing a leg, he left me alone in the waiting room. I wish I had lied and said I was his son or grandson or something. Why do I always lie, except when it might actually be helpful.

I reach into my jacket pocket to grab the phone and realize I have three missed calls from "the Diner." The phone must have been on vibrate.

"Thank you for calling Beer n' Burger's diner; this is Holly speaking."

"Hey, Holly, put Jimmy on the phone."

"Jimmy left an hour ago hon." That was when the last missed call was from.

"He what? Where did he go?"

"I don't know but he was pretty shaken up. Is this Sam?"

"Yes."

"He said he hadn't heard from you and he kept trying to call you. You guys supposed to have a date or somethin'?"

"Something like that. Look, if he comes back, tell him I'm sorry and that he needs to call me right away."

"Sure thing, hon."

Shit. Jimmy was probably thinking I had another episode. I'm sure that's the only thing he can be thinking of. Hell, that's what I'd be thinking if I were in his shoes.

But with me having his phone I have no way of calling him.

I go through his contacts and find the one marked home.

"Hello?"

"Alex. It's Sam. Has Jimmy stopped by?"

"No, but he called a while ago. He was looking for you. I thought you guys were together?"

"We got separated. Look, did he mention where he was going to look for me?"

"Well, sort of."

"What do you mean 'sort of'?"

"I mean that he said he knew where to look for you, but he didn't mention it. After I told him I hadn't seen you, he said, 'I think I know where he is,' then he hung up." What could that mean? Where was he going to look?

"Okay, thanks. If you hear from him let me know. I have his cell phone."

I hang up and try to think. Where would he be looking for me? He would have just walked next door and seen I wasn't at Ronnie's. But he also would have seen that Ronnie's car wasn't in the driveway. Perhaps he realized we had gone somewhere. But where would I have gone? He called his house, so he didn't drive out there. Where else would he have gone? I look through his contacts, but they are a bunch of places and people I didn't know.

Then I realize I shouldn't look for where he would go. I should be looking for where I would go. Or better yet, given that I wasn't answering my phone and therefore possibly having an episode, where would Kevin go.

The house.

I jump up and run over to the nearest nurse that I recognize. She had been one of the ones talking to Ronnie's doctor. I don't know for sure if she was Ronnie's nurse, but I didn't have time to wait around and find out.

"Hey, I need you to tell Ronnie to call—"

"Do you mean Mr. Mills?"

"Who?"

"Ronald Mills. Is that who you're talking about?"

"Oh, yes." Now I remember looking for and finding his license. It had been the beginning of the distrust from the doctor's given that I didn't even know his last name. "Tell him to call the diner when he wakes up."

"Call the diner?" She looks skeptical.

"Yes. He'll know which one."

Heading out of the hospital I call the diner and let Holly know to give Ronnie Jimmy's number. It takes some convincing to get her to agree.

"Why are you giving out Jimmy's number?"

"Look. I don't have a phone, and Jimmy and I are sharing his."

"Why are you—"

"Because we are. Just give Ronnie the number."

I hang up on her before she can protest and get into Ronnie's car. I never told the people at the hospital that it was his car. I hope he doesn't mind me borrowing it one more time.

It isn't until I get out on the road that I realize I don't know where I'm going from here. The hospital is outside of town and I have only been to the house one time as myself. The first time I was Kevin. For half a second, I almost wish I could turn him on. But no. That would be a bad idea.

But then again, if Kevin knows, then I should, too. I mean somewhere in my brain I have to know where the house is. Otherwise, Kevin wouldn't have driven straight there. So, on some level, that address or at least the way to get there is imprinted in my brain. I just need to be able to get at it. I pull over to try and decide what to do.

I look at the intersection that is about fifty yards ahead of where I've pulled over. I don't recognize the street name or anything around me. I know that if I follow the road, I'm on I will get back to town because this is the way I came to the hospital. But beyond that I'm lost.

I think back to when me and Jimmy drove out to the house the second time. It had taken us a long time because even Jimmy hadn't remembered how to get there, but we had made it eventually. I close my eyes and try to think about exactly how we got there but I can't remember. Jimmy had been directing most of the way there and all of the way back to town. It has to be in my memory, though. I have to remember something. I think back to anything we might have driven past that day, but it is dark and even if I remembered anything I'm not sure I'd be able to find it. I curse at myself for not remembering the address. We had used it that day to find my connection to the Cartwrights, but I don't remember now what it was.

That's when I remember I have Jimmy's phone. It has connection to the internet and Robert is still listed at that address. I pull it out and type in the name and the search engine pulls up the address. Sure enough, it comes up with the address. 5871 Plymouth Road. I quickly pull back out onto the road and head out, using the maps app on Jimmy's phone.

It takes me about thirty minutes to get there but when I do I see Jimmy's truck in the driveway. I don't see any lights on in the house, though, as I walk up to the front door. Instinctively I almost knock, but instead, I just open the door and walk inside.

"Jimmy?"

I get no answer, so I turn on the light and begin to look around, but I don't see Jimmy or anyone else, for that matter. In the darkness the house has a creepy almost haunted feel to it. I guess any place that doesn't have anyone in it for so long would get that feeling.

It's in the kitchen that I notice movement out the window in the back yard. I look out the window and notice that the yard goes all the way back and actually ends at the edge of the lake. You can't see the lake from the front of the house because it's built into the tree line of the forest surrounding it. I open the kitchen door that leads out to the back yard and I realize I was partly wrong.

The lake isn't exactly the right word. It's more a small inlet from the lake. I can see the other side of it, but the lake does extend out to my left further. There is a dock and Jimmy is sitting on the dock. He is just sitting there looking past the boat that is tied to the dock, *Freedom* written on its hull in fancy letters. I think of calling out to him but I'm afraid to startle him, so instead, I walk up and sit next to him.

"I figured you would show up here eventually," he says, not looking at me at all.

"Jimmy. It's me." He doesn't answer for a long time.

"What does that mean?" He looks at me finally. "I mean is it really you? I've been thinking." Another long pause but just before I respond he looks away and begins to talk again. "Do we really even know who you are? We think we know what you might have been doing here but obviously your name isn't Sam. The license that the detective had said Kevin. That's what you initially answered to. So, that's obviously your name.

"But what else do we know? What else do I know? I don't know anything about you. When I couldn't get a hold of you earlier and I was trying to think of how to find you, I couldn't think of anywhere to look."

I don't say anything because I feel like he doesn't want a response, but I wish I could come up with something to say to get that sad look out of his eyes.

"You just stepped into my life and turned it on its head. I realize now that you waking up on the dock in my backyard didn't just change your life. It changed mine. I'm not sure any of it is going to be the same ever again and it's all because of you. I don't know if it's for better or for worse, but it just is.

"And I don't even have any idea of who you are. What am I supposed to do with that? What am I supposed to do when the person who has become a central player in my life, I have no clue about who he is." My heart flutters at what he is saying, but it breaks at the same time because I understand his struggle. "I don't know what to do. I don't know anything. I'm not even sure how I feel."

He is quiet. I tentatively place a hand on top of his on the dock. He pulls away at first, but then returns his hand, this time on top of mine. I hear a distant roar of thunder coming from across the lake.

"I don't know how to explain how I feel. Everything seems to be moving so fast around me and the only constant I have is you," I say, looking at him even as he stares into the water. "You're right. Both of our lives changed that night when I woke up. I don't know if it was for better or for worse either. I can't say for sure because I have nothing to compare it to. But I do know this. In one way my life is better now because I have you in it. I can't imagine a life without you in it. You are the one thing good right now. The one thing I wouldn't change."

"I was so afraid today when you didn't answer." He still won't look at me, but instead, blinks rapidly as he stares at the water. "I was afraid you had forgotten me." I feel a singular drop on my forehead. "I kept thinking, what if he has an episode? What if he forgets all about me? What if I never see you again?" He finally looks at me.

I see all the pain in those hazel eyes. I see the turbulence of his thoughts. Everything from his stress about me and his family and his worry about the future; his, mine and ours. There is also a happiness, the relief in seeing me here with him. It all swirls together in his iris to form a mysterious storm. A storm that has taken him out of Kansas into this Ozian future where nothing seems to make sense.

"I could never forget you. Forgetting you would be like forgetting how to breath." It's a truth I feel in my bones. A rock I cling to in the hurricane that surrounds us. "And you do know me. You know me better than anyone else. Because the only thing that is me. The only thing that defines me. The only thing that keeps me from knowing I haven't completely lost it is my feelings for you. Without you I'm nothing. I may have woken up on that dock, but I was born when I sat in that booth with you at the diner. Until then, I was nothing but a shell."

I hadn't noticed as I was talking that the drop on my forehead had become three and then five, and now the rain was coming down in droves heading across the water towards us. You could see where it started; that's how quickly it moved in.

But neither of us cared. We were too busy staring into each other's eyes. But when the line of rain finally hits the dock, it hits us like a brick wall. Suddenly, we go from mostly dry to looking like we have both been swimming. It takes us a half a second to register what has just happened and for us to jump up. He gets up faster and pulls me up with one hand. We run to head into the house not saying a word but as we come to the edge of the dock, right next to a post with an old lamp on top, I stop and pull him back.

In the wet and rain our lips meet and all the words we said before become just that, words. Suddenly, we no longer need to speak anymore, but instead, our lips send messages in a quicker more efficient way, through electricity and waves of emotions. I run my hand through his sopping hair and the rain suddenly feels miles away. I don't care about anything, not the weather, not Ronnie, not Callahan, not the dead girls, nothing can distract me from the two of us kissing in the rain. He pushes me up against the post, and our bodies get pressed together.

He pulls his face back less than an inch. Not because he wants to stop but because he wants to look at me. I can see in the way his eyes rush across my face. Like he is eating up every inch of what I look like in this moment. Every dripping bit of me. Suddenly, he is laughing. Not just a giggle, not even just a laugh, but a whoop. I get sucked into it and soon we are both trying to catch our breath from the powerful joy and happiness that we both feel. The strength of which is so strong we have no other way of letting it out but by literally laughing and dancing in the rain.

It's not until lightning strikes in the trees by the house and thunder crashes immediately after that we are brought down from cloud nine. A large branch falls in the woods with a resounding boom. It's no more than a hundred yards from us.

"We should go inside." He screams at me over the rush of the wind. When did it get so loud and strong? Suddenly, I feel like the hurricane I imagined just moments before in his eyes has arrived at the shore of the lake and is threatening to take us both out over the water. He takes my hand and runs towards the house again. This time I don't stop him.

We slam the door behind us, shutting out the noise and the storm. He hasn't dropped my hand, but we are both simply standing there trying to catch our breath. I shiver as the dryness of the house turns my soaking skin to chills. The light in the kitchen is on, but it flickers and goes out.

"There goes the power." I can't see him in the sudden darkness, but I could feel his smile from a mile away.

"I guess we have no choice." I reach my empty hand out towards him. "We will just have to feel our way." My hand touches his wet shirt as it clings to his chest. I feel it shudder under my touch.

"It's cold in here."

“We can change that.” I pull him in closer feeling the wet clothes between our bodies. I already feel my body warm against his.

I kiss him once again before leading him blindly out of the kitchen and towards the stairs. Partially using memory and partially light from infrequent lightning strikes, but mostly using blind faith we struggle our way upstairs to the king size bed, stopping only a few times to hold each other close and remind ourselves of our ultimate goal.

Or perhaps a few more times than a few.

Jimmy’s mouth slams into mine and causes a flurry of fireworks to explode along my lips. The burning, lusting needing sweat drips down my neck onto his knuckles. I blindly tear at his clothes searching for something to hold onto as we fall together through the ecstasy that is each other’s bodies. The world spins more times than it should as we flip over each other falling onto the bed, the springs squeaking under our weight. Over the sound of thunder, I moan. I moan with pleasure I’ve never known before. I know I’ve never felt it because I know in that moment that I could never forget this feeling. This feeling of being absolutely completely safe.

His mouth explores my body and finds crevasses I didn’t even know existed and brings me pleasure to those places that one forgets exist; the nape of my neck right where the jawline disappears. That miniscule area becomes an everlasting puddle of pure delight under his tongue. My back arches in pleasure forcing me closer to him, closer to life, closer to joy.

My ever-searching hands find a grip on his belt and throw it against the wall in my desperation to get as close to him as possible. I feel him against me, then, and my mind goes blank for the first time. I don’t think about my past I don’t worry about my future. I’m here. Here and now with him and no one else. The storm freezes around us as we love each other, as we love ourselves with each other. In this moment, I know it needs to happen and, more importantly, I want it to happen.

I had no way of knowing for sure, but I believe it is my first time. I want it to be because I want nothing to take away the special feeling that courses through my veins and touches every fiber of my being. We are finally as close as possible. Me and him have become one. We fit together like two pieces of a broken puzzle that suddenly becomes whole again. I kiss him and look him in his eyes. We pause our rhythmic movement for a moment to simply look at each other. To take in the pure wonder in each other’s eyes.

He almost says it. I see the words itching to come to the tip of his tongue. I silence him with a kiss. Words would ruin it; put it in reality. This act is of another world. I cannot let him rip it back into this one. Not until I am finished. Once I fall off this high he has me under, I will let him ruin it. I will let him say it. I might even say it back. There will be no reason not to. Even if the words haven't been uttered doesn't mean they aren't there hanging between us like a golden thread. A golden thread like that of the ancient Greeks tying us together. A single living soul. Break it and we both die.

He has become my life source. My raison d'etre, my soul purpose. And I have become his. There is no going back from this. No stopping. And so, I press onward and pull him ever closer.

Chapter 20

"What was your mother like?" I sit back in his arms afterwards, staring into the darkness. There isn't even any moonlight. Just the occasional flash of lightning to remind us of where we are. Neither of us move to put on clothes, we simply sit there basking in in each other, soaking ourselves in.

"She was beautiful. She was the most generous person I've known. She used to bake apple pie on the weekends. She would always give me the biggest slice and anything that was left over she'd take to the diner. She worked there when I was little."

"I didn't realize the diner was that old."

"It's really old. It dates back to the sixties. It's been through a couple of owners and a couple of names, but it's always been a diner."

"You must miss her. I'm sorry I asked."

"No. I do miss her but I'm glad I have the memories of her. It's better than Alex. She doesn't even remember her at all. Flashes, but nothing solid.

"She's got more than I do." I snuggle closer to his chest and close my eyes. "Tell me more memories."

"I remember one Thanksgiving, we had my grandparents over for dinner. Mom wanted to make this huge turkey, but she accidentally left it in too long and burnt the whole thing. The kitchen was full of smoke by the time we noticed. She was so embarrassed she was almost in tears. But all dad did was laugh. He went into town; thank goodness the grocery store was still open. He bought turkey T.V. dinners and brought it home and we each had our own dinner trays. From then on, every thanksgiving we would always buy a bunch of them and keep them in the fridge. Just in case. I never tell anyone, but I still do it even now. But we don't really do the big dinner anymore. Not since… It just doesn't seem right. And Dad's not aware what day of the week it is let alone if it's a holiday."

"So, you don't celebrate it at all?"

"Not really. We don't celebrate a lot. Pretty much we do birthdays and Christmas. But with only my tips and trying to pay for school and everything. I mean I get a check from Dad's Social security every month, but it isn't much. We got some money from selling off the farm land but there isn't much of that left after paying for all of the hospital bills. Uncle Ben used to help but now he just drinks it all away."

"That's a shame."

"It's okay. I'm just grateful that we haven't had to lose the house yet. Though it might come to that. I'm not sure we can continue like we are until I graduate."

"You'll figure something out. I'm sure of it."

"Sorry. My memory turned kind of depressing."

"That's okay. It's better than nothing. I'm jealous of your memories. The good ones and the bad ones."

"Really? I'm jealous of you."

"What?" I sit up at this and give him an incredulous look.

"You aren't held back by anything. You don't have anything to control who you are. You can be whoever you want to be."

"No, I can't."

"Yes. You can be whatever you want. You can make up your past. You're not controlled by it."

"I feel like I'm controlled by my lack of a past." I lay back down and feel the rise and fall of his chest.

"Then you need to give yourself a past. You tell me a memory." I chuckle at this.

"I don't have any."

"So, just make one up. Come on I'll help you. What's your dog's name?"

"I don't- I don't know if I have a dog."

"You aren't getting the rules of this game. Make" He kisses me. "one" Kisses me again. "up."

"Okay.... Spot."

"No. Wrong. Too bland. You have a dog named... Hector." I roll over so that I'm on top of him with my chin resting on his chest.

"What kind of a name is Hector for a dog?"

"I don't know you tell me. There's got to be a story behind the name." I think for a minute before I answer him.

"How about this…. When we found him. He was a mutt on the side of the road. I found him while I was out walking. Anyway, when we found him, he was chewing on…. A baseball. And One of my favorite Baseball players name is Hector. How about that?"

"So, now you like baseball?"

"I guess I do."

"Favorite team?"

"New York Yankees."

"Have you ever been to New York?"

"I don't—" He stops me mid word with a kiss.

"You're not allowed to say that. You have to answer. No 'I don't knows.'" I laugh and look him in the eye for a moment.

"No. I've never been but I've always wanted to go."

"Favorite food?"

"Pizza."

"Boring, try again."

"Falafel."

"Better. Where did you grow up?"

"Umm…. Minnesota." I shrug.

"Siblings?"

"Oh, bunches. My parents were catholic. I have so many you can't even count them."

"Got to give a number."

"Okay. Uh… twelve."

"Oh, that makes thirteen of you. That's not lucky."

"Yeah, and I was number thirteen."

"Oh, the baby?"

"Gotta love me!" I vaguely remember having heard that from somewhere. Almost as if it were a quote. "I was also the only boy."

"Oh, were you?"

"That's why they finally stopped with me. They finally got what they wanted."

"Thirteenth time is the charm." We are both giggling at this point. I sit up as a crack of lightning flashes across the window.

"My mother was a circus acrobat."

"A catholic circus performer?" He raises an eyebrow.

"You said I could make up anything. And besides I'm sure it's happened. In fact, I know it did. Because she would hold mass every Sunday for all the circus freaks at our house. The clowns would all sit in one row and the performers in another. My sisters would sit in a row by themselves, but I would shift between the rows."

"You must have had a huge house to host such a large congregation."

"Massive. My father has lots of money, so we had a huge mansion. That's how my mother was able to go after her dream of acrobatics."

"I see."

"But then there was a huge fight. It was so big that it broke up the circus."

"Oh, dear what happened?" He mocks shock and awe.

"My sixth eldest sister…. Helga."

"Horrible name."

"They had thirteen children they couldn't all be named well. Anyway, Helga… She fell in love with the magician. But he was married to the lion tamer."

"Ooh, scandalous."

"When the lion tamer found out about the two of them, she got so upset she let out the lion in the middle of a show and it trampled through the big top."

"Oh, no! Not under the big top!"

"Yes! But luckily, no one was hurt. But it knocked over the clown that was on stilts and he spooked the elephant, and he trampled the ropes that were holding up the tent and the entire thing fell down trapping everyone in the tent!" With that I grab hold of the sheets and pull them over us like the made-up tent collapsing on top of us.

I begin to kiss him all over his face, but he is having none of it. He begins to tickle me until we are a mad knot of arms and legs tangled up in the bed sheets, giggling till we are out of breath and collapse laying sideways on the bed.

"I wonder what my parents really did. Do?" I take a few deep breaths to try and calm my beating heart.

"You'll find out someday. We'll figure it out together." He takes my hand and kisses the back of it.

I wake up to the pounding of the front door. Jimmy is absent from the bed. I quickly grab my pants from the floor and slip on a shirt as I walk down the stairs. I pass Jimmy running up the stairs. He is only wearing his underwear, He didn't get the door from the sounds of the continued knocking.

"Who is it? Where are your clothes?"

"I left them upstairs. I didn't anticipate company. It's detective Callahan." He runs up the rest of the stairs without another word.

What is Detective Callahan doing here? Shit. This isn't going to go over well. I'm positive it's not going to be a good thing that we have spent the night in an abandoned house.

I don't know what I'm going to say, but I have no choice but to open the door. He knows we are here because of the cars.

"Good morning, Detective Callahan." The first thing I notice as I open the door is that the detective is not alone. There are about five squad cars in the front driveway all with their lights going. There are a few of them standing in the bed of Jimmy's truck. "Isn't this a little excessive? We broke into an abandoned house. It's not like we—"

"Like you what? Killed someone?"

"Look. We will get our stuff and go. We just needed shelter from the thunderstorm last night. I didn't want to drive all the way home, and this was the closest place."

"You have a lot bigger problems than staying in an abandoned house my friend. I think the two of you are going to have to come down to the police station with me. Where's your boyfriend?"

"*Jimmy* is upstairs. He'll be down in a minute. Tell me what's going on."

"Callahan, the coroner is on his way!" One of the officers yells.

"What does he mean the coroner is on their way?"

"Oh, don't you know what your boyfriend was hiding in the back of his truck?"

I don't bother waiting for him to tell me. I push past him and run down in my bare feet across the gravel driveway. I hop up onto the tailgate of his truck and look at what is waiting at the feet of the officers.

It's Dany. The waitress from the diner.

Pale white and surely cold as death.

Chapter 21

I find myself back in the same interrogation room as before. This time I sit for an hour or so alone before Detective Callahan comes in.

"I'd like to see a lawyer."

"So, quick to end the party?"

"A lawyer." I had a lot of time to think this through while I was riding in the car here and then while I was sitting in the room alone. They didn't let me and Jimmy exchange a single word. They handcuffed me on the back of the truck and threw me in the back seat of a car before he even had a chance to come out of the house. I did see him put up quite a fight trying to get to me, but he was eventually cuffed, as well.

I now sit with my still bare feet flat on the cold hard laminate floor, and my hands cuffed in my lap. Callahan sits across from me with a manilla folder in his hand.

"We can definitely get you one. I'll give a call over to the public defender's office."

"Call Philip King. He's my lawyer." I'd rather have someone I know than some random lawyer. I'll figure out how to pay for it once I get out of here.

"Okay, then. I'll give him a call. While you wait, could I get you a glass of water?"

"How about some shoes?" He chuckles and stands up.

"I'll see what I can do 'bout that. But I want you to think about something while you wait for your lawyer. You aren't the only one who's gonna need one. It wasn't your truck we found the girl in."

It takes about twenty minutes for Mr. King to get here.

"I need a minute with my client before you start questioning him."

"By all means. Take all the time you need." Callahan gives us the room. King sits across from me where Callahan had sat before.

"I'm not your lawyer."

"I'll pay you once I get out of here."

"I'm not worried about the money."

"Then what's the problem?"

"The problem is I don't want to do it."

"Then why did you come when I called?" He doesn't have a response to that. Instead, he sits there for a minute, chewing over his words.

"I'm not going to ask if you did it."

"I didn't."

"But I need to know your alibi for last night. If you have one." He pulls out a notepad and pen from his briefcase.

"Jimmy. We were at the house all night together. Neither of us left."

"What time did you get there?"

"I don't remember. It was before the storm started."

"Before that, where were you?"

"The hospital. Ronnie was there. I took him there. He drove me out for an errand, and he passed out and I couldn't wake him up."

"And Jimmy? I assume you want me to represent him, as well?" He clearly doesn't want to, but I nod my head yes. "Where was he before you met him at the house."

I realize I haven't got an answer for that.

"We will have to remedy that. I'll have to meet with him after we get done. Okay. Did you happen to see if the girl was in the bed of the truck before this morning?"

"I didn't look." Suddenly, my mind begins to race.

"Did you know the girl?"

"She worked at the diner with…"

"With Jimmy?" He writes that down. I barely even look at what he is writing. It can't be anything good.

"Yes. I don't want to put all this on Jimmy, though. That's not how I want to get out of this."

"I figured as much." Philip sighs as he crosses something off on his notepad.

"Is there anything else? Did anyone else come to the house last night? Did you see anything unusual?" I rack my memory but all I remember is Jimmy.

"It was storming really badly. We lost power. We couldn't see anything outside except lightning and rain." He writes something else down.

"Alright, then. I'll go get Callahan. I can't promise anything, but I'll do my best." He stands up but, then pauses. "I have an idea. You won't like it, though."

"What is it?"

"You two came in separate cars, correct?"

"I don't want to pin this on Jimmy. I said that." He shakes his head.

"That's not what I'm suggesting. I'm just saying that *technically* speaking, all of their evidence points to Jimmy. We aren't pinning it all on him, but *technically* they have no reason to keep you on the murder charges. I can worry about Jimmy next, but I can at least get you out of here. How does that sound?"

I don't know what to say. On the one hand I feel like I'm deserting Jimmy, but someone has to be on the outside, so we can figure this all out. One of us out is better than neither of us.

"Is there any way that you can get me a chance to talk with him?"

"Absolutely not. They'd never allow it."

"Can I give him a message?"

"Legally no." He pauses for a moment and puts his pen in his breast pocket. Then he stops, pulls it back out and sets it on top of his notepad on the table. He looks me in the eye as he does this and then turns and walks out of the room.

I immediately grab the pen and paper. I don't know how long I have, so I write quickly and simply. It isn't easy writing with my hands cuffed but I don't care about my handwriting as long as Jimmy can read it.

Philip is getting me out. I'll get things figured out at the house. We will figure out a way to get you out. I know you didn't do it. I'll do everything I can.

I pause before adding. "I love you."

Just as I finish writing, I see the door handle turn, I swivel the notepad back around and drop the pen on top. It begins to roll, and I panic that it will roll to the floor before it stops an inch from the edge, just as the door opens and Callahan comes in followed by Philip.

"Let me get those hand cuffs off your wrists." Callahan comes around the table and unlocks my hands.

"Do we have another chair?" Philip asks.

"Don't worry I'll stand this isn't going to take long."

"Let get this over with," I say forcefully.

"Well, for starters the lawyer was a little unnecessary. The charges against you have been dropped." Initially I want to jump for joy, but then I see the smile on Callahan's face, and I know this isn't good news.

"Why?"

"You're boyfriend confessed. He said you had nothing to do with it."

"He's lying!" I jump to my feet. Philip puts a hand on my arm and gives me a glare.

"Would you care to throw your hat into the ring? I'd gladly charge you both for it. Regular Bonnie and Clyde? Or I guess in this case it's two Clydes. Tell me how does that work?"

"Don't answer that." Philip says.

"You know I don't see how I didn't figure it out sooner. I mean, it makes sense now. Why one of the bodies was dumped in his own back yard almost." He smiles that ruthless smile of his.

"He didn't do it. He's just—"

"If you aren't charging my client with anything, then we are going." Philip glares at me.

"Be my guest."

"I'd like to see the transcript from your interrogation with Jimmy. I'm going to be representing him, as well."

"Gladly. We have the whole thing on tape. I'll get you a copy." The two of them stare each other down like cowboys in a western about to have a shootout.

"I would like to speak with my client before I leave. Where are you holding him?"

"Just next door in the other interrogation room. We haven't moved him to his holding cell yet, although I'm sure it won't be long." This last bit he directs at me as if to stab me with the information. I take Philips advice and keep my mouth shut, but in my head, I'm cursing the detective to the ends of the earth. "Don't glare at me boy. I'm being really nice, not charging you for breaking and entering into the old Cartwright house. I could you know. But one arrest is enough for me." He winks and opens the door for me.

"I take it you'd like a ride somewhere?" Philip joins me out in front of the police station.

I haven't exactly been waiting for him, more just trying to figure out my next move. I'm barefoot without a car or a phone. Not that I would know exactly where to go or what to do if I had any of those things. I know I need to go to Jimmy's and explain to Alex what's going on. Figure out a way to make sure their father gets what he needs while Jimmy is unavailable. I'm not sure how long Jimmy will be locked up. It's only a matter of time till I'm able to clear his name, I'm sure.

Unless I can't.

I try not to let my mind wander off that cliff. There has to be a way to prove he didn't do it. Because if there isn't any way, then that would imply that he…

No.

Don't think that. Don't even put that idea into motion.

But how do I prove he didn't do it?

"Where do you want me to take you?"

I didn't even notice getting into Philip's red Cadillac. Sitting on his leather seats that are so pristine, it makes me feel dirty just being surrounded by so much cleanliness.

"I guess take me out to the Cartwright place to get my, or rather, Ronnie's car. I can take it from there. It's just out past—"

"I know the way. I've been before."

I remember, then, his history with the Cartwright's.

We sit in silence for most of the ride. I can't attest to his thoughts, but I know mine go round and round like a carousel going and faster and faster but trying to not fly off the rails. How did Dany's body get in Jimmy's truck? How can I prove he didn't kill her? If he didn't, there has to be a way. Who else could have put it there? How can I find them whoever they are? How long till it's too late?

"I don't know what I'm supposed to do," I say as we pull into the gravel driveway and come to a stop. I don't look at him. Instead, I stare at the spot where Jimmy's car is supposed to be. It must have been towed away by the police. It wasn't a question, but at the same time I really wish he has an answer.

"I can't tell you what to do but I can give you some advice." I don't respond but I look at him, pleading with my eyes for him to solve this puzzle. "If you truly don't think he did it, which I assume you don't, then let the police do their jobs. As long as there isn't anything you're hiding from them, then all this will work itself out. They can't convict Jimmy if they can't prove anything. And if he really isn't involved, then they will figure that out."

"But what if—"

"No 'what if's.' If he didn't do it, then there won't be enough evidence..."

"What about the body in the back of his truck? How did it get there? They aren't just going to ignore that!"

"They aren't going to, but *someone* put it there. And they are going to figure out who it was whether it was Jimmy or someone else."

"It wasn't Jimmy." I defiantly look away from him.

"Look, you going around trying to play Hardy boy is only going to screw up the police investigation further and that's going to get you in even deeper trouble. Just be patient, let the police do their job and let me do mine."

He sits waiting for me to leave. I finally open the door but then stop.

"What if I don't have anything else to do?"

"Do whatever you were planning on doing before the police showed up. Go home."

He leaves me standing in the driveway. I turn and face the house, the house that I came to when I was out of my head. The house where I think my birth parents lived. Is this home?

What about Jimmy's house? Where the man I love lives?

Where is my home?

If nothing else, I need to return Ronnie's car. I head inside to grab my shoes, ducking under the yellow tape they put across in front of the door. I also pick up some of Jimmy's things that he left behind. His wallet, his phone.

Just before I leave, I step out into the back yard and look out at the lake. The back yard is littered with fallen limbs from the storm. I step out onto the dock and remember. I remember last night. I take the memory and freeze it in my mind.

I have so few memories and even less are good ones.

But this one I will not lose. I will never forget it.

It will be mine forever. Just like he will.

Chapter 22

"Liver cancer?" I'm sitting next to Ronnie's hospital bed.

"That's what the doctor said. And from the looks of it, it's been there a while. Not much I can do at this point but wait." He eats out of a little cup of Jell-O as he says this. He grimaces with each bite but eats the entire thing.

"Isn't there some sort of treatment?" I ask him.

"I'm not going to lose my hair and spend the next few months next to a toilet puking my guts out only to die at the end anyway. No. I'm not getting any treatment. And don't try to talk me into it." With that he throws his Jell-O cup into the trash can next to his bed. Subject closed.

"Now what happened yesterday? Did you talk to Cartwright?"

"He didn't have any answers for me, but he told me where I might be able to find some. I was wondering if you'd mind if I continued to use your car?"

"Go ahead. They said I shouldn't be driving anyway. Wouldn't want to pass out again behind the wheel. I may be dying soon but I'm not dying that soon."

"You're not dying."

"We're all dying Kiddo. Some of us are just better at it than others." With that he winked at me and pressed the call button for the nurse.

"Did they give you a timeline?"

"The doctor said he could, but I told him not to bother. I don't want to know. Would you?" He pressed the button again this time with a little more force.

"No, I guess not." The nurse finally walks in.

“What do you need hon?” She is about forty and has bright red hair tied up into a bun. Her smocks have little kittens all over them.

“I need some more of that awful Jell-O.” She giggles in that way that only some women can pull off once they become adults.

“If it’s awful, then, why do you want more?”

“Cause it’s the least awful thing you got here. If you wanna go out and get me something else feel free.”

“I’ll see what I can do.” She leaves with a smile.

“Now you get out of here. I need to get some sleep. And don’t come back here without some answers about your parents. I ain’t got forever for you to figure this all out you know. Don’t let me die wonderin’.”

I wonder what awaits me at the end of this drive as I watch the exit signs fly by. I went back to Jimmy’s house and made sure that Alex had enough food and told her that Jimmy was going to be gone for a few days. I didn’t tell her he was in jail.

That seemed altogether too much. She didn’t need to worry about it anyway, he would be out soon. I hope so at least.

So, now I’m driving out towards the orphanage. I’m not sure what I am going to find when I get there. I’m not even sure what is even there. I looked up the address before I left the house, and it is still an active church, but it apparently no longer works as an orphanage. They stopped taking in children in the mid-nineties and then sent all remaining children off to foster care.

But they are still open so perhaps someone will know… what?

I can give them my name, or at least the name that was on my driver’s license, but who’s to say that they would have any record of my new name or that they would give it to me with no form of identification.

This might all be a wild goose chase. But it’s the only thing I have.

I pull into the complex and immediately have an uneasy feeling of deja vu. I don’t remember it or anything, but I feel like I should. The dark brick church and the matching building behind it are both covered in moss and look like they need some severe restoration. But you can still see the cracked letters above the front door. St. Elizabeth’s Catholic Church.

Beneath it is a statue of, I assume, St. Elizabeth herself. She is surrounded by children dancing and playing in a circle. The statue was obviously supposed to convey the happiness of the children that were staying at the orphanage but due to years of neglect it doesn’t do its job.

Several of the children have been dismembered either by weather or by vandalism. There is a Burger King bag sitting at the foot of one of the girls and all of their faces have been worn away leaving them as dark grey shadows of children.

I walk inside and find the chapel empty. There is a set of candles off to the side where you can light a prayer for a loved one. It is dark and only the light of the candles and the colored rays streaming through the stained glass light up the pews. It isn't a large church, but it still echoes when I close the door behind me.

I don't know where to find anyone and I can't call out. The quiet of the church quells any desire to break the silence. Instead, I walk down the aisle and find myself a seat in one of the pews.

I don't know what to do. I should go and check the other building. See if I can find someone who can help me, but instead, I sit here staring at the cross at the front of the room.

I don't feel any familiarity in the room. I don't know if this is because I don't remember this particular church or if I don't remember churches in general. I'm not sure if I'm religious or if I was before I lost my memory. Can I be religious now? Can you believe in something beyond yourself if you don't even know yourself? Does that make it easier?

I don't know if anyone is listening, so I pray. I bow my head and pray to anyone or anything out there that may be listening. I pray for my memories to return. I pray for me to be able to find out the answers to my past. I pray that Jimmy will be exonerated. I pray for the dead girls and pray for forgiveness in any part that I may or may not have had in their deaths.

I pray for some sign that I didn't do it.

I pray for a light to guide my way.

Almost as if in answer to my prayers a nun enters. She is not in a full habit, but she is in a simple blue dress with a black hat covering her hair. She doesn't acknowledge me but simply walks from the rectory towards the front door of the church. I stand up and almost miss her for fear of saying anything. Finally, as she reaches the last row of pews, I get the courage up and I call out to her.

"Excuse me."

She turns to me and the feeling of deja vu I felt in the parking lot returns in full force. In fact, it's stronger. It's the same feeling I had when I woke up next to Elizabeth.

I know her.

"Yes?" She looks at me curiously, then begins to walk back towards me. We meet halfway down the aisle.

"This may sound weird but…. Do I know you?"

Now that she is closer, I get a better look at her face and am even more sure that I know her. But she looks different. I don't know how I can know she looks different than last time when I can't remember last time or even if it actually happened. For all I know I'm making this all up in my head.

Her azure eyes stare at mine. There is a moment and then I see her face change. She was initially just humoring me, but suddenly, recognition is there.

"Samuel?"

Suddenly, it's there. That feeling I'm sure others have. When you hear your name and you instinctively respond. That feeling in your gut. Samuel is my name. Kevin may be on my driver's license, but Samuel is my name. And this sister knows me.

"Yes." And for the first time I'm not lying or guessing.

"You came back! You told me you would. But I'd given up hope." I'm suddenly being hugged. It's amazing how a little nun can have such a powerfully strong hug, but it is comforting. Suddenly, I pull out of it.

"Look. This isn't… It's not what you think…. I… I don't know who you are."

"What? It's Alice! Don't you remember?" She is confused. I can see tears in her eyes.

"I've lost my memory. I… I don't know you. I recognize you but I don't know you."

"Lost your memory?"

"It's a long story. Why don't we sit down?" I sit down with her on one of the pews.

I tell her the whole story. Well, almost the whole story. I leave out waking up next to the dead body because I'm not sure that the privacy of confessional applies here and I'm not even sure it would apply given that she is a nun and not a priest. I also leave out my romantic relationship with Jimmy. I don't know how she might take that given her beliefs.

"So, now your here looking for answers?"

"Well, you have given me some already. I apparently was an orphan here. I assume that's how you know me?"

"Yes. We both were. I wasn't adopted, so I stayed and became a novice instead. We were very close while you were here."

"How old was I?

"You were about two when you came here, and you were here for a few years. I think I was seven when you were adopted, and you were a bit older than me so you must have been eight."

Six years. I was here for six years. No wonder I remembered it when I pulled in.

"But you told me, when you were adopted, you promised me you would come back for me. We were kids and didn't know anything but St. Elizabeth's. We were almost frightened of being adopted rather than excited. You swore you'd escape from your new parents and come back. And now you have."

"I have. But I'm looking for information. Do you think there might still be records of who dropped me off here? I'm trying to locate my birth parents."

"I don't think so. There was a big flood a few years back and all the files were in the basement. Almost everything was lost. And it's such a shame because we were just in the process of putting everything into computers."

"Another dead end." I regret saying this the minute it exits my mouth. The look on her face shows the pain it's caused. I forgot for a moment that while for me she is just another person, for her I am her long lost friend. "That's not what I mean."

"No, I understand. You don't remember me. But in time you will. I'm sure that God will grant you your memories back one day. And when he does you will remember everything. Oh, goodness! I remember something!" She jumps up suddenly.

"What is it?"

"This may not be a dead end for you after all! I had completely forgotten about the diary! Hold on. Don't move! I have to run to my dormitory." She doesn't wait for a response but instead bolts down the aisle and through the rectory, leaving me all alone in the church.

I look up to Jesus on the cross and wonder if Alice is the answer to my prayers after all.

She returns quickly with a little leather book in her hand.

"You had this when you were little. We couldn't read it at first because we were too young, but the sister's let you keep it. It was your mother's and she left it when she dropped you off. I don't think you ever actually read it, it was a lot for an eight-year-old to try and read. And it was in cursive, but you kept it. But then when you moved, you forgot it. I kept it for you in case you ever came back to get it. God must have told me to keep it because He knew you would come looking for it."

She hands me the little leather book. It is a simple black book with a piece of ribbon attached to the spine to keep the place. I flip through the pages and see them all covered in a smooth beautiful handwriting. The words of my mother.

"Thank you so much, Alice. This will definitely tell me something!" Suddenly, the church bells begin to ring.

"I've got to go to prayer. Are you going to stay?" I see the hope in her eyes.

"Do you think it would be okay if I sat somewhere and read this?" I suddenly want to read it cover to cover in one sitting. All the questions I've been wondering about my past could be in this book. I know it's silly to think that. It can't have the answers to questions about the dead girls, but I still feel like I have found the key to everything.

"Come this way. There's a sitting room where you can sit and read as much as you like. I will let Sister Martha know that you will be staying for supper, yes?" She leads me out of the chapel and through a few rooms before we come to a stop in a little room that has an ugly green couch in it. It may be ugly, but it's comfortable, so I sit and after giving Alice a quick hug, I open up the book and begin to read my mother's words.

Before

April 19, 1991

"There are so many stars" Angela says not necessarily to Drew but to the air, to the world, to herself. "Makes you feel kind of small, doesn't it? Almost inconsequential." His hand clasped hers between them.

"You're anything but inconsequential. Especially to me." She turned and smiled at him. They were lying on the dock in her back yard. The sounds of the party behind them seemed far away. It was like the dock was not attached to the shore. Like they were in their own little world on top of the lake, floating away to another time and place.

"I think it's comforting to be inconsequential." Angela said.

"How in the world," Drew sat up on his elbow, his gorgeous hair fell in his face as he turned to her. "Would you find that comforting?" He chuckled as he said this. Angela loved it when he chuckled like that. She could hear adoration in his laughter. It wasn't that he was laughing at her, it was him laughing at the thought of her. And it was laughter of joy.

"Because" she propped herself up on an elbow in order to face him, almost nose to nose with him, "if I'm inconsequential than I can do whatever I want. None of it matters anyway. Suddenly, the world is my oyster because there are no repercussions, no consequences." She smiled at him coyly asking him to question her logic.

"So, tell me Miss Cartwright. What do you want to do?" He moved ever closer without actually getting any nearer. His face was so close to hers that she could see nothing else but him. She broke away from his eyes so that she could take in every inch of his face from his strong jawline, to his eyebrows, one of which had a cowlick in it giving the impression that he was leering at all times. His lips that were only one shade away from his cheeks and pursed closed in anticipation.

"I…" Angela returned her gaze to his strikingly blue eyes and held his sight making sure he looked nowhere else. "Want…." She licked her lips to prepare herself. "To…" She fluttered her eyelids down like she was going to close them. "Go back to my party." In one swift movement she pulled away and hopped up, almost hitting him in the face with her shoulder as she rose so quickly.

"Really?" He laughed, rolling back onto his back, and staring up at her.

"Yes." With a twirl of her blue and red polka dot dress she turned back towards her house and ran up the grassy hill towards the lights of the party.

They were having a double party that night. It was not only her birthday, but it was her father's coming home party. All of her friends and family and a bunch of people from town that were somewhere in between were on her back lawn. Her mother had put up hundreds of Chinese lanterns with candles in them, or rather she had told other people to do it. Her mother hadn't actually *done* much in preparation of the party other than organize it.

"Some people are born to do things; some people are born knowing what needs to be done," her mother would always say to her. Usually, her father would pipe in with "And then there's your mother." But he never said it loud enough for Elizabeth to hear.

Angela peered through the crowd, looking through the waves of familiar faces for the red hair that would highlight Melly. The minute she caught sight of her over by the buffet table, Angela headed in her direction. She peeked behind her to see Drew making his way up to the party. She giggled at him but did not wait for him.

"Chris has really outdone herself with this spread Angela." Melly hadn't even turned her emerald eyes around to see Angela's approach. They almost had a sixth sense about each other that they knew exactly when the other came close. Melly was three years Angela's senior but they had been best friends for years. No one quite understood what kept them so close.

They hadn't even flinched when Melly had gone to school in Columbus. They had simply written letters and paid the long distance to call each other whether their parents had approved it or not.

They had spent each of Melly's breaks together while she was at home and she had even come home secretly without telling her parents once or twice to visit only Angela. They could finish each other's sentences and enjoyed doing anything as long as the other was along for the ride.

"You have to try these meatballs they are absolutely to die for." Melly stabbed one of the delicacies on her paper plate and held it out for Angela to take a bite. She had not lied. It was delicious. Angela took a moment to savor the flavor before swallowing it, so she could speak.

"You sure have a plateful" And Melly did. In fact, Angela could see that she had doubled up her plate in order to hold the extra weight.

"Well, I am eating for two remember?" It seemed unimaginable that Melly's belly was as big as it was. She looked like she was hiding a balloon under her shirt. She was only six months along, but Angela swore it looked like she could pop any day now.

"Well, Little Danielle must be really hungry if you're going to finish that entire plate." Angela said putting a hand on Melly's stomach. It had only been a few weeks ago when Angela had first felt the little girl kick. Melissa insisted it was a girl, even though they had chosen not to find out. She had no reasoning behind it, of course, it was merely "mother's intuition."

"You'll understand when your time comes," she said for not the first time and probably not the last as she took a bite of the homemade coleslaw on her plate.

"That won't be for quite a while I can promise you that." Angela said as she grabbed a plate of her own and began to put food on it.

"You now it's funny, but I remember saying those exact words just about a year or so ago." Melly said with a devious smile and a wink.

Melly had had a runaway romance with her now husband, Harry Evans. She had met him when she was home for summer after her freshman year. She had ended up dropping out the spring of her sophomore year and moved back home to Fareport, got married in August and was pregnant before the first snowfall. They now lived on the Evans family farm with her brother-in-law.

"Don't be putting ideas in her head now, Melly." Drew had finally found his way through the throngs of party guests. "We decided that school was to come first." Drew put his hand on the small of Angela's back.

It was true they had discussed their future. After they had been dating for six months, it was impossible not to. Especially since being a senior in high school, Angela's future was all she could think about. Now, Drew was only a junior, so he had another year yet to decide what to do, but Angela had already applied and gotten accepted into Ohio State University. She had visited Melly a few times during her one and a half years there and had loved the campus. Plus, they had a wonderful art program.

Drew's idea of a future was of a much grander and insanely beautiful sort, but at the same time much more naive and perhaps unattainable.

"I want to walk along the wall of China." He had said to her when she asked him what he wanted to do with his life. "I want to swim in the coral reef in Australia. I want to feel the sands of the Sahara between my toes. I want to leave this town and never look back for a single second." She had felt her heart skip a beat when he said this. While yes, Fareport was a small town in boring old Ohio, it had something special about it to her. Yes, she wanted to get out just as much, she wanted to grow and live and do amazing things. But to never look back, to never come back, even for a visit. It was a little more than what she wanted.

But that was what made Drew.... Drew. He was wild and crazy and fun and never thought about what he was doing he just did it. If there was anyone in the world who would just run off into the sunset and never look back, he was going to be the one to do it. If he could, he probably wouldn't even bother with high school. Wouldn't probably even have bothered with her.

But his next words had gotten her heartbeat back in sync with his own.

"As long as you're by my side what would I ever come back here for?" And with that, Angela fell even further into the rabbit hole that was their relationship. A hole she didn't think she could ever, or would ever want to, climb out of.

"Angela!" Angela was shaken back to the party. Melly was waving her hand in front of her face.

"Sorry. I must have zoned out for a second." She flashed a smile and went back to piling her plate full of food.

She wasn't sure if she could eat all of it but it all just looked so good that she had to have a little of everything.

From then on, the party became a blur. She just finished dishing up her plate when her mother came by and stole her away to parade her in front of relatives and the like. She began answering the same questions multiple times in a row, thinking all the while how much easier it would be if she simply held up a sign with her relationship details and the information about her school and what she was planning on going for.

"So, you're going for art? I didn't even realize that you drew?" Said her Aunt Kelly at one point. Lovely Aunt Kelly with her chunky jewelry and thick glasses that made her eyes grow two sizes too large for her face. She lived alone down in southern Ohio and had come up for the weekend. She was staying at a hotel because it would be "too much of a hindrance on her parents to stay with them, what with the party and everything they had to plan." Angela secretly thought it was because she wanted to be alone with her cat. Mr. Whiskers.

Aunt Kelly had had a husband a number of years ago, but he died before they could ever have any children, so all Aunt Kelly was left with was their grey cat. She took Mr. Whiskers with her everywhere. She had even brought him to the party, although Angela's mother had insisted that he stay cooped up inside rather than disturb the guests.

"That's fine," Aunt Kelly had told Elizabeth. "He wanders if he's left outside and I'm not around. He goes looking for me and he can't find me and gets scared. I just can't stand to leave him alone at the hotel." How alone at the hotel was any different than alone up in her bedroom, Angela had no idea. Perhaps Aunt Kelly was sneaking up there to visit with him throughout the party.

"I don't. I want to be an art critic."

"They have classes for that?"

Suddenly, she was thrown into the same dialogue yet again. No one seemed to understand exactly what it was she wanted to do with her life or why she wanted to do it. Of course, how could they when the closest thing that Fareport had to an art exhibit was the Spring Festival when the local elementary kids did finger paintings and put them on display for the whole town to coo over and brag about how beautiful the seven-year-olds' smudges were.

Angela wasn't even a hundred percent sure that was what she wanted to do but it was her best answer at that moment. She just knew she wanted to be involved in art and as her Aunt Kelly had so keenly pointed out, she didn't have much artistic skill innately built in.

But she just remembered the first time that she had spent the weekend with Melly down in Columbus visiting OSU campus. Melly's roommate was a painter and had invited them out to a showing of one of her friends at a gallery downtown. They had dressed up super fancy and made a night of it. They had had so much fun pretending to know what they were talking about when they were wandering through the various paintings when, suddenly, Angela had turned a corner.

She had come face to face with a painting that was so large it filled the entire wall. It was a painting of an empty birdcage. The door hanging open and a chain hanging where the bird had been restrained. Now she knows it would have been considered a still life except for the hint of a flutter of wings in the top right corner. It wasn't much but it was enough to suggest that it was anything but still. It was a moment. It was the exact moment as the bird had finally achieved it's eponymous Freedom.

Suddenly, Angela's life had changed in that moment the way that the fictional bird's had. She felt such a rush of emotion from the sight of the empty cage, with the bird droppings and feathers left forgotten and the rest of the world at the non-existent wingtips of the captive who was no longer chained. She wanted to be a part of that transferal of emotion. She wanted to bring that to others. She wanted to move people in such a way that they were brought to tears, or to rage, or to smile.

She had immediately gone home and tried to find a way to bring this new desire to life. But she couldn't draw, she tried but her sketches looked like they would fit right in with those spring festival finger paintings. But that didn't stop her need to immerse herself in this newfound world of art. She went to her school and got out books by the armful filled with pictures of paintings from every genre and movement. She threw herself into the one art class they offered at Fareport High. As hard as she tried, she never could get the hang of creating any art of her own, but she spent hours looking and finding art.

Once she cracked that pandora's box she discovered that there was very little art that she didn't enjoy. Even the more modern painters with their abstract paintings of dots and splashes, pulled at her emotional heartstrings and made her head spin with thoughts of multiple meanings and interpretations. Her mother got tired of her constantly showing off the newest piece that had become her obsession, her father humored her, but she could tell that it all went over his head. He didn't have any sort of appreciation for emotions and things. He was more of a down to earth kind of person. He couldn't understand why someone would pay that kind of money for a mere picture. "And a picture of nothing but colors at that."

But he had been her biggest supporter last year when she announced that she wanted to pursue art in college. Her mother had been the one who had fought against it. She wanted Angela to pursue something more suitable, something that would make her money, something that she could make a living at. What her mother didn't understand was Angela wasn't interested in making a living, she was interested in making a life.

But she would not be altered in her decision. She had found that OSU had a program within their art department. It wasn't a huge program by any means, the art department was, of course, predominantly about creating art, not interpreting it. But it was a good program and she looked forward to next year when she would be learning about art every day instead of having to worry about passing chemistry.

There was a crash of glass and gasps from the party guests pulled Angela out of the dull conversation with Aunt Kelly. She looked in the direction of the crash.

Chrissy stood at the door to the back of Angela's house, over the remains of one of the casseroles she had gone into the house to retrieve to refill the buffet table. But Angela couldn't pay any attention to the lost broccoli. Her eyes were stuck on Chrissy. She looked like she had seen a ghost. Or rather like she was still seeing one.

"Oh, dear." Angela's mother headed over to help clean up the mess, but Angela followed Chrissy's line of sight and saw that it fell on her father, standing over with some of the men around the bonfire as it crackled in the almost darkness of twilight.

"Chrissy, what's wrong?" Angela said as she walked over and put a hand on her shoulder. Chrissy hadn't stopped staring over at the bonfire. Now that Angela was standing next to her, she could see that her angle had been slightly wrong. She was looking in that direction, but it was a little to the left of her father. One of the other men. He was currently clouded in smoke and Angela couldn't tell who it was.

"I'm so sorry." Chrissy suddenly broke herself out of her trance and bent over to pick up the pieces of glass and broccoli.

"It's okay, Chrissy. it was an accident. It could have happened to anyone." Elizabeth said standing up with a handful of the wreckage in her hands. She headed into the house to dispose of it as Angela and Chrissy continued to pick up the pieces. Slowly the party around them returned to its usual rhythm as they cleaned up the mess.

"Ouch!" Chrissy cried as she picked up a sharp piece and red entered the mix of green and yellow.

"Oh, Chrissy! Be careful. Here let's get you inside." Angela took her by the arm and led her inside to the kitchen sink and turned on the hot water to run over the wound. It wasn't too deep, but it was long, and it was still bleeding.

"Let me see if we have any bandages." Angela turned to the cabinet next to her where they kept the medicine.

"Son of a bitch!" Angela was momentarily shocked by Chrissy's language. Chrissy was not the kind of person to drop curse words.

"Does it hurt?" Angela found a box of Band-Aids and pulled out a few. It was going to take more than one to close up this cut.

"No, not that." Chrissy wasn't looking at her hand now. She was looking out the window above the sink. Angela couldn't see much through the glass besides the party returning to its original vigor.

"What happened out there Chrissy?" Angela hoped that this time, with no one around she might get a real answer.

"Nothing. Nothing happened. I just.... I just slipped." She took a band-aid from Angela's hands and tried to open it one handed.

"Here let me help."

They got her bandaged up and Angela sent her back to the party while she grabbed paper towels and returned to get the rest of the broccoli mess. She was dumping the remains into the trash in the kitchen when she felt the eyes on the back of her head.

"Quite the little cleaner, aren't you?" Drew stood in the doorway.

"You scared the bejeezus out of me!" Angela laughed as he walked over and drew her into a kiss. The last dirty paper towel was still in her left hand as her right found the side of his face. "Let me finish cleaning up."

"I'd prefer it if you didn't." He smirked and cut off her protest with another kiss, this one longer and more passionate.

"Drew." She broke away with great effort and regret. "I have to go back to the party."

"They haven't missed you yet. Let's go."

"Go where exactly?" she said coyly dropping the used towel onto the counter.

"I have a present for you," he said, then pressed himself closer to her as their lips met again. With two free hands, she was able to explore the waist of his blue jeans and find the strip of bare skin between them and his tee shirt.

"And what might this present be?"

"You're going to like it I promise." His hand was between them, palm on her chest, not grabbing, just resting, caressing.

Then as if a switch had been flipped, he had backed away and was holding something in front of him. It was a gift, complete with wrapping paper and a bow.

"Oh." Angela gasped. "It's an actual… gift." She was startled. She had anticipated that it would be something… else.

"I said I had a present for you. What did you expect?" His smile showed that he knew exactly what she had expected.

They had talked about being physical and had agreed to wait until the time was right. But then they had never decided what made the right time… right. So, now Angela was apparently of a different mind than Drew.

"Well, are you going to open it or not?" He tossed the gift to her and she had to fumble to catch it. She struggled at first with the bow but then the paper slipped right off and revealed a black leather book. It took Angela a moment before she realized.

"A diary."

"A journal," he corrected. "A diary is for little girls. A woman deserves a journal."

She smiled as she flipped through the blank pages. Pages she was going to fill.

"Make sure you put in there how amazing your boyfriend is." he slipped his arms around her again.

"Oh, I will." She smiled. It may not have been what she wanted but she still appreciated it.

"And that's just part one. Part two you'll get later." He whispered in her ear.

"Oh, there's more?" The spark in her heart didn't die out but began to grow.

"It'll be good enough for the first entry in that book of yours." He winked as the door to the back yard opened to her father standing there.

"Angela. You need to come back and rejoin *your* party!" He said his eyes assessing what he walked in on and whether he should give her a scolding. He apparently decided not to since he didn't say anything about Drew's arms around her waist. Angela noted the beer in her father's hand only because of the fact that she couldn't remember ever seeing him drink a beer.

"Coming Daddy." He smiled at her but dropped it when he gave Drew a look before closing the door and returning to the party.

"He doesn't like me much." Drew said as Angela untangled herself from him.

"He just doesn't know you that well. He will get to know and love you the same way everyone does. Remember he's only heard about you in my letters until now." She threw the paper towel from the counter into the waste bin and headed towards the door.

"Come on, you can give me the rest of my present later." And with that, they rejoined the throng of people out in her back yard.

Slowly the swirl of the party began to slow as the night wore on and eventually there was only a handful of relatives saying goodbye to the Cartwrights and Chrissy was attempting to clean up with her damaged hand.

"Mrs. Cartwright, may I steal your daughter for a bit?" Drew interrupted the farewells.

"Oh, I guess..." Her mother, she could tell, was about to say "however." Drew noticed and was quick to take Angela's hand and drag her away before either of them could hear the end of her mother's thought. But they did hear her father's bellow from across the yard.

"Have her home by eleven!" Angela hadn't even noticed that they were headed towards the front yard where Drew's car was parked.

"Thank you," she said as they got to the Jeep.

"You're most welcome. I figured it's time for the second part of your present." He smiled as he started the car.

"And we have to get in your car for that?" Angela said, suddenly confused, as they pulled out of the driveway and headed towards town.

"Well, yeah. You can't walk there." He pushed the button on his radio to start the tape player.

Bonnie Tyler's strained voice began to pour out of the speakers as they barreled down the road towards town. Her cries for a hero were engrained in Angela's ears. It was one of the songs on her mixtape that she had made for Drew for their one-month anniversary. If you were to ask Drew, he would tell you that the tape deck on his car was broken and that he couldn't get the tape out to replace it with anything else, and you might believe him given the fact that the tape deck wouldn't be the first or the last thing to be broken on his car.

However, if you were to ask Angela, she'd tell you that she had checked it once while he was getting gas. He had left her alone for a few minutes to get a soda form inside the store and she had pressed the button that used to have the little triangle with the line beneath it. The tape popped out perfectly fine without even so much as a struggle. She had slipped it back in with a smile just before he came back out.

"Can you give me a hint as to what it is?"

"My lips are sealed. Besides, if I gave you a hint, then you'd just figure it out and that wouldn't be fun for either of us." He rested his hand on her thigh.

"It would be fun for me." She mumbled and began to pay attention to where they were driving to try and figure out where they were heading.

They were driving into Fareport, passing the town square and heading towards the river, but then they turned and headed south, passing the diner where she worked.

"Are we headed to your house?" Drew lived outside of town with his father in a junk yard. They didn't actually live in the junk yard, but they lived on the same property and they worked the junk yard. It wasn't good money, but it was enough that Drew's father had saved up some money for Drew to go to college when he graduated. He may not be able to afford OSU, but Drew wasn't lucky enough to have a mom that came from money like Angela did.

Drew wasn't lucky enough to have a mom at all. Drew's dad never talked about her, but Angela had gotten Drew to tell her that his mother had ran away after he was born, abandoning his father and him alone. She had never brought it up again.

"No. But you're getting very warm."

They turned and headed north towards the lake. It wasn't long and they passed the sign that told them there was no outlet.

"There isn't anything out this way?" Angela protested, confused by Drew's smirk.

"Oh, yes, there is." He continued driving even as the shore came into view and ultimately the only thing that was in front of them was the water and…"The lighthouse? My gift is in the lighthouse?" There were actually two lighthouses in Fareport, but she didn't need to make the distinction between the two. Anyone who said 'the lighthouse' would be talking about the Grand Lighthouse. The Fareport Lighthouse was actually on the other side of town. This one was called the Grand Lighthouse because of the river but it was the only one that was still in use. The Fareport lighthouse had been out of commission for decades and was converted into a museum about the town.

"Sort of." He parked the car next to the fence that blocked the way out to the lighthouse. It was a huge ten-foot fence that had barbed wire across the top. There used to be issues with local kids from the town breaking in and vandalizing the light house. They had even accidentally cut the power and the light had gone out. Luckily, nothing happened but out of fear, the town had put up the fence.

Drew got out of the car and walked over to the gate. It had a chain with a lock on it. But unfazed he pulled out a key and put it into the lock.

"How in the world did you get a key to the lock?"

"Come on, I'll explain inside." He closed the gate behind them, and they headed, hand in hand, to the tower on the edge of the water. Somehow, he also had a key to the door at the bottom of the lighthouse. Stupefied, Angela followed him inside and up the metal spiral staircase. She wondered if they needed to be quiet. Surely there had to be a security guard or light operator here. But Drew didn't seem to worry, so she just followed suit; besides, he was climbing too quickly for her to catch up and be quiet.

When they came to the top, the light made its way past them and was so bright it blinded her for a moment, so that when she followed Drew out onto the balcony, she had to look through the colors on her corneas. She blinked them away to reveal the gorgeous view of Lake Erie that lay in front of her.

"Oh, my God." Angela had been up in the Fareport Lighthouse, it was a field trip for the elementary kids, but it's view was obstructed by the docks and boats that sat on the coast. This view had no such obstruction. Instead, there was nothing but water for as far as she could see from the edge of the handrail onward till it hit the horizon.

"Beautiful, isn't it?" Angela barely noticed that he wasn't looking at the water. She tore her eyes away from the water to look at him.

"How are we able to be up here?" Angela wouldn't put it past Drew to break in here illegally. It was just the type of thing he would do, but something told her that wasn't the case. Maybe it was the keys, or his assured attitude climbing the stairs, or maybe it was the fact that he had that smirk. That smirk that said he was up to something.

"I got a job. You are looking at the new Lighthouse custodian."

"What?" Angela threw her arms around him and kissed him on the cheek, then on the mouth.

"I started last week," he said as she pulled out of the embrace.

"Wait... so what do you do?"

"I just clean everything and check the fuel gauges every day. Make sure everything looks good. Ideally, I don't have to do anything. It's all automated now, but they just need someone to check everything and make sure all is going smoothly every day." Angela beamed at him with pride.

"I'm so proud of you!"

"The best part is I can still work at the yard with father. This takes maybe an hour a day and I get a weekly check. It isn't much but it's something." He smiled, but this wasn't his usual smirk. This was the smile of someone who was happy with themselves. Someone who wasn't up to no good, but rather had done something good.

"But hold on a minute, mister." She back up and tried to pretend to be upset but she couldn't keep the smile off of her face. "I thought this was a present for me?" He chuckled.

"It is. Come and look." He led her around the balcony the eastern side and pointed along the coast of the town. At first, she was too distracted to see what he was pointing at. This view was almost better than the view out to the lake. You could see all of Fareport and all the lights of the houses where night owls were still up reading or watching television lit up the view like a hundred fireflies.

"See that light way out there, right by the water? The last light as you head east along the coast?" She followed the direction of his finger and found the light he was referring to. It was a ways away from town and it was a tiny little pinprick of light but sure enough you could see it there.

"Is that..."

"That's your dock light. We can see it from here." Angela racked her brain but finally she turned away from the coast and looked at him.

"I still don't see the gift."

"You can sail over here, silly. You can sail over here and meet me here anytime we want, and your parents will just think you're out on the boat."

The genius of his plan began to dawn on Angela. She had been sailing since she was little and just a year or so ago, she had begun to sail on her own. In fact, her father almost never sailed the year before his deployment, so the family boat had quietly become Angela's. It wasn't uncommon for her to take sail day or night, by herself, and sail out onto the lake. She never really went anywhere, she simply sailed to get away from stress, but now she had a destination.

"There's a small dock big enough for a single boat."

"It's perfect." She put her arms around him again and pulled him into another kiss. This one was the passionate romantic kind. She even kicked up her leg a little. He pulled out of this one, however.

"You're perfect." He smiled at her, and in that moment, she couldn't have been happier. Everything in her life seemed to just fit together like the pieces of a puzzle.

"I think I'm ready." She threw the words out with hope in her heart. She didn't want to ruin this moment, but at the same time, she had the potential to make this night an even bigger night. Luckily, she had gambled on a game she could win.

"I think so, too. I love you, Angela Michelle Cartwright."

"I love you, too, Philip Andrew King."

May

1

Staring at the little stick in her hands, Angela felt her blood pulse through every vein. She could feel her eyes dilate. She could feel every single hair on her skin stand on edge.

There are certain moments in our lives that seem to go by in slow motion. This one moment felt like it took a whole year to survive.

Her brain went into hyperdrive as she ran through everything that had led her to this moment. Not just the moments and decisions of the last month but all the moments of her life from birth onward seemed to culminate with this. This stick.

She felt a chill crawl its way up her spine and her legs skipped the liquid stage and went straight from solid to gas. She lost all feeling in them so quickly that her torso fell to the toilet faster than she could realize that she was sitting down. The cold porcelain brought back a momentary feeling of having thighs, but it didn't last long. Nothing could last long except that stick. That stick killed any sensation, any thought.

She tried to tell herself to breath. Take in one breath. Just one. Just open your mouth and suck in air into your lungs. Isn't it funny how in your biggest moments the smallest things, the things you do a million times a day, things that take no brain power whatsoever, suddenly become nearly impossible? She couldn't convince herself to breath. She couldn't do anything but stare at that stick in her hands.

Every nerve of her body from her littlest toe to her right kidney stopped working and focused all of its attention on the five inches of plastic in between her fingers; the five inches of plastic that dictated the rest of her life.

Nothing was ever going to be the same, ever again.

Her life was not just flipped on its head. Because that would imply that all you had to do was flip it back. It wasn't altered or rotated or changed, it was obliterated. It was completely annihilated, decimated, wiped off the face of the earth. Her life as she knew it was gone. It was never ever coming back. All she had now was her future. Her future, as dictated by this stick.

More specifically, the little window on the right side of the stick and the little symbol that it contained. A little plus symbol. She didn't think she could ever see a plus symbol the same ever again. She couldn't finish her math course. How could her mind process the simplest formula with that little cross staring at her, judging her, controlling her.

Plus. That meant positive. Positive that she was pregnant. Positive that she had a little body growing inside of her. A body that was not hers. A body that was both hers and his but also neither. An entirely new person, currently in her stomach. Probably no larger than a pea but it was there, nonetheless.

After what felt like ages, she was able to slowly rip her eyes away from the stick and focus on something else, anything else. What they landed on was the mirror across from her. The girl in that mirror seemed a stranger now. With her blonde hair pulled back into a ponytail. Sitting there in her matching pale pink bra and panties.

She stared into her own blue eyes in complete shock and terror. Suddenly, her brain began to be capable of coherent thought beyond the little addition symbol. She began to wonder at how this could have happened.

She, of course, knew how it had happened. She had paid attention in school. It wasn't physically a question of how, but rather a more profound question of how in this enormous universe that this could have happened to her. She, the straight A student. The girl who was applying for colleges, the girl who was going to go out into the world and do things. The girl who had the world at her fingertips. How could this happen to her?

She wasn't so ignorant to think that this was some kind of cosmic punishment for some previous mistake, but even if she were to follow that line of thinking, where would that lead her? To what decision would that point her? She had made all the right decisions.

She had been a good student. She was involved in school. She was popular but she wasn't a bully about it. She was nice to everyone. She was class president. She had a job and helped out around the house. Her parents loved her, and she loved them back. Everything she did was right in line with what she was supposed to do.

And she couldn't comprehend how the actual physical act that led to this could have been the cause of this. How could that have been wrong? It had been absolutely perfect. She refused to allow herself to regret that decision or to think that it had been a mistake. Nothing about that night had been a mistake. It had been the happiest night of her life. How could she regret that?

But what other choice did she have? Sitting here in the bathroom with her mother's cross stitch that hung above the toilet staring at her. "Girls are made of sugar, and spice, and everything nice." She had made it while she was on bed rest when she was pregnant with Angela. Apparently, there are a few other ingredients because sugar and spice and everything nice does not add together to make this little plus sign appear on a plastic stick.

Like a dam that breaks after one too many leaks, her brain became a cascade of thoughts that ran together and had no through line. What was her mother going to say? What was she going to do? What about college? Should she give it up? How would she keep it a secret at school? Would she have to quit the diner? How could she graduate? What would her father think? How could she tell Drew?

Drew.

Wonderful Drew. Handsome Drew. Perfect Drew. Drew who would do anything she asked him to. Drew who would see her through anything and everything. Drew who would follow her to the ends of the earth if she so much as asked. How could she have done this to Drew?

She felt tears welling up in her eyes. They poised on the edge of her eyelids ready to fall like rain. She blinked them away and bit back the need to bellow with pain.

The bathroom walls seemed to close in around her and the small space that had always been comforting suddenly became much too small. And it kept getting smaller, or rather she was getting bigger, at least her belly was. She couldn't stay here any longer. With a surge of energy, she yanked the door open, and her room hit her like a brick wall.

Her four-poster bed was covered in a light pink bedspread. She had four throw pillows on it along with her stuffed teddy bear. What the hell was she doing with a stuffed teddy bear at seventeen? The floral wallpaper seemed to mock her with its prettiness. Her desk, covered in Polaroids of her and Drew, her and Melly, her and her mom, seemed so trivial. Quickly she grabbed pants and a t-shirt. She threw on sandals without even caring if she looked presentable. But hesitated when she got to her door.

Once she walked out that door this would stop being a bad dream. It would start being a reality. A reality that she would have to face. Once she left this sanctuary that was her childhood room, she would have to tell her mother. Maybe not right away but at some point. She would have to admit to herself that this really was happening.

Maybe she could just stay in here forever. If she stayed then, perhaps, every minute would feel as long as that first minute did. If they did, she would die before she would have to deal with anything surely.

But she couldn't stay cooped up in here she had to get out. She had to go somewhere, anywhere. Just not in this perfect pretty, cute room. Away from her flowers, from her teddy bear. Away from her childlike decorations. Away from the pink and the frills. She had to get out. She had to run, to scream.

So, she pulled open the door and stepped out into her new reality.

"Where are you going Angel?" Her father called out his pet name for her as she barreled down the steps and headed to the front door, grabbing her mother's car keys off the wall where they hung next to the door.

"Melly's." Her instinctive answer flooded her with panic. Was that where she was going? Was that where she wanted to go? Did she really want to turn to Melly with this? With anything else her answer would always be yes. Melly was her best friend, her closest companion, her confidante. But with this she was possibly the worst person to turn to.

Melly, who was almost seven months along with a growing child of her own. Melly who would never judge her but would be nothing but a constant reminder of her future. Melly who wouldn't let her forget anything for even a moment.

Melly was out of the question. But that was where her parents would have to think she was. It was the only place she would run to on a Tuesday night at ten o clock at night. It was the only place her parents would allow her to run to.

"Okay, well, don't forget you still have school in the morning." Her father chuckled at himself as she stepped out into the night.

Where was she going? If not to Melly's, then she had to go somewhere. She couldn't just get in her mother's station wagon and just drive without a destination.

Unless she did. What if she just drove away and never came back. Just moved to a new town and changed her name and never looked back. She could just disappear. But then what would she do with the baby? Raise it herself? She wasn't sure what she was going to do with it here let alone in another city. Moving wouldn't solve the problem. At least here she wasn't alone. At least here she had Drew.

Drew.

She could run to Drew. She could run to the light house. He'd be there checking on his equipment about now. If she hurried, she could catch him.

And tell him what?

You're going to be a father. No, she wasn't ready to tell him yet. She wasn't ready to tell anyone. She needed to go somewhere where no one would ask her what she was doing there. She needed to go somewhere safe where she didn't have to talk about it and could forget for a while.

She was driving up to the diner before she even registered in her brain where she was going.

She parked the car in the almost empty parking lot and headed inside while trying to decide on a reason for her showing up so late. Trying to come up with some logical excuse that would explain without telling anyone that she was actually not alone. That she wouldn't be alone for a very long time.

But in the end, she didn't need one.

"What will you have tonight hon?" Chrissy didn't give her a menu since she obviously knew what they had. Angela had started working at the diner about a year ago. She never worked more than two shifts a week, but it gave her some money of her own, so she wouldn't have to ask her parents for everything.

"Just a burger and fries." Chrissy wrote it down and headed to the back to tell the cook. Angela sat in the booth and stared at her hands. She wasn't the only person in the dining room. There was an older couple, as well, who were sharing a milkshake, a man who was covered from head to toe in dirt who must be on break or just off work from the factory.

"I got you a Coke." Chris sets the cold glass bottle in front of her and sits across from her.

"You don't—" She started, but Chris wasn't buying it.

"Look, you don't need to tell me why your here, or why your mascara is running down your face." Angela hadn't even noticed that she had been crying. "I just wanted to sit with you. Is that okay?"

Angela hesitated for a moment before she nodded.

"Do you want to talk about it?"

Angela shook her head.

"That's fine. Do you want to talk about anything else?" Angela's eyes landed on Chrissy's bandaged hand. It looked a lot better than it did two weeks ago but it still looked like it hurt. "Anything but that." Chrissy noticed her gaze and put her hand in her lap instead of on the counter.

"No, I'm okay," Angela lied.

"Well, you sit here as long as you'd like." Chrissy got up and began to walk away. But just before she got to the counter she turned. "Just letting you know. Not saying it out loud doesn't make it go away. Whatever it is."

Angela wanted to tell Chrissy to take her own advice, but instead, she sat silently with her cola.

2

It grew the way a lie does. You tell a little lie to one person and you think it is so small and minuscule that no one will ever know. But then they ask you a question you cannot answer. You have to tell them another lie. You tell yourself it is nothing but another small little lie and it is whiter than porcelain so there is no shame in telling it, even if it's to someone you trust the most. Someone who trusts you just as much.

But it isn't another lie. It is merely an extension of the first. An appendage that has grown out from the same base lie. And pretty soon that appendage is joined by another and another and another until what was once a small sapling of a lie has grown up and is now a tree. And you think it will finally stop because a lie cannot get any larger. But just when you think it's done, it sprouts flowers and drops seeds to grow more trees and soon it becomes a forest. A forest of lies that is so large you can't get out of it and you can't see the tree where it all started. You literally have lost the tree for the forest.

Angela had gone to the library, telling her mother that she was going to Melly's; One of the branches of the first tree. All the meanwhile, telling Melly that her mother needed her to stay at home; yet another one of her many growing trees. She looked up all there was to know about the little lie growing in her stomach. Or at least all that she could find in the public library. The books there were remarkably out of date it seemed.

She wasn't sure why, but the size of the thing seemed the most important thing to her. And there were lots of comparisons made in the books she was reading. luckily for her she knew exactly the date that it had been created. There was only one date that was possible. Having been her birthday it wasn't hard to remember at all.

So, working from that day onward, she figured that she must be in her fourth week which according to the book sitting in front of her, meant that it was the size of a raspberry. A little tiny raspberry, growing in her stomach. Her hand settled on her abdomen without her intending it to. Quickly she snapped the book shut and looked around to make sure no one was watching.

She didn't dare to check any of the books out. Her mother was on the PTA with Mrs. Krawley who was the head librarian. She didn't want word of her research getting back to her mother. She would much rather Krawley be confused by her prolonged stays at the library than be more confused by her reading material. So, after an hour or so more of researching the same things she had the time before, Angela closed up the books and returned them to their rightful place on the bookshelves. All the while keeping one eye searching around for anyone who might notice where she was getting books from.

She knew she was being paranoid. No one knew the Dewey decimal system enough to be able to know what she was looking up just by her location in the bookshelves, but still the voice in the back of her head told her she needed to watch her back and keep her eyes peeled for onlookers.

Logically she knew in her heart that she couldn't keep this lie going. Soon the trees would become so many that someone was bound to notice. Even if they didn't catch on to her lies and avoidances, it wouldn't be long, and that raspberry would become a watermelon. Only about thirty weeks according to the book she had just put away.

Thirty-six weeks, to be exact. She tried to do the math in her head, but her brain refused to do it, so she pulled out her school planner. Her father had bought it for her for Christmas. She was extremely meticulous about her schedule and liked to write all of her school activities down using color coded pens. She opened up to the front where it showed an overview of the entire year of 1990. She began counting from April 19 and counted all the way through the spring and into the fall ultimately overlapping into 1991 on the next page.

That couldn't be right. She counted again and then yet a third time but sure enough, it wouldn't become a watermelon, the last stage of the fruit cycle, until January of the next year. It was a whole year away. Not really, but it was in the next calendar year.

This alleviated a little of the weight on her shoulders. Oddly enough, thirty-six weeks didn't seem so short anymore. It felt more manageable. She would figure a way out of this mess in thirty-six weeks. She had time. Time to think.

She stepped out into the warm air.

June

1

"I have to tell you something." Angela sat across the table from Melly at her house. Melly had her chair sitting at an angle, so her large belly wouldn't bump against the edge of the table. She was about to pop very soon now, and she was more than ready to not be pregnant anymore. Little did she know she wasn't the only one who was ready.

"Hold on." She closed her eyes like she was concentrating. After a moment, she sighed. "I thought I was having a contraction, but I think it was just lunch." She was very clearly disappointed. "Anyway, you were saying?"

Just as Angela was working up the courage yet again to spill the beans, she was further interrupted by the entrance of Melly's husband.

"How you ladies doing in here?" the farmer said as he bent over and kissed his wife on the cheek. He was dressed in flannel with dark blue jeans that were all covered in little bits of dirt like his face, slick with sweat.

"Oh, you know just gossiping." Melly smiled at the peck on her cheek. Angela saw her pregnant glow shine brighter in her happiness. Would she glow like that? "Now you get out of here Harold Evans. We can't talk about you when you're right here. That would be rude."

"Alright." He chuckles and heads back out after grabbing a cookie out of the jar on the counter.

"Anyway, you were saying something important?"

Angela had gone over this conversation in her brain a thousand times. She knew she had to tell someone eventually and of all the people in the world, Melly was the logical choice. She had considered not telling her until she started to show but she risked the possibility that someone else might notice first, someone like her mother or Drew. She was not ready for them to know. She wasn't sure she would ever be ready for them to know. But here she was ready to tell Melly and she couldn't find the words.

"I'm..." Might as well not sugar coat it, "Pregnant."

She waited for the shocked face. She waited for the wide eyes and the freak out. She waited for Melly to get so hysterical that she would go into early labor. All of this she had prepared for.

None of it happened.

"Have you told Drew yet?" It was as calm as if she had asked Angela to pass the sugar. It was like Melly could sense Angela's stress and knew that freaking out would only add to it. Angela silently thanked God for Melly.

"I haven't told anyone yet. Other than you now. I just haven't felt like I could." She waited while Melly mulled it over in her head.

"Okay. What do you want to do about it?" Angela could feel the weight behind this question. She knew what Melly was asking without her having to come out and ask it. She was asking if she wanted to keep it.

"I don't know." She knew it was a horrible answer to a question that she needed to find a good answer to. It wasn't just a question on some exam that she could skip and come back to. It was a decision that could alter the rest of her life.

"Well, do you want my advice?" Melly was always like this. Very separated. She knew that sometimes you didn't want advice, sometimes you just wanted to be able to say something out loud. This was not one of those times for Angela.

"I want your advice."

"You need to tell him. I'm assuming it's Drew's?" Angela nodded. "It's as much his decision as it is yours. You can't leave him out of it." Angela had a feeling that that was what she was going to say. She had been thinking the same thing in the dark recesses of her mind and Melly had a knack for finding those quiet thoughts and giving them a voice.

"I already know what he's going to say," she said weakly, knowing that it was no excuse.

"He still has the right to say it, whatever it is."

That night, after dinner Angela felt as if she were being tested by fate. She had told one person and now it seemed the universe wanted her to tell it to the world. Maybe not the world but at least her mother.

"Honey, are you okay?" Her mother asked from the kitchen sink where she was washing dishes. Angela was putting away clean dishes and hesitated at the cabinet where they kept the plates before answering.

"I'm fine." She knew this wouldn't end the conversation. Her mother was like a dog with a bone.

"You just haven't seemed yourself for the last few days. Is something on your mind?" she said this without taking her eyes off of the dish in her hands.

"I'm just tired is all." Angela hoped that would be enough to throw her mother off the scent, but she knew that the conversation wasn't over even if it was simply postponed to another time. She would need to either tell her or come up with some sort of excuse to tell her. For now, she searched for an excuse to change the subject.

"Where did you get that bruise mom?" She honestly hadn't noticed the bruise before now and while it acted as a convenient subject trajectory, she was also genuinely curious. It was a small bruise, but it looked pretty dark against her mother's pale forearm.

"Oh, I slipped last night while I was getting a glass of water. It's nothing." Every once in a while, Angela was shocked by how alike her and her mother were.

2

Melly's baby boy arrived on June 15. He was a large baby coming in at eight pounds and nine ounces and measuring a whopping twenty-two inches. Melly had ended up having to have a Cesarian because he was folded up like a contortionist just to fit in her too small belly.

When Angela came to visit her in the hospital, dressed in one of her loose tops that had become her mainstay in order to try and hide her own ever-growing belly, she was almost afraid to enter the hospital room to see the two of them. She was afraid that perhaps visions of what might happen in January would lead her to showing signs of panic and perhaps letting something slip to her parents who had joined her for the visit.

Her concerns turned out to be false as everyone's eyes were on the newborn baby.

Little Daniel James.

Melly had had to alter her previously chosen name slightly. Harold had apparently pushed for James, after his father, but in the end Melly compromised by having it be the middle name.

"I just think James is such an old man's name. I much prefer Daniel," she said, never taking her eyes off of the small child in her arms.

Angela was mesmerized, but not only by the baby that was not even a day old, but by her best friend who had become a mother in the last twenty-four hours, and it appeared had become a different person in doing so. She had adopted a glow ever since her pregnancy began but now that glow had strengthened into a beam and it was all directed towards the little life she had created. She never took her eyes off of him for longer than a few heartbeats and the smile on her face was the biggest and most purely joyful smile that Angela had ever seen.

Suddenly, for the first time in the last two months, she looked forward to this child growing in her stomach with something akin to joy as opposed to fear and anxiety. She knew that her situation was worlds away from Melly's. She was not married, she wasn't sure she was ready to handle being a mother or having a child to provide for. She knew the father of that child was not ready. He had not even graduated from high school yet.

But she knew that when the time came, she would be able to experience the joy and happiness that Melly was feeling right now. The knowledge that there was a small being who without her, would not exist. Knowing that to someone, even if it's just a little someone, a little someone with ten little fingers and ten little toes, you are the world. And to you, they are yours.

Harold's brother Benjamin handed Angela a tissue before she even realized that she was crying. She accepted and thanked him. She hadn't even noticed he was tucked away in the corner on one of the hospital chairs. Her eyes like everyone else's had been drawn to Melly on the hospital bed.

"Do you want to hold him?" Melly said, and it was a moment before Angela was aware that it was her Melly was speaking to. She nodded and pulled up one of the chairs and sat next to the bed.

As Melly passed the infant into her arms Angela felt a weight lift off her shoulders. Suddenly, there was no more question in her mind. She knew what she wanted to do.

She wanted this.

Whether she had to back out of school, or whether she had to do it by herself. She wanted this. She needed this. Little Daniel James reached out his little pudgy hand and gripped onto her ring finger and let out a yawn that was almost too big for his little head.

Yes. She wanted this. There was no question. Now she just needed to find out if his father felt the same way.

July

1

The wind whipped her hair out her face as she stood on the deck of the Freedom.

She always loved to go out on the open water whenever she needed time to herself to think. This was where she had decided what she wanted to go to school for, and this was where she had decided what school to attend. This was where she had gone when she had missed her father while he was overseas, and this was now where she was to go while deciding what to do about what her mother said last night.

Angela had told her mother everything.

She had still yet to tell Drew. She had avoided it like it was a plague. She knew she needed to go through with it and tell him, but she was so terrified of what he would say. Especially now that she had decided to keep it.

That was ultimately why she had decided to tell her mother. She knew that there was no way she could continue to lie to her parents when she lived with them. They were going to notice her growing size eventually if they hadn't already noticed her frequent trips to the bathroom to lose her lunch. She had mentally prepared herself for getting sick in the morning, but she didn't realize that it would happen at all times of the day and night.

She had waited until her father was out with an old work buddy so that she could tell her mother woman to woman. She thought it would be simpler this way. In a way she had been right, but in another way, she couldn't have been further from the truth.

"Can I tell you something mother?" Angela asked from across the antique wooden dining table. She waited for her mother to finish a bite of her chicken before continuing but she never got a chance.

"You've finally decided to tell me I'm going to be a grandmother?" Her mother says without any judgement but also without any joy or any emotion at all. If there was any emotion it was disappointment. But it didn't seem to be in the predicate but rather in the first two words. Like she was hurt that it took Angela so long.

"You knew?"

"Of course, I knew Angela. I'm your mother. I know these things. It also doesn't help. that you've gone three months without putting pads on the shopping list." Angela almost kicked herself for not realizing how obvious she had been. She apparently was not as good as she thought she was when it came to lying.

"Well.... I've decided to keep it." At this her mother seemed taken aback. But Angela was ready for this. She had prepared in her mind talking points about how she was going to drop out of OSU and how she was going to pick up more shifts at the diner and Drew had this new job.

"Of course, you will. Was there ever any question?" Angela had not prepared for that.

"You... want me to keep it?" Angela's mother was the perfect wife and mother. She was the type of woman who wrote thank you cards when she borrowed a cup of sugar. She baked cookies and homemade apple pie while her husband was at work. She attended church every Sunday and never cursed. She had morals and standards that bent for no one. The idea that she would be okay with her daughter dropping out of school and raising a child out of wedlock had never occurred to Angela.

"Angela. Come with me. I want to show you something." She stood up from the table and headed towards the front door of the house. Angela wasn't sure where they were heading but she silently put on her shoes and followed her mother out into the dusk. Even though it was almost the height of summer, it still got cold this close to the lake at night time.

They walked along the driveway a short ways and then turned into the little path that cut into the woods. Angela knew where this path lead. She remembered running along it when she was younger and thinking that she had discovered a secret kingdom of rocks. She had run back to tell her father and he had smiled at her, almost not wanting to ruin her naivety. But in the end, he had told her that those rocks were not alive but rather dead like the bodies that rested beneath them. Bodies of her ancestors.

Now as her mother lead her to the family cemetery without a word, Angela began to wonder what all this death could possibly have to do with the little life that was growing in her belly.

Her mother took a moment and just looked at all the stones in front of her. This property came from her side of the family, so these were her ancestors rather than Angela's father's. Angela wondered if her mother knew most of the dead or if they were merely names on stones the way they were to Angela.

"Do you see these flowers?" And honestly Angela almost said no because she hadn't. Whether because she was preoccupied with the stones or because they hadn't been there when she came when she was younger, she had never noticed the flowers. She hadn't even seen them when she walked up until her mother pointed them out. They were in a row in front of the first line of stones. There was five of them. They were pink lilies that were at the end of their perennial life span and wilting before disappearing for the year.

"What about them?"

"After you were born, your father said he wanted to have a baby boy." She walked up to the far left flower. "We got pregnant the summer after you were born. We were so excited. We immediately redecorated the guest room in blue before I was even far enough along to know it would be a boy. We decided on a name. He was going to be Luke. We lost Luke in September." She reached out and touched the wilting lily like she was caressing the cheek of her unborn child.

"But we didn't give up. A lot of women have miscarriages. Even after they have one successful pregnancy. So, after we planted Luke's flower, we tried again the next year. Your father still wanted a boy and I still wanted to give him one. Besides, we had already done up the room." She stood and took a step to the next flower.

"We had Timothy for a little longer. I actually started to show. We began to tell people. We even had a baby shower planned. I never went to the doctor and found out if it was a boy. But I knew. I could just tell in my heart. But we lost him in the middle of the night in April." Angela isn't sure if the memory that pops into her head is real or if she is making it up, but she vaguely remembers her mother acting funny after one of her birthdays when she was extremely young. She remembers asking why she was crying.

"I'm just so happy you're another year older baby girl," she had said.

"Jessica lasted the shortest. I decided to give her a girl's name because..." She sniffs back a sob before continuing. "Because we hadn't even named her yet and I didn't want to waste another boy's name." She took an extra-long moment with the third flower. Tears were streaming down her face.

"Then we had Eli. Eli was our little miracle. He was so close. You probably don't remember. You were only five. He was going to make it. He even made it to the hospital. It was the right date. Everything was right. It was going to be the one." She smiles at the memory. "But when the doctor pulled him out, I knew. He tried to hide it from me for a moment. He tried to smile and let me be happy for a moment longer. But I knew. A mother knows. They let me hold him. He was so cold. It was like he was a baby doll. I kept expecting him to open his eyes. But he just... he never did. Your father had to pry him away from me."

Angela felt tears running down her own cheeks. She had never known that her parents had even tried for another child. Obviously, she had wondered why they hadn't had another one, but she had always just thought that maybe she had been enough. Suddenly, her parents' absolute devotion to making sure she had everything she ever wanted made sense.

"And then there was Matthew. You are the only person who knows about Matthew now. Your father doesn't even know. I didn't want to get his hopes up again. Not after Eli. Eli was the hardest. We had gotten so close to only have it ripped from our hands. I couldn't do that to your father again. So, I didn't tell him when I missed my period. I kept it a secret and tried to hold on to him with all my might. But I lost him, too. Matthew was a good boy, though. He waited until your father was at work before he left. That way I could... That way I could clean up and hide it away before his father came home. He knew I didn't want to tell anyone. He was such a good boy." She gave the last flower a kiss before standing back up and facing Angela.

"You have to keep it, Angela. You have to. You might never get another chance." She walked right up to Angela and hugged her. "You hold onto that baby with all your life. You hold on to it and never let it go."

When they got back to the house and were cleaning up dinner, her mother told Angela that she shouldn't tell her father.

"Let me tell him. I'll make sure he understands," she said. Angela wasn't sure what that meant but she decided to trust her mother. If she thought she could make things easier with Angela's father, then she was going to let her.

So, now she is out on the boat while her mother is presumably telling her father that they are going to be grandparents. While she lets the wind point her boat, she lets her mother point her father. Meanwhile, the small child in her belly continues to grow next to the pit in her stomach. She knows that the next person she needs to tell is Drew. But instead of telling him, she just keeps sailing, enjoying the wind against her face and her hand on her stomach.

2

When Angela arrived at home, her parents were waiting for her at the kitchen table. The screen door closing was the only sound as she walked in.

It had never occurred to her, but it now seemed strange that her father hadn't returned to the force. He had been a police officer her whole life. Even had been a chief for a year. But then he had suddenly decided that he wanted to join the war effort overseas. He had been too old, so he had to join with an independent company rather than with the actual armed forces. And yet now that he was home, currently living off of the payments from Darkwater, coupled with his wife's inheritance, he still got up every morning and dressed as if he was going to the office, but he never went.

"Sit down, please." Angela could tell from the tone of his voice this was going to be a difficult conversation. She had always been much more susceptible to the quiet disappointment form of punishment rather than the loud anger, and her father's voice was almost a whisper.

"I wanted—" Angela was going to say she wanted to tell him earlier, but he held up a hand to silence her. He took a moment before he said anything, the entire time looking at the oak of the kitchen table.

"We have decided what we are going to do," he said with authority. Angela looked to her mother, but she was looking out the window. She was clearly allowing Angela's father to have his way of things. All Angela could hope for was that she agreed with whatever he said.

"We are going to keep this... child." He clearly struggled to let the word pass his lips. "But we are not going to let this ruin your life." Angela didn't understand what he meant by ruin her life. Once again, she looked to her mother for answers, only to receive nothing in return as Elizabeth stared out the window silently.

"You will stay at home and let no one know. You will tell your friends that you are sick. I have a cousin who works at OSU. I will give him a call and explain that because of your... illness, you will need a year off. I'm sure with a donation of some sort we will make them understand." When he said illness, it didn't sound like a lie he was giving to excuse her; it sounded like his actual feelings on the pregnancy.

"When the... the child is born we will take it on as a second child, and we will act as if your mother had a... another child." It was as if the word baby was poisonous to his mouth. "I'm sure some will question it, but we will give them no choice but to believe us."This is the first time he looked away from Angela. He glanced at her mother, who continued to avoid the conversation by looking at the forest through the window. Angela realized that she was looking in the direction of the cemetery.

"That is what we will do." He then stood up. He never looked at Angela again. Instead, he simply walked out of the room without waiting for a response.

Angela was dumbfounded. She didn't understand what she was supposed to say. How could he expect her to stay in the house and not tell anyone? How could he expect to keep this a secret? And to make this decision for her without even asking her opinion or thoughts, it was like she was a five-year-old who was being put in time out, except this time out was going to last six months.

"Mother you can't let him do this. I can't—"

"Your father knows best, dear. This is what's best. You didn't think you'd be able to raise this child alone, did you?" She finally looked away from the window, but the loving woman who had caressed flowers the night before was gone. Instead, she was cold and demeaning.

"I wasn't going to do it alone."

"That *boy*" she said it with a look of distaste like she had just taken a sip of spoiled milk "Will not have anything to do with *our* child." The possessive pronoun cut through Angela's heart like a knife. "You are never to see that *boy* again."

"You can't—" This time it was her mother's hand that silenced her slamming hard on the laminate countertop.

"There will be no arguments. This is what is best for everyone. Now please go up to your room." Her mother did not sound herself. It was almost like her father was speaking through her. Angela couldn't remember a time when neither of her parents would listen to her voice. Suddenly, the void in her stomach that had grown full of lies plummeted to the depths of her soul.

As she stood up to leave the room her mother turned back to the window.

August

1

"You can't let them do this, Angela!" Melly's voice had been almost a cry over the phone. Angela had put off telling Melly in hopes that maybe her parents' plan had been an idle threat and once they realized that their plan would never work that they would let her go and see Melly. It would all be a bad dream that she could tell Melly about after the fact. But they hadn't woken up and it was mid-August.

Melly had apparently been over to the house to check on Angela two weeks ago. This was the longest they had ever gone without speaking to each other and she had been worried, But Angela had been upstairs and hadn't heard the door. Her mother had told Melly she wasn't allowed over anymore and closed the door in her face. This had prompted Melly to call incessantly to the point that Angela's mother started leaving the phone off the hook effectively cutting them off from the rest of the world.

Her mother was like her security guard. She watched Angela like a hawk and made sure she did not leave the house or pick up a phone. Angela had tried to weasel her way out of the house with excuses about wanting to go sailing alone but her mother didn't buy it. She had tried to say that she needed to go and give her two weeks at the diner or at least explain to them where she was, but her mother said her father had taken care of it.

She finally got a hold of Melly by waiting till the dead of night and sneaking downstairs to call her and whisper through the phone line of her imprisonment.

"I don't know what to do Melly. What should I do? Just leave? Where would I go? I have no money. It's not like I made any good money at the diner and I wasn't exactly saving up for anything." She kept her voice the smallest whisper she could in order to not wake her prison wardens.

"Come and stay with us. We have plenty of room. Just walk out the door now and I'll wake Harry up and he will come and get you."

"I can't do that to you. You have a houseful with Ben and the baby. Besides, that still doesn't give me any money." Angela had to resist the urge to jump at the idea of running away to Melly's house.

"Angela. I'm telling you. You need to get out of that house. They can't keep you captive. Come to my house and we will help you figure things out." Angela sat on the couch in the living room where she grew up playing, and contemplated leaving.

She had mentally prepared herself to leave for school, but this was something different. This wasn't just leaving, this was fleeing. Was she prepared to leave her house and her parents and her home? Did she really have a choice?

Her hand went to her stomach. She had noticed that it had begun to do that anymore whenever she was worried or frightened. She tried to think of what was best for the child.

If she went through with this it would be the first real act of defiance she had ever done against her parents. She had never broken curfew, she had never actively gone against their wishes, she had always been a good girl. But desperate times called for desperate measures and it wasn't like she was doing this out of spite. She was a prisoner in her own home and that was no way to live.

"Wake Harry up."

Angela packed a duffel bag with a few things she knew she would need but she was afraid to take too much time packing and possibly wake up her parents. She only hesitated once as she came to the front door her hand on the door handle.

Was she really ready to do this? Suddenly, this felt like more than just defying her parents. It felt more like she was growing up, becoming an adult leaving her childhood behind. But isn't that what we are supposed to do? Isn't that the natural progression of things? If so, then why did this feel anything but natural?

She walked out to the road and stood waiting for her knight in shining armor to come and rescue her from the castle. But that wasn't exactly right. She tried not to think of it that way because in that metaphor her parents became the evil king and queen and that wasn't what they were. They weren't evil they were just confused. Maybe once she got out and her parents saw that she wasn't a child anymore they would understand.

That had to be what would happen. They would understand. This wasn't the end of everything. It was the beginning. That's what it was. That's how she would have to look at it. A new beginning. A new life, like the one growing inside of her.

2

Living at the Evans' was anything but the end of a fairytale.

Daniel was nothing like he had been in the hospital. In the hospital he was a beautiful ray of hope for Angela. A sneak peek into the beauty of what was possible for her and her child. A loving mother holding her perfect little angel in her arms. But now he became the antithesis of all that hope. Instead, of beauty he was full of disgusting gunk that seemed to come out of every orifice, his mouth, his nose and, of course, into his diaper. There seemed to be no end to it. And if that wasn't enough, Angela was convinced that the only time she had ever seen him sleeping was that day he had been born.

The nights were filled with his screams adding a dissonance to the melodious lullabies that Melly hummed and sung as she paced the living room bouncing him up and down trying to get him to fall asleep for at least an hour, so they could all get some sleep. Angela was in the study on the couch towards the back of the house, but it didn't seem to matter where you were in the house. Daniel's cries seeped through the walls till they filled every nook and cranny so that not even the mice could sleep.

Angela lay awake in the middle of the night listening to his cries, but the screams of the infant was not the only reason she couldn't sleep. Her belly was churning, but this wasn't morning sickness. This was guilt. Guilt and regret.

She hadn't spoken to her parents since she ran away. They had tried to call and talk to her. Melly had answered the phone and told them Angela was there, but when they asked to speak to her, she declined. She knew they were only going to try to convince her to come home and she was not ready to come home yet. She wasn't sure she would ever be able to go home.

She also wasn't sure if she would ever be able to afford not to. Melly had refused to allow her to contribute to the groceries or rent since she had moved in. Angela had started keeping her tips in the empty cookie jar in the kitchen. She had quite a bit of money in there now. When she eventually left, she planned on leaving most of it there. Melly would never take the money but perhaps if she just found it one day, she would be able to accept it.

That was if Angela ever did go back to her parents. She resisted it with every fiber of her being, but she also couldn't see an alternate future for herself.

Even though she didn't want to return, she felt that it was expected. She felt pulled by some imaginary force that told her that she needed to do what her parents said whether she agreed or not. She knew this was just her subconscious following the trend of what she had done for most of her life, but it was difficult to resist, nonetheless.

So, she lay listening to the ear-piercing screeches coming from the little boy in the living room and tried to concentrate on the harmony of her best friend's voice to help soothe her to sleep.

When the birds outside decided to chime in their two cents on the matter, Angela decided it was time to give up and headed downstairs for some coffee or tea. When she entered the kitchen, she found that she was not alone in her effort to escape the cacophony with a soothing mug of warm beverage. Benjamin sat at the table with a mug of coffee.

"Good morning," she said as she pulled out a mug. It said number one dad in red letters. It was a gift for Harry. Harry was the only one who seemed immune to his son's cries. He never had issues sleeping through the night. Melly said it was because he snored so loud, he couldn't hear anything over top of it.

"Does it count as morning if you haven't been to sleep yet?" Benjamin said without turning to look at her. Angela sat down and suddenly the screams from the other room became dulled by the silence between them. Angela had never had much interaction with her best friends brother-in-law. They had never had any reason to converse and had never been in this close quarters for this long before. The only interaction she could ever remember having with him was when he handed her the handkerchief in the hospital the day Daniel was born.

She tried to search for something to say but nothing came to mind. She didn't know anything about Benjamin other than that he was Harold's brother. The two of them had inherited the farm from their parents and had decided that instead of splitting it and having to deal with the financial issues, they would both just continue to live there together. There was more than enough room and it wasn't like either of them could tend to the fields by themselves.

"Wonder when he'll ever stop." Angela finally said just to fill the void. Benjamin didn't say anything in response. In fact, Angela couldn't even be sure he had heard her given his complete lack of response. But the longer she looked at him the more she began to feel like it wasn't the screams from the baby that were blocking her words from reaching him.

He was staring at the table with such an intense look, and he was clutching his mug of coffee like it was his last chance for survival. He was almost shaking with the exertion. Something about him just wasn't right. It was like he was grappling with some terrible something in his head and nothing beyond his head mattered to him at the moment.

"Ben, are you okay?" She reached out a hand to touch his and it was like popping a bubble. One minute it was there, and then suddenly, it was gone. He flinched back like she had almost scared him and then recovered quickly and acted as if nothing was wrong.

"Yeah, just tired." He laughed it off and stood up and walked over to the sink. He poured out his coffee which Angela noticed was almost completely full. "I'm gonna go out and get an early start on the day. Lots of work to do." He didn't look back as he walked out the screen door towards the barn.

Angela almost made a joke about him getting more sleep in the barn than in the house, but she didn't feel like the moment would welcome humor.

Just then, Melly brought the cacophony with her into the kitchen. She was bouncing the poor baby so hard she was probably doing more harm than good in the way of calming it down.

"Oh, good, you're awake. Can you hold him for just a second? I have to pee like a race horse. Please? Harold is still asleep." Angela wanted to say that Melly should go wake her husband up, so he could suffer like the rest of them, but instead, she was the good houseguest and nodded yes before taking the baby in her arms so Melly could run to the restroom.

Angela tried bouncing him on her shoulder as she walked in circles the way that Melly had but it didn't seem to be doing anything except gyrating the pitch of his wails with the up and down motion and on top of that made her empty stomach do somersaults. So, she only did a few bounces before she gave up and transferred him to a lateral position, so she could look him in the eye.

"You need to be quiet, so we all can get some sleep," she said sternly to his open mouth, not expecting any response, other than the caterwauls he had been spewing for the past twelve hours.

Much to her surprise, though, he snapped his mouth closed and opened up his blue eyes and looked at her completely bewildered. Whether it was because he had expected to find his mother and didn't, or because she had simply spoken to him without putting it to melody, something had confused the poor thing and he was now looking at her as if she were some foreign object from outer space.

But he kept his mouth closed and didn't make a sound.

The silence was beautiful in its serenity. It was as if the world had stopped moving, time had stopped and nothing else mattered except that there was no sound.

"Angela!" She heard through the walls of the house followed by thumping and scrapping as Melly scrambled and bolted her way down the hallway back to the kitchen running at full speed until she barreled through the door and saw her child in her best friend's arms.

"I thought for sure you'd killed him." She whispered to herself staring dumbstruck at the young woman holding the younger infant in her kitchen. "Is he asleep?" She whispered as she walked on tip toes towards Angela.

"No. He's just... He's quiet." Angela said, at least she thought she did. She was so enraptured with the little blue eyes staring back at her. They still looked confused at her, but she was afraid to break eye contact for fear that it might bring back the screaming.

"How did you do it?" Melly asked as if she were almost afraid of the answer, like she expected Angela to say that she had made a deal with the devil or had sold her soul for silence.

"I... I don't know." Angela sat down on the chair behind her careful not to change the angle of the baby in her arms. "What do I do now?" She yanked her eyes away for a moment to look at Melly. She braced for the screams, but they didn't come.

"Now? Now you have a new job. Call in and quit the diner right away. You're not putting this baby down for the next two years." A smile broke across Melly's face as she tried to control her joy.

"No, but seriously, though, what do I do now? I can't just sit here like this. In case you didn't know I haven't slept yet either." Angela was suddenly terrified. Afraid that Melly would leave her and go sleep while she was stuck on this wooden kitchen chair with the child in her arms unable to move or do anything for fear of waking the dragon.

"Maybe he'll let you get in the La-Z-Boy?" She said this, almost asking the infant for permission. He didn't respond, which was as good as a yes, so Angela carefully stood up and slowly walked into the living room with Melly following closely behind like someone who was "helping" to move an extremely heavy piece of furniture by not really doing anything other than directing.

"Be careful! Don't bump the door! Here I'll get it. Don't sit so fast. Do you need a pillow? A blanket? Are you cold? Do you wanted to take off your shoes?"

"Melly. Quiet." Angela hissed at her.

"What?" Initially Angela had said it because she had been enjoying the silence only to have the screaming replaced by Melly's directions, but then, as she said it, she noticed Daniel's eye lids slowly sink to meet his cheeks and his thumb slid up into his mouth.

"He's... asleep." Angela breathed.

"Thank God. No, not God. Thank *you*." Angela let out a slow sigh as she relaxed back into the blue comfy chair and Melly pulled the lever at the side to kick up her legs.

The last thing Angela remembered before falling asleep was telling Melly to go get some rest.

3

"This isn't what I ordered." the old man barked as Angela placed the food down in front of him, but she didn't hear him at first. She was distracted, her head someplace else completely.

"I'm sorry?" she said, still not really paying attention or looking at him.

"Here I'll get it fixed for you sir." A hand came in form out of nowhere and grabbed the plate form in front of him. It took Angela a moment to realize that it was Chrissy who had come to her rescue and was now leading her to the back of the restaurant back behind the wall that separated the customers from the cooks.

"Sorry Chrissy. I'm not feeling myself today." She apologized and shook her head trying to clear her mind.

"Today? Honey you haven't been yourself all summer. Come on let's sit down." She led Angela to the break room, not that you could really call it that. It was a little alcove at the back of the kitchen that had two chairs and a table that was always covered in dirty dishes and food that looked like it had been there since the last owners had sold the restaurant.

Angela had started picking up shifts again, not many but a few a week. Melly wouldn't let her do more than that since she seemed to be the only one with the magic touch for Daniel, but Angela insisted that she needed to put some money towards the food for the house. She was obviously costing them money by giving them yet another mouth to feed and while Melly insisted that it was unnecessary Harry had told her that it was probably a good idea. Besides, it gave Angela a chance to get out of the house.

"Now you take a break. I'm gonna go check on my tables and yours, and then we will chat. Here eat this." Angela wasn't sure where Chris got the candy bar from, but she was grateful for it.

Angela had been sleepwalking her way through work for a while but today had been especially difficult. She had received a letter on the Evans' doorstop from OSU. Apparently, it had arrived at her house and her father had brought it by for her. He had not stayed to try and talk to her. The phone calls had stopped a week or so ago, so her parents apparently had either decided that they respected her decision to isolate herself from them or they were punishing her with their silence. Either way he had left the opened envelope on the welcome mat and gotten back into his Cadillac and driven off before Angela could even put the baby down.

Her postponement had been approved. On the one hand it was comforting that her father had still gone through with his plan enough that she could still go to OSU next year. However, it didn't seem all that plausible under her current situation. She couldn't take the baby with her and she couldn't leave it at the Evans.' It was almost like her father was baiting her. Telling her she could still come home. She could still go with their plan and go to school. All she had to do was turn in her freedom for the next five and a half months.

The Hershey bar in her hand helped to wake her up but it didn't bring her mind back to the present. She shook her head to try and focus but all she could do was see images of her with the baby. She had begun fantasizing about it ever since she had become Daniel's caretaker. However, every time she pictured her child it was like one of those children you saw on television from some third world country, and she looked like she hadn't washed her clothes since before the child had been born.

If there was one thing living with the Evans' had opened her eyes to was the cost of a child. She was amazed how quickly they went through diapers and formula and wet wipes. It seemed like every other night Melly was going to the grocery store and coming back with bags and bags and bags of baby stuff. She didn't know how they were affording it, let alone housing four adults, of whom two didn't have full time jobs. Melly had talked about going back to work but Harold had told her no.

They had fought about it the other night and it had kept Daniel awake. Even Angela could do nothing to get him from adding his screams to theirs. Between her cooing at the baby and the three of them yelling the only quiet one in the house was Benjamin, who simply sat on the front porch whittling.

"Now tell me what you are doing here?" Chrissy snapped Angela back with a question.

Angela didn't know how to respond. At first, she wanted to say that she was scheduled to work but she knew that wasn't what Chrissy was asking. She knew that Angela wasn't in it. Something was off and Chrissy wanted to know what it was.

"I need the money." This was true. it may not be the whole truth, but it was the part that she felt like she could talk about.

"No, honey, I'm not talking about work. I'm talking about here in this damn town. What are you still doing here? Aren't you supposed to be heading to Columbus? Ain't you supposed to be getting your pretty hiney outta here?"

Chrissy was right. Angela still hadn't made her situation public knowledge mainly because she didn't want things getting back to Drew. The two of them hadn't spoken in over a month. There had been no fight or even anything that was approaching a squabble. It was simply that she had started avoiding him, being afraid to tell him what was going on and between her parents keeping her locked up and then her subsequent move she assumed he had no way of knowing how to get a hold of her.

She didn't know what exactly she would tell him when she finally got a chance to talk to him. She guessed that the truth would have to be enough, but it might not be. He may not forgive her keeping this from him for so long which, of course, made her all the more hesitant to talk to him and officially tear them apart. But was this any better? Was it better to have a ghost of a relationship than to officially stab it with a knife?

She tried to focus on the here and now, that was all she could fathom to be capable of at the moment. Chrissy was wondering why she hadn't gone off to school. Angela hadn't thought of that when she went back to work. She had figured that if she wore baggy shirts and tried her best to not stand up too straight no one would think anything was wrong. But her mere presence was telling even without her distracted demeanor.

"I'm taking a year off." She could see in Chrissy's eyes that she wasn't going to accept that as an answer. She was like a hawk hunting its prey. She could tell there was more to the story and she was going to hear it.

"I've moved out of my parents' house." She suddenly felt close to tears. She didn't know if it was sadness from the rift that had been driven between her parents and her or if it was the fear of what she was going to do when the baby eventually came or if it was simply exhaustion from keeping up a facade of knowing what she was doing or even pretending to think that she knew what she was doing.

"Now why would you do something stupid like that? Your parents are great parents." Angela almost laughed with how simple Angela made it sound. She, of course, didn't know the story. She didn't know that her parents had made her a captive in her own home. Whether they had done it for good reasons or not that was what they had done.

"It's a complicated situation." Was all that she could muster. She could feel the tears brimming her eyelids and even felt one or two break the barrier and cascade down her cheeks.

"Well, you need to talk to someone, honey. You can't bottle all this up inside and try to deal with it all by yourself. You can talk to me or you can talk to someone else, but you need to talk about it." She reached out a hand, but it didn't feel comforting it felt intrusive.

Angela suddenly didn't want to be there. She didn't want to be asked any more prying questions or given any more life advice. She just wanted to get out and run away from it all she wanted to escape like the bird from the cage and never come back.

So, that's what she did she stood up and bolted. She pushed past one of the dishwashers who was getting something out of the freezer and ran through the back door and out into the bright sunshine.

She hadn't driven since she didn't have a car; she had instead ridden in with Melly while she went to do some errands around town and make the rounds to show the baby off around to friends and family who hadn't seen him smile yet, so she did not have any mode of transportation other than her two feet. So, she began to walk. Then she began to run. Without realizing it she was bolting. She was pumping her legs up and down so hard that her legs began to scream at her, but she didn't listen she just kept running.

She gasped for breath but would not stop to catch it. If she stopped, she would have to face her problems and right now she didn't want to face them she wanted to run away she wanted to escape.

If she could have, she would have flown.

But she wasn't a bird escaping a cage. She did not have wings to take to the air. She also wasn't a runner. She had never been athletic, and it wasn't long before the screaming muscles could not be ignored. She bent, doubled over by the side of the road. She didn't bother to take in her surroundings and see where she was. She hadn't even been paying enough attention as she was running to know in which direction she had headed. She glanced at the fields to either side and tried to figure out where she was, but she didn't recognize any of the landmarks.

She knew she was out of town and probably had headed south since she couldn't see the lake anywhere, but that didn't help her much in the way of knowing where she was. She was exhausted to the point that she wasn't sure she would be able to walk back to the restaurant besides that wouldn't do her much good given that she probably no longer had a job. They probably did not appreciate her literally running out in the middle of a shift.

She would have kicked herself if she had the energy. Here she was with no money and no future and she squandered the one way she had of making money. Now she really was going to end up in the poor house and maybe take her best friend's family down with her.

And for what? To run away from a nagging waitress? And was she really nagging? With the clarity of a pounding head, she could push aside her emotions for a moment, long enough to see that Chrissy had simply been concerned for her. She had wanted to help, and Angela had run away from her. What was wrong with her? Did she want to ruin her life?

She couldn't stand it anymore, literally or physically, so she simply sat. Sat down on the side of the road, gravel digging into the back pockets of her jeans.

Jeans that were already almost too tight. She had almost went without buttoning them today. As she thought of that she went ahead and unbuttoned them. What did she care now? No one was going to see her out on this road.

She sat and caught her breath and tried to decide if she was ready to head back into town. That was the logical place to go. Sure, she couldn't go back to work, but she could at least get back to the diner so Melly could come pick her up and take her home. Maybe she could even go back and talk to the manager and see if she could keep her job. They hadn't actually fired her yet. She had only been gone maybe fifteen minutes. Though it would be half an hour by the time she got back if not more. She still hadn't started walking yet, so her odds of getting back before her tables all left wasn't looking good.

After her heart beat resumed a normal rhythm, she got up off the hot pavement and started to walk. She hadn't seen a single car drive by the entire time she had been sitting but after only two minutes of walking a cop cruiser slowed down on its way towards her. She didn't really feel like talking to anyone but given that it was a policeman she felt obligated to at least let him know that she was okay and hadn't broken down or anything.

"You okay, miss?" The young guy, leaning across his passenger seat to look at her, didn't look old enough to have a driver's license let alone be a police officer.

"I'm fine. Just out for a little stroll." She almost laughed at herself.

"You sure? You don't look dressed for a walk." She hadn't even thought of the fact that she still had on her name tag and apron. She realized how absolutely silly she looked walking along the side of the road with her uniform on. Talk about being in the weeds.

"Oh, you know, chasing down someone who forgot their change." She attempted to laugh at her own joke but even she didn't find it funny.

"Would you like a ride somewhere?" He offered, and suddenly, he looked different. She saw his blue eyes as youthful and caring instead of childlike and curious.

"Sure. Why not?" She reached out and opened the door and let herself into his car.

Sitting in the cool interior of the car she realized just how hot it was outside. She figured she was probably sweaty and gross from her impromptu run and tried to avoid looking at herself in the side mirror. The tie in the back of her apron pressed uncomfortably into her lower back as she leaned back in the seat, so she reached behind her and untied it, balled it up and held it in her lap.

"So, where would you like me to..." He had looked over at her and his eyes had been pulled down by her movement. She looked down and remembered that she had unbuttoned her pants.

"Shit!" She hastily buttoned her pants back, sucking in her stomach as far as it would go in order to do so. "I'm sorry."

"No. You're fine." She could tell he was laughing at her inside. She felt herself go red with embarrassment.

"I'm having a really shitty day. I'm normally a lot more..." Angela hesitated trying to find the word she was looking for.

"I think you're just fine miss." This time it was his turn to turn red. "Not fine. I mean you're fine, but not like... Not that you aren't but I just." He turned back to the stationary road in front of him and put both hands securely on the steering wheel and took a breath. "You're—"

"Fine." She interrupted him to try and alleviate his awkwardness. Yet again he appeared like a pubescent teenager instead of a police officer.

"Where would you like me to take you?" He asked this without looking at her. She could tell he was anxious to end their interaction and avoid any further embarrassment on either part.

"Why don't you take me..." She almost said home but then realized that he didn't know where that was. But then again, neither did she. No, that wasn't right. Her home was still her home. She just wasn't living there at the moment. "Just take me back to work."

He nodded and checked both ways before attempting to turn around, he ended up having to do a three-point turn which only made the poor boy even more red in the face. Angela figured work was best. That way Melly didn't show up and worry about her, she could see about getting the manager to forgive her, and best of all could get out of the cop car of awkwardness.

"Some days I wish I could run away from work, too," he said as they came to a stop at a stop sign. She didn't remember running through an intersection, but she had been pretty out of it when she had been running. She counted her lucky stars that she hadn't been hit by one of the ten cars that would drive around Fareport at any given moment.

"Sadly, we always have to come back eventually, don't we?" she said. She didn't understand how he could drive around in this car. There was no radio, except for the one used to communicate to the police station which was nothing but static at the moment. She figured not much other than static ever came over its speakers. Fareport was a quiet town if there ever was one. The last time she had heard about a crime being committed was when someone stole some firewood from the grocery store last winter and Tom, the owner of the store, had decided not to press charges.

"Yep, I guess so," he said, though she felt he only agreed because he didn't have anything else to say.

In the awkwardness between them, she suddenly felt very intimately close to him. She wasn't sure how many people normally sat up here with him. If he ever picked anyone up, don't they normally sit in the back? Why wasn't she in the back? She had let herself in, so maybe he just had been too awkward to correct her.

"Don't you usually have a partner? I mean not you specifically but don't cops normally travel in twos?" Angela wasn't really sure of what she was talking about. Most of her knowledge of the interior of a cop car came from watching Miami Vice and she didn't even watch that very much.

"We don't have enough officers to travel in partners for regular patrols. If we have a situation we are supposed to go in pairs, but that happens so rarely, we don't bother driving together." She realized with a smile that those thirty or so words came out so much easier than anything else he had said.

They pulled into the parking lot of the diner and parked right beneath the neon sign advertising Beer n' Burgers.

"Well, I really appreciate the ride. It would have taken me much longer to walk back. So, thank you," she said, hesitating to get out of the car. She wasn't sure if it was her trying to capture as much of his cool air conditioner as possible or if it was fear of returning to work, or perhaps something else, but she didn't quite want to get out of the car yet. Initially when she got in, the awkwardness had been so tangible that she had wanted to get out at the next opportunity, but now she wasn't so sure.

"I'm Angela, by the way." She wasn't sure what made her say it, but she suddenly didn't feel like a stranger to him, and she felt the need to tell him so.

A burst of static exploded the silence from the radio.

"We have a sixteen over on Water Street." It was a young woman's voice. "Any officer near the location, please report and follow up. I repeat, we have a sixteen over on Water Street." Another burst of static signaled the end of the call.

"Well, Water Street is just over there. I'd better let you go do your job." Angela said, opening the door but still not fully getting out of the car. It was like there was some sort of gravitational pull that kept her on the black leather seat.

"Probably, although a sixteen is just an animal situation. It's probably Mrs. Thompson's cat got out again. She files a report about it every other week claiming it was stolen but it always turns back up." He chuckled. Angela noticed he hadn't exactly asked her to get out. If anything, he was reassuring her that it was okay if she stayed for a moment longer.

Finally, the awkwardness got the better of her and Angela got out of the car.

"Thanks again," she said before closing the door and walking around towards the diner. She was halted by his voice behind her.

"Hey!" He had rolled down his window and was leaning out with an outstretched hand. There was something small and white in it. "If you ever need a ride again. Ask for Matt" She reached out and took his card, her hand briefly brushing against his as she did so.

She stood out in the parking lot for a few minutes after he pulled away to go save the cat, just staring at the small card. It was a very plain business card, didn't even have a logo on it. All it said was Lake County Police Department and below that a four-digit badge number followed by his name and the number for non-emergency situations.

"Officer Matthew Callahan," she said to herself quietly under her breath before heading inside.

4

Angela sat behind the wheel of Melly's van contemplating what she was going to do. She had put this off for way too long and now she needed to face her fears and simply do it. She looked out the window at the junkyard in front of her but could not bring herself to get out of the car.

What was she so afraid of? No matter what he said the situation wouldn't be any different. She was still going to stay with the Evans.' It wasn't like they could afford to move in together. He didn't make enough money even if you added in her tip money, which luckily was still coming in. Chrissy had thankfully covered for her and said she had gotten sick and needed to go home.

But telling him couldn't make things any worse. In fact, it had the possibility of making things better, because then she wouldn't feel so alone in all of this. Besides, he deserved to know.

She took a deep breath in and let it out as she stepped onto the dirt driveway. When she slammed the door closed, it drew his attention from the car he had his head inside of. He was covered from head to toe in grease and dirt but even in all that dirt and grime he looked gorgeous to her. She was used to him smiling when he caught sight of her, but this time, he didn't. Instead, he slammed the hood of the car and took a small rag out of the pocket of his overalls to wipe the oil off of his hands.

"Well, look who decided to drop by for a visit?" The anger in his voice did nothing to cover up the hurt that was underneath.

"I'm sorry—" she started as she walked up to him, but he cut her off.

"Don't bother." He leaned back against the hood of the car. She could tell he was trying to put on a brave face to show he wasn't hurt but his eyes were his tell. She could tell he was upset with her more than he was angry at her.

"Can I explain?" she asked quietly, suddenly full of shame and guilt.

"Explain what? Explain why you haven't returned any of my phone calls? Explain why I haven't seen you in over a month? You know I went to your house?" This came as a shock to Angela. If he had stopped by her house, it was after she had left.

"I moved out," she whispered, knowing that was no excuse.

"I know. Your mother told me. Right before your father came out and told me to get off of his property. They wouldn't tell me where you went. Your mother told me you never wanted to see me again." Angela hadn't thought of the possibility that he would have spoken to her parents or that they would have lied to him. She knew why they had. They wanted to drive a wedge between them.

And Angela hadn't made it hard for them to do so.

"Can you please just let me explain?"

"Your father almost called the cops on me. If I hadn't hightailed it out of there, he probably would have." His voice was loud now as he pushed himself off the car. His spark of anger had caught flame and was building slowly into an inferno.

"That's why I ran away from them! I couldn't stay there with them anymore!" She had told herself she wouldn't cry, that she would be strong, but she could already feel the tears falling.

"Then why didn't you come to me! Why didn't you ever call? What was I supposed to do? Just sit around and wait for you?"

"I… I couldn't." A lump in her throat kept her from saying the words she needed to say.

"Why the hell not? You know where I live! I don't know where you do apparently!" He was shouting now. She vaguely saw the door into the office open across the red dirt parking lot. Drew's father filled the doorway. He didn't step out, he just stood there watching.

"I'm living with Melly for now," she said quietly, trying to bring the energy of the conversation down. She didn't want to tell him while he was yelling. Not like this.

"And what about school? Are you just giving up on all that? What's happened to you? What is going on? Was it something I did?" He was still angry, but the sight of her crying seemed to cool the flame.

"I'm going to take a year off." She kept saying things that weren't important. Why couldn't she bring herself to say it? Why couldn't she just say it out loud? Why couldn't she just say the words. Just two words. Three syllables.

"When were you going to tell me these things? When were you going to tell me you had ran away from home? That you weren't going to school? What about your plans?"

"Plans change." She couldn't even look at him now. The pain in his eyes was too much. She didn't want to cause him anymore. She didn't want to hurt him.

"You know what? I'm done! I don't know what's going on with you and at this point I don't even care. I obviously mean shit to you so go. Just go!" Angela had been wrong. It could be worse, and it was. Seeing him stand there looking at her now with not just anger but a complete lack of caring.

"I'm sorry." She truly meant it. But he couldn't hear her.

"If you won't go, then I'm going." He turned to storm off and then paused. "I'll give you one more chance. If you just tell me straight forward what's going on."

This was her chance. He had his back turned, so she didn't have to see the hurt in his eyes. She could do it now. She could tell him. She could say it out loud.

But her voice didn't come.

He didn't bother to say anything he just walked away. His father stepped aside and let him inside. She stood there watching him walk away from her in tears and just as she was about to chase after him, to call out to him, to scream at the top of her lungs, his father stepped out from the doorway and walked out to her.

"I'm sorry, Mr. King." She didn't know why she said it. She just felt so wrong standing in his junk yard sobbing.

"Don't be sorry, little lady," he said, standing there in his wife beater and jeans, his ball cap pulled low down over his face. "You want me to talk to him?" He handed her a handkerchief. She was reminded of the one handed to her by Benjamin but this one she did not take. She wiped the tears away with the back of her hand, instead, and tried to straighten her back.

She had had her chance and she had blown it. She was utterly alone in this now.

"Look. It's going to be okay. Whatever you're going through is going to pass. You'll get through it and you'll move on and you'll find someone. High school romances don't ever end happily." He said the words, but he didn't have any heart behind it. Angela had never been very close with Drew's father, this was probably the most he had ever said to her in a single instance.

She wasn't sure what made her say it. Maybe it was intended for Drew, but it just took too long. Maybe it was because Mr. King had as much right as her parents to know. Maybe she wasn't even saying it to anyone. Maybe she was just making sure she still had a voice to speak with. But regardless of the reason, it came out of her mouth anyway.

"I'm pregnant." She expected this to cause a change in Mr. King. She expected him to console her, she expected him to run in and get Drew and bring him back out. She expected him to understand the scene suddenly and to come to her rescue. Maybe that was what she was hoping for. Maybe she had been hoping he would do her dirty work and tell Drew for her.

She was wrong yet again.

"Now listen here missy. You leave and never come back here." His tone was suddenly filled with emotion, but it wasn't empathy, it was anger. She looked him in the eye shocked but there was nothing but cold hatred there. "That boy of mine has a real chance of doing something good with his life instead of being stuck in this godforsaken shit hole and I'm not going to let some whore like you ruin it for him. So, you take your slutty little ass out of here and never speak to my son again. I don't want you coming around here looking for handouts to help pay for that bastard child of yours."The venomous tone of his voice scared Angela and she backed up away from the man.

"I wasn't asking for—" Her hand stretched out behind her and found the edge of the van behind her.

"You tell that stupid child of yours that it doesn't have a father. Cause my son's gonna get out of this shit hole. At one point I thought you were gonna help him but apparently your no different than his whore of a mother. A pussy just looking for a meal ticket. Well, my son isn't gonna be no baby daddy. So, I suggest you close your legs and run." He had stalked closer to her as she slowly grabbed the handle of the van. But she was so terrified she couldn't move. He came close enough that she could smell his body odor. It reeked of sweat and dirt.

"I said run."

She didn't run but she didn't bother to take the time to put on her seatbelt as she put the gas pedal to the floor and drove out of there as fast as she could.

September

1

"I'm running," Angela said as she laid down the six of hearts and picked up her foot.

Harold had gone to bed, and Melly had put the baby to sleep about an hour ago. The night had just gone full dark and she and Melly sat at the kitchen table playing Hand and Foot. It was a version of Canasta that Melly's mother had taught them.

"I wish I could get rid of these freaking pairs, but I haven't got a single wild. You know I haven't had one all game?" Melly said as she picked up cards and threw one on the pile in the middle.

"What were you and Harold arguing about earlier?" Angela asked without looking up from her cards. She didn't have to look up to see the surprise on her best friends face. "Thin walls." She had been reading in the guest bedroom which had sort of turned into her room over the past month and she had heard raised voices coming from downstairs. She had respected Melly's privacy and not listened in, but she also knew her best friend. She would want to talk about it.

"Me and Harold weren't fighting." Melly bit half of her lip. Angela knew this meant that she was lying. Maybe she didn't know her friend as much as she thought.

"If you don't want to talk about it that's fine. I just assumed—"

"It was Ben," she said, and when Angela looked up from the cards in her hand, she could feel like Melly was trying to say something to her with her eyes.

"Why were you arguing with Ben?" Ben was currently in his room. He hadn't gone to bed necessarily, although he never really came out to say goodnight, so Angela couldn't say for sure. However, when she had gone out to the garage to get something to drink, she had walked past his room and the light was still on and shining through the crack between the door and the floor.

"We were fighting about Harold." This was strange to Angela. She normally didn't need to pry things out of Melly. Ever since they had become best friends, they didn't hide anything from each other. Except for Angela's pregnancy which she only hid for a month or so. And that was hard enough on her. That was a special case.

"What's wrong with Harold?" It was like she had said a curse word. Melly dropped her cards and went over to the sink and poured herself a glass of water.

"Nothing's wrong with Harold. Benjamin just.... Benjamin is just being stupid." She wasn't looking at Angela when she said this.

"Melly... What are you talking about?" Angela set her cards down, the game forgotten.

"Can I ask you something?" Melly suddenly turned to face Angela and the look on her face was so pained. She took a deep breath before continuing. "Is thinking about doing something as bad as doing it?"

"Melly what are you telling me?" Angela was so confused. She had no idea what was going on or what they were even talking about.

"I'm not *telling* you anything. I'm simply asking. Is it the same thing? To think about doing something?"

"No, I guess not." She couldn't pick up any bread crumbs of what they were discussing no matter how much she searched her friends face. "Melly what is it you're thinking about doing?"

"Even if you think about it... all the time? From the moment you wake up to the moment you go to sleep?" She seemed like she was pleading with Angela like she was begging her to give her the answer she wanted but Angela wasn't sure what she wanted.

"Someone just parked their car out front." Angela almost let out a cry when Benjamin spoke from the doorway. She had been so intent on what Melly had been saying that she hadn't heard him approach or the engine of the car in the driveway. Although now she could see the headlights and, oddly enough, she recognized them.

"I'll go look and see who it is," she said, taking a moment to notice the glare that was mutually sent between Benjamin and Melly. They looked like they were having a conversation with their eyes and it wasn't a conversation she wanted to be a part of. She left them to their silence and went into the living room and to the front window. Looking out, she saw why she recognized the headlights.

Her mother's car was being put into park and the engine was being turned off.

"It's my mother," she said more to herself than to the two silent combatants in the kitchen and then walked over to the front door and stepped outside into the cool evening air. It was beginning to cool down finally at night, although it still wasn't quite that autumn chill yet.

Her mother got out of the station wagon and stood there for a moment. Angela could tell her mother hadn't planned on meeting her out on the porch. She must have expected a few more moments before confronting her. Angela wasn't quite sure why, but she felt a bit of happiness surge in her when she thought that she had the upper hand at the moment.

"Angela."

"Mother." Angela didn't move to leave the porch and for a moment her mother didn't leave the side of her car. But eventually she decided that she didn't want to have this conversation in the driveway and walked up the wooden steps to the porch.

"Can we go inside?" She reached for the door, but Angela didn't stop her she simply walked along the porch to the little wooden swing that hung in front of the living room window.

"The baby is sleeping inside. Let's talk out here." She also didn't want to involve Ben or Melly. Not only because they were obviously dealing with their own... whatever they were dealing with, but also because she wanted to do this on her own. She needed to know that she could stand up to her mother. She could fight her own battles.

"Alright. We can talk out here, then." Her mother came and sat beside her and they slowly started to swing without saying anything and without looking at each other.

"I'm not coming back." Angela knew the minute she saw the car in the driveway that her mother had come to try and convince her to come home. What other reason would she have for being here?

"I know. I told your father as such." This wasn't what Angela expected, but she didn't let it show. She kept her face a cold stone. "I told him this was a useless effort but us mothers we don't care if things are useless. You'll come to find that soon enough. For our children, a mother would go to hell and back even if it was futile." Angela didn't know which made her angrier. The implication that coming to talk to her was like going to hell and back or if it was the condescending tone that said she would understand soon. Soon but not quite yet.

"Well, you can say you've tried." Angela almost got up then, but her mother clearly wasn't finished.

"I'm sorry." She said it as a blanket statement without any specifications to tie it down. As if those two words made everything better.

"I appreciate that but—"

"You need to understand, Angela, we were only trying to do what we thought was best." She put a hand on her daughters between them, but Angela pulled her hand back as if it had been burned.

"No, you did what Dad thought was best. You didn't lock me up after we talked about it that night. You didn't lock me away until Dad told you to. I notice he isn't here apologizing." Perhaps that was what angered Angela. That her mother had come alone. Like he had sent her to do his dirty work.

"I told him not to come." Her mother was full of surprises, it seemed. "I knew that if he came, he would try to force you to come back. He would make threats. He would…" She looked down at her lap for a moment. "He would do something he would regret. So, I told him to stay at home. I told him to let me handle it."

Angela tried not to let it get under her skin that she was a problem that needed to be handled.

"You know this is our first time doing this. Your father doesn't have any younger siblings and mine are well… well, my family was just different. We don't know how to handle a young adult." At this her gaze left her lap and turned to her daughter. "Or an adult, for that matter." Angela smiled at this compliment, but she steeled herself not to let flattery sway her.

"I understand but I'm still not coming home. Not yet."

"Do you want my honest opinion?" Her mother asked and then didn't wait for a response. "I don't think you should. Did I ever tell you about the first time your father and I got engaged?"

"The first time?" Angela had heard the story of their engagement, her father proposing at her family Christmas by giving her a ring hidden at the bottom of her stocking, but that was the only story she knew.

"The Christmas story was the second time. You see he asked me earlier that year. He asked me in September, actually." She chuckled to herself at the irony. They swung a few times before she continued. "He asked me, and you know what? I got so scared. I was terrified. I hadn't had a single boyfriend before him. And I was young and naive. I thought that I shouldn't marry the first horse out of the gate you know? So, I said no." Angela couldn't imagine her mother saying no to her father, especially not when he asked her to marry him.

"We didn't speak for a week or so and I was so distraught over the whole thing. Your grandmother was no help at all she told me I was stupid and had ruined my life. She said he was the best I could ever get. Your grandmother was not a very nice woman. At least not to me." She seemed lost in thought for a moment before continuing, "But anyway, I finally went back to him and apologized. I told him I just wasn't ready yet. But then, by Christmas, I had agreed to think about it. So, when he gave me the ring that morning, I said yes."

Angela wasn't quite sure why she was getting this history lesson, but it was at least better than her mother chastising her for not coming home.

"Saying no that first time could have been the biggest mistake of my life. Your father really is the love of my life and I almost threw it all away because I was scared. But you know what? I'm so glad I did it. It sounds crazy to say it out loud but I'm so glad I told him no and if I had to do it all over again, I'd do the same.

"We are a product of our mistakes, even the big ones Angela. One day you might look back and see this leaving home as one of yours. But it's your right to make it. And I think you need to make it. You need to learn from it. I'm not quite sure what you are learning, but I trust you. I trust that you'll come back from it the same way I came back to your father."

At that she stood up abruptly and Angela felt the lack of weight send the swing into slight swivel. Her mother didn't look back at her but simply walked to the steps of the porch.

"Until you decide you want to come home would it at least be okay if we saw you some?" She heard pain in her mother's voice at this. She hadn't noticed her mother crying but she could hear it in her voice. "We miss you."

"I miss you, too." She wasn't sure if she intended the you to be plural or singular, so she didn't bother to specify.

"Well, I won't keep you. Please call me. You can even stop by if you'd like. We won't kidnap you." She smiled over her shoulder at Angela before descending the steps and walking over to her car.

When Angela came back inside, Benjamin was gone but Melly had returned to the kitchen table and was looking at her cards as if the game hadn't been forgotten. She wasn't sure what had transpired between the two in laws while she was out on the front porch but Melly didn't seem to want to talk about it. So, Angela trusted her to say something if she needed to talk about it. But they played the rest of the game in silence.

Angela barely even spoke above a whisper when she finally said, "I'm out" and won the round.

2

"Thank you, hon." Chrissy said as she removed the sparkly purple paper from the set of new baking pans. It was her birthday and a bunch of the servers and various friends all congregated in the dining room of the diner to watch her open the myriad of presents they had bought for her. They hadn't exactly closed the store down, but it was a Sunday, and they didn't really expect that many people to come in. Most of the regulars were here anyway with presents for their favorite waitress.

Angela handed over her present. It wasn't much since she didn't have much to spend right now. She was trying her best to not spend any money and to save everything for the coming expenses of the baby. But she had at least done something for her friend.

"Oh, Angela. It's beautiful!" She smiled as she held up an emerald necklace. Angela had found it in a thrift shop when she and Melly had gone shopping earlier in the week. They had went to see if they had any baby clothes, but they hadn't come back with much.

Angela *had* come back with an ever-growing sense that there was definitely something going on with Melly that wasn't being shared. They had never again discussed what was going on between Melly and Benjamin from last week. Angela hoped that Melly would come to her eventually, not only because she was curious but also because she was worried about her friend.

Melly had not come that day to the festivities because she didn't want to bring the baby and she didn't want to leave him with Benjamin.

Benjamin.

He was somehow wrapped up in this issue with Melly and Angela couldn't quite figure it out. She barely even saw Benjamin, it was almost like he was trying to avoid her, but from what she saw it wasn't only her. It was everyone in the household. He didn't normally have meals with them. He never came out and played cards with them. They would watch a movie in the living room, and he would say he'd rather be alone in his room doing God knows what.

The other day Angela had been tempted to sneak into his room when he was out in the fields with Harold and she was home alone, but she had ultimately decided that it would be a bad idea. She didn't want to put her nose where it didn't belong and ruin the homeostasis they had developed. As imperfect as it was, it was still a good situation for her while she tried to figure out what to do next.

Something that she was nowhere near being able to do.

She still wasn't sure if she wanted to go back home or if she wanted to remain at the Evans' or if she wanted to try and find a place of her own. Ever since her official break up with Drew she was even more lost. She felt so alone and so inept. Slowly the idea of returning home to her parents' house had started creeping back to the forefront of the race. It was the most economical decision, as well as the easiest.

The ringing of the front door opening brought Angela back to earth. Angela hadn't even noticed that they were down to the last present, she had been so wrapped in her own little world. She watched as Chrissy opened a book when, suddenly, the tome fell out of Chrissy's hand and hit the floor. Chrissy's face glassed over as her stare held fixed to the front door of the Diner. Angela looked over her shoulder and she saw a man that she didn't quite recognize. He seemed vaguely familiar in that she thought she saw him once, but she didn't think she had ever spoken to him.

Chrissy obviously knew him. When Angela turned back to see if Chrissy had picked up the fallen book, she saw her friend instead stand up from her chair with a look of almost hate on her face.

"What the hell are you doing here?" she said quietly. If it weren't for the hush that had fallen over the dining room, Angela wouldn't have been able to hear her, let alone the gentleman at the front door. He did hear her, though, but he didn't say anything. He simply walked over to the group with a small package in his hand. He walked with a strange limp, almost like he couldn't bend his left leg.

"Happy birthday." He placed the package on the white table in front of Chrissy. His face had a strange expression. It looked almost hopeful. It was the face you made while reading the end of a book when your hoping that the characters are happy in the end. The face that hopes everything turns out okay.

Chrissy didn't say anything in response to this, she simply continued to stare at him with disdain. He took that as a cue and turned and limped back out of the diner. Chrissy waited until he had walked out of sight of the dining room before sitting back down. The package in front of her was very small but wrapped pristinely with a bow on top. Chrissy pushed it to the side but someone in the gaggle of friends piped up.

"At least open it." A few more people put in their two cents about it and finally Chrissy opened the small box.

As she unwrapped it Angela realized what the box was. It was a ring box. She could feel Chrissy's hesitation as she held the closed box in her hands. Angela didn't know who the man was, and she didn't know the meaning of this box, but it was clear that Chrissy was afraid of what she would find inside.

She opened it up like Pandora would have and revealed a simple silver ring with no diamonds or gems of any kind. Judging from the size and the lack of decoration, it appeared to Angela to be a man's ring. This seemed an odd gift to give to a woman but apparently Chrissy disagreed.

She was in tears.

Angela couldn't decide if they were happy tears or not. They seemed a slight mixture of elation and despair. Chrissy closed the box with a snap and wiped her eyes.

With the snap of the little box, the party was over.

"Thank you, everyone, for all the gifts. Now I'm going to head home," she said as she stood up and put all the presents into a big bag that one of them had come in. The bag had a picture of a birthday present on it, and the letters that spelled out Happy Birthday seemed suddenly too happy for this occasion.

No one felt the nerve to ask about the man in the doorway as Chrissy led the exodus of the group. But when Angela headed out to her best friend's van, she saw that Chrissy was sitting in her pickup truck all alone with the big bag sitting next to her. She seemed to be crying again.

Angela walked over and tapped on the passenger window to get her attention. When Chrissy looked up and unlocked the door, Angela climbed in.

"What was that?"

"Just an old... friend." She seemed to not like her choice of title for the man, but she didn't want to spend any more time searching for an appropriate word. She was trying to wipe away her tears and bite back anymore that wanted to follow.

"A good friend of mine once told me that just by not saying something, that doesn't make it go away," Angela said, and Chrissy looked at her with a small smile.

"I don't want to make it go away." Chrissy said tearfully. "I just want *him* to go away."

"Who is he?" Angela didn't want to pry but she also wanted to help.

"He's my ex," Chrissy said. At first, Angela thought she was going to leave it at that, but then she decided that it warranted an explanation.

"We started seeing each other a few years ago. We dated for almost three whole years. We almost got engaged even. Well, that isn't true. We had kind of talked about it and I had expected it. But then I drove over to his house one day last spring without calling first. He lived over close to Cleveland. Well, when I got there, I saw a woman through the front window sitting in the kitchen with..." She almost couldn't bring herself to continue. "With two little girls. He had a wife and two daughters. And he hadn't told me. He just let me be the other woman without even letting me in on the joke." Angela was heartbroken for her. She hadn't heard of Chrissy even having a boyfriend.

"I hadn't heard from him for almost a year after we broke up. I told him never to contact me again, and I guess until today he really hadn't but... he did show up at your party. I don't know what exactly he was doing there but... Well, it doesn't matter. Nothing changes anything. Not even this." Angela hadn't noticed that Chrissy had been holding the little ring box in her hand. She tossed it into the bag next to her.

"You know." Angela reached in and grabbed the ring box herself. "This is a man's ring. It must be his, so he must not be married anymore."

"It was never the marriage dear. It was the lies. He lied to me and I can never forgive that." Angela looked into her eyes and saw true pain there. Angela wished she could say something to appease it, but she couldn't come up with any words of wisdom to give.

"I'm so sorry," she said for lack of anything else to say.

"But enough about me. You have much bigger issues to deal with than unrequited love." Angela wanted to say it obviously wasn't unrequited since he had shown up at her birthday, but she didn't want to put salt in the wound.

"I don't have any issues."

"Dearie, you never have had any sort of a poker face. You moved out of your parents' house, you didn't go off to school. Drew's out of the picture, apparently, and word around town is you're sick on top of it all." Angela was confused at the last part but then remembered that that was what her parents had planned to use to excuse her disappearance. They must have started setting the groundwork in case she came home and decided to go along with their plan.

"I'm not sick." She gulped back the little fear that was left in her stomach. "I'm pregnant."

"Oh, honey, I know. I'm not stupid. I just didn't want to take away your right to tell me." Chrissy smiled at her for the first time since she got in the truck. "And the father?" Images of Drew walking away in the junkyard crossed Angela's mind, followed by the last words from Drew's father.

"He's not gonna be any help."

"Well, even then, honey, just remember, you're not alone in this. You're blessed with family and friends who care about you. You'll figure this all out I promise." She reached over a hand and took Angela's in a fist. "It'll all be worth it I promise."

It was so nice to have someone tell her that. Angela had been so stressed and worried and distraught the last few months that she sometimes forgot that at the end of this she was going to have a little baby in her arms and while that would bring its own set of challenges it would also bring its own set of joys that would make the whole thing worth it.

"Now you head on home. We can't sit in the cab of this truck crying all day." She started the engine as Angela got out of the truck. "Thank you again for the necklace." She called as she pulled out of the parking lot leaving Angela alone on the pavement.

"No, thank you," Angela said to herself before heading back to Melly's van.

3

"I brought home some groceries!" Angela cried out to the seemingly empty house. She had been cut early from work, so she stopped by the grocery store on her way home. She had expected to find Melly in the living room with the baby, but instead, she found him napping by himself in the bassinet. She gave him a loving smile before continuing through the house to look for Melly.

She assumed that Harold and Benjamin were out working in the fields as she saw the tractor on the way in. She had honked at Harold as she drove by and he had waved. Benjamin had been in the wagon behind organizing the straw, so she only saw his backside and he didn't see her at all to wave.

She ran out of rooms downstairs, so she headed up the creaking stairs as a strange feeling creeped up her spine. It wasn't fear as much as it was dread. It wasn't grounded in any logic, but she felt that feeling you have when you sensed someone watching you late at night, even after you have turned to find the empty house behind you.

Nothing awaited her on the landing but when she turned to the right and saw the door to Melly and Harold's room closed, her mind began to put together the pieces.

In her mind's eye, she saw Benjamin's far off stare as she approached the door. She considered his avoidance of social situations that included Melly as she reached out a hand to grasp the door handle. She could still hear Melly's words as she tried in vain to turn the handle: "Is thinking about something as bad as doing it?"

Angela's breath caught in her throat as she leaned forward to place her ear on the door, all the while remembering the small bit of red flannel that had stuck out of the top of Harold's wagon of straw.

Benjamin didn't have a red flannel shirt that she knew of.

If there had been any doubt in her mind, it was extinguished by the quiet moans in the bedroom beyond the panel of wood against her ear. She distinctly could hear her best friend and the recognizable grunts of her brother-in-law.

Angela didn't know what to do with this information. She stood in front of the door for a few minutes trying to process. She had pulled away from the door quickly, unable to continue listening to the sounds of their love-making.

Can you call it love-making when it's breaking the vows of marriage? But oddly enough the vows of marriage weren't what Angela was struggling with. Instead, it was the vows of sisterhood.

Prior to this summer she and Melly had told each other every single thing. Melly had told her about the first time she had drank illegally when she went to school. Angela had told Melly first when she had decided to go to OSU. Melly had come to her first when she got engaged and then again when she got pregnant. Angela had gone to her the very next day after she had sex for the first time with Drew.

But then she had hid her own secret from Melly.

It had taken her a month to come clean about her pregnancy to Melly. A month in best friend years was a decade. Did she cause this? Or if not the act itself, the secrecy of it? Was Melly not confiding in her because of her own secrets?

She suddenly felt so much further away from her best friend than she had ever felt before. Standing on the other side of the door from her suddenly felt farther away than when they had lived hours apart.

She couldn't stand there anymore, so she walked calmly downstairs and began to slowly unpack the groceries trying to push away the thoughts of what this meant for her and Melly's relationship.

Then, as she was putting the milk away in the fridge, she paused. The cold air hitting her face helped to slow the blood that was still pumping through her veins at full speed. She began to think of what she needed to do now with the knowledge of her friend's adultery.

She could no longer stay here. It wasn't that she had a moral compass that made her unable to remain in the house where a woman slept outside of her marriage, although that did bother her. The bigger issue was that whether it was given to her or she had taken it of her own accord, she was now entrusted with a secret. A secret that she intended to keep. Even if her best friend had not felt the need to open up to her, she was still her best friend. At least Angela hoped she was.

As Chrissy had said, she had no poker face.

Perhaps that was why Melly had not said anything. Perhaps she was afraid of Harold finding out through her. Angela couldn't let that happen. She had to get out of the house, and not just for a bit because this secret wasn't going to go away. She didn't know all of the details but even if this ended the secret would remain like a stain on a white shirt. Bleach and time might get it out but if you held it up to the light a faint outline would remain for all time waiting to be noticed by someone.

She didn't want to be the one to point it out.

She finally closed the refrigerator and put the last of the groceries away quickly, fueled by the need to get away. After she put the last box of cereal away, she headed upstairs to her guest bedroom. She walked significantly faster past the master bedroom, although she could no longer hear what was going on behind the door. She wasn't even sure it was still going on, although did the act stop when the moaning did? Or did the act continue into the calm afterwards? The bare-naked silence when the lovers lay apart or together, regardless of how, closer than they were when they were physically connected mere moments before. Wasn't that in a way more intimate and therefore more damaging?

She took the few pieces of clothing that she had brought with her and returned them to the duffel bag. It seemed almost funny to her that a mere month and a half after she had run away from her home she was now running away from her sanctuary.

But what was she running to? Was she going to return home? She had not put that thought to work yet. All she had considered was needing to get away from the affair that was occurring as she threw her clothes into the bag. She did not have anywhere else to turn to.

Which was worse? Living with a secret here or living with a secret at home?

She held a yellow blouse in her hands as she contemplated her options. If she went home, she would have to go along with her parents' plan of secrecy and solitude. She would not be able to leave the house and she would not be able to tell anyone else that her child existed. But how constricting was that now in her current situation?

Melly obviously already knew, and her parents would know that she knew. There would no longer be any reason to hide from her, not that there had been to begin with. Drew was out of the picture so that eliminated another reason to get out of the house. She thought about the last month and a half and tried to think of how things would have been different if she had stayed indoors. The only thing she would be missing out on is the diner and while she needed that income to help out financially with the Evans' household, that would be an unnecessary gesture at her parents' home.

She would no longer be interested in coming to visit Melly, for obvious reasons. But there would be nothing stopping Melly from coming to visit her in her prison.

Ultimately that was the biggest issue with returning home. It wasn't the fact that she had no reason to leave it was whether she was willing to give up her right to leave. Whether she chose to use it or not, the choice was more important than the action.

But she looked down at her ever-growing belly and remembered that she needed to take into consideration the welfare of her child more than her own selfish need for freedom. Wasn't it more economical and therefore more beneficial to her unborn baby to go home? She could not provide a sustainable home for it alone and she had been fooling herself when she thought she could do it here in this house, secret or no secret. This house, while physically large enough, was barely big enough for the lives of the three adults and the one baby living here. Adding another baby to that mix could destroy what little symbiosis they had here.

The answer was staring her in the face. She just had to bite the bullet and take it. So, she threw the yellow blouse in her bag and zipped up the top, her mind finally being made up.

This time she did not run past the master bedroom at the top of the stairs. Instead, she paused and looked at it, not close enough to even consider trying to eavesdrop to the colluding that was going on behind it, but not far enough away that she couldn't reach out and touch it if she wanted to. If she dared. She didn't know if she could face them right now, or if she wanted to. Their secret had been passed off to her like a baton in a relay race but when it did it was duplicated. Now she had a secret of her own.

They did not know she knew. She knew that she would not be able to keep the secret from Melly, nor did she particularly want to. She did not want any more secrets between them. But Benjamin was a different story. She did not know how he would react to her knowledge of his affair. Would he be guilt-ridden? Would he be angry? Would he decide it was a sign they should stop, or that they should continue?

She did not know him well enough to judge. Melly, it appeared, would probably be better equipped to answer those questions so perhaps she should be the one to do so.

So, instead of facing them right now, she went downstairs and left them a note.

It was a simple one. It said that she was going home. It would cause them to question her reasoning for returning home but the only one who would come looking for answers was the only one whom she wanted to confide them in.

She paused in the living room by the basinet, her duffel over her shoulder. Looking down at the young life that currently was traveling through dreamland, she felt a tear roll down her cheek. A month and a half was a long time even in normal time, and in that time, she had grown attached to this house and the people in it. The little boy before her especially, held a significant place in her heart. She smiled down at him as he shifted in his sleep. She wondered what he was dreaming of and if he would remember that she was the one who calmed the storm when he became a thundercloud.

"Be good for your parents. I can't be here to keep you quiet anymore." She whispered to him. "You'll have to do it all by yourself." She leaned over and kissed him lightly on his forehead, careful not to wake him up.

She got into Melly's van and started the engine. She cursed her dependence on other people's vehicles, and she even paused to consider the idea of either calling her mother to come and get her or walking, but both those options seemed impossibly long. She needed to leave now while she still had the courage and while Melly and Benjamin still lay upstairs without the knowledge that their secret had a new keeper.

Melly could get her van back later. Angela pulled out of the driveway and onto the country road headed into town. She wondered if she would ever be able to return to this house. Was her sanctuary tainted by the secret tryst that she was now aware of? Perhaps in time she would return. Even if it was just for a visit.

Her heart hardened to her decision as she barreled down the road towards town. She turned on the radio, but she did not listen to it over the sound of her own thoughts of her decision. She was so lost in her own mind and the possible consequences of her decision that she did not even realize there was a cop behind her until his lights began to flash.

She wondered if this was a sign from above that she had made a wrong choice. Perhaps this was telling her she should have remained at the Evans'. Regardless of its meaning, she pulled over and waited for the bearer of her first consequence to approach her car.

"Did you know how fast you were…" The policeman trailed off as he recognized her.

"Officer Callahan?" She almost thought it was ironic but then remembered that she lived in a town of less than a thousand people.

"Where you headed to?" She saw him adjust his demeanor back to its appropriate candor so that he could reassure himself that he was still doing his job. It was almost cute the way he tried to continue being the officer who had pulled her over, even though they both thought of him as the officer who picked her up.

"I'm headed home actually," she said, her heart rising towards her decision now as her omen suddenly took a much brighter turn.

"Well, you were trying to get there awfully fast," he said, and she could barely contain her giggles at his attempt at authority.

"I'll try to slow down I promise." She smiled at him and, even though he was wearing sunglasses, she could see a definitive brightness in his face when she did so. There was a definite redness that rose to his cheeks, as well.

"Well, okay. I guess I'll let you go this time. Just slow down." He was skirting close to ridiculousness with any implication that he would have given her a ticket.

"Thank you, I will." He walked back to his cruiser and she pulled back out into the road to head home. This time she kept the car at exactly the speed limit, but her heart was flying faster than an airplane.

4

Angela is sitting in the kitchen eating a bowl of cereal when Melly pulls up in the truck. Angela can see her through the window and wonders to herself why she brought Benjamin with her. Obviously, she needed someone to drive the truck home, but did it have to be him? Would Harold have realized something was going on? Was she afraid Angela would tell him? Or was she over analyzing it and it had simply been out of convenience that she had chosen her lover instead of her husband to drop her off. She gets out of the truck at the same time as Benjamin, and for a moment, Angela fears he will come inside with her. She didn't want to talk to him.

On the phone she had told Melly that she wanted to talk to her when she came to get the van. She had even made sure her parents wouldn't be home, so they could talk privately. She had waited until Tuesday when her parents went and played euchre with one of her mother's old college friends and her husband.

But she had never imagined that Benjamin would be a part of the conversation, at least not physically. Obviously, he would be discussed but it didn't necessarily have to include him. She didn't want it to. She wanted to talk to Melly and Melly alone.

Her rush of fear turned out to be unnecessary as Benjamin was only getting out of the cab to switch sides and get in the driver's seat, so he could drive the truck home. Melly walked up to the front door alone. Once she passed out of sight Angela got up from her chair and headed to the front door. She stood at the door and waited for Melly to knock. She imagined that they must look pretty silly both waiting on opposite sides of the door, but she didn't want to be the one to initiate the conversation. She wanted it to be Melly's decision to let her in.

Finally, Melly rang the doorbell. Angela didn't let the tone even get to its lower note before she swung the door open. At first, she stood there with the door open, but then, like a rush of wind, Melly took her breath away with a swift and tight hug. It caught Angela off balance, and she had to remain holding onto the door to keep her feet.

"I thought you'd never speak to me again." Melly sobbed into Angela's shoulder. She had not even noticed she was crying but her shoulder was quickly wet with her friend's tears.

"Why would you think that?" Angela said putting her open hand on Melly's back to try and comfort her. After a moment, Melly pulled back and looked Angela in the eyes.

"You know now, don't you?" Melly's eyes were red with tears and her jaw shook as she asked.

"Let's go inside Mel." Angela stood back and let Melly walk into the foyer and then into the den where they sat on the couch together. They sat silently for a moment while Melly contained herself. Luckily, Angela's mother always kept a box of tissues next to the couch, so she handed them to Melly with a smile.

"I knew the minute I came downstairs what had happened. What must have happened. What was going to happen eventually. I don't know what I was thinking!" She blew her nose with a blast and looked at Angela sideways, almost afraid.

"What exactly did happen?" Angela didn't know how to ask the questions she wanted to know. "I mean, I know what happened… but I guess… How did it happen?" She had told herself she wouldn't be judgmental, and she was trying very hard to maintain that promise.

"Oh, Angela, I don't know how it happened. I mean I do but it was just so fast, but at the same time it has been happening for a long time." She looked away like she was searching for the answers herself, but Angela could tell she was just trying to avoid putting them into words out of shame or guilt.

"When did it start?"

"It started just after Daniel was born. Before you moved in. When he was screaming all the time. But it didn't really start till long after that. I mean we talked about it, but we didn't…. we didn't follow through until the other day."

It dawned on Angela that this was more than just a one-time thing. Yes, it had only happened the one time, but it clearly was an ongoing situation that had only reached a climax the day that she happened to come home from work early.

"So, you only slept together the one time?" The words had an almost bitter taste in Angela's mouth. She wanted to be judgment free for her friend, but it was hard for her to understand Melly's thinking. She had seemed so happy with Harold.

"Yes. But that isn't the worst part. I mean it's obviously bad and it's the biggest slip in judgement on my part, but it isn't the hardest part to admit." Angela tried to follow the thread of the sentence, but she didn't understand. Her face must have shown it because Melly didn't wait for a response.

"I'm in love with him Angela."

The piece of the puzzle fit into her head suddenly. She had thought that it was a dalliance. She thought it had been a tryst. Some lapse in sense that would have long lasting effects but, in reality, it was so much more than that.

"Do you no longer love Harold?" Angela hated to ask because she didn't really know if she wanted to hear the answer. She was afraid she already knew it.

"I do. But not in the same way." Melly looked at Angela pleading her to understand. "Harold changed after the baby came. I don't know if it was because of Daniel, I don't know if it was because of something with me, or if he had been this way before and he just never showed it before.

It's like he is a shell of who he used to be. We haven't made love in almost a year." She whispered the last sentence almost as if she was afraid of saying it too loud.

"At first, we said it was because of the pregnancy. We didn't know if it would hurt the baby or not. They tell you it doesn't but… I just couldn't picture it working. But then it continued after he was born. And it wasn't just the sex. Harold used to be so romantic. He used to take me out. He used to buy me flowers and…" She looked like she was searching for examples to justify herself.

"He's different." Angela finished for her. Looking back on it, she had noticed an absence of Harold in the house while she was living there. She had been too wrapped up in her own thoughts to notice or to infer anything from it, but between his absence and Benjamin's secretiveness it had seemed like she and Melly were living alone in that house with the baby.

"He is. And I didn't know what to do with it, so I turned to the only other person who might be able to help me understand. Bennie." Angela had never heard Melly call him anything other than Benjamin before. It took on a melodious sound to it when she called him Bennie. She could hear the happiness in the tones of Melly's voice, and it lit up her face in a way that Angela hadn't seen before. That isn't true. She had seen it whenever Melly looked at Daniel.

"It started from there. He became my confidant. I mean you were here dealing with your own problems and even when you moved in, I didn't want to bother you with my problems. You had enough of your own. So, I leaned on Bennie. And he leaned on me. He confided in me about growing up in his brother's shadow. He may have been older, but he was always the lesser of the two."

Angela realized that Melly was almost like a salesman trying to convince her that what she had done was right. But then again, when it came to situations of the heart, when is anything really right or wrong? Isn't everything somewhere in between?

"At first, I just thought it was simply a confidence. We were just growing closer almost like brother and sister. But as we grew closer, and me and Harold drew apart, it suddenly became clear what was really happening. But by the time I realized, it was already too late." She took a deep breath and waited for Angela to put in her two cents.

"Please say something. Please tell me I'm not crazy for saying these things."

Angela poured her thoughts over one another trying to figure out exactly how to put into words how she felt. She wanted to be an objective voice of reason, but the truth of the matter is that objectivity doesn't exist when it comes to friends. And attempting to fake it is impossible to do.

"I can't say that I completely agree with what you did." She emphasized the last word to try and imply that she was hoping it wasn't continuing or that it wouldn't in the future. "But I love you and I understand why you did it."

A look of relief crossed Melly's face, and she leaned in to hug Angela, but Angela put up a hand first.

"However, I think you need to make a decision." Melly was taken slightly aback at this statement. True she hadn't asked Angela's opinion on what she should do but Angela felt it was her duty to tell her friend the hard truths that she didn't want to hear. "You can't do this to Harold or Benjamin."

"I know." Melly collapsed slightly into herself with regret.

"The longer this continues, the more it will hurt both of them. So, you either have to end it with Benjamin or you have to end it with Harold." Angela tried not to sound like a stern teacher as she said this, but she wanted to be clear that there shouldn't be any leeway in this. It was the only way that she could morally condone her friend's actions.

"I know," Melly said again.

"Now, you don't have to decide right this second." Angela wanted to alleviate her friend's anguish and also felt that any answer that came out now would be forced rather than thought out well. "But you should do it sooner rather than later."

"I will."

"In the meantime..." Angela wanted to diffuse the situation suddenly. She could tell that any more discussion on the topic right now would drown Melly's emotions and make it all the harder for her to make a decision. Besides, it was something that, like Angela had to about talking to Drew, Melly would have to do on her own. "Let's play some cards." She pasted a smile on her face to try and brighten the mood.

"So, we're still friends?"

"Of course."

"I'd like that," Melly said, that look of relief crossed her face again.

October - December

1

Returning home after living with the Evans' was definitely an adjustment. Angela had become used to feeling on equal footing with her housemates and, suddenly, she was back to feeling like a child. She had expected to begin feeling cabin fever when she moved back in because of the strict rules on her remaining in the house but she didn't think that she would begin feeling it so soon.

She had never felt it necessary to join the Evans for dinner if she chose not to and when she did it was when they all decided they were hungry, sometimes being as early as five and other times as late as nine. Lunch was a free for all and you ate whatever you could find, whenever you were hungry. At her parents' home, however, dinner was served promptly at eight every evening and her mother expected her to be there every night.

When she had been living there before, she had never questioned it. She had grown up that way and she had the excuse of work to get out of it every couple of days, so it didn't matter to her very much. But now that she was cooped up in the house twenty-four hours a day the strict schedule became monotonous.

Her father had gone back to work which she was not aware of prior to moving back. This left her and her mother alone all day. Her mother would leave the house to run errands sometime which was nice because it was the only time she was able to go outside. Even going out to the back yard was strictly prohibited in case someone were to drop by and see her ever growing belly.

That was another adjustment. Up until now her pregnancy had been a fact that she was aware of but other than a very brief bout of morning sickness it wasn't something that she was reminded of every second. It wasn't that she ever forgot but it was more that it was pushed to the back of her mind. Now it was in the forefront at every moment because she walked around with a melon on her stomach. She started having to pee all the time and she woke up during the night with the strangest cravings.

One beneficial thing was that her mother waited on her hand and foot when it came to the pregnancy. She would cook anything that she was craving, and she did not balk when Angela had to get up five and six times during dinner to go to the bathroom. She didn't even give her any issues when Angela started walking around in sweatpants all day every day. It wasn't like anyone would see her anyway.

One day her mother came home with a car load of baby clothes and toys. Everything was yellow, green, orange, and red. She said since they couldn't take her in to see if it was a boy or a girl, they had to go gender neutral on everything. Although Angela did find a blue onesie hidden amongst the stack.

That was one thing they had discussed the first week that Angela had come home. There was to be no doctors. Angela's mother had a cousin, Carol, who was a mid-wife, and she came out to the house and checked Angela out head to toe. Everything seemed to be right according to her, and she said that they shouldn't have any issues. She taught Angela some prenatal exercises and said she would come back periodically and check on her and help her get ready.

"The idea is if you stay here, then no one ever has to know," her mother said when Angela mentioned going to the hospital the night of the birth. "Martha says you shouldn't have any issues doing it right here, so that's just what we will do. I wouldn't allow it if I didn't think we could handle it." But there was a small part of Angela that feared that her mother would insist on the secret even if it was safer to go to the hospital.

As the days on the calendar drew closer and closer and her pants grew tighter and tighter her worries about the baby ballooned almost as much as her stomach did. She began to worry about what was going to happen when it was born. Would she know what to do? Would it scream constantly like Daniel had? What if it got sick? What if it wouldn't eat? What *would* it eat? Should she breast feed, or should she do formula?

What was going to be its name?

"You can stop worrying, angel," her father said as he entered the kitchen.

"I wasn't worrying," she quickly said.

"Oh, well, you've just been standing there washing that one dish for the last five minutes." He chuckled as he sat down at the kitchen counter and undid his tie.

"Oh." Angela looked down and realized that he was right. The dish in her hand sparkled like it was brand new. She set it aside and grabbed another plate.

"Put down the dishes for a moment, Angel. Come here for a minute." He patted the seat next to him. She wiped her hands with a towel and came to sit next to him. She was nervous suddenly, but not about the baby anymore. She felt like she was about to get a lecture and she wasn't even sure what it was going to be about.

"Do you know what I always said to your mother whenever she came to me with her worries? It didn't matter what they were, whether they were about you when you were growing up, or about this house, or about your future, or when you told us you were pregnant, it didn't matter. I always said the same thing. You know what I said?" She wasn't sure if she was really supposed to respond, and even if she was, she didn't know the answer, so she shook her head no.

"I said, 'I'll still love you.'" He smiled at her like that solved all her problems in a moment.

"But what—?" He held up a hand.

"I'll still love you. I need you to know that. No matter what happens I'll still love you. And everything I do, for you and for your mother, I do it because I love you both *so* much." He reached out a hand gripped her arm on this last statement.

She smiled at that sentiment but also inwardly winced as his grip and his determination to show her how much he loves her hurt her thin forearm. It didn't last long, so she said nothing as he leaned back in his chair.

He nodded to her as if that was the end. Like he had, with an easy statement and a hard hand, fixed all her worries about the unborn child growing in her stomach. She appreciated his sentiment, but love would not feed the child or ease it when it cried.

But rather than contradict him she stood up and went back to the sink to continue her dishes. She reached into the hot soapy water to grab the next dish and grabbed at the first thing her hand touched without thinking. She yelped and yanked it out of the water and dark red dripped from it where she had gripped the knife that was in the sink.

"Robert!" Her mother suddenly barreled into the kitchen looking like she had just seen a ghost. Angela was so shocked by her mother's unexpected entrance that she momentarily forgot about her sliced finger. The pain brought it back to the front of her mind, however. She sucked in a breath and grabbed it with her other hand to put pressure on it and try to stop the bleeding.

"What happened?" her mother asked with a tinge of panic in her voice.

"I cut myself on a knife in the sink," Angela said, sucking the blood off the tip of her finger while still keeping pressure on it. "Will you get me a Band-Aid?" She gestured to the cupboard that she was unable to open with no free hands.

"Oh." Her mother breathed a sigh of relief and put a hand to her chest. Angela noticed her throw Angela's father a quick glance as she walked across the kitchen to open the cupboard. Her father hadn't moved from his seat, but he noticed the glance. "Let me get that for you. I don't think I have any Neosporin." She searched through the cupboard and eventually found a Band-Aid.

Once they got the wound covered and wrapped Angela turned back to continue washing the dishes, but her father stood up.

"You head on upstairs Angel. Your mother will finish the dishes," he said, but it oddly sounded like an order to her mother rather than an offer for Angela to rest her wound. She opened her mouth to protest but her father didn't let her. "I said, you go upstairs, and your mother will finish the dishes!" She could tell that there would be no swaying him in this.

When she got upstairs, she heard raised voices coming from downstairs. She couldn't make out any words, and while she couldn't figure out how it could have anything to do with her or her bleeding finger, for some reason she felt like whatever they were arguing about was her fault.

The first snowflake of the season fell outside Angela's window.

2

The weather men had said that Christmas would be unseasonably warm but as the sun set on Christmas Eve the flakes began to fall. By nine o'clock, there was at least three inches on the ground. It was going to be a white Christmas.

Angela was putting the last of the decorations up on the Christmas tree, her belly kept knocking the ornaments off the bottom branches. It had been years since the tree had presents underneath it. She no longer, of course, believed in good old Saint Nick coming down the chimney and her father felt that at a certain age spoiling your children on one day of the year was too much. They exchanged gifts but they did it on Christmas Eve instead of Christmas morning.

In previous years, they had a dinner on Christmas day and invited relatives from her Mother's side, but not this year.

Angela was "too sick."

That was, of course, what they told them. In reality they couldn't hide the baby anymore if they tried. She looked like she constantly was keeping a watermelon under her shirt. And it was a large watermelon at that.

So, instead, they planned on having a quiet Christmas alone.

It happened when she was reaching up high to put an ornament up near the top of the tree. It felt like maybe it was just her stomach acting funny at first, but it didn't feel like anything she had ever felt come from her stomach before. She panicked for a half of a second before she realized that it wasn't painful, and it didn't last more than a moment.

The baby had simply kicked her.

She dropped the ornament in her hand and let her hands fly to her stomach, hoping and praying for it to happen again. She closed her eyes and tried to will it to kick again but nothing happened. When her mother came in with cinnamon rolls on a plate for her, she gave her daughter a quizzical look.

"I was trying to get the baby to kick again."

"Again!" A smile spread across both women's faces. Her mother quickly set the plate down on the table and ran over to Angela to place her hand on her stomach, as well. They both stood there waiting with their hands on her stomach, but nothing happened.

"He must be shy," Angela said.

Angela had been referring to him as a boy for a while now, but she really didn't care one way or the other. It was going to be a beautiful baby whether it was male or female. She did secretly hope for a little boy if for no other reason than for her parents' sake.

"Robert! The baby kicked!" Elizabeth said as Robert entered the living room, but a smile did not cross his face. Instead, his face was cold and stern.

"There is someone pulling in the drive." The two women quickly went to the window and peered out the curtains at the arriving car. In the darkness and snow Angela couldn't tell what kind of car it was but only one person got out of the driver's seat.

"Go upstairs, honey," Elizabeth said calmly to Angela. Angela was about to protest but she decided against it. She wouldn't win anyway.

So, she trudged upstairs, grabbing a plate of cinnamon rolls first in case she had to be up there awhile. She closed herself in her room and quickly went right to the window. She couldn't see the front porch because of the overhang over the top, but she pushed the window just slightly open, not enough to let in too much cold but enough to let in just the right amount of wind to carry voices.

"Merry Christmas," her father said.

"Merry Christmas." It was a man, but she couldn't place the voice. She didn't think she'd ever heard it before.

"What brings you all the way out here?" Her father had a defensive tone in his voice. Angela hadn't expected to hear much more because she figured they would invite the man in from the cold, but her father didn't seem to want to do that.

"I came out to wish you a Merry Christmas," the man said as if he needed no other excuse.

"Well, you've done that." Angela didn't know who this man was, but her father clearly did, and did not like him, or want him at his house.

"I also wanted to check on you."

"I don't need you checking up on me." The defensive tone in her father's voice was sharp enough that it could cut.

"Dr. Horvath says you haven't been in therapy for months."There was a strange mixture of accusation and concern in the stranger's voice.

"What business is that of yours?" Angela heard the front door close, but she could tell they were still on the porch. Her father must have closed the door, so her mother would not hear what was said.

"Come on Robert. You know we were all supposed to have six sessions at minimum. Especially now that your back at the station, even if they have you on desk duty."

"Keeping tabs on me?"

"I didn't mean to sound like that. I'm just worried is all."

"I think you've made your point. You can leave now." Her father's voice was slowly spinning from defensive to offensive.

"Now look, Robert, I am just trying to look out for you. There's no shame in needing a little help." Angela, of course, couldn't see but she could feel this stranger trying to appease her father, perhaps with a hand on the shoulder or simply a smile.

"Did I say I was ashamed?" If he had put his hand on her father's shoulder Robert would have shrugged it off for sure with that statement.

"Look, why don't you just do one more session. For me? What happened over there…" Angela didn't know what the stranger was talking about. She hadn't heard about her father taking therapy or even needing it. And what was this business with 'what happened over there'? She hadn't heard of anything happening out of the ordinary while her father was overseas. Maybe that was all it was. "You can't get over that in one or two sessions."

"Who are you to tell me what I can and can't do? You don't have a medical degree, do you?" Her father was downright angry at this point. Angela wasn't even sure she needed the window open at this point, but she was frozen in place, so she left it open.

"It was simply a suggestion, Robert. Listen. I wasn't trying to offend you or anything. But look I was talking to Mr. Horvath about it—"There was a sudden scuffle. Angela wasn't sure what happened, but she heard rustling like there was some sort of physical action going on between the two of them.

"What did you tell him?" Even though it was the voice that Angela recognized, her father's voice sounded like a stranger. It was a tone she had never heard before.

"I didn't tell him anything Robert! I told you I wouldn't!"There was a pause while they both caught their breaths. "I simply told him I was worried about you. And he said that it would help us both if I came out here and told you of my concerns."

"Well, your concerns aren't necessary. Now have a good holiday."

"Can't I come inside? It's cold." Angela could hear in this other man's voice that he really wasn't cold, but rather wanted to see for himself exactly how fine her father was.

"No." Her father didn't expand on the matter or offer any sort of reason. It was simply negatory.

"There's no reason to shut me out, Robert."

"I said you could leave."

"I'm not leaving until I know—" Angela wasn't sure what happened next without the benefit of seeing but she heard another scuffle, this one lasted longer and sounded louder. It also came to a peak with a loud grunt from the stranger. She suddenly saw him appear in the yard at the edge of the overhang. All she could see was his head and it took her a moment to realize that he was in the snow and his nose was bloody. Her father had punched him and threw him off the porch or pushed. She couldn't be sure exactly how, but he ended up in the yard.

He took a moment before he got up, but when he did, he didn't return to the porch he simply walked over to his car. He didn't even bother to beat the snow off of himself, even though he was covered in it. He did pause by the door of his car.

"Merry Christmas," she heard her father say as the door closed.

The man stood there and stared at the door then, for some odd reason, he decided to look up and his eyes hit her like a brick. It took the breath right out of her chest. Suddenly, she recognized him. It was the man who had crashed Chrissy's party. But that wasn't what scared her. It was the look on his face.

It looked like he was warning her.

It looked like he was seeing a ghost. But he wasn't looking at a ghost. He was looking at her.

January 7, 1992

After it was all over, Angela couldn't believe it had only taken the few hours that it did. If you had asked her during it, she would have said it had lasted for at least a week.

The pain was so strong that it brought tears to her eyes. It felt like someone was taking her pelvis and squeezing it, as well as stretching it simultaneously. It was so excruciating at points that she screamed.

The screaming helped, but it didn't make the pain stop. Nothing did. You had to wait it out until you hit the break between contractions. When that happened, Angela walked.

She walked and walked and walked. She felt like she was walking a marathon in between bouts of screaming in pain. She cursed herself and her mother for putting her through this. She cursed Drew for doing this to her. But most of all she just cursed.

Angela had never been one to curse. In her whole life she had probably cursed enough times to count on one hand. But on that winter's night, she cursed like a sailor who had lost all of his winnings in a poker game. Her mother continued to be shocked every time an expletive came out of her mouth, but Carol didn't bat an eye. She had seen enough women give birth that she understood the pain.

They had set up snacks in the kitchen and Angela kept finding her way into there to try and eat some, but she would always get one bite or so, and a contraction would start, and she would be brought to her knees in pain.

She was drenched in sweat almost the entire time, and it was everything her mother could do to wipe it away with towels. Her father had opted to stay out of the whole affair and was closed up in his study upstairs. Angela tried to scream loud enough for him to hear her. She wanted him to know the pain this was causing her.

Carol showed her how to kneel in front of the couch and put her elbows up to help ease the pain. She swung her hips back and forth in rhythm with her moans but even the two together couldn't stop the pain completely.

She just wanted it all to be over. She wanted the baby to get out of her, so it would stop ripping her lower half apart.

After what felt like years and years of walking and moaning, Carol said they were getting to the final laps. Angela at first was relieved, thinking that this meant it was almost over, but she was wrong. It only meant that the brief respites between contractions had gotten shorter and shorter and were now almost non-existent.

Her mother tried to get her onto the bed to push out the little baby, but she protested the minute she laid down. Carol suggested squatting over the disposable towels she had brought instead and that was much more comfortable.

Angela had only a moment to notice her mother's look of terror as she squatted and began to push. She was sure Elizabeth was thinking of her precious carpet. She wanted to tell her that they should have gone to a hospital, but instead, she was overcome with another contraction and the pain drove a guttural moan from her chest instead of words.

As she was talked through the process of breathing and pushing, and breathing and pushing, Angela tried to focus, but her brain was so intent on escaping the pain that it was like it refused to listen to her. Her attention and thoughts bounced around constantly trying to find a distraction that was big enough to make her forget the fact that there was a giant hole between her legs that was almost baby sized now.

With each breath in and each push out, she tried to will Kevin out. She had discussed names with her mother and while her parents had advocated for Samuel, she had decided on Kevin. Samuel was a family name on her mother's side, but Angela didn't want her baby to have a family name. She wanted him to have a name all his own. She wanted him to have a life that wasn't overshadowed or copied. She wanted her son to be his own person.

But at the moment, all she really wanted was for Kevin to get the hell out of her.

It came as almost a shock. Suddenly, her final push happened and there was a sudden release. If it hadn't been for Carol crouched next to her, the baby would have hit the floor. She had not been fully prepared for it, secretly thinking in the back of her head that it may never actually happen. She looked down at the child in Carol's hands next to Angela's one knee that was on the floor.

He was there. And he was beautiful.

Carol wiped him off with one of the towels and then handed him to Angela. They were still connected by the cord and it was a strange out of body experience. She felt like they were closer than they had been when he had been inside of her. His eyes were closed tightly and now it was his turn to be screaming at the top of his lungs.

She didn't even notice that the pain was gone because all of it was replaced with warmth and adoration for the little miracle that sat in her arms. She was still covered in sweat, and tears were dripping down her cheeks, but they had become tears of joy rather than pain.

Then, suddenly, time decided to catch up with itself and after almost seven hours of moving at a snail's pace it decided to take the next hour in a single bound. It felt like it was ten minutes later when she found herself in her bed with her child in her arms. In reality they had cut the cord and cleaned both of them up and while she had showered her mother had watched the baby and Carol had cleaned up all the towels and disposed of the mess.

Angela sat up in bed not wanting to sleep. She didn't want to take her eyes off of the infant for even a moment, for fear that he might disappear, or that she might miss something. She stared into his dark green eyes.

"I love you." She whispered, and while he obviously did not understand her words, she felt sure that he understood her meaning and responded in kind.

Finally

I barrel down the country road heading back to Fareport with thoughts of the diary running through my mind, faster than the car does down the pavement.

I understand so much now.

True, there are things that I still do not know, but there is so much that I do know. Including who my parents really are. They were not Robert and Elizabeth Cartwright as I had originally thought. And while I had thought that I had met my father in meeting Robert, I had met him before.

I had met him multiple times, in fact.

And yet I had had no idea. I couldn't even be sure that Philip had known. I couldn't even be sure that Philip even knew that his son existed to begin with. The journal didn't include any indication that Philip knew he was a father but there was some things missing from it, namely everything from my birth to my mother's death, as well as everything after.

This is still a mystery to me, but I can just feel that I am getting closer and closer to the truth. Almost the same way I am getting closer and closer to Fareport.

I left the convent in a hurry immediately after I finished reading the journal. I'd had to take a small break in the middle of reading so that I could rest but it was a restless sleep. I kept waking up and wanting to return to my mother's story. The pages burned in the back of my mind from when I read the very first page till I closed it on the very last.

It is like I had a glimpse of my mother. Like she was speaking to me from beyond the grave across the many years that separated us. And while I learned about her struggles, I felt like I was learning about so much more, the people in my life gained a whole new dimension through my mother's words.

I can't wait to tell Jimmy that not only had our mother's known each other but they had been best friends. I felt a much stronger connection between us like we were no longer chance partners in this mess, but like we had been destined to meet one way or another. It wasn't chance that had me wake up in his backyard.

It was fate.

But now I have to get him out of his cell more than ever. I am so much closer to the truth than I ever was before. With the strides I had made in discovering my past I feel like figuring out my future should come naturally.

Now that I know who I am and where I came from, then where I'm going should be simple.

Right?

As I get closer to Fareport I try to decide what my plan is. I have to get Jimmy out of jail. That is my number one priority. But I also have to use the information I gained form the diary to try and see if I can figure out what happened before I lost my memory. As great as I feel for having found out about my past and my heritage, I still need to find out if I killed Sarah.

But first I need to exonerate Jimmy somehow.

I'm not sure if it is the adrenaline from finishing the diary or if it is some sense of wanting to be a white knight for him the way he has been for me, but I suddenly disagree with Philip. I can't sit back and let the police figure this out. This is my story. This is my mystery to solve.

If I didn't solve it no one would.

I'm not quite sure how I would solve it. I'm not even sure how I'm going to try, but somehow, I have to. For Jimmy's sake, as well as for my own.

As I enter the town that has begun to feel more and more like home, I realize that the cars in front of me have slowed way down and are pulling over to the side, making way for something. Confusedly I follow suit and wait for the sounds of sirens, but they never come.

What does come is the long black Cadillac followed by a steady stream of cars with their lights on and little flags on their hoods. I don't count them but there aren't that many. As they pull away, I get a sudden urge to follow them. I'm not sure where it comes from or why, but it takes over me from my toes to the tips of my goose bumped hair.

I quickly pull out after the last one and join the slow procession before any other cars can get between me and the trail of mourners.

My intuition begins to grow as we turn onto Westchester Street. I've been here before. I know what is on this road, and more importantly who is buried there.

This time, however, when I read the stone, I will know her as a person rather than a simple name and date. I will know who she was, not only as a person but to me. I will be able to mourn her as my mother.

I pull Ronnie's car over to the side of the path, a ways back from the other mourners. I don't want them to wonder who this new tag along car is and disrupt their mourning. I simply get out of the car and head over to my mother's gravesite. I wish I had flowers or something to put on her grave like all those at the funeral do, but I don't. All I have is my heart and feelings.

I stand over the same grave I stood over a week ago and read the same words I read before but now I feel tears break loose from my eyes. I feel like I'm losing the mother that I never had and while twenty-four hours ago I didn't even know her name, I feel like I've known her forever.

And I have a sinking suspicion that I did know her. At least in name. Why else would I have been searching so hard for her. Perhaps I didn't have evidence as I do now, but I had to have known. That was why she was haunting my dreams those first few days after I woke up on that dock. She may have been taking the form of Sarah but that was only a substitute for the woman that I was truly searching for. And when I found her, because of my memory loss I didn't even know what I had found.

I almost feel guilty for not remembering, for not knowing before.

I look up from the gravestone and it's like I can see her face. Across the many slabs of granite with inscriptions of so many lives the ghost of my mother stares back at me.

But, once again, it isn't really her, it's Sarah. And it isn't her ghost; instead, it is a portrait of her. It takes me a moment to put the pieces together and realize why there is an easel with her portrait among the funeral service.

I had unknowingly followed her funeral procession.

I whisper a quiet goodbye to my mother's grave and promise to come back with flowers. I head over towards the mourners in order to pay my respects to the first person I ever knew. We may have known each other at different times, but I feel a strong connection with her. She has been my silent partner in this mystery, and I feel like this is where I leave her and pursue the truth alone and for that I have to say my thanks and whisper my goodbye.

As I stand in the back of the mourners, trying to stay invisible as the priest says words of comfort to the family and friends gathered, I catch the eye of a man standing on the other side of the congregation.

While I don't recognize the blonde young man staring back at me, I can tell by the way he is looking at me that he knows me somehow. I avert my eyes for a moment, but when I look back at him, he is still looking at me with curiosity and intrigue.

After a while, the congregation begins to morph and change as those closest move ever closer to the hole in the ground where Sarah's body is being lowered and those on the outer ridge begin to leave. I suddenly feel very out of place among the suits and black dresses. My clothes are not only out of place but also a day old among all these people who are dressed in their Sunday best. I duck out of their sight and try to act like I wasn't just crashing their funeral and head back to my mother's graveside as if that were the only thing of interest to me in the cemetery.

I intend to return to Sarah's side to pay my respects after everyone has left but I never get a chance because I am not alone at my mother's grave. I am followed by the blonde man with whom I made contact across the services.

"You're Kevin?" He says from behind me. I almost crawl out of my skin when he says it. He not only recognized me, but he knew my name. And it must have been from before I lost my memory since he knows me as Kevin instead of Sam.

I turn to him and nod wondering how we knew each other. Logic said that we knew each other through Sarah since I obviously was working with her, but I have no idea who he is to her, whether a brother or a friend?

"You don't know me," he says. This is a strange experience for me to actually be able to believe my own memory in that I don't know someone. "I'm… or rather I guess I was…" He struggles with how to say what he wants. He takes a moment, then continues, "I was Sarah's boyfriend." As he says the word, I recognize the odd taste in his mouth. Like he doesn't quite feel like the word does his relationship justice but at the same time is too strong a word. His face is similar to mine whenever I try to think of what mine and Jimmy's relationship is.

"My name's Thomas." He extends a hand out to shake mine. I take it and suddenly feel very awkward for not having said anything. But I don't know what to say. He already knows my name, although how I'm not sure, so there is no need to introduce myself.

"I'm sorry for your loss," I say, and the awkwardness grows in the pit of my stomach as I remember that I am infringing on a moment that should be only for family and friends of the deceased. Not some guy who doesn't even fully remember her and also may have helped to cover up her murder.

"Thank you," he says respectfully. "I've been actually trying to find you, but I didn't know how." I give him a quizzical look. Why would he be trying to contact me?

"I've been…" I don't know how to describe the last few weeks in a single word. "Unavailable." I feel weird. I'm struck once again that this situation where I have been looking at myself as a victim had effects that went much further than myself. Ripples that caused my memory loss and confusion also caused the death of not just Sarah but others, as well. Even though my memory hasn't been lost again, I seem to always forget that.

I'm not the only victim.

"Sarah left some stuff that… well, I think you ought to have it. I'm not sure what to do with it anyway. I'm honestly not even sure what it is." Sarah had things of mine? My heart begins to race as I think of the possibilities. Sarah was investigating my past, who knows what she might have found. She might have found some of the final missing pieces between the end of my mother's diary and now.

"Okay, sure." I'm not sure if I'm supposed to ask for it. I highly doubt whatever he has for me he would be keeping on him especially at his dead girlfriend's funeral.

"I'm going to go and have lunch with her family, but you can stop by for it a little later, say around two?" I nod, and he begins to walk away before I call out to him.

"Where am I picking it up from." Now it's his turn to look confused.

"From our apartment. You've been there before, haven't you?" I don't really want to get into the whole story of my amnesia right now with him standing there in the early morning chill in his suit and tie. Sarah's friends and family have noticed his absence and are looking over at us making me feel all the more uncomfortable. I shake my head no and hope that that is enough.

"It's 3005 Skylark Drive, Apartment 3." He tells me but it's like there's an echo in my head that goes a half a second after he speaks. Like I knew it before he said it, I just simply needed help retrieving it. He asks me if I will remember it, and I nod my head yes as he returns to the family. They clearly are asking him who he was just talking to. I wonder what he tells them.

Does he tell them that I'm a friend of Sarah's?

A client of hers?

What does he say, given that he has no idea that the correct thing he should have said was the man who found her dead body and covered it up?

I shake my head and tell myself no. That may be who I was but that isn't who I'm going to be. I'm *going* to be the man who finds her killer.

No matter who it is.

Angela woke with a rush. She wasn't sure what her dream had been about, but she felt that there was something strange about it. It had felt both new but familiar. It had been scary but also exciting, both frightening and exhilarating. It was like Deja vu but different somehow. The details of the dream disappeared before she was able to grasp them like fog through her fingertips.

She got out of bed and wanders through the quiet house. It was too early for anyone else to be awake. Perhaps seven o'clock on a Saturday. She wouldn't even be up if it hadn't been for the dream. It was strange, it felt so real but at the same time so surreal. She remembered falling but she was also floating and there was a lot of water and a lot of light.

She tried to shake off the weird feeling it gave her, but she couldn't seem to take her mind off of it, so she found her way to little Kevin's room.

He was so adorable laying there on his back sleeping. His little hands clenched tight as if he were holding onto something for dear life. She wondered if he was dreaming and, if so, what he was dreaming about? Did babies have dreams?

She stood there and smiled at the little life that she had created and replayed the few images she could recall but even those were slowly dying away in her mind's eye like they were being eaten away by bugs till there was nothing left.

She remembered a dock over water but beneath it was a reflection of a lighthouse that wasn't there. She seemed to think that she had reached out to touch the lighthouse through the water but maybe it wasn't her. Perhaps it was someone else. Maybe that was when she had fallen. That would explain floating right afterwards because she would have fallen into the water.

Oh, well, it was only a dream, right?

She went downstairs and made herself a bowl of oatmeal for breakfast. If she was going to be awake this early, she might as well do something, so she went over to one of the bookshelves in the living room to find a book to read.

She decided on one of her old favorites, The Hobbit, and was sitting down in her favorite reading spot on the couch, getting ready to delve into Middle Earth again, when suddenly, there was a knock at her door.

She glanced at the grandfather clock to reaffirm that she was right in that it was seven in the morning. She was. Who would be stopping by for a visit this early?

They hadn't had any visitors for a long time. Unless you counted Christmas Eve and her father's encounter with Chrissy's ex. And now for someone to show up this early unannounced seemed exceedingly strange.

She went over to the window and looked out through the curtains to see if she knew who it was.

It was Drew.

He stood in front of the door waiting for her to come and answer it. She had not seen him since their fight, and she didn't know what to do. She knew what she wanted to do. She wanted to go back upstairs crawl into bed and try to start this morning over, with no nightmare and no Drew on her doorstep.

But should she do that? Was that acceptable? He obviously wanted to talk to her. It wasn't like he was coming by to talk to her parents. The only logical person for him to be looking for was her. What did he have to say? He had seemed to make it clear last time they talked that he didn't want to talk to her again.

Oh, God.

He still didn't know that Kevin even existed. Her lie of omission had been bad enough last time when she had been five months pregnant, but now, she had actually had the baby and had never even mentioned it to him. Had never picked up the phone and called or stopped by. She hadn't even written out a letter, sent or unsent.

How could she even talk to him now? How would the conversation go? "Good morning. Want to come upstairs and meet your son?" No, she wouldn't say that. She'd say, "our son." He was as much hers as his. Angela shook her head. What did it matter which pronoun she used? She had to tell him if she opened that door.

He knocked again.

He wasn't going anywhere, apparently, so she would have to answer the door eventually. Maybe she could tell him to leave, that she didn't want to see him anymore.

But was that true?

Even after he left her crying in the parking lot, she still cared about him. She still loved him, and he was still the father of her child whether he knew it or not. He turned towards the window and she quickly let the curtain fall and backed away hoping that he hadn't seen her peeking through and looking at him. He knocked a third time this time was more of a pound. If she didn't go out and talk to him, he was going to wake her mother.

She walked up to the front door and put her hand on the door handle.

She took a deep breath and opened the door.

Momentarily she hoped that perhaps she had been wrong. Maybe she was still dreaming, and he wouldn't be there on the other side of the door. But there he stood in his jeans and leather coat. He looked just as charming as ever but at the same time he looked different. His hair was cut shorter than she remembered, and his face didn't have the same look that it did before.

She opened her mouth the say something, but he put a finger to her lips to silence her and leaned in and kissed her. In that moment, all the emotions came rushing back through her veins. It was like the last nine months had never happened and they were happy young teenagers with the world at their fingertips. It took her breath away and made her hairs stand on edge.

She relaxed into the kiss just in time for him to pull away and stare at her longingly.

"I'm sorry." He whispered. It was then that she realized she didn't need to tell him. She had agonized at the window for nothing. He already knew. Somehow, he knew.

"No, I'm sorry. I should have told you." She felt even more guilty than she had before.

"I didn't make it any easier for you. I'm sorry. You shouldn't have had to go through it alone." He grabbed her and held her against him, and she felt his warmth breathe life into her soul.

She didn't want to leave his arms. She wanted to stay exactly like this forever, standing in the doorway with his arms around her, protecting her from everything.

"Do you want to meet him?" She asked into his shoulder and he immediately pulled back as if she had bitten him.

"Meet him?" He sounded so confused that she didn't understand what had happened. He knew she could see it in his eyes. "You mean you didn't." He let the silence after his sentence complete his thought for him and the pieces connected in Angela's mind.

"No. No, I didn't." She wanted to feel upset that he would think she would ever consider that, but she couldn't fault him for thinking that. He had been out of the loop all year and she couldn't blame him for not knowing what she had decided to do. "He's upstairs. Do you want to meet him?" She asked him again and this time the realization crossed his face.

She saw him grow ten years in that one moment. He went from an adolescent into an adult in that moment. He changed from young to old in that instant. He grew from a boy into a man, from a child into a father all at once.

Suddenly, excitement built between the two of them. She took his hand and led him into the house. She held up her finger to her lips to tell him to not make a sound. He nodded with a huge smile on his face as she led him up the stairs. When they got to the guest room, which was acting as the nursery for right now, he let go of her hand and went to the crib clutching the side with both hands to help keep him standing.

He stood there staring at the child he hadn't known existed until that day. And Angela stood at the doorway staring at the man who didn't exist until a moment ago. She began crying with joy at seeing the transformation of the man she had fallen in love with.

"What is his name?" He asked her not taking his eyes off the little child. She walked up and joined him at the crib, nuzzling in close to him.

"Kevin Andrew." He squeezed her closer to him, as they stood there and watched their son sleep. She wished that she could freeze his moment. Finally, she felt like she wasn't all alone. She had Drew there with her and they both had Kevin. Darling little Kevin with his little puff of hair and little pudgy arms.

Together they could make it. Together they would make it work. However, they wanted to continue, they would do it together. As a family.

As soon as I pull into the driveway, I see someone lying on the front lawn. I am not exactly sure who it is at first or what he is doing laying in Jimmy's front yard, but I immediately fear the worst.

I throw the car in park and hop out and run over to the body lying in the grass. I run through the possibilities in my head. Did Harold come out and fall asleep in the yard? Did something happen to Uncle Ben? Or, God forbid, did the murderer change his pattern and kill a man this time?

It is only Uncle Ben. But he lays there unconscious and reeking of alcohol. I lean over him and almost gag on the fumes that are seeping out of every one of his pores. I immediately put a hand under his nose to check and make sure that he is alive. The last thing I need is to be found with yet another dead body.

Thankfully, he is still breathing.

I try to think of what to do. I can't leave him laying out here in the yard, but I can't get him up by myself. I hold my breath and shake him to try and wake him up. He doesn't respond except to open and close his mouth as if he had a nasty taste in his mouth that he needed to get rid of.

"Alex!" I call out, but she can't hear me inside the house. I'm not quite sure that I really want her there or if she would be able to help at all, but I can't think of anything else at the moment.

I leave him there for a minute to run to the front porch and open the door yelling for Alex. She comes down the stairs like she just woke up in her pink pajamas which I would imagine she did given that it is only ten o'clock on a Sunday morning.

"What's the matter?" She says rubbing the sleepiness out of her eyes.

"It's your uncle. See if you can help me get him inside." I leave the porch and return to Ben in the grass. I shake him again trying to wake him up. He finally opens his eyes as Alex makes her way over to us. He doesn't look like he is able to focus on anything let alone know what's going on.

"Help me lift him up." Alex isn't able to help much but it is enough that I can at least get him sat up which wakes him up a little bit more. He looks around and his eyes are able to fix themselves on each of us. He still looks like he has no idea where he is or how he got there.

"Whas' goi'on?" he slurs as I move around behind him and slip my arms under his shoulders.

"I'm trying to get you up Ben, so I can get you inside." He is little help as I try to lift the two-hundred-pound man to his feet. Luckily, he is not any bigger or else I probably wouldn't be able to do it. As it is, once I get him standing, it is everything I can manage to not drop him down to the ground again.

"Ye kno' hoo you loo' like?" He slurs noticing Alex as if she hadn't been there before. I don't try and figure out what he is saying as I try to steer him into putting one foot in front of the other. He isn't cooperating very well. Alex tries to help but she's too little and since she has to take two steps for every one of ours it causes this weird rhythm that makes the whole process even more difficult.

"Come on, let's get you inside so you can sleep this off." We finally make it to the porch after what feels like an eternity of walking and that is when I realize I have to get him upstairs. He is currently leaning on me for balance and I'm not sure I can leave his side, so we take the stairs together like we were dancers in rhythm. I put one foot up with his and we lift together to make it up the step. Finally, after a few wibbles and a few more wobbles we make it to the top and are standing in front of the door. Alex slips in front of us and opens it.

"I liv'ere" He mutters more to himself than to anyone in particular. It's in that moment that Uncle Ben and Benjamin become one person for me. It is such a sudden realization that I almost lose him to the ground but I'm able to hold him still and keep him upright.

I, of course, had known that it was the same person, but it had never meshed together for me until now. I had thought of Uncle Ben as nothing more than a drunkard who may or may not be abusing his niece. Now I see the hurt man beneath the drunkard. The man who lost the woman he loved and whom no one felt any sympathy for because he wasn't the husband. All they saw was the brother-in-law when, in reality, he was the lover.

I felt such pity for him in that moment. But I didn't have time to be having an emotional blossoming on the front porch. I push him through the front door into the house that so many people seem to call home. Not only Harold and his family but his brother and my mother and now myself.

I decide to lead him towards Alex's room since it is the only one on the ground floor. Besides, it seems fitting given that it used to be his room back when he lived here. Alex apparently has the same thought since she goes and opens her door for us. He is more and more awake now, so he is able to help more, and we cover the distance to the bedroom a lot faster than we did the yard.

I take a moment to take in Alex's room. It is the first time that I've ever been inside. I don't know what I expected but it is just like any twelve-year-old's room. There is a wilting poster of some boy band on the wall above her bed which has a light blue cover. Her desk is littered with notes and drawings. The floor is covered in clothes and things, which makes it all the harder for our little three-legged race to get Ben to the bed. But get him to it we do, and I get him to lay down.

"Go grab the trashcan out of the kitchen." I tell Alex. She goes to grab it and I try to keep Ben sitting up until she comes back with it. She is just in time as the alcohol in Ben's system realizes that he isn't going to sleep it off so, instead, tries to shoot out of his mouth and into the plastic bag inside the trashcan.

I make a face unintentionally and turn away from the sight of it. Alex leaves the room, and I don't blame her. After a few minutes when I think he is done, I grab all of Alex's pillows and set them up behind him so that he can lay back without laying all the way flat.

"Just go to sleep." I tell him but he doesn't seem to want to.

"I love'r s'much," he says as I nod and lean him back onto the pillows.

"That's right, just get some sleep." He finally closes his eyes and begins to snore in almost a moment. I watch him for a few minutes to make sure he isn't going to wake up and start vomiting again before I head out into the living room.

When I do I find that Alex is not alone.

Harold is sitting on the couch with her. They look like they are waiting to be seen at the doctor's office. Both of them sitting there not talking and not looking at each other just staring straight ahead, only reacting when I enter.

"Is he okay?" Alex asks, and she becomes a twelve-year-old again. It's so hard to remember how young she is sometimes.

"He will be," I say because I don't know what else to say.

"Why don't you go upstairs Alex dear." This is the most lucid thing I've ever heard come out of Harold's mouth. I don't know what has caused it, but he doesn't seem himself. As Alex heads upstairs he looks at me with the deepest concern on his face.

"I apologize for my brother." He says this to me, and I wonder if he has been swapped with a clone in the one night I have been away. "It was awfully nice of you to stop by and help him. Would you like some money in return?" I realize he thinks I was some random good Samaritan who stopped by. In the one night I've been gone he has completely forgotten that I have been living in this house.

"Harold. It's me, Sam. I'm Jimmy's friend." He looks at me slightly confused. He stares at my face and tries to place it, but he doesn't seem like he can. Finally, he simply gives up and pushes on with what he wants to say.

"Look, you don't have to worry about my brother. He is just depressed. Our family has been going through some… Trials lately." I don't know what exactly to say to this. I am about to say something to try and make him remember that I'm plenty aware of what has gone on in the family when he presses onward. "I myself have struggled. You see I just lost my wife" He says this so matter of factly that if I didn't know that she had actually died years ago I would wonder if he was really even mourning the loss.

"Harold. I know that." He doesn't even seem to hear me.

"She was killed in a car accident. A drunk driver drove her off the road. It's been hard on all of us, but Benjamin blames himself. She was on her way to meet him when it happened."

It's like I got a smack in the face. I hadn't had any indication of it, but I had assumed that the affair had ended years before Melly had died. It was the only possibility that I had considered. Otherwise, why would she have stayed with Harold? Raised a family with Harold? My shock must have shown in my face because now he looks had me and smiles a knowing smile.

"I'm fully aware that they were sleeping together. I knew years ago. In fact, I even told Melly that she could leave me if she wanted but I just wasn't going to be the one to make that decision. I'm not the kind of person who quits things just because they aren't perfect you know?" My eyes grow ever wider as he continues, "Just because you break something doesn't mean you buy a whole new one and throw the old one out. No, you fix it. You paid for it and it's yours now whether it works the way you wanted it to or not."

I don't know what this is that is going on with Harold. I don't know if he is confused or if he really did feel this way when she had been alive. Either way, I suddenly understand his desire to take all the drugs. With the knowledge that your wife was sleeping with your brother for so long I'm sure kills your outlook on life regardless of who you are.

"But what about the children?" I whisper, almost playing along with the time traveling he seems to be doing by referring to both of them as children, even though Jimmy hasn't been a child for years.

"Oh, the children don't have any idea. And besides if it weren't for Benjamin there would only be Jimmy." He says this as if he were telling me the weather and not dropping a bomb in his living room. I sit down at this, unable to keep my feet under me.

"Alex is…"

“Benjamin’s child yes.” He still shows so little emotion I feel like at any moment he might yell ‘syke’ and laugh like it was all some big practical joke. “Me and Melody didn’t have sex after I found out about the two of them. And in a way it almost worked. Benjamin and her never would have worked as a couple. Benjamin is too wild for Melly. She wanted a family and solidity. He wanted to party and enjoy his life to the fullest. So, she got what she needed from him and just came home to me and the kids.

“So, when she came up pregnant again, I knew what had happened. I may not have gone to college but I’m smart enough to know how a baby is made. So, once again, I told her. I said, ‘You can leave, or you can stay. It is up to you,’ and she stayed. And I got my dear Alex out of the deal.”

Suddenly, the whole situation with Ben and Alex makes so much more sense now. What looked like unconventional affection from a drunk uncle suddenly makes sense as a father trying to show his love to a daughter who doesn’t even know he’s her father.

The pity that I had for Benjamin grows ever stronger in my heart as I sat on the couch in the house where his family had lived. I suddenly can see the progression for him form wild party animal who enjoyed life to the depressed drunkard who had lost the love of his life, as well as his own daughter to his brother and then to have Melly die so tragically. And, of course, he blames himself.

“Do you need a tissue?” Harold seems really confused by my crying. I myself hadn’t even noticed it until now. I shake my head and wipe my eyes. “Anyway, you’ll probably want to be on your way.” He stands up as if to escort me out of the house in his bathrobe.

“Harold. I live here with you.” He stares at me as if I had spoken a different language.

“Well, you have a nice day. I’m sure you can find your own way out, I guess. I’m going back to bed.” He walks over to the stairs and heads up. He stops about halfway up.

“Please don’t tell them.” I can’t be sure but I’m almost positive that he knows who I am in this moment. His lucidity certainly seems true. “It would break his heart. And I don’t want them to ever think that Melly and I didn’t love each other. We did. She just… She just had so much love to give that there was enough for both of us.”

Angela and Drew spent the next hour talking about their options and their hopes and dreams for the little life and family that they had created. Angela could barely believe it. It was like Drew had been on board with this from the very beginning. He sounded so sure of himself. He wanted to drop out of school and find himself a job to help support them. Angela, of course, would have to work, as well, but they talked about maybe in a few years once they were more settled, they could talk about her going back to school part time.

She wasn't sure any of what they talked about was really possible, but it seemed like it might be. And in that moment, all that mattered was that there was some hope left. Just a little light at the end of this long dark tunnel that she had been in since she found out she was pregnant.

"We will have to find ourselves a place to live. I can't stay with my father. He wouldn't have it." Angela could tell from his tone that there was more to his statement than met the ear.

"He told you, didn't he?" The realization dawned on her in a moment. It was the only logical explanation.

"We had a fight and he brought it up to try and hurt me. Told me that I was useless. That no one ever actually cared for me, not him, not my mom, not even you." The hurt in his face was so painful for Angela to look at. She knew what it was like to be on the receiving end of his father's wrath.

"You know that's not true." She took his hand in hers to try and comfort him.

"Maybe not for you, but my mother did run away, and my father... well... " He trailed off without even dignifying his father with an example. "I don't want that for our son. I want him to know how much we care about him. I want him to know he's loved." He looked her in the eyes with the utmost urgency in those blue irises.

"I promise, I will never allow him to think we don't love him," she said, vowing it not only to him but to herself. "I have a crazy idea." Suddenly, she wanted to turn the conversation back to their hopes and dreams instead of the dread of the past.

"Let's go away. Let's go far from Fareport. We'll start over someplace new. Take your car and drive it till the gas runs out and just figure things out." She almost laughed as she said it. It sounded so crazy coming out of her mouth, but it also sounded so... exciting.

"Where would we go?" He chuckled.

"I don't know. I don't care. Let's just get out of this stupid town. Get away from our stupid parents. Let's just go." She was gripping his arm now with excitement.

"How could we ever afford it?" He asked, she could tell he was trying to be the voice of reason, but his eyes told her that he wanted it just as much as she did.

"We'll figure that out. You can work and I can serve just about anywhere. We can figure it out. Sure, it won't be easy, but it'll be better than this. And we'll have each other. And Kevin. That's all that matters." What had started out as a crazy idea in her mind suddenly began to be so much more than that to her. She wanted to do it. She wanted them both to do it. No, not both, all three.

"Okay." He smiled at her with the biggest smile she had ever seen on his face. "Let's do it." She almost shrieked with excitement as she threw her arms around his neck. Sitting there on the floor of the semi-nursery in her parents' guest room with her two-month-old baby and her recently reunited boyfriend, that was the happiest and most hopeful moment of her life.

And it lasted all of five seconds.

"What the hell are you doing here?" They were both shocked out of their excitement to find Angela's father standing there in the doorway.

"Dad, we were just—" Angela started to tell him that they were just talking about the future. She wasn't sure it was the best idea to mention their plan to start over, but it didn't matter because her father didn't let her finish her sentence.

"Get the hell out of here!" He took two steps into the room and grabbed Drew by the neck of his shirt. He drug Drew out of the nursery despite Drew's attempts to fight back. Drew may have had youth on his side, but Angela's father was a well-built man. He had gone through extensive training before being shipped overseas, and his many years on the force didn't hurt, so he was able to take any of the hits that Drew threw at his sides as he drug him through the hall.

"Let him go!" Angela chased after him, smacking her father on the back trying to get him to listen. But he could not be reached. He got to the front door and opened it just wide enough to chuck Drew out onto the front porch.

"And don't ever come near my daughter again!" His words were not said at a volume that could even overpower the cries from Kevin upstairs who had been woken up by the excitement, but they were intense enough to silence Angela and Drew's protests.

Angela looked from her angry father to the father of her child on the floor of the front porch. She didn't know what she was supposed to do but she needed to do something.

"If you're throwing him out, your throwing me out, too." She stepped out onto the front porch and defiantly turned to face her father looking through the open doorway. His hand was on the door like he was about to slam it.

"Don't listen to his lies Angela. He doesn't love you. Come back inside." Angela forced down the tears, so that she could do this without fear, or at least without showing it.

"No." She remembered the courage it took to run away from home before. Now she called upon that courage again. She wasn't going to sit idly by and let her father dictate her life or the life of her child. She was going to stand up for herself and she wasn't going to do it in the dark of night like last time. She was going to do it here and now in the morning light.

"We are leaving. We are taking Kevin and we are leaving. You can't stop us." She bent over and offered a hand to help Drew up to his feet. He stood next to her and while it was comforting to feel his strength standing with hers, it was even more comforting to know that she didn't need it.

"Who are you? What happened to my little girl? My little girl who listened to her father? Who had respect?" His words sounded like venom pouring out of his mouth. She could feel the disgust and disdain laced through his voice and it cut through her chest right to her heart. She wanted to curl into a ball right there on the porch, but she couldn't. She knew that this was her one chance to have the life she wanted. This was her opportunity to be that bird in the painting and to break free of the cage her father had created for her. If she didn't take it, she would live the rest of her life chained to him and this house.

"I'm the woman she grew up to be." She tried her best to keep her voice from cracking, but it did a little anyway. She powered through and kept her face from showing her pain.

"Fine. You want to run away from your life, from those that love you, those that have cared for you? You want to throw it all away for this piece of trash that you call a man? Then do it. No one is stopping you. But you're not taking my son." She didn't even have time to register his words as he slammed the door in her face. It was a half of a second before she began beating on the front door of the house that she had just escaped, begging to be let in.

They were free from her prison, but Kevin was not.

I sit there in the living room for five minutes, unsure of what to do with this new information. Everything seems to be turning on its head. I don't know how to process it all as fast as it seems to be happening.

I vaguely hear Benjamin groaning from the other room. I hear him lurch into the waste bin and quiet down and go back to sleep. I wonder if he is even aware. Harold made it sound like no one knew but him. Surely Melly would have told Ben that he was Alex's father but if she had why hadn't he ever said anything? Even before she died, he must have wanted to be a part of Alex's life. He must have wanted to be a father to her.

I look out the window and see her sitting on the porch. She is sitting in between the two posts where Benjamin had tackled Jimmy a week ago. It still hasn't been fixed yet. Just like the wreckage of this family, it will take time before things are healed, if they ever are right again.

Perhaps that was why he never fought to tell her. Perhaps he was sacrificing his own pride for her to have a solid home. If he had forced the issue the family could have been torn apart. Suddenly, this unit that Melly and Harold had created would be torn apart. Not by hate, but by love.

I realize that in this moment the man vomiting into the waste bin in Alex's bedroom is one of the strongest men I know, to be willing to put aside his own happiness like that for his daughter. No wonder he drinks. You've got to escape somehow.

Escape.

That's what I want to do right now is escape this whole mess. Escape it with Jimmy and get away from everything that's going on. But how am I supposed to do that when he is locked away and there is a murderer on the loose? And no matter how I felt driving back to Fareport this morning I'm still really nowhere closer to finding out who the murderer is.

I'm still really no closer than I was three weeks ago when I woke up on Jimmy's dock. I may know who I am, and I may know who Sarah was but that still doesn't explain what we were doing on that dock or how she ended up with a knife stuck in the back of her neck.

I feel like a complete failure.

I need some air, so I get up and walk out to the front porch. The cold September morning pulls at my skin. I sit down next to the young girl without saying anything. We sit there for a few moments before either of us speaks.

"Where is Jimmy?" she asks it without looking at me. I can tell by her tone that she doesn't want to know the answer, but she needs to know at the same time.

"He's in jail." She doesn't react at first. I wonder if there is ever a bottom to the amount of strength this little girl has. I'm sure she hates me for bringing all of this drama into her life, but she hides it well.

"I don't blame you." She's apparently a mind reader, as well.

"I do." I search for the right words to explain what I'm feeling. "I'm the one that should be locked up. They only let me out because Jimmy took the fall for me. I'm the one who… who woke up next to a dead body." I've lost track of exactly what Alex knows but at this point I'm sick and tired of lying. I'm sick and tired of having to watch every word I say and put up this facade. I just want the truth to come out, so I can stop having to search for it.

"I'm sorry I had to come to your house. I wish I had thrown myself in that lake along with her." She finally looks at me when I say this.

"Don't say that. It's not true and you know it." Her glare is enough to shatter glass. "And I for one am glad you chose our house if you really did *choose* it. Jimmy hasn't been happy since mom died. And while he's not… Happy exactly, I guess right now, he's at least living. And it's because of you. He's a different person since you came along. He's not…" Now she seemed at a loss for words.

"Dead inside." I finish for her.

"So, how are you going to get him out?" she asks as she gets to her feet. Her question catches me off guard. Not that I hadn't been planning on trying to do that very thing, but I hadn't put together exactly how, and I wasn't quite ready to be put on the spot like that.

"I… I don't know."

"Well, you'd better figure it out. Because of you, I finally got my big brother, and it's because of you he's locked up, so it's your job to get him back." She doesn't seem to think that that warrants any further discussion as she marches into the house and closes the door behind her.

This leaves me all alone on the front porch wondering what to do next.

I know where I want to end up, with Jimmy by my side on the outside of a prison cell with the murderer inside of one but how can I get there? How can I get Jimmy out of jail without the murderer or at least evidence of who it is? How can I find evidence if I don't even know who the murderer is? I keep circling around my options in my head, but I don't know what to do or where to go to figure it out.

I try to concentrate and think of any possibility no matter how crazy. I think of breaking Jimmy out but that wouldn't solve the problem. We'd still be stuck with a murderer on the loose and all it would do is make things look even worse for me. If Callahan didn't have solid evidence that I was a criminal, breaking my boyfriend out of jail would certainly give it to him.

I want to scream. I want to rant and rave. I hate that I have caused this and, no matter what, Alex says I feel like I've caused more trouble than I'm worth. Why did this have to happen to me? Why couldn't some other random guy end up on that dock?

And suddenly, the answer locks into place in my brain.

I jump to my feet with a sudden urgency. My brain starts to try and figure out the ramifications of what this means as I run into the house and begin to call out for Alex.

"Alex!" I scream almost making myself hoarse looking for her. She comes tearing down the stairs looking like I had been yelling that there was a fire in the house or something.

"What? What's going on?" She looks completely dumbfounded when she sees me standing at the bottom of the stairs with a huge grin on my face. She doesn't understand because she is just like I was until a minute ago. She's only looking at the two problems as individuals instead of looking at the bigger picture.

"The killer knows me!" She continues to give me a confused look.

"What are you talking about?" I try to calm myself enough that I can put my thoughts into coherent sentences.

"He didn't kill me. Why wouldn't he have killed me?" It's a while before she realizes that I expect an answer.

"I don't know."

"Unless he tried." I point to my head. "My memory loss! It was probably caused by a blow to the head! He probably tried to kill me and failed!" She still looked at me like I was talking gibberish. I didn't know how much of this I needed to spoon feed to her.

"Why would the killer be trying to kill me? Look at all of his other victims! Sarah, Emily, and Dany. They are all women. I'm the only man! Why would he have tried to kill me?" Realization dawns on Alex's face as she finally puts the last piece of the puzzle together.

"You must have known who the murderer was!"

"Exactly! And if I knew then how could I have figured it out?" Alex is at the bottom of the stairs and is almost as excited as I am.

"I have no idea!" She, of course, doesn't. She hasn't been a part of my search for my past, so she only knows tertiary details.

"I must have figured it out while I was looking for my parents! Somehow, I don't know how but my search for my parents and my search for the murderer is all tied together! It's the missing link between the two! I must have found out something I wasn't supposed to find out and that's why he tried to kill me!"

"Okay." Her excitement starts to die now that she sees this is as far as I have gotten. But she doesn't know what I do. She hasn't read the diary. She doesn't realize just how close I am to figuring out the story of my parents. "But you lost your memory, so you no longer know who it is."

"No, but if I continue trying to figure out the story behind my parents and why I was put up for adoption then I'll come across the same discovery! *That*'s how I'll catch the murderer! The same way I did before this whole mess started. Only this time I'll be on the lookout and I won't lose my memory."

"So…. Now what are you going to do?" Alex still seems wary of this new plan, but I didn't let that kill my motivation. I know exactly what I need to do next.

"I am going to go and talk to my father."

Angela paced around Melly's kitchen as Melly tried to calm Daniel with a pacifier. He hadn't stopped crying since Angela and Drew had gotten there. The tension in the room was just too much for him apparently. Angela had tried holding him but not only were her magical powers not working today but also holding a baby only kept her mind stuck on her poor baby stuck in that house without her.

They had pounded and pounded on the door for what felt like forever, surely waking her mother up, as well as Kevin, but no one ever opened the door. Too late she had thought of the back door and when she got there it was already locked by her conniving father.

After an hour of pounding without any response, Drew had convinced her through her tears that they would do best to go somewhere and decide what to do rather than continuing to beat a dead house. So, she had had him drive her to the only other place she felt at all at home. But now, almost an hour later, after having told Melly everything that had happened, they were still at a complete loss as to what to do.

"I have to go back and get Kevin," Angela said without preamble and headed for the door but Melly reached out with her free hand and grabbed her arm.

"That isn't going to solve anything. Drew is right. They aren't going to let you back into that house by screaming and pounding on the door." She let go of Angela's arm rather quickly to return to her attempt at soothing the crying child in her arms. She shifted him from being cradled to over her shoulder and began to bounce him which didn't exactly stop the crying, but instead, made the sound bounce in rhythm.

"That's it," Angela said, realization dawning on her face.

"What?"

"We have to change our plan. We can't go in pounding." Drew saw exactly where she was going with this before she said it and immediately his face turned into an unspoken no. "Why not? It's the smartest plan."

"Maybe I'm too busy with a screaming baby in my ear but I don't hear an actual plan yet. What is it you're proposing?" Melly asked in between shushes in her son's ear.

"I'm going to go back alone."

"Definitely not!" Drew slammed his hand down on the kitchen counter in anger at the thought of it, but Angela plowed onward.

"I'm going to go back and beg forgiveness. I'll lie and tell them that I was a stupid little girl and that I want to come back home. I did it once why can't I do it again?"

"What says you will be able to get Kevin and actually leave?" Drew clearly was still against the idea.

"They are my parents Drew, not monsters." She said this, even though when it came to her father after his explosion this morning she somewhat disagreed with her own judgement. However, this was the only way she could see of being able to get their son back.

"You know she has a point, Drew." Melly said. "It's not the best plan but it could work."

"I wouldn't even stay very long. I'd wait until tonight when they go to bed and sneak away in the middle of the night. I'd just take the baby and run. By the time they wake up, I'll be long gone and what are they going to do then?"

She didn't want him to answer because she honestly didn't want to think about it, and she could tell from his face that while he wasn't saying it he was thinking some of the same things that she was.

They could come after them. They could try and take the baby legally or by force. Technically this would be the best time for her if they were to try and take it legally because she still could prove that she had recently given birth, but in a few months, it would become more and more difficult to prove that their story of her being sick and her mother having a miracle child wasn't true.

That was if they even got the law involved. They could simply do exactly as she was doing and come in the middle of the night and take her Kevin away. She couldn't understand how her father had become this villain in her head seemingly overnight.

"I just hate the idea of you having to go back there. After this morning, I'm not sure I want to know what your father will do if you go back. He looked like he really wanted to hurt me this morning." Angela almost laughs at this.

"That was you. No matter what happened this morning my father loves me. He may have thrown you out of the house, but I left on my own. He wouldn't hurt me. I'm his little Angel."

Angela was confident in her words but deep down in the core of her being a very small voice whispered that she hoped she was right.

I stand outside of the King household. It feels strange that this was where I went that very first night that I stayed at Ronnie's. It feels like it has been so long since I came here and saw Helen through that window. The entire situation feels totally different now. Not only is it the height of midday now as opposed to the dead of night, but I feel like a completely different person, and I am looking for a completely different person now. I still need someone who might know me, but now, instead of just a strange feeling leading me here, I actually know exactly who I am here to see.

I'm here to see my father.

I stand outside for a few minutes just gathering the courage to go in and talk to him. It's strange because I have spoken to him on two occasions previously, so I shouldn't have any issue talking to him, but now my tongue is like cotton, and my throat is contracted to the point that it's difficult to breathe. I wish Jimmy was here with me to hold my hand and give me support.

Alex had offered to come with me, but I told her that someone needed to stay at the house with her father and with her uncle. I didn't want to leave either of them while they were in their current states. Besides, this is something that I need to do on my own, no matter how difficult it was going to be.

I walk up the steps to the porch and raise my hand to knock but the door opens before I get a chance to. Helen stands there in a flowery blouse and capris. She is wearing gardening gloves and for a moment I wonder if it was just a coincidence that we met at the door, like perhaps she was on her way out to do some gardening and had not expected to find me on the other side of her door.

The look on her face tells me otherwise, however.

"What are you doing here?" she asks with a very cold tone, just loud enough to let me know that she isn't scared of me but quiet enough to let me know that her husband is home, and she doesn't want him to come to the door wondering who is there.

"I need to talk to Philip." It suddenly feels weird calling him Philip. Not that I would call him dad or father but at the same time our relationship has changed since the last time I spoke of him. Also, because I kind of want to call him Drew.

"I thought I told you—" I don't want to have this conversation with her again, so I cut her off.

"I have to see him. Things are different now, and I have something to tell him, and he needs to know. You probably need to know, as well." This catches her off guard. She, of course, has no idea of what I'm about to tell him but she has no idea how it could concern her. But I figure, even though it's not like I'm asking them to take care of me, it still pertains to her that her husband has a child that he didn't know existed.

"Can I please come in?" I say it with as much authority as I can muster so that she isn't able to say no. She opens the door and stands back and I walk into my father's home. I see the kitchen to the right where I watched Helen that night so long ago and see the living room to my left. I walk into it and take a seat without being offered one.

"I'll go get Philip." She goes up the stairs as she takes off her gardening gloves, realizing, I'm sure, that she wouldn't get to go gardening for a while.

I sit on the couch and look around the living room and try to get a feeling of how the Drew that I read about grew up into the Philip that was about to come downstairs and have his world turned upside down. I see pictures on the wall of him and Helen. A wedding picture and pictures from the different places they had visited over the years. Some of them I can tell where they were taken but some I can't. One looks to be in a back yard, whether it is theirs or someone else's. Another looks to be on a college campus, perhaps that was where they met.

There is a piano in the corner of the room, and I wonder which of them is able to play if either of them. Perhaps it is simply a furniture piece that they purchased with the intention of learning to play but never actually did. It's amazing to me how little I actually know about this man that I am about to call my father.

"I thought I told you not to play Hardy Boy?" Philip says as he comes down the stairs. He is in a black T-shirt and blue pajama bottoms. It's strange to see him out of a shirt and tie and out of the office. I feel like his normalcy is gone. When I sat in his office, I felt like he would blend into the background if I saw him in a crowd but now in his own home, he becomes an individual, a person with a story of his own. I notice his T-shirt is faded but has the ACDC logo on it and I feel like I'm talking to Drew as opposed to Philip.

"I did what you told me to, and I went home. Or rather am trying to." Helen looks confused at this. Perhaps he hasn't told her that we have spoken. Perhaps he couldn't because of client confidentiality or perhaps he didn't feel he needed to. He had no idea me and her had spoken. He probably didn't realize that she knew of my existence.

They were both going to be fully aware very shortly.

"Helen says you said you have something to tell both of us?" He looks very confused at this.

"Please, you'll want to sit down." I feel strange asking them to sit in their own living room, but they do so anyway. Angela sits on the love seat and Philip sits on the piano bench. I feel like this is a perfect example of what Helen was talking about. If it weren't for me having brought back thoughts of Angela over the last few days, I'm sure that Philip would have joined her on the love seat.

"I came to you asking about my sister Angela, but I was misinformed." Philips face has no noticeable change but Helen's shifts just slightly. Perhaps she already had an inkling of a thought, but she refuses to admit it just yet.

"Angela wasn't my sister. She was my mother." Helen cringes at the word as her worst nightmare comes to life. I'm sure I can imagine exactly what is going on in her mind. The ghost of Angela that has haunted her marriage for so long has suddenly taken corporeal form and risen from the grave to snatch her husband away. "Which makes you my father."

Philip's reaction is a lot harder to read because his face remains unchanged. I'm not sure how he feels but whatever way it is he doesn't want to show it to me or to anyone else. I can't tell if he is surprised by this revelation or if he somehow knew. I need him to fill the gaps that exist in the timeline between my birth and my mother's death.

I give them both a moment to digest the information. Helen looks at Philip to see his reaction and both of us wait on baited breath but he still continues to be a statue, almost as if I hadn't said anything at all.

"Honey?" Helen reaches out a hand, but Philip doesn't take it, so it hangs there between them.

"My son is dead." Philip says with finality and a hint of anger. At this Helen retracts her hand and shows the first bit of shock. She may have feared that I was Philip's son, but I don't think that it ever crossed her mind that he knew he had a child. I didn't know that he knew either but am not as shocked. Instead, I am ecstatic because this means that he must have met with Angela before her death or at least somehow had contact in order to find out my existence.

"I found my mother's journal. It never mentioned her telling you." His eyes grew more and more angry as I continued to speak.

"I have no son." I don't know where to go from here. This is by far a different reaction than I expected. I had prepared for tears. I had prepared for questions about what had happened and why it took so long for me to come to them. I may not have been able to answer many of them, but I was prepared to explain why I couldn't remember.

I was not prepared for this outright denial of the truth.

I decide to just get him to tell me what he knows and try to connect the dots.

"When did your son die?" I venture the question out as an olive branch hoping to take the anger out of his eyes.

"The same night that his mother died." His anger is still there, but instead of burning, it has begun to simply simmer. Perhaps he realizes that I don't have all the facts. Perhaps what he will tell me will clarify all the confusion.

"Angela told me about Kevin the day she died. Her parents refused to let us take him away from that hell hole." His anger suddenly had a new victim; even if they weren't in the room, I saw a wrath directed at the Cartwright household. "We were supposed to meet at the train station that night, but she never showed. I don't know why but she ended up out on her boat and there was a storm, and she never came back. Our son went with her."

Something didn't quite compute with what he said. I didn't understand why she would have gone out on her boat in the middle of a storm. And how he knew that that was what she had done.

And besides, I felt there was something that he wasn't telling me.

"You are not my son, and I don't know what kind of sick joke this is to you, but you need to leave." He stands as he says this and the anger in his voice becomes redirected at myself again.

"I'm sorry, I just—"

"Leave!" Panicked I listen and head towards the door before he physically forces me to.

"Are you sure that your son—" I keep thinking maybe he was misinformed. He wasn't there when Angela died that night. He doesn't know for sure that she took their son.

I realize in that instant that even in my head it has shifted from myself to him.

Philip slams the door in my face leaving me standing on the front porch confused. This whole time I had been running under the assumption that I was the same Kevin in the journal. But what if I'm not? What if that Kevin died and I have been deluding myself into thinking that that was the solution? I try to think of what evidence I have.

The journal.

I was given the journal by my mother when I was dropped off at St. Elizabeth's. At least that is what Alice said and she recognized me, and I recognized her, so I had to trust that.

I consider pounding on the door to try and talk to Philip again, to try and convince him that what I said is true, but I decide that it would probably be best to simply let him have his space and see if he realizes the possibility of what I said.

Besides, this makes me wonder where he would have gotten the idea that I had died. The only logical place he could have gotten that from would have been from Angela's parents. But why would they have lied to Philip all those years ago and then the other day, her father came right out and tell me the truth, or at least a partial truth. He did claim that it was his son that he put up for adoption rather than his grandson.

It's astounding to me that after so many years he is still clinging to the lie that he created to keep the world from knowing his daughter got pregnant out of wedlock. I guess you can't teach an old dog new tricks.

I walk back to Ronnie's car and decide that in the now free time I have before meeting with Thomas, I will go and visit my grandfather and see what he has to say.

But when I drive over to his apartment and begin knocking get no answer. I don't find this odd given that I am dropping by unannounced on a Sunday afternoon. He could be out. As I'm leaving, however, I almost bump into a woman who is carrying groceries into her apartment that is across the hall from Robert's.

"Oops, I'm sorry," I say as I skirt around her to avoid bumping into her.

"No problem," she says, then pauses for a minute. "Hey, were you trying to get into 104A?" Her tone sounds strange like she couldn't believe that that was what I was really doing.

"Yes, why?"

"Well, it just seems strange that in the last three years I've never seen him have a single visitor." She shifts her groceries over to the other arm and tries to pull her keys out of her pocket. "And then to get one the day after he moves out." She finds her key and sticks it in her lock.

"Moved out?"

"Yep, just up and moved out. I didn't even see him moving boxes or furniture. But I saw him turning in his key yesterday when I went by the front office to do my laundry."

Angela stood in front of her house. Drew had just dropped her off. The plan was simple. She was going to go back into her house begging for forgiveness and then tonight, in the middle of the night, she would sneak out and run away with their child.

She wasn't sure what they were going to do after that, but they would figure it out.

But first she had to go back in there and face her parents. Specifically, her father.

Angela and her father had always been close. She had been daddy's little girl. He was wrapped around her finger from the day she was born. Whenever she was in trouble, she wanted her father to be the one to catch her because she knew he would roll over on her and let her get away with little or no punishment.

But something had changed since he went overseas.

Angela had a sinking suspicion that it had something to do with whatever he and that man had been talking about on Christmas Eve, but she couldn't be a hundred percent sure.

Regardless, her father was a different person now and that person had taken her child hostage in his home. And she couldn't let him do that. She would do whatever she had to do to get him back. Even if that was to face this new father of hers.

She walked up to the front door and calmly rang the doorbell.

She had been so prepared to face her father that it threw her for a loop when her mother answered the door. But there she stood in her satin robe with flowers on it. Angela's mother looked her age, but she had aged well and had always looked attractive. When Angela saw picture of her as a young woman, Angela thought she could have been a model if she had wanted.

She didn't look like a model now.

She had a black eye over her left eye; her arm that was holding open the door showed a nasty bruise on her forearm. She had clearly been crying but more than that her face had a weary look on it. A look that told Angela this wasn't the first time that bruises like this had appeared. A tired look that hurt almost as much as the bruises.

"Mom." Angela didn't know what to say, so instead, she took her mother into an embrace and tried to hug the hurt away. It, of course, could never work, but she had to give it a shot.

They stood like that hugging in the doorway for a few minutes before her mother broke away and walked silently into the house. Angela followed her and they took a seat at the kitchen table, where there was a cup of coffee and a lit cigarette in an ashtray. Angela hadn't seen her mother smoke in her entire life. She knew that she had in the past, but she had stopped when she got pregnant with Angela.

"He's not here," she said as she sat down. Angela wasn't sure which 'he' she meant. Whether Kevin or her father, but either one meant the same thing. Her father had taken Kevin somewhere else. The shocked look on her face must have shown. "They are coming back. Your father just went into town. He said he didn't… didn't trust me not to take Kevin to you. He blames me for this whole business."

She took a drag from her cigarette as Angela sat down next to her.

"Why didn't you ever tell me?" Angela and her mother had never been exceptionally close. Her father had always been her favorite parent. But she still felt like they had had a good enough relationship that her mother could have come to her with something of this magnitude.

"I was so ashamed. And you were so happy. I didn't want… want to ruin that. And besides, I knew that it would make him angry. It used to not be this bad. It's gotten worse." She took another drag of her cigarette. Angela noticed the open pack of Marlboros on the counter. It was half empty.

"Why didn't you ever leave?" Angela tried to understand what her mother had been thinking but it just wouldn't process.

"And leave you? I could never take you away from your father. He loved you and you loved him. It would break your heart. And mine. I still love him. He still loves me. He just …gets angry." She fumbled with her robe and didn't meet Angela's eyes.

"You can't possibly think that."

"You don't understand what it's like to be in a marriage for twenty years Angela. There are certain… compromises you make. You do things for each other. Things that help one of you but hurt the other. This is just… just that. A compromise."

Angela was dumbfounded to hear the words coming out of her mother's mouth. The fact that this abuse had been going on and she had no idea was shock enough but to add in the fact that her mother was making lame excuses for it and accepting it as an unavoidable fact was worse. She'd never thought of her mother as particularly weak. She was a stay-at-home mother, so it wasn't like she was one of those powerhouse women with a career and a life of her own, but she wasn't this shell of a human being that was sitting across from her.

"Come with me." She reached across the table and grabbed her mother's hand. "Me and Drew are running away." She hadn't planned on telling her mother about their plan, in case she would tell her father, but now she felt a need to protect her. She wanted to take her far away from her father and never come back.

"You know my grandmother lived in this house." A weak smile reached her lips but fell short of making it to her crying eyes. "And her grandmother before that. This house has so many memories in it. I don't know how it can contain them all and still have room for more." Angela wasn't sure what her mother was saying. A small part of her worried that she had had some sort of mental break.

"I could never leave this house. This is my home. And I could never leave your father. I love him too much to… to hurt him like that." She stubbed out her cigarette as if to say that was the end of the discussion on that topic.

"Well, I'm leaving, and I'm taking Kevin." Her mother looked at her in shock at that.

"Don't do that to him. To me. You'll only make him angry." There was fear in her mother's face now. Angela noted that she hadn't argued with Angela running away. She was only afraid of her father's wrath over the loss of Kevin.

"I'm not going to let my child grow up in this house. Not with him." Her anger bled through her voice and her mother matched it.

"You had a good life here, didn't you?" Her words were scalding. "You never wanted for anything. He loved you. And this is how you repay him? By taking away our one chance?" Angela suddenly remembered the flowers and the cemetery.

"He's my chance. Not yours. He's my child. And I refuse to have him in a house where a man beats his wife. Not to mention where his own father is not welcome." Her mother looked appalled at Angela's defiance.

"What are you going to be able to give that child? You have no money. Where are you going to live? You have no home. Don't you see that it would be so much better for him, for both of you, to just stay here. You can go to school next year like we planned and get your degree and— "And meanwhile, he'll be home watching dad beat the crap out of you?"

The smack came out of nowhere. Angela hadn't seen it coming, and so she hadn't been able to brace for it. But she wasn't sure it would have helped if she had. The sting of the smack was nothing compared to the sting of the fact that it happened at all.

"Your father and I provided a good home for you and will do the same thing for Samuel." Angela felt like she had been smacked again.

"Samuel?"

"We discussed it and have decided that it would be better if we named him. I don't like the name Kevin. Samuel is a stronger name. It's my father's name. It suits him better." Angela was shocked at how quickly her mother went from wrath to simply sitting there discussing names as if it were an everyday conversation.

"You do remember that Kevin is my son. Not yours. I'm his mother." Angela had a burning urge to run away now just to get away from her mother.

"You have to do more than just get yourself pregnant to be a mother, dear." The condescension in her tone hurt Angela right down to the bone. "You have to learn how to be a mother. It's okay, it took me a while myself. You have to learn to put your child's needs above your own."

"That's what I'm doing."

"By taking him away from a home where he has loving parents who will provide for him?" Angela noted the absence of the grand. "Taking him away to what? You have no place to stay. You haven't got a job. Are you going to stay in the junkyard where that boy grew up?" The dig at Drew was expected but it still hurt when Angela heard it.

"We may not have much but at least Drew doesn't hit me. At least I won't have to worry about finding bruises on my child." She stood up, done with this conversation. "I'm leaving and I'm taking Kevin with me."

As she walked upstairs without waiting for her mother's response, she hoped that she wouldn't tell her father what had happened. Or at least would keep quiet about Angela's plans to leave. She had to hope that somewhere deep inside the denial that consumed her mother, there was a piece of her mother that knew she was wrong. That knew it was better for Kevin to leave this house.

I stand in front of the house on Skylark Drive. It had been converted with Apartments 1 and 2 on the ground floor and Apartment 3 on the top floor that was only accessible by a wooden staircase outside. I walk up the wooden stairs wondering to myself if perhaps this is where I am going to figure it all out. Presumably, I knew who the killer was prior to losing my memory and logic says that means that Sarah would have known, as well. So, would I discover the final clues in her notes?

I knock on the door with the brass number three on it.

It takes a few moments before Thomas answers, and when he does, I almost don't recognize him. He looks totally different in casual clothes than he did this morning in his suit and tie. He is wearing jeans and a tee shirt for some band I don't recognize.

"Oh, hey. Come on in," he says as if it were just anyone that he was letting into his home. I feel guilty for not telling him about the last time I saw his girlfriend, but I realize that if I told him right now on the day of her funeral I'd probably be kicked out of his house if not sent away in handcuffs by the police he would surely call.

"I'm good, thanks," I respond when he offers me something to drink. I don't want to stay long. I decided on the way over here that I would come and get the stuff that he wanted to give me and then get out. I didn't want to stay long for fear that I might slip up on something. I had to keep reminding myself that he has no idea of my amnesia and while we never met before, he obviously knows some things about me. He knew my name; at least so his girlfriend mentioned me to him.

"Well, I don't know exactly what she was helping you with." He says as he leads me through the small living room and into a small study off the hallway. It was absolutely pristine. Everything on the desk had its place and everything was in its place. The pens were in color order in the cup and the one sheet of blank paper left on the desk was in line exactly with the edge of the desk. "She was very tight lipped about her work. I only knew your name because I looked at her day-planner when the cops were asking about her whereabouts." I am silently grateful for this.

"She was kind of a neat freak." He chuckles half-heartedly remembering her. Another wave of guilt flows through my veins. "She kept all her notes and everything locked up in this closet." He pulls out a key and unlocks the sliding door to the closet. Inside there were file boxes that each had names on them. Right there on top was mine.

Kevin Price.

"This one's you." He pulls it off the top of the stack and places it on the desk. "I haven't let the police see anything in the closet. I've been talking with the lawyers about if I'm even allowed. I mean technically private detectives don't have the same kinds of confidentiality assurances that lawyers and doctors have but at the same time I feel like this isn't her stuff. It's really yours. Anyway, it's not like it's any business of the police. She said she was helping you find your parents." A look crosses his face like he is feeling guilty. "She didn't say you, but I mean, she just said one of her cases, and well, you were the only open one she had."

"Right." I'm not sure what I should say. I want nothing more than to rip the top off the file box and see its contents, but I try to contain my excitement.

"Well, I'll leave you in here to look through it. If you want to keep any of it, you're more than welcome to. If you leave it, though, it might get turned over to the police soon. The lead detective called me yesterday and said that they may have a suspect in custody. They want to look through the boxes and see if he has any connection to her old clients." He gives me a kind of half smile, then realizes he doesn't have anything else to say and walks out into the hallway closing the door behind him.

I sit at the desk and stare at the box in front of me.

I'm not sure what I'm going to find when I open it, but I feel a bit like the mythical Pandora as I lift the lid off the cardboard box. Instead, of all the darkness and pain of the world pouring out, however, all that is inside is a bunch of papers.

They are organized into three folders. The first folder is marked "Official Documents." I open it up to look at the few things inside. It has my birth certificate marking my grandparents as my parents. It also gives me the name of Samuel Robert Cartwright. Along with it is some documents detailing my adoption from St. Elizabeth's, as well as the forms that my grandmother filled out when she dropped me off there. I note that the date that I was dropped off was not long after my mother's death. Perhaps a few days if not a week if I remember correctly. That's all that's in the first folder and while it is interesting to see on official documentation it doesn't give me any new information, so I put the first folder back in the box.

The next folder is the thickest of all three and it is marked evidence. I open it and immediately all the misshaped contents fall out to the floor. It is filled to the brim with newspaper clippings. If it weren't for how organized and precise Sarah's office was, I would assume that these were misfiled.

The clippings are assorted from different publications, but most of them are from *The Fareport Gazette*. There are a few that are from *The Cleveland Daily*, but those are few and far between. I don't see what any of them have to do with me, however.

There are articles and pictures and a lot of obituaries. Rather than try to pick them up off the floor I get down on my hands and knees and begin to spread them out further on the floor to try and get a better look at all of them, hoping that maybe looking at them as a whole will give me a hint at why they are included in my box.

Initially nothing connects for me. I skim some of the headlines, however, and soon a pattern begins to emerge.

"Car Accident Kills Local Girl" one clipping reads while showing a picture of a flipped pickup truck. Another one reads: "Young Girl Dies in Boating Accident." And yet another says: "Two Found Dead After Apparent Murder-Suicide." This one doesn't include a picture, but when I skim the short article, it appears that the couple were both shot, and the husband was found with the gun in his hand.

As I grab more articles, I notice that all of them are about dead girls. None of them are labeled as murders, all of them instead are deemed accidents except for a few suicides. And beyond it being a bunch of dead girls and all of them being in Fareport, I don't notice any connections.

I find an obituary of a Kelsey Hughes that matches up with the boating accident article. I put the two together and begin looking through the articles and trying to find the names of the girls to match up the obituaries. Not all of them have them but most of them do. If I hadn't already been on the floor when I found the third one, I would have had to take a seat.

"Local Woman Found Dead After Drunk Driving Accident" the matching article read. The photo at the top of the obituary was a cropped version of the wedding photo that I had seen in Jimmy's house. It was Melody Evans.

I also find the paper copy of the obituary for my mother that I read online.

My mind begins to race as I start to question the reasoning behind these clippings. It doesn't take long for me to fall on a theory, but I push it out of my mind.

It couldn't be possible.

Finally, I have matched all of the obituaries with their corresponding articles and have spread them out across the floor. There are fifteen dead girls in total, as well as three other extra victims. There is the one husband from the murder-suicide, as well as a little sister and a boyfriend who both died in car accidents. Other than those three, however, all the victims are young women between twenty and twenty-five and, judging from the photos in the obituaries, all of them look similar to Sarah: blonde, skinny, and pretty.

I feel my heart pumping at an abnormally fast rate as I reach into the box to grab the last folder. This one is marked "notes" and is almost as thick as the newspaper clippings folder. I open it to find a stack of notebook paper with writings covering almost every inch of them. Sarah's handwriting is loopy and feminine and cuts a severe contrast from the content of her notes.

As I skim through, I catch phrases like "murder weapon" … "two found dead in the woods" … "47 missing person cases." Most of it is detailed outlines of the fifteen girls in the articles but there are references to many others like the three in the woods and quite a few missing person cases. I find a page that lists all of them. She seems to have copied it down from somewhere and the title of the list is “unsolved missing persons.” Either the list she found was curated or she only wrote down the women. But even some of the ones she wrote down were crossed off. Perhaps she found out after that they were too old or too young.

I skim through the list looking for the name that I know will be there. The name that confirms the rampant theory growing in my brain. I find it at the very bottom and it’s underlined in red ink: Emily Bradshaw.

If I’m reading these notes and clippings right, then Sarah believed that the serial killer had started long before I came to town. I looked through the clippings again and the earliest one I found was from 1992. If Sarah is right, then the serial killer has been killing for over twenty years.

I look through the notes and find a timeline that she has drawn. It starts in 1992 and has different colored points on it leading all the way up to present day. Each point has a name hovering over it and it is there that I find the first hint at how it all connects.

The name next to the first point is Angela Cartwright.

I don’t understand why but Sarah seemed to believe that my mother was the first victim of this serial killer. Which doesn’t make sense since she died in a boating accident, but then again, as I look back over the clippings, it dawns on me that that is exactly what connects them all. None of them were seen to be related because all of them looked to be accidents or suicides.

Until the last few murders no one even knew there was a serial killer on the loose.

At least according to Sarah. I remind myself that regardless of what the folder says, all this is a theory. None of this has any true evidence.

I go back through the notes and look at the notes on the specific cases.

Lisa Cost was another boat victim. She died in 1998. Sarah wrote that apparently there were no storms the night she died and that her parents said she was a “talented swimmer and sailor.” Her body was never found.

Amanda Wintrow was the female half of the murder suicide. Steven Wintrow was her husband and apparent murderer. They were newlyweds who had just purchased a new house and were planning to start a family. They had scheduled an appointment with a fertility clinic for the week after they died. They died in 2012.

Susan Young had just been accepted into Yale the week before she drove her car off the road. The cause of the crash was a faulty break line.

She had reported to the police that she had been followed but they had never found any evidence and it had happened a month before her attack so was considered unrelated. She drove off the road and into a tree in the winter of 2001.

Erin Thompson was never found but her parents say that she would never have run away from home. She was studying to be a nurse at Fareport community college. They never heard anything from her or any sort of communication from her kidnapper and now apparent killer. She went missing in 1995.

The list went on and on and the stories were all different but eerily similar. They were all freak accidents that had something that seemed a bit off about them. It was never anything strong enough to suggest foul play but when put together in a list it seemed enough to suggest that something was amiss.

I couldn't find anything strange about Melly's outline beyond the odd feeling seeing her name on the list. If Sarah was right, it seemed curious that Melly had been a victim of the same man that killed her best friend years prior.

I was apparently not alone in assuming the gender of the killer as Sarah wrote plenty of notes off the sides referring to the killer as a *he*. *Who is he?* or *How does he pick his victims?* And also, *Why does he choose these girls?* were written across the margins sometimes circled or underlined.

Nothing in the notes seemed to indicate any possible suspects or even any ideas about how to find him. Apparently, Sarah had as little idea about who the murderer was as I do now. She simply knew more about his numerous victims.

It does seem strange to me as I continue to look at it that, according to Sarah's theory posited in her notes, the murders started in the spring of 1992 with my mother. It is strange because she does not even have any possible victims listed for before then. I don't know if this is because my mother was the starting point in her research or if she thought that my mother was the first murder.

I hear a knock at the door that makes me glance at the clock on the desk and realize how long I've been reading through these notes and clippings. It has been almost an hour.

"I wanted to make sure you were okay in there," Thomas calls through the door. At first, I don't know how to respond. Do I tell him that his girlfriend may have been chasing her murderer before he killed her? Do I tell him that her murderer also murdered my mother, and tried to kill me, as well?

"I'm doing fine." I decide to say none of these things. I don't want him to think I'm some crazy person. I need to show this all to someone who will believe me. I need to find proof of this.

I quickly put all the clippings and papers back into their respective folders and throw them in the box. Standing up I decide exactly where I am headed next. I know exactly who to talk to.

"Do you mind if I take this box with me?" I say to Thomas on my way out.

"No, go right ahead." I feel like I ought to tell him that I might have figured out who killed his girlfriend, but then again, do I really want to add any more stress to his already difficult day? Especially when all it is at this moment is speculation.

"Thank you very much," I tell him as I head out the front door.

"You're welcome," he says with a small smile. I hesitate in the doorway. He looks like he could use a hug, or some sort of affection, but not from me. Instead, I give him a sympathetic smile and leave him to his mourning.

When I get to Ronnie's room, I walk right in with the box in my hands expecting to find Ronnie alone in the bed. Which is why I am so thrown when I find Chrissy sitting next to him with a newspaper in her hands doing the crossword.

"Three letters, Actor Shepard," she says, not noticing my entrance at first.

"Sam?" Ronnie says sitting up.

"Doesn't fit; has to start with a D," Chrissy says not looking up and chewing on her pencil.

"No," Ronnie says, almost barking, trying to get her attention. "Sam! What's with the box?"

"What are you doing here, Chrissy?"

"I heard that Ronnie was…" she looks at him and a funny look crosses her face, "wasn't feeling well. I thought he might like a visitor." Ronnie takes his eyes off of me for a moment, and I'm able to witness a half a heartbeat between the two of them and another puzzle piece falls into place.

The limping man. Chris's ex-lover. The man who had showed up at the

Cartwright's on Christmas Eve. They were all Ronnie.

Ronnie was the missing link the entire time and he had been sitting here in the hospital just waiting to be found. I can't believe my own luck at having come here right when I needed him most.

"An… old friend," I whisper more to myself than aloud.

"What's with the box?" Ronnie repeats, taking us both out of our respective moments. I hesitate with Chrissy there, but I don't want to ask her to leave either, so I sit down and set the box on the floor.

"I've figured it all out," I say, then realize as his face brightens that that was simply one of my lies. "Well, almost. But you can help."

"I can?" He looks confused at this.

"Yes." I quickly explain to him about the journal I found and explain how I found out who my mother was and who my father really was. I make sure to leave out the fact that I now know their history and I also try not to lead him towards my conclusion on who I think killed my mother. I need to know that he reaches the same conclusion I do without any coaching.

"Okay, so how can I help?"

"You visited my grandfather on Christmas in '91." He looks slightly taken aback at this, and at first, I think I might have been wrong.

"How do you know that?"

"Because the girl you saw in the window was my mother. She saw you and overheard your conversation." I notice his eyes dart to the door, almost as if he is checking to make sure no one else was in the room.

"Okay, and what about it?" I feel like he is trying to dodge my questions before I have even fully posed them.

"What were you talking to my grandfather about? My mother wasn't sure and only wrote down bits and pieces. But it seemed extremely important." He shifts in his seat before responding.

"I don't particularly remember, it was a long time ago." He doesn't look me in the eye when he says this.

"Ronnie, look, whatever it is, I need to know. It's extremely important." He looks at me and then at Chrissy and then at the door before opening his mouth.

"Look, before I tell you this, I want to make sure we are clear that this was a long time ago, and if I had known, then what I know now I would have done things very differently." I nod to let him go on.

"Your grandfather and I knew each other from the Gulf War. I was part of the actual ground troops and he was part of the private security detail that helped us out sometimes. It was my first and only time overseas, his, too.

"We were still kids practically. I mean we weren't, but we acted like we were. Him more so than me. He was getting paid big bucks to be over there and most of what he was doing was easy stuff. Neither of us were doing anything remotely near the main fighting. We were in charge of watching this one town: Baqubah. It wasn't an exactly militant city but at the time we were worried about everything.

"We were doing a routine patrol one night. They always sent out three of us. Two of us Army men and one hired mercenary." He begins fiddling with his IV at this point. "It was me and your grandfather and one of my buddies. Greg Howard." He closes his eyes at this point and pauses.

I almost call for a nurse, but he comes out of his moment and continues, "We were just doing our regular patrol, when suddenly, out of nowhere, this kid comes running to us out of the desert. And Robert—" He coughs at this point and almost chokes. I reach for the call button, but he smacks my hand away from it. He takes a moment and controls himself.

"You have to understand. At this point none of us had had much sleep. We were the first patrol that night, and so we had been up since six that morning and the heat. The heat does things to you. You get antsy, you see things. Not mirages like in the movies but…" He trails off and sighs. "We kept hearing stories from where the fighting was going on and we kept expecting it to reach us at any moment. They were teaching us to be constantly vigilant. Always ready. Fingers on our triggers all the time. And, well, in the end it was... It didn't matter. But…" He stares off through the window for a moment.

Robert shot the boy dead.

"The boy didn't have a weapon. He was unarmed. He was just a kid. Maybe eight years old. I don't know what he was doing out so late or coming from the desert. But there he was, dead." I saw the heart monitor spiking and I worried that a nurse might come anyway but none did.

"So, we did what any sensible men who valued their freedom and reputation would do: we covered it up. We buried the kid out there in the desert and then continued our patrol and pretended like it never happened. We were like brothers over there. We were closer than brothers. We stood up for each other. If Robert had been found out he would have got sent home and sent to jail. He had a daughter, your mother. He had a wife. He was a good guy, I thought. He didn't deserve to go to jail for what happened. I could have done the same thing. Probably would have…." He takes a moment and wipes his eyes dry.

"It wasn't more than a week later, and the fighting finally reached us. That's when I lost my leg. So, I got to go home. Gregory did, too. He got sick. Robert was the only one who stayed till it was all over. It wasn't long but it was long enough.

"When he came back, he was …different. I came to his house for his party, and he put on this face of being happy, but I could see something was off in his eyes. It was tearing him up. We were forced to go to therapy, but the private sector men weren't required. Highly suggested but not required. They got paid either way.

"He never went. Insisted he didn't need it. I went to his house that Christmas to try and convince him to go. If I had known… I might have said something…. but then, by that point, by that point, I'd have lost my pay and disability benefits. How was I supposed to live with only one leg? I didn't have as good of a leg as I do now. I couldn't have gotten a regular job. I couldn't be on my feet for longer than twenty minutes or so. Besides, who wants to hire a guy with one leg." I feel like he is apologizing to me.

"I needed that paycheck every month. Otherwise, I would have said something. And it's not like I had any proof. I only had a hunch. Not even a hunch. Just a feeling. And no one else seemed to have any issue with it, so I kept my trap shut and my eyes open. I mean it's not like I watched him, but I paid attention.

"But nothing ever happened, and I never heard anything. Until now. I have a feeling you know what really happened. You know that he killed your mother?"

The sentence hits me like a brick to the face. Ronnie had been heading towards this the entire time and I had been thinking the same thing since I found the box at Sarah's apartment. It was the only theory that made sense. He was the only person who had motive to kill her and was still around to murder all the other girls. Ronnie, of course, didn't know about those other girls, but I did.

But something about hearing it said out loud like it wasn't a theory, like it was an absolute fact. It shocks me to my core.

Chrissy apparently had not come to the same conclusion and gasps, her hand flying to cover her open mouth.

"Yes, I think he did," I say as the shock wears off and righteous anger begins to build in the pit of my stomach. I may not have the evidence that I need but I have my ally. "And that's not all."

I open up the box of secrets that has been closed this whole conversation. I try not to move too quickly and to cover everything, but everything comes pouring out like a waterfall. I show them the articles and the notes. I show them the timeline and the list of names. I try to explain it to them in such a way that I don't leave any room for dispute.

I can already feel I'm rehearsing for the next time I explain this when I'm telling Officer Callahan to let Jimmy out of prison and to go after the right man.

My grandfather.

"You need to take this to someone. You need to go to the police right away!" Chrissy says at the first opportunity while I take a breath and try to reorganize the clippings and papers.

"I can't yet. I haven't got any proof. I have an idea but beyond that all I have is newspaper clippings and a thirty-year-old story that has one eyewitness." Ronnie looks downcast as I say this. I can tell he wanted to finally redeem himself and be able to catch my grandfather for what Ronnie had assumed he had done for twenty-odd years.

"What's this photo in here?" Chrissy asks reaching into the empty box. But it must not have been empty because when she pulls her hand out, it has a photo in it. I haven't seen it before, so it must have been underneath the folders and I never noticed it before.

"What is it of?" I ask and take it from her hands.

The photo is eerily familiar. It's a candid photo of my mother on the dock in her back yard. She and her father are cracking a bottle of wine over the front of the sailboat that ultimately will be hers. Someone, I assume Sarah, had taken a pen and circled the sailboat, so I look closer at it.

The word *Freedom* is written across the hull of it.

The photo is eerily familiar because it is the exact same boat that is still docked there now.

I quickly flip through the clippings in my hands to find the one that told of my mother's death to clarify that my memory served me correctly. I find it and read through it one more time to make sure I remembered right and sure enough I had.

"Neither Angela nor her boat were recovered. It is assumed that her boat was damaged and sank in the storm."

If *Freedom* had sank when my mother died, then how could I have seen it the day before yesterday at my family's dock?

"Chrissy. You just gave me the proof I need," I say quickly throwing all the clippings and everything into the box and standing up. "You don't mind if I borrow your car for just a bit longer, do you, Ronnie?"

"If you catch that son of a bitch, you can keep it."

Drew was heading back to the Evans's house after he dropped Angela off when doubt began to creep back into his mind.

He had not been for this plan of sending Angela in like a Trojan horse, but it was impossible to talk Angela out of it once she had come up with it. It also didn't help that Melly had been in support making it two against one.

He didn't trust Mr. Cartwright one bit around his son so why send the love of his life over there, as well. Angela was naive to think that familial ties would keep him from hurting her or seeing through her facade. If there was one thing that Drew's father had taught him, it was that blood meant nothing when it came to affection.

While his eyes watched the dark clouds on the horizon, all he could see in his mind's eye was the look on Mr. Cartwright's face that morning when he had thrown Drew out of the house. It had shocked Drew how strong he was. Sure, he had been trained and had served overseas, if not in the actual armed forces, in a similar sense nonetheless, so he was clearly fit. But there was a difference between being fit and the strength that anger and derision gave a man.

Mr. Cartwright had been fueled by hatred.

It was when he saw a cop sitting by the side of the road clocking speedsters that Drew made the decision to go against the plan. He wasn't going to sit idly by while Angela was taken hostage in her own home and God knows what else.

He pulled over next to the car and got out of his truck. The cop got out, as well, Drew noticed that his hand was uncomfortably close to the firearm at his waist. Drew put up both hands.

"I need your help."The cop immediately relaxed.

"What's seems to be the problem?" He looked into Drew's truck trying to see if Drew was alone.

"It's my girlfriend. I think her father is going to hurt her."

"What makes you think that?" Drew could see that the cop was not much older than him. and looked rather skinny and wiry. It wasn't exactly the kind of person he had been hoping to find to help Angela, but it was better than nothing.

"Well, he physically threw me out of his house this morning. And previously he was keeping her hostage." The officer gave Drew a quizzical look.

"Hostage? In her own home?" Drew could tell his story was weak.

"Look, I know it sounds crazy and strange, but I'm telling you, something's going on in that house, and I need you to go and make sure that no one gets hurt."

"Who's your girlfriend?" He pulled out a little notebook and pen and began to write something down.

"Angela Cartwright." Drew couldn't be sure, but it appeared that this officer recognized the name.

I quickly pull into the driveway of my grandparents' house. When I get there, I see that Detective Callahan beat me there. Or at least there is a cruiser in the driveway. I assume it is the detective's. Next to it is Jimmy's truck, yet to be towed, and on the other side of that is another car. It isn't Philip's Cadillac, it's a Saturn Ion, but I assume it's his wife's car. It's the only other person that would make sense. I had called them both from the hospital. Either because of sheer luck or because it was the hospital phone that showed up on their caller ID, they both had answered right away.

I feel the first drop of rain as I get out of the car and head towards the house. The wind bites at my neck as I climb the front steps As I close the door behind me, I hear a distant roar of thunder before the click of the door.

"Detective?" I call out to the quiet house and get no response. The hairs on the back of my neck begin to stand on edge.

Angela is locked upstairs in her room when she hears the front doorbell ring. She sneaks to the edge of the landing at the top of the stairs to listen.

"Everything doing okay tonight?" She heard the familiar voice of Officer Callahan at her door. Unsure of what he was doing there she quietly waited rather than go downstairs and let her presence be known.

"Everything's fine tonight, officer. What can I do for you?" It's amazing how nice and Rockwellian her father can sound when he wants to.

"Just wanted to let you know that a big storm is coming in tonight. They're saying it might be tornado weather. Wanted to make sure everyone out here away from town was prepared."

"We have a basement we can go to. But thank you for the heads up." Angela could tell from her father's tone of voice that he didn't buy for one second that Officer Callahan was there to check on their severe weather readiness.

She didn't buy it, either. Something told her that she should go down and let him know that she was here, but she wasn't sure if that would help or hurt matters.

"Well, I just wanted to make sure everything was fine. Hey, you have a young daughter, don't you?" The tension in the quiet after his question was so intense that Angela could feel it all the way up the stairs.

"What business is that of yours, officer?" It was amazing how he could make a threat with just the tone of his voice.

"I just wanted to make sure everyone was at home. Wouldn't want anyone out driving in this weather." His voice almost cracked as he said it. Angela could picture in her mind's eye, Matthew's palms getting all sweaty, the way they did any time she talked to him.

"Well, in that case, you'd better head on home then, officer. Wouldn't want to get caught in the rain." Her father presumably gave a facade of a smile before he closed the door. Then he came to the bottom of the stairs and glared up at Angela. She could feel the glare cut straight down to her soul.

I feel trepidatious as I walk down the hallway towards the kitchen at the back of the house. I feel as if my senses are in hyper awareness mode as I try to catch any sign of movement or sound in the house. So far, however, I see and hear nothing but an empty house.

I get to the kitchen and get a strange feeling that someone has been in it soon before me. It isn't so much something that I can see as it is something I feel. Like someone had come in and moved something then put it exactly where it had been before leaving no trace of their trespassing.

One thing that is not in the same place that it was before is the boat. I can see through the back window that the dock is empty of all vessels. I remember the lady at the apartment building saying that Robert had left the day before. Realization dawns on me that he must have known the boat was the one thing left that proved Angela hadn't died in a tragic accident.

He must have come here and taken off in the boat. That's whose car was out front; not Philip's, Robert's.

But what about Detective Callahan?

"Detective Callahan!" I call out once again, now sure that Robert isn't here and no longer as afraid of the silent house, although still concerned. Why hadn't he responded earlier when I called out to him.

I make my way through the living room back to the front of the house and look up the stairwell. I pause to listen, but I don't hear anything at all except the patter of the rain begin to hit the roof of the house.

I step on the bottom stair and begin my ascent one step at a time, the apprehension taking over again as I creak my way to the second floor. Something is amiss, and I'm almost afraid to discover what.

As I come to the top of the stairs, I see that the master bedroom door is closed. The room where me and Jimmy had made love just two nights prior. The door was definitely open when I left it last. While the house is old it is not drafty and would not have closed the huge oak door on its own. I make my way across the carpeted floor and reach out and open the door.

Detective Callahan lies on the bed in a pool of blood.

I explode into a run and check to see if he is still breathing. I almost cry out when I put my hand to his neck and feel nothing except the warmth of life that has yet to leave his dead body. I pull my hand away quickly after realizing and come back with red droplets on my hand. I wipe it on my pants without thinking about it.

I get deja vu flashbacks to the last time I discovered a dead body and accidentally got covered in its blood. I back away slowly trying to check and make sure I didn't get any more blood on me.

I begin to breathe heavily. I don't know what to do. I can't stay another moment in this room with a dead body and I can't stand to be in this house of death a second longer, so I barrel down the stairs and out the front door into the now pouring rain.

Robert stalks up the stairs towards the frozen Angela taking one step for every word.

"What was that policeman doing at our house? Did you call him?" He now towers over her, hunched as she is on the landing.

"No," she is able to manage before shaking her head. Something about the look in his eyes makes her extremely terrified of him in that moment. She had told Drew that she did not believe her father capable of hurting her but in that moment on the stairs she become unsure.

"Then why was he here? Did your boyfriend send him?" She shook her head again and tried to gulp down her fear. "By the way, your mother told me about your little 'plan.'" He made quotation marks in the air as he said it. Her mouth went suddenly dry. If her mother had been there, she would have been so angry with her, but then again, she was sure the terror she felt at that moment was similar to what her mother had felt for the past twenty years.

"You're not going to take away our child. He is ours now. We have sacrificed enough; we deserve this. You deserve nothing, you little whore." And with that, he kicked her.

She fell across the floor, not having been prepared for the attack. It took the wind out of her stomach and sent a cold chill down her spine. As far as she could remember, it was the only time she had ever been physically attacked in her life. It hurt a lot more than she thought it would, but even more than the physical pain was the emotional hurt due to its source.

She let out a whimper as she heard him creak his way back down the stairs. When he finally made his way back to the kitchen where her mother waited, she heard muffled sounds of conversation. She couldn't tell what was said but she could tell by the tone that it was concern on her mother's part and lies on her father's.

A crack of lightning flashed outside the window in the yard, and it stirred her into motion. Angela quickly got up immediately and clutched her bruised stomach. She leaned on the bannister for a moment before leaning against the wall and making her way over to the nursery. She looked over her shoulder before going inside to make sure her father was not heading back up the stairs.

When she got inside, she went to the dresser and grabbed the warmest, thickest onesie she could find and the biggest blanket. She grabbed Kevin out of the crib slowly so as not to wake him up and alert her father downstairs.

She tried not to let her son hear her whimpers as she got him dressed and bundled him up slowly without waking him. Then she went into her room and grabbed the only jacket she had upstairs. Her big winter coat was downstairs in the hall closet, and it would be impossible to grab it. Once she got downstairs, she would never be able to take the time to put it on.

She would just have to bear the cold.

When she finally came back to the top of the stairs, she was ready to never return. She had considered trying to pack a bag but there wasn't enough time.

She had intended to do this in the middle of the night, but she was almost afraid to lose this chance that she had. Especially with the storm blowing in, she didn't want to have to leave in the height of it. Right now, it was nothing but a little wind and rain.

She didn't know if Matthew's references to a tornado were legitimate or if he was just trying to talk his way into the house. Regardless, she didn't want to chance it. She had to leave now.

She tried to walk as quietly down the stairs as possible and made sure to skip the one step halfway through that always creaked.

After what seemed like forever, she was standing in front of the door. She took one last look over her shoulder before opening it and heading out into the darkening night.

I am whipped by the cold wind as I step off the front porch.

The wind hits me so hard that I almost lose my balance. I almost turn to go back into the house when, suddenly, I notice something strange about the cars in the driveway. I had pulled up right next to the Ion, and I remember that when I got out of Ronnie's station wagon it had been almost the same height.

It is now visibly lower to the ground by a few inches.

I grab a hold of the bannister and step down, trying to not let the wind catch my clothes like sails and drag me out into the storm. When I get to the bottom of the stairs and get to the car, I can see that the tires have been slashed.

I'm not as alone as I thought.

I quickly turn around a complete 360 degrees to see if I see anyone. I don't, so I step back up the stairs to head towards the house but stop at the last moment.

That is exactly what Robert would expect me to do. He is probably inside waiting for me right now. He knows the rain and wind, which are getting stronger by the minute will cause me to run back inside where he is probably lying in wait. I back down the stairs and into the rain.

I try the door into his Saturn, hoping against hope that he might have left it unlocked. I had hot-wired a car before. Maybe I can call on Kevin again to save my life. It doesn't matter as the door is locked.

I turn and try Jimmy's truck, but it is locked, as well. I run around it and try Callahan's cruiser and thank my lucky stars when the door opens. There are no keys in the car, but I do hear a new sound added to the cacophony around me.

The sound of the radio on his dashboard.

I grab a hold of it and press the button on the side.

"Hello! Is anyone there?" I say as loudly as I dare.

"Who is this on this line? Over." The lady on the other end sounds confused.

"I don't have time to explain. Send police and an ambulance to 5781 Plymouth Road. There's a dead police officer here!" Suddenly, a crack of thunder hits and the front door to the house bangs open. I duck down into the seat hoping that whoever had just opened it had not seen me.

"We are sending help now. Don't leave the vehicle." Easy for you to say, I think to myself. I don't know that I'll have any more luck out in the rain but at least I will be able to run if I see him. I drop the radio and let it dangle and head back out into the storm.

I look around and try to see if there is any sort of shelter I can use to hide and get out of the storm while also stay away from the murderer inside the house. The only shelter I see is the trees, so I quickly make my way over to them and push my way through the underbrush heading deep enough into the trees that I won't be visible from the house.

Where I expect to find more brush, however, I find myself in a small clearing. The trees around me are dense enough that I'm semi dry and protected from most of the wind at the moment. The middle of the clearing, however, is getting down-poured on.

Causing the man standing in the middle of the clearing to be completely soaking wet.

I'm not sure if Robert didn't hear my approach or if he is simply choosing to keep his back to me. I know it is him in my gut if not by sight. I can't see any defining characteristics with his bright red rain coat on and the hood pulled up.

He stands in front of the row of lilies. I count and notice that there are six now instead of the five. Someone must have planted another one after Angela died.

I step back into the underbrush, and a twig snaps under my foot.

Angela ran around the house to the back quickly as the first few drops hit

her. The rain was steady at the moment, but it was far from strong. Luckily, the wind had taken a quick reprieve for the moment, which is exactly what she needed.

She realized, standing on the front stoop, that not only did she not want to draw attention by starting any of the cars, she didn't have any of the keys with her. She would have to use some other means of escape.

Freedom.

She immediately thought of the lighthouse. Philip had said that he was going to run home and try to pack up some stuff before they were supposed to meet. She might be able to catch him over by the junkyard. It wouldn't be easy, but it would be better than trying to walk to town from here. Besides, if she needed to, she could radio for help from the lighthouse. It had a radio.

But first she'd have to try and navigate this storm. Luckily for her the storm was coming from the opposite direction than the lake so as she walked towards the lake the rain lessened. She tried to quiet Kevin in her arms, but it was to no avail. She hopped onto the boat and opened up the cabin. Inside she set Kevin down and took a moment in the warmth to catch her breath and to look out the little window at the house. She didn't see any movement. The sound of the storm must have drowned out Kevin's screams, so no one knew she was gone.

Yet.

She didn't have any time to lose, so she quickly ran out on deck and began to get ready to set sail. She didn't know if she could make it in this storm, but she knew for sure that it was her only option at this point.

"I didn't want to hurt him," Robert says without turning around. He only has eyes for the graves at the moment. I am not sure if he is talking to me or to the dead children.

"You've driven me to this. It's your fault what I've become. All I wanted was for you to be good. For you to follow the rules but you broke them. You didn't do as I wanted!" He screamed this last one and spun around to face me.

"You're just as bad as the others!" He takes a step towards me with a menacing look on his face. I am frozen in place in fear and cold. "All I want is a child who will listen! Someone who will do as I ask! Someone who won't lie, or cheat, or be a filthy whore!"

My mind races through all the girls that he had killed.

All the replacement daughters who he had carefully chosen; all the ones who disappointed him.

"You were going to be it! And how perfect it was going to be! But then you had to stick your filthy faggot nose where it doesn't belong! You and that stupid girl!" With that he takes another step and I quickly take three into the woods heading back towards the house. He cuts me off, however, by using the path which while longer, does not require you to push through foliage.

He stands between me and the house getting soaked but not seeming to care. I head to the left, then quickly change direction and head towards the back of the house instead. He falls for it and slips in the wet. He doesn't fall over but he stumbles enough that I have time to get ahead of him. I try not to slip the same way he does, so I make a large arc to turn around and head back to the house but when I do I find that he is, once again, between me and the house, and I'm at a dead end.

The giant cold lake is behind me and my mother's murderer is in front of me.

"So, you're just going to kill me like all of the others?" I shout above the storm.

"Oh, no. I'm not going to just kill you. You see I've come full circle now. I get to kill the last remaining eye witness." I take a step back from him and step onto the dock, realizing that all I am doing is tightening his trap.

"Then just do it!" I scream trying to throw him off guard maybe get him to run towards me. Maybe if I do, I can dodge his attack and he'll go flying off the edge of the dock.

"Oh, no. I'm not going to do it here. No. You deserve someplace special. The place where it all began." His gaze moves past me; I turn and look at what he's gazing at and I see the lighthouse off in the distance. I don't know what he means by the fact that it all started there but I don't have time to figure out his deranged mind at the moment.

By the time I've turned back, he's directly in front of me. He grabs my head and slams it into the light post next to me, making me see stars.

Things start to dim around the edges of my vision as I fall to the ground. My head begins to spin as I am curiously levitated off the ground. My mind tries to focus, and I realize that I'm being lifted. This is it, I realize. This is how I'm going to die. He's going to pick me up and throw me in the lake.

But no, no he's not. He's taking me to the lighthouse. There's still a chance. Someone can come and save me.

But how? No one will know to look at the lighthouse. The backup is on its way here. I'm surprised they aren't already here. Neither is Philip, for that matter.

Philip.

My brain isn't working correctly, and I struggle to remember who exactly Philip is. I reach out and grab the post in a vain attempt to keep Robert from taking me away, but my arm is barely strong enough at the moment to grab a hold of the post.

I clutch onto the last thing I can: the string to the light at the top of the light post.

It slips through my hand as Robert walks me off the dock and into the yard, but not before I feel the click of the light and see the light turn on.

I smile.

Philip. Philip is Drew. Drew is Philip.

Philip will know.

Drew will come.

I sink in and out of consciousness going black, then grey, then white, then coming out of it all. Sometimes I feel like I am on a boat sometimes I am in a car. I toss and turn with the curves of the road and the rocking of the waves. I can hear myself, but I hear it through the sound of the storm as if it is coming from outside myself.

I also hear him.

"She never should have had you. She never should have slept with that dirty boy. She was a dirty filthy whore just like her mother."

The waves crash against the side of the boat. I run over and try to keep the lines from snapping and to keep the boat from flipping.

I see a light. At first, it is rotating like it's on a top, but then it is stationary like it's on a post.

"If she had just listened to me, I could have forgave her but, then she tried to take away my boy! My beautiful perfect little boy! She deserved exactly what she got that night!"

I try to sit up in the back seat of the car, but I don't have the energy to lift my head more than an inch off the seat. Suddenly, the light becomes two lights coming straight towards us till they fly past us and disappear into the storm.

I hear a rope snap and see a sail go flying. I leap across the deck to try and catch it before it goes flying out of control. Sailing solo is difficult under the best of conditions, these are the worst.

I can hear the baby crying, but perhaps if the murderer would just stop yelling, it would quiet down or maybe if it would just stop raining. I have to get to the spinning light. Otherwise, Drew won't know where I am. that's what the light on the dock means. That I'm at the spinning light.

But I have to get there first. He won't find me if I'm in the middle of the lake.

But I'm not on a lake. I'm on the road.

Blackness overtakes me again for a few moments, but then I fight my way back to the spinning light.

I have to get to the spinning light before Philip gets to the standing light. It's the only way he'll be able to save me.

My head stops spinning long enough for me to sit up when the car stops. I look out and see the spinning light of the light house. Robert opens the back door and lets in the cacophony of sound that is the storm. His arms reach in and grab a hold of me and drag me out.

Angela finally got close enough to the dock that she could throw a line and try to catch to edge of the dock to pull herself in. She's wasn't sure she could with the waves pulling her back out into deeper water, but she had to try. She couldn't do anything else.

Robert carries me through the metal gate and towards the tall brick lighthouse. He opens the door awkwardly with the hand that is supporting my legs. I reach out a hand for the door jam and grab hold. This time I have enough energy to put up some sort of a fight, but it is still no use. Robert easily yanks me away from the door and kicks the door shut. At least most of the storm is quiet in here. We only hear the whistling coming from the opening up at the top of the tower. Robert begins the long ascent up with me in his arms.

Angela was able to pull herself in to the dock and tie the boat off. She quickly dipped into the cabin and grabbed Kevin, who was miraculously asleep, and climbed onto the dock. It felt good to have her feet on dry land again. There

were moments in that storm where she feared that all had been lost but she had found her way to the lighthouse and all she had to do now was get inside and radio for help.

She started the hike up the little incline to the door at the base of the lighthouse. Either because of her determination or because of her elation or perhaps simply because of the storm she did not see the car parked twenty yards away from the base of the lighthouse.

I begin to more fully come to my senses as Robert climbs the stairs. The edges of my vision are no longer as blurred and my head stops feeling so fuzzy. The pain by my left ear becomes stronger and it almost helps by giving my brain a single thing to focus on rather than the crazy mess swirling around me.

We reach the top of the stairs, and I am suddenly blinded by the light for a moment before it spins away from me and flashes in the other direction in it's slow but steady tilt a whirl, going round and round.

Robert sets me down against the wall. The sound of the storm is back, as is the wind, but the rain does not get inside.

"I gave her another chance when she got here you know? I told her she could come back." I don't know if he thinks that I care or if he is simply trying to justify it all to himself but regardless, I let him ramble as the clarity begins to grow in my brain and I see a fire extinguisher a few feet away from where he has set me down. I don't think he sees it. his eyes on the storm and his mind on the past.

Angela climbed the steps to the top with her baby in her arms. It wasn't until she got all the way to the top that she saw him.

Her father stood there staring at her like some sea monster blown in from the storm.

"Did you think I didn't know where you were? Did you think I didn't know what you were hiding?" Her father took a step towards her and she almost fell down the stairs by taking a step back from him. "Such a stupid girl you are. To write every little detail in a book that anyone can find." He shook his head at her.

"Give me the child," he said quietly, barely audible over the thunder behind him.

"No." She took a defiant step toward him.

"What are you going to do?" Angela's eyes darted to the railing that

was only five feet behind him. It was a low railing. All it would take was a single push with just the right amount of force. But she had to put down the baby first.

"Let me put Kevin down and we can talk about it."

"His name is Sam." Angela didn't have time to argue about names.

"Fine. Let me put Sam down, then."

I drag myself a few inches closer to the red barrel. I can just see myself lifting it up and slamming it over his head. It may not finish the job, but it might be enough that I could get away. My head is getting clearer by the second and all I need is to grab hold of that silver handle and pick it up.

Meanwhile, I try to close my ears to the incessant ramblings of my Mother's murderer.

"You were so good. I believed you could be the one. The one to redeem me. The one that would make all this worth it! But you and that little brat were going to let loose my little secret! That's what you two were canoodling about out on that little dock that night. You don't remember, but I do."

I am only an inch away from the handle. If I can just reach a little further.

"She had found out that I had dumped that Emily girl off at a dock. She had a friend in the police department, you see. She had you meet her there, so she could show it to you. Prove to you that her theory was right. But the stupid slut had the wrong fucking dock!"

I can feel the cold metal under my fingertips, but it's wet from the spray of the storm and I can't get a grip.

"But it worked out for me! I finally had my moment! I could kill you both and no one would know your dirty little secret!" He laughs maniacally into the rain at the thought. I finally grab the silver medal in my hand.

Angela placed Sam down on the floor over by some machinery and quietly gave him a quick tearful kiss.

I stand up and slowly walk behind him as he stands with his face out in the storm.

"At first, I thought I was so stupid. I couldn't kill you. You were my own flesh and blood. My only son. I couldn't bring myself to do it. So, I simply knocked you unconscious and framed you. I figured your story would be so outlandish, so ungrounded. No one would believe you!"

Angela took a step towards her father, the spray hitting her in the face. She braced herself to run. For once not away from him but towards him.

I lift the metal extinguisher above my head.

"But I was smart! It all worked out so much better than I planned! You practically framed yourself! And now I get to kill you right here. Right where I killed her!"

"Come to Papa."

I slam the extinguisher down on his head with a loud clunk, but he doesn't fall to the floor like I anticipated.

Angela ran with all her might at her father.

He swivels around and grabs hold of my shoulders.

Her father caught her and diverted her energy to the left sending her toward the railing herself, instead of toward him.

We grapple with each other for a moment, but the knock to his head, like mine earlier, has weakened his ability to control his body.

Angela caught herself just in time on the railing.

I drag him ever closer to the edge of the railing.

Angela hung over the side her face pointed directly down, rain hitting the back of her head.

I get him so that he is hanging over the railing, I finally have enough hold over him that I can overpower him.

In that moment, Angela had a realization. The painting she so adored. The

one with the bird finally escaping the cage. The only time you take a bird out of its cage and let it go is when the bird is dead.

"You're just like your grandfather, aren't you, my boy? My pride and joy," Robert slurs. "My little Samuel."

"Kevin!" they screamed as he flipped them over the edge of the railing and sent the body down to its death at the bottom of the tower.

My head spins as I watch my grandfather's body hit the ground and hear his neck snap. I'm immediately sick over the edge of the railing. I tell myself it was in self-defense but, suddenly, that thought that I had that first night comes flying back to me.

I'm a murderer.

I have taken another life.

I turn and stumble my way back to the inside of the lighthouse.

The edges of my vision begin to get blurry again, but this time, it's different. It's familiar but different than before. I try to focus on something to keep the shadows at bay, but I can't. I fall to my hands and knees and dry heave trying to throw up what I already sent over the edge of the railing.

I close my eyes to try and blot out the pain in my head, but nothing can stop it. The cacophony of sound becomes a hum as my ears begin to ring louder and louder. I lose my breath and have to force myself to open my eyes and mouth and to breathe.

I crawl my way over to the stairs and look down just in time to see the door open. It's Jimmy. I don't know how, but it is. I wonder if he's a figment of my imagination as he's running up the stairs to me. He's taking two or three at a time. I feel tears coming down my face as he gets ever closer. I beg the shadows at the edge of my mind to cease and let me have this moment. Just a moment more, I beg.

But they don't listen. They never listen.

Jimmy gets to the top of the stairs just in time to grab my face. His touch almost brings me back. Almost.

"I came as fast as I could. I heard you over the radio in the police station. I wouldn't let them go without me. Oh, God. Are you okay? You're bleeding." I only hear half of what he says but I see all of him. I see his eyes and his smile. I see his soul touching mine. I feel his heart beating in rhythm with mine.

"Help! I need help up here!" He yells but it's too loud. I wince at it and that brings the shadows in closer. "I'm sorry. I should have been here sooner. Please. Please be okay. I love you." He cradles my head in his arms and squeezes with all his might as if the shadows will be held at bay by love alone.

"I..." I whisper because it is all I have strength for at the moment. "Love..." He is beautiful, even with tears streaming down his face. I don't know what waits for me in the shadows, but I hope that I can remember his face there. I hope that I can remember his love there. Because I may have never been able to remember anything in this world, but in the next, I want to remember him.

"You."

The shadows overtake me.

Epilogue

Three Days Before

"What is it?" I'm confused as Dr. Green closes us in alone.

"I wanted to forewarn you of something." She looks oddly apprehensive.

"What?" I don't understand why she insisted on the privacy. She looks to the door and then back at me almost as if she isn't sure she wants to tell me now.

"I don't want to dash your hopes. I also don't want to ruin your… relationship with Jimmy." I suddenly am very concerned.

"What are you talking about?"

"In all the cases I've studied where people claimed to have DID, the main personality, the main identity, the one that was the original before the psychotic break…" She trails off and looks away.

"What about them?"

"They were the ones that were always aware. They knew what the others did. They had no memory loss. It was the other personalities. The ones that weren't original. The false identities. They lost their memory." She looks me in the eye as she says this.

"Wait, what are you saying?"

"I'm not saying anything. It's not an exact science and it hasn't been studied extensively yet. All this is simply speculation." She bit her lip almost as if she regretted telling me.

"But what your suggesting is…" I don't need her to say it, I don't want her to. But I make her say it none the less.

"What I'm suggesting is the possibility that in order to make you get better and fix your psychosis… it means getting rid of Samuel and leaving only Kevin."

THE END

July 30, 2016

CPSIA information can be obtained
at www.ICGtesting.com
Printed in the USA
LVHW080824210322
713945LV00004B/57/J